THE BESTSELLING COZY MYSTERY SERIES

AGATHA FROST

Stories in this book:

Chocolate Cake and Chaos
Shortbread and Sorrow
Espresso and Evil

Other books in the Peridale Café Series:

Pancakes and Corpses
Lemonade and Lies
Doughnuts and Deception
Macarons and Mayhem
Fruit Cake and Fear

CHOCOLATE CAKE AND CHAOS

BOOK 4

CHAPTER 1

"Try this one," Barker said, handing Julia a small sample of dark beer. "I think this is my favourite so far."

Julia looked unsurely at the beer, the taste of the last sample still staining her tongue. She looked back at the long line of barrels, sure each new beer had been Barker's favourite. Julia's taste buds had always been uncertain of beer, but it had taken the first annual Peridale Craft Beer Festival to assure her she was more of a peppermint and liquorice tea kind of woman.

"It's certainly malty," Julia said, wincing after taking a small sip. "I'm not sure I have the tongue for the subtleties this requires."

"You're just not an IPA beer kind of girl," Barker said defiantly, taking the sample from her and placing it back on the table. "There's a drink out there for everyone."

Julia wasn't so sure, but she followed Barker to the next barrel, smiling her apologies to the brewer for not choosing his batch.

"This should be a little smoother." Barker picked up two samples from the small tray sitting in front of the barrel on the next table. "Smells fruity, don't you think?"

"Smells like ale," Julia mumbled as she inhaled the amber liquid. "*Bottoms up!*"

They clinked their plastic shots, and instead of sipping this one, she tossed it back like Barker had been doing, hoping it would affect the taste. She swallowed, wincing as she had with the others. It didn't leave as strong an aftertaste, and it was definitely smoother, but Julia couldn't detect the fruitiness Barker had assured her of. Glancing over her shoulder at the dozen more ales to taste in the white tent outside of The Plough pub, she opted for half a pint of the one she had just tried in hopes it would appease Barker. If he hadn't looked like a kid in a toyshop when he had first heard about the festival coming to Peridale, she would have stayed home and spent her Sunday afternoon de-weeding her daffodil beds.

"I guess you weren't one of those teenagers who drank alcohol on street corners?" Barker asked as they took their drinks to one of the free benches.

"I was more of a stay home and bake girl."

"I should have known," Barker said with a wink. "That's why you're so good at it."

Most of Peridale had turned out for the festival, which had been organised by Shelby and Bob Hopkins, the owners of The Plough. They had been talking about pulling something together for years, but life in Peridale moved slowly, so most people expected it to stay nothing more than just talk. Julia suspected a lot of the visitors were showing their faces to see if there was anything worth gossiping about for the coming week, but so far the event had run a lot smoother than the alcohol Julia was forcing down.

"Here comes trouble," Barker whispered over his pint, nodding towards the opening of the tent. "*Code Grey.*"

Julia followed his eyeline to a group of senior women, fronted by her gran, Dot. They were decked out in brightly coloured and mismatched tracksuits, with even brighter neon sweatbands pushing their permed curls away from their faces. It reminded Julia of the 1980's workout videotapes her gran had tried and failed to complete when Julia was a little girl.

"I see you're polluting your body with the rest of them, Julia," Dot called out loudly enough for everybody within earshot to hear as she marched over, her knees and elbows lifting dramatically. "It's a beautiful day out. Why don't you put down that poison and join our fitness group?"

Dot continued to march on the spot, squinting at the expensive new exercise watch on her wrist that she had recently purchased. Julia had tried to teach her how to use it correctly, but the technology had gone over her head. She missed the days when devices had buttons and not just touchscreens.

"I think I'll pass today, Gran," Julia said, smiling to the rest of the girls behind Dot, who didn't seem as enthusiastic about their new club. "Clocking up lots of steps?"

"Eight thousand so far this morning," she announced

proudly. "I've decided we should do one hundred steps for every year of our age. Since I appear to be the oldest, we've got another three hundred left."

There was a grumble from the girls as they adjusted their sweatbands and sluggishly attempted to copy Dot's eagerness. It had only been a week since Dot had started her new health-kick club, but Julia was sure the numbers were already dwindling.

"You should take it a little easier," Julia suggested after sipping her beer. "Remember what the doctor said about your tricky hip?"

"My hip has never felt better, thank you very much!" Dot cried. "We've got another lap of the village green before we can sit down. Barker, you should stop eating so many of Julia's cakes. You're starting to get fat. *Must dash.*"

Dot twirled around, pushed through the girls, and power-walked out of the tent, her head held high and her shoulders forced back. The rest of the girls followed, some of them eyeing the barrels of beer longingly as they left.

"Am I getting fat?" Barker mumbled as he prodded the tiny bit of softness poking through his white shirt.

"Ignore her. She saw some documentary about fitness for old people on the telly, and she hasn't shut up about it since. She's already warned me about the dangers of heart disease four times this week. Sue and I went to her cottage for dinner last night, and she lectured us about meat and dairy while we ate steamed asparagus and kale. Knowing Gran like I do, she will be bored in a couple of days and she'll already be onto the next thing."

"You didn't answer my question."

"Of course you're not getting fat!" Julia insisted with a chuckle. "You're in better shape than most men in this village."

"Only *most* men?"

"Do you want me to tell you you're in the best shape to make you feel better?"

"Yes, please."

"You're in the best shape, Barker," Julia said, glancing down to his barely there stomach. "Although maybe she's right about the cakes."

"That's your fault!" Barker cried, readjusting his posture so he could suck his minuscule stomach in. "You know chocolate cake is my weakness."

"I'm trying to perfect my recipe," she said casually. "Nobody is forcing you to eat it."

"Maybe if you weren't such a great baker, I wouldn't need to. Perhaps you *should* have been that teenager who drank beer on the street corner?"

He winked and kissed her on the cheek, the malty scent of ale lingering on his breath. Julia felt her face flush as the kiss sent the pit of her stomach into a wild swirl. It had been three weeks since they had confessed their love to each other after only a couple of months of dating, but it was the small things that kept taking Julia by surprise. After twelve years of marriage to a man whose idea of romance was buying Julia a bottle of whatever perfume was on sale once a year on Valentine's Day, Julia was enjoying the feeling of being in love.

"Oh, more trouble," Barker mumbled, nodding to the opening of the tent once more.

Julia turned around with his kiss still fresh on her cheek. Her heart skipped another beat when she saw Jessie, her sixteen-year-old lodger, sneaking in, a hood pulled low over her pale face. Leaving her beer, Julia hurried through the crowd and across the tent, her pastel yellow dress fluttering behind her.

"What are *you* doing here?" Jessie demanded, looking down her nose at Julia, her lips snarling into a scowl.

"*I'm* the one who should be asking that."

"You hate beer."

"I'm here with Barker."

"Oh," Jessie said with a roll of her eyes. "I was bored at home. Thought I'd come and see what was happening here."

"And not to try and sneak some underage alcohol?" Julia asked with a smirk as she folded her arms across her chest. "You're right, I don't like beer. Let me grab my bag, and we'll head home."

Jessie grumbled as she slid her hood back to let her dark hair fall over her shoulders. She had been living with Julia and working in her café for four months now. Their relationship had begun with Jessie breaking into Julia's café and stealing cakes because she was homeless, but it had developed into something that resembled mother and daughter. Julia hadn't expected to suddenly have a teenage girl in her life to look after, but it was a challenge she was enjoying. Jessie was a good kid, most of the time.

Leaving Jessie lingering by one of the barrels, Julia headed back to the bench she had been sitting at with Barker. Her half-full plastic cup of beer was still there, along with Barker's now empty cup, but Barker and her bag had disappeared. She spun on the spot and was relieved to see him getting a refill of the IPA that had almost made Julia gag. That relief turned into a steel weight when she didn't see him carrying her handbag.

"Barker! Where's my bag?"

Barker walked back to the bench, his fresh pint crammed firmly against his top lip. After a deep gulp, he set it down and looked under the bench, a little less urgently than Julia would have liked.

"You had a bag?"

"*Men!*" Julia cried, pushing her hands up into her hair as she spun on the spot. "I think somebody has stolen it!"

They both scanned the tent, their eyes landing on the same thing at the same time. A hooded figure in a red tracksuit was hurrying through the tent and towards the opening, clutching Julia's bag under their arm. They gazed at each other, frozen for a moment before they set off at a run. The figure looked over their shoulder, revealing the face of a teenage boy.

"*Stop him!*" Julia cried as she felt the nauseating sinking of despair. "He's stolen my bag!"

The boy began to sprint, but as he approached the entrance to the tent, he slammed into two men who had just walked in. There were gasps from the watching crowd as he was thrown to the ground, dropping the bag as he landed in a heap. But just as Julia breathed a sigh of relief, the nimble teenager scrambled to his feet, grabbing the bag in the process before either of the thick-necked men could figure out what was happening.

Side by side, Julia and Barker burst out of the tent, the bright May sunshine blinding them. They stood outside of The Plough, looking up and down the crowded village street.

"*There!*" Barker cried before setting off at a sprint. "He's heading towards the village green!"

Julia kicked off her kitten heels, hitched up her dress, and set off running, catching up with Barker in seconds, her tights-covered feet pounding into the cobbled road. She didn't care about her phone, or even her café's takings that were in her bag from the busy Saturday shift the night before, but she did care about her small notepad, which had all of her recipe revisions and notes for the chocolate cake she was working on.

The boy's hood flew down as he darted across the village green. Dot and her speed walking group all stopped to gawp at the commotion.

"Stop that boy!" Barker cried through bated breath. "*Stop* him!"

The women all looked to one another as they fumbled from side to side, none of them appearing to know what to do. Dot, on the other hand, charged at the boy, seemingly forgetting the existence of her eighty-three-year-old tricky hip once again. The boy smirked over his shoulder, eyes wide as Peridale's finest came at him from both directions.

"*Stop*!" Dot cried, letting out a tribal scream as her Day-Glo green sweatband flew off, unleashing her recently permed curls. "*Thief!*"

Like a rugby player going for a below the belt tackle, Dot dove in, but like an even better player, the boy darted out of her way. She fell into the neatly mowed grass and rolled over onto her side. Julia gave up on her recipe notepad and ran to her gran's aid.

"I *almost* had him!" Dot said through shallow breaths. "I was — I was *so* close."

"It doesn't matter," Julia said, crouching down to her gran. "I'm calling an ambulance."

"You'll do no such thing!" Dot cried as she stumbled up to her feet, instantly checking her watch. "I've just finished my steps for the day. And a new calorie-burning

14

record to boot! Ladies, another lap around the green for you!"

As though nothing had happened, Dot scooped up her sweatband, reapplied it, and marched back to her group. Julia turned her attention back to the boy, who was sprinting full force towards St. Peter's Church with Barker lagging behind. Resting a hand on her forehead, she wanted to cry out to tell Barker to leave it, but at that moment, a black blur darted in front of the boy, knocking him clean off his feet as he entered the church grounds. The figure flicked their dark hair back, and Julia was startled when she saw that it was Jessie who was pinning the boy into the ground.

With renewed energy, Julia ran over, overtaking Barker as he paused to clench his knees and pant out of control.

"*Apologise!*" Jessie screamed, shaking the boy with fistfuls of his red tracksuit. "Apologise to the woman, you worm!"

"Get off me!"

"*Apologise!*"

"I said, get off me."

"I ate idiots like you on the streets for breakfast!" Jessie yelled as she shook him even harder. "Apologise, *now!*"

"*Fine!*" the boy cried, pushing Jessie's hands off him. "I'm sorry, alright?"

For a moment, Julia thought Jessie was going to plant a fist in the boy's face, but she relented and jumped off him. She scooped up Julia's bag and tossed it over the boy to her.

"Billy Matthews," Barker mumbled through his pants. "I should have known it would be *you*."

Billy's eyes widened when he saw Barker. He glanced from Jessie to Julia before darting off again. Jessie went to

15

chase him, but Julia put her hand out and shook her head.

"I can get him!"

"Just leave it," Julia said, checking in her bag, relieved to see everything intact. "I owe you."

"Somebody had to stop him," Jessie said with a roll of her eyes. "It was like witnessing an old folks fun run watching you two."

"Maybe your gran was right," Barker mumbled as he leant against the church wall. "I'm so unfit."

"You are getting fat," Jessie said casually. "Being suspended isn't a good look for you."

Barker looked up at Jessie, his eyes narrowed and his cheeks red. Julia stared sternly at Jessie, who shrugged and shook her head as though she didn't know what she had said. Jessie might not have been blood-related to Julia, but she shared her gran's bluntness and brutal honesty. She usually appreciated it when it came to critiques of her cakes, but less so when it came to Barker's recent suspension from the police station, which seemed to be her current favourite topic to joke about. If Julia and Jessie were like mother and daughter, Barker and Jessie were more like brother and sister.

When Barker had finally caught his breath, they set off walking up the winding lane towards Julia's cottage. They reached Barker's home first, so Jessie set off on her own and left them alone.

"She didn't mean it," Julia apologised as they stood outside of Barker's gate. "You know what Jessie is like. She can be a little – *prickly*."

"It's nothing that's not true," Barker said with a small shrug as he circled his foot around on the smooth pavement. "I went to the station yesterday to see if they were any closer to deciding on my future, but nobody would speak to me. It doesn't look good, does it?"

Julia's stomach knotted inside her as she bit her lip and looked down at the ground to stare at her filthy and torn tights. It had been three weeks since Barker had been suspended and there hadn't been a day that Julia hadn't blamed herself for getting him into this mess. She was pouring her energy into baking the most perfect chocolate cake for Barker, but it didn't disguise the fact it had been her actions that had caused his suspension. Dragging him into helping her solve the murders of homeless men without official police support was a decision she was regretting every day.

"No news is good news," Julia offered pathetically.

"I've never heard of a Detective Inspector being suspended and getting their job back," he said with a small smile. "I need to face the reality of the situation."

"*Temporary* suspension," she reminded him. "That's what they said. They would be stupid to let you go."

Barker smiled at her, but she could see the worry in his eyes. He had been trying to hide it the best he could, most likely to ease her guilt, but they had been spending a lot of time together since he had been without a job, and she had seen the silence from the station chip away at his hope day by day.

There was nothing Julia could say to ease his worry, so she stood up on her tiptoes and pulled him into a hug. He nuzzled his face into her neck as she squeezed him tightly while the bright sun shone down on them. Julia wished she could make everything better, but behind her words of support, she was just as worried. She couldn't live with herself if her stupid actions lost Barker his career.

"It'll be okay," she whispered as she opened her eyes. "Everything will be -,"

Her voice trailed off when she looked ahead at Barker's cottage. She pulled away from the hug and walked around him to unhook the gate as she squinted at what appeared to be flowers on Barker's doorstep.

"What's that?" Barker asked as he followed her down the garden path.

Julia shielded her face from the sun and narrowed her eyes, her vision not what it had been in her twenties. The flowers were arranged in a circular design, with a black sash across its middle adorned with decorative silver lettering. When she figured out what the letters spelt out, all of the moisture vanished from her mouth. She parted her lips to speak, but no words came out.

"What the -," Barker mumbled.

"'*R.I.P. Barker*'," Julia read aloud in a small voice as they looked down at the flowers. "It's a funeral wreath."

CHAPTER 2

B arker paced back and forth, the wreath filling his coffee table. Julia caught herself chewing on the ends of her short nails, something she only found herself doing when she was incredibly stressed. During her divorce, she had practically chomped them down to her cuticles.

"It's probably a joke," Barker said hopefully. "Right? A joke?"

"It's not very funny," Julia said, avoiding looking at the wreath. "Who do you know that has this particular brand of humour?"

Barker paused for a moment while he stared down at the wreath, his brows tensed tightly. He shrugged and continued to pace as he ran his fingers compulsively through his hair.

"Who does this?" Barker asked, straining a laugh. "It's sick."

Julia fearfully looked down at the wreath, as if it was a bomb that might explode at any moment. It was clearly a threat. It had felt dirty and strangely weighty in her hands when she had brought it into the cottage.

The doorbell rang, offering a distraction for both of them. Julia jumped up, and Barker headed for the door, giving her a troubled look as he passed her. Alone with the wreath, she forced herself to read the words again. '*R.I.P. Barker*'. She bit hard into her index fingernail, catching the skin underneath it. Muttering under her breath, she crammed the end of her finger into her mouth, the cut stinging against the edge of her tongue.

"Julia, this is Detective Sergeant Forbes."

A man who looked to be in his late fifties walked into Barker's sitting room. He was of average height, with a large stomach pushing through his suit jacket. He had a head of thinning, grey hair, combed over from what was left on the sides. His face reminded Julia of Santa Claus, with plump red cheeks, and a grey goatee framing his smiling mouth.

"Please, call me Bradley," he said, his voice squeakier and higher pitched than Julia had expected. "I've heard a lot about you from this one. He's quite smitten."

"Thanks for coming, Bradley," Barker said, slapping the man on the shoulder. "I didn't know who else to call."

"You sounded rather rattled on the phone, old friend. Is everything okay?"

Julia stepped to the side, glancing down at the wreath as she did. Bradley squinted at the flowers before pulling a pair of thick-rimmed glasses from his upper pocket. With his eyes magnified to the size of large saucers, he leant into the wreath, teasing the sash with a finger.

"Who died?" Bradley asked. "Does that say -,"

"*Barker*," Julia said with a nod. "It was on the doorstep when we came back from the beer festival."

"Oh, how was it?" Bradley asked with a cheerful grin. "I meant to drop by, but I shouldn't really drink on the job. You know what it's like."

Bradley chuckled as he took off his glasses and slotted them back into his pocket. Julia looked desperately to Barker, wanting him to stress the seriousness of the situation.

"The thing is, Bradley, somebody left this on my doorstep," Barker continued. "Why don't I make you a cup of tea?"

"I'm parched, that would be great," Bradley said, already sitting on Barker's creaky white leather sofa. "A wreath, *eh*? Is this someone's idea of a practical joke?"

"I hope so," Julia whispered, sitting next to Bradley as Barker rushed into the kitchen.

"Not very funny, is it?"

"That's what I said."

Barker returned with a cup of tea for Bradley, a cup of coffee for himself, and a cup of peppermint and liquorice tea for Julia. She had never been more grateful for a mug of her favourite comforting beverage.

"How are things at the station?" Barker asked as he sat in his armchair, perching on the edge, dividing his attention between Bradley and the wreath.

"Oh, you know," Bradley said with a small shrug. "The usual."

Barker nodded and looked down into the black surface of his coffee. Julia could tell he was disappointed with Bradley's answer. He missed the station so much, he probably would have liked to hear the boring in and out details of their usual daily routines.

"Heard anything from the gaffer yet about my – *ya'know* – suspension?" Barker urged, twitching in his seat.

"You know the Chief Inspector," Bradley said with another small shrug. "Jim is a man who works at his own pace. I'm sure you'll be back soon enough, although not too quick I hope. I'm enjoying playing inspector while you're away."

"So they haven't replaced him?" Julia asked. "I'm sure that's a good sign. Right, Barker?"

Barker nodded as he sipped his coffee, his eyes firmly on the wreath. Julia could tell it didn't reassure him as much as she had hoped.

"Rough business, this suspension," Bradley said as he blew on his tea. "It will sort itself out. You watch. You don't get to be my age in the force without ruffling a few feathers."

"Have you ever been suspended?" Barker asked.

"Well, not quite. But I've had my fair share of slaps on the wrist!" Bradley replied with a soft chuckle, his bright red cheeks glowing. "Any idea who sent this thing?"

"Not that I can think of."

"Somebody you've upset?"

"You don't make many friends in our job, you know that."

"I do indeed," Bradley said, nodding in agreement as he turned and smiled at Julia. "I once had a steaming bag of – *well* – since we're in the presence of a lady, I won't go

22

there. But it's not a job that wins you favour with the people. Anybody you arrested recently that you might have given enough reason to want to scare you?"

Barker gawked at the wreath and seemed to rack his brain for a minute.

"There's a couple," Barker said with a heavy sigh. "Peridale's a quiet place. Most of the time it is trouble with the kids from the Fern Moore Estate."

"I said they should never have built that awful place," Bradley said, his squeaky voice deepening suddenly. "Brought my house value down thousands back in the eighties. Of course, it's fine now, what with our beautiful village being so desirable, but that's not the point. Nothing good comes out of Fern Moore! They're all slippery little buggers from that place!"

"Billy Matthews, for example," Barker whispered under his breath.

"You said that name before," Julia said, her ears pricking up. "That kid who tried to steal my handbag?"

"Billy Matthews pinched your bag?" Bradley cried, shifting awkwardly in his seat, his large stomach not allowing for much movement. "Did you report it?"

"Well, he didn't steal it. We caught him, but he tried. That boy can run."

"He's a little toad," Bradley mumbled after sipping his tea. "Might as well get him a permanent cell at the station. Arrested more times than I've had hot dinners. Always let off with a caution or a fine though. I say lock him away and throw away the key, even if he is only seventeen!"

"I arrested him for stealing Denise Andrews' tractor from Peridale Farm not long before I was suspended," Barker said, suddenly snapping his fingers together. "He was here in the village today. It's got to be him!"

"I wouldn't put it past him," Bradley affirmed. "Aren't these wreath things on the pricey side? When my dad died, the flowers for his send off cost us a small fortune, and that was ten years back."

"He could have stolen another bag?" Julia offered. "He seemed to know what he was doing."

"This isn't his style," Barker said, talking himself out of it. "He's more likely to put a brick through your window. He doesn't have the brains for this."

They all sat in silence again as they tried to think of how the wreath could have turned up on Barker's doorstep. Julia didn't know the ins and outs of Barker's list of enemies, but she did know that whoever sent the wreath meant to seriously scare Barker, and if not frighten him, to warn him. She looked at the writing again, then gulped down her warm tea, not wanting to think of what it could really mean.

"It's probably nothing," Barker said, breaking the silence. "Can you look into it, old chap? *Unofficially,* of course. No point kicking up a fuss over some flowers."

"Leave it with me," Bradley said with a wink and a tap on the side of his nose. "I'll get to the bottom of this. Just call me Detective *Inspector* Forbes. Can you imagine?"

The man chuckled again, finished his tea, and stood up. He shook Julia's hand once more and headed for the door with a promise that he would look into it the second he was back at the station. When he reached the front door, he stopped in his tracks and turned back to Barker, his brows pinched, a curious look in his eyes.

"I've been meaning to ask you this for a while. Does the name '*Jeffrey Taylor*' mean anything to you?" Bradley asked as he brushed down the wispy stray strands of hair on the top of his head.

Barker's face turned a deathly shade of white right before Julia. Eyes wide and jaw gritted, Barker looked more terrified by the name than he had at the wreath.

"Where did you hear that?"

"Your name came up in conversation with his earlier this week. He's just moved into the village, and they usually let us know when new releases come to our corner of the world."

"Jeffrey Taylor is *here*?" Barker asked quickly. "In Peridale?"

"Staying at Evelyn's B&B last I heard," Bradley said, the twinkle in his eye growing ever more curious. "Anything we should be worried about, boss?"

Barker appeared to be somewhere else, his eyes completely glazed as he stared through Bradley, through the door, and out of Peridale entirely. Julia nudged him, and he blinked forcefully, suddenly looking down into Bradley's face again. He forced a smile, which Julia recognised as his '*everything is fine*' smile, and shook his head.

"He's nobody," Barker said confidently. "Thanks for coming 'round. If you hear anything about my job, you have my number."

Bradley shook Julia's hand for the third time, and then left them alone in the cottage. When Barker closed the door behind him, he leant against the wood and banged his head against the frosted panel of glass.

"Who's Jeffrey Taylor?" Julia asked, her voice suddenly shaky. "Barker? Are you okay? You don't look well."

Barker's eyes glazed over again, and he seemed to be somewhere else entirely until he blinked and looked down to Julia, this time without the forced smile he had given Bradley.

"He's somebody I put away on a murder charge years ago, and last I heard he was serving a life sentence in prison," Barker said, his voice gritty. "Last time I saw him was in court for his sentencing. He said if he ever saw me again, he'd kill me, and now I guess he's in Peridale."

Julia felt a fist tighten around her heart as the village she adored suddenly became a dangerous place. She pulled Barker into the living room, sitting him back in his chair. She forced his cup of coffee into his hands. He stared down into the dark liquid, but he didn't drink it. Julia had so many questions to ask, but Barker had experienced enough stress for one day so she decided she would wait until he wanted to talk.

Instead, she went through to his kitchen and made ham and cheese sandwiches with the few ingredients in Barker's fridge. When Barker started to eat, Julia's nerves eased a little. She looked at the wreath once more, something new catching her eye. A small white tag was poking out from under the sash, which must have been disrupted by DS Forbes' brief examination. She reached out and read the stitched writing on the small tag.

"At least we know the florist," Julia said, a small smile lifting up the corners of her lips. "It's from Pretty Petals, the only florist in Peridale. I think we need to pay them a visit and get to the bottom of this ourselves."

CHAPTER 3

Mulberry Lane was the oldest known street in Peridale. Its golden Cotswold stone buildings, with sagging slate roofs, and tiny windows and doors, dated back to the 1700s. The shops and cottages contained within the winding lane were impossibly crammed together, as though they had been built on top of each other. They looked like they could crumble without a moment's notice. Despite this, they had stood the test of time.

Julia pulled up outside Pretty Petals in her aqua blue Ford Anglia. She crammed her stiff handbrake into place, and she peered through the single-paned bay window of the tiny shop. Just seeing the flowers made her feel uneasy.

"We're taking my car next time," Barker mumbled as he unbuckled his seatbelt. "This thing is ready for the scrap heap."

"She's vintage."

"She's close to death."

Julia almost laughed, but the mention of death stopped her. The wreath was still burning a hole in the pit of her stomach, as well as Barker's coffee table.

They climbed out of her petite car and stood on the narrow pavement outside the shop. They both stared at the small hand-painted sign, its peeling lettering matching that of the tiny white tag on the sash. Barker pulled it out of his pocket, and held it up to the sign, just to make sure.

"Let me do the talking," Barker said as he adjusted his stiff white collar. "It is my wreath, after all."

Julia nodded and pulled an invisible zip across her lips, locking it at the corner. She wondered if she should have told Barker that she knew the owner of the shop, but it hadn't gone unnoticed to her that he had dressed for the occasion in a freshly ironed shirt, pressed trousers, and his shiniest shoes. She hadn't seen him dressed so smartly since his suspension, and even though he didn't have his job back yet, it warmed her to know he had a purpose again, even if it was under morbid circumstances.

A bell tinkled as Barker opened the door. He ducked into the shop, holding the door open for Julia. She stepped inside, and the scents of a dozen different brightly coloured flowers fought for her attention. A bucket of unusually bright yellow roses caught her eye, which she thought would look nice in her kitchen window. She made a mental note to pick up a bouquet for herself if things went well.

They weaved in and out of the displays towards the

counter, where Harriet Barnes was peering over the top of her hot-pink glasses as she re-potted a bright orange plant with thick green leaves. Barker cleared his throat, but she held up a finger without looking at him.

"Just a second," she mumbled. "This part is *critical*."

Julia bit her lip to stop herself from laughing. With a frown deep in his brow, Barker puffed out his chest and stiffened his back, the top of his hair almost touching the low-beamed ceiling.

"*Perfect!*" Harriet exclaimed, holding the plant up to the light. "Don't you think? Nothing makes me happier than a healthy guzmania. They are beautiful, aren't they? *Oh*! Hello, Julia! What can I do for you today?"

Julia smiled her acknowledgement, but she kept true to her promise to let Barker do the talking. She stepped to the side and allowed him to take centre stage, something that caused Harriet to pull off her glasses so she could assess him suspiciously. Harriet was a regular in Julia's café, always ordering a cup of camomile tea with a slice of fruitcake. Aside from her amazing florist skills, she was well known in the village for her crazy patterned cardigans and her frizzy silver hair, which was always held up in a bun by two pencils. She was also known to call upon them if anybody ever needed something to write with.

"I was wondering if I could ask you some questions, Mrs. -,"

"*Ms.* Barnes," Harriet corrected him firmly. "I kept my husband's name after divorcing him. It was a darn sight better than Harriet Hudders. I can't tell you how many cow and milk jokes I had to endure as a child. And *you* are?"

"Detective Inspector Barker Brown," he said, a quiver in his voice. "I'm here unofficially to ask you about a wreath

I think you might have made."

"I should hope it's unofficial," Harriet said casually as she put her glasses back on before flicking through a large appointment book in front of her. "I heard the new DI was fired quite recently."

"*Temporarily* suspended," Barker muttered with a cough, his cheeks blushing.

"Yes, well, even the most hopeless looking plants can be brought back from death, but root rot is still root rot, no matter what you call it. I have five minutes before I need to start on my next job. A wreath, you say?"

Barker glanced to Julia, who was still biting her tongue. He looked as though he wanted her to jump in, but she decided it was best to keep her lips locked, even if Barker had just embarrassed himself.

"Somebody left a wreath on my doorstep yesterday," Barker said as he placed the sash on the counter, the letters facing up and shining under the spotlights in the ceiling. "A funeral wreath."

"I know," Harriet said through pursed lips. "I put it there."

"Oh."

"I don't usually do deliveries for single items, but they paid extra, so I was more than happy to oblige, even if it was out of my way. I forgot you lived up that lane, Julia. I would have popped in for a cup of tea."

"The thing is, this wreath is for me," Barker said, the frustration obvious in his voice.

"Didn't you like the flowers?"

"I did, but – *well* – I'm not dead, you see."

Harriet peered over her glasses, her brow arching even higher. She looked Barker up and down, even leaning over the counter to peer at his shiny shoes.

"I can *see* that."

"Maybe there was a mix-up?" Barker asked, a glimmer of hope returning to his voice. "Is there another Barker in the village?"

"Are you suggesting I can't do my job, Mr. *Detective Inspector*?"

"No, not at all, it's just -,"

"I was given *very* specific instructions, all handwritten and *very* detailed. I followed them to the letter, including leaving the wreath on *your* doorstep yesterday morning. *Your* address was underlined and written out *very* clearly."

Barker looked to Julia again, the fear from yesterday returning to his eyes. Julia stepped forward and decided it was time to unlock her lips to help him out.

"Can you tell us who ordered the wreath, Harriet?" Julia asked kindly.

"No can do, I'm afraid."

"Why not?" Barker asked rather loudly.

"Client confidentiality."

"They're *only* flowers!"

"And the law is *still* the law!" Harriet snapped back. "Not that you care much about the law! I'm almost *certain* it's illegal to pretend to be an officer, temporary suspension or not!"

Barker's cheeks darkened as his nostrils flared. Julia had suspected this might happen. Being a trader herself, she was familiar with the law concerning customer records and privacy, even if it was something she had never encountered in her café.

"I understand that," Julia murmured, resting her hand on Barker's arm to let him know to leave it to her. "The law *is* the law, but it's put Barker in a tricky situation. As you can understand, seeing your name on a funeral wreath can be quite distressing, and we're just trying to get to the bottom of things without wasting police time."

"You know I can't tell you, Julia."

"I know that," Julia agreed. "But the man who ordered these flowers might be -,"

"I never said it was a man," Harriet jumped in, shaking her head and pulling off her glasses.

Julia concealed her smirk, glad Harriet had fallen into her trap.

"So it was a woman?" Barker asked suspiciously.

Harriet exhaled severely, her eyes darting between them. She sighed, licked her finger, and flicked back through the book.

"Listen, I can't tell you who ordered them because quite frankly, I don't know who ordered them," Harriet said through pursed lips as she scanned her bookings. "A girl came in here on Saturday with a handwritten note and cash. She wouldn't leave a name or a contact number. I wouldn't usually stand for that, but she came in the last thing on Saturday and didn't stick around. I thought maybe her family had sent her down for a funeral that was happening on Sunday, so I put the order together and delivered it at the time that was written down."

"So she was a young girl?" Julia asked, glancing to Barker, who was looking more and more confused.

"I never said that."

"But you thought her family had sent her, which suggests she wasn't old enough to come into a florist and order funeral flowers on her own."

Harriet's lips twisted into a taut snarl, her expression

growing more serious, clearly frustrated by the incessant questioning. Julia knew they didn't have long until they permanently made their way into her bad books.

"She was a teenager," Harriet said, slapping the book shut. "Thirteen, maybe younger, maybe older. It's hard to tell these days. That's all you're getting from me because that's all I know, and I'm confident that doesn't break any laws. Now if you don't mind, you've wasted enough of my time, so if you're not buying flowers, you can leave."

Julia decided against buying the yellow roses, although she made another mental note to bake a particularly rich fruitcake to give to Harriet on her next visit to the café, if she ever showed her face again. Barker led the way out of the florist, leaving Harriet to start gathering the flowers for her next job.

"Well that was a waste of time," Barker exclaimed as he shielded his eyes from the sun.

"Not necessarily," Julia said, pulling her car keys from her bag. "We know it wasn't Jeffrey Taylor who ordered the flowers."

"I almost wished it were him. At least that would make sense."

They climbed into the car, but instead of pushing her keys into the ignition, Julia held them against the wheel and stared ahead to the end of the lane, where two men were loading a grandfather clock from the antique barn into a white truck.

"Are you going to tell me about this Jeffrey Taylor?" Julia asked, shifting in her seat to face Barker. "He seems to have you pretty rattled."

Barker glanced at her out of the corner of his eyes before running his hands down his light stubble. He looked ahead at the grandfather clock, following its journey into the truck.

"You know how Superman has Lex Luthor?" Barker asked, turning fully in his seat, his brow wrinkling deep in thought. "Jeffrey Taylor is my Lex Luthor."

"Okay?"

"He was my first case after I passed my inspector's exam eight years ago. I had just turned thirty, and I was living in Hull at the time. I had the world at my feet, and I felt unstoppable. In my first month, I was put on a serial murder case with another DI, Steven, who had thirty years experience on me. He was under pressure from the big dogs to close the case before the press grabbed hold of the story and made our jobs ten times harder. Women were turning up dead all over the city, and we couldn't figure out a pattern. It was like trying to finish a crossword puzzle without the clues. It felt like we would never get a break, and then we found Jeffrey Taylor at the scene of one of the murders. He was arrested and processed. Turns out his DNA matched one of the samples taken from another one of the victims. He didn't have alibis for any of the times of deaths, and he fit the rough profile of what we had managed to put together. Steven was sure we had our guy, so that meant I was sure. I was fresh into the job, and I didn't want to ruffle feathers by going against the grain. The evidence was purely circumstantial, and aside from the DNA, we had nothing else. It was enough though. It turned into a witch-hunt, and he got life in prison. It all happened so fast, and then when no more women were found dead, it felt like we had our guy safely behind bars."

"So what happened?" Julia asked, her stomach writhing as she edged closer to Barker, her keys clenched tightly in her fist. "Why is he suddenly out of prison?"

"I looked online last night and it seems new evidence recently came to light putting another man in the frame. From what I could gather, the new guy even confessed. Jeffrey's lawyers called for a mistrial, and he won. Got a healthy payout by the sounds of it too. I transferred out of Hull to London soon after the first trial, and I moved on. The case was passed on, and they never called on me, but I never forgot his words on that last day in court. '*I'll make you pay for this! I'll kill you all.*' He looked me right in the eyes when he said that. I had nightmares of him killing me for weeks, but eventually, I forgot. I had that nightmare for the first time again last night, knowing he was in Peridale. I barely slept."

"Do you think he's innocent?"

"I don't know what I think, I just know that he's here at the same time somebody warns me of my death. It's all a little too creepy to be coincidence, don't you think?"

Julia thought about it for a second, not wanting to believe that Barker could really be in danger, but also not wanting to scare him any more than he clearly already was. Instead, she reached out and grabbed his hand in hers. Their eyes connected, a smile flickering between them. A loud sound of crashing wood snapped them both back to reality, and they turned to see the grandfather clock shattering against the cobbled road.

"Coincidences do happen," Julia stated as she slotted her key into the ignition. "Maybe he's come to Peridale to start a new life like you did?"

"Or maybe he's come to ruin my new life," Barker whispered, almost under his breath.

They drove back to Barker's cottage in silence. When

they pulled up outside, Julia jumped out of the car and opened her boot, pulling out a plastic cake box.

"The latest version of my chocolate cake," Julia said as she handed it over. "There's a gooey chocolate ganache centre in this one."

"You always know how to cheer me up," Barker said with a soft smile. "Join me inside for a slice?"

"I need to get back to the café," Julia said regretfully, glancing to Barker's cottage, where she knew the wreath was still sitting on his coffee table. "If I leave Jessie alone any longer she'll burn the place to the ground."

Barker kissed her goodbye, his lips lingering against hers a little longer than usual. When she climbed back in her car and drove down the lane, she peered through her rear-view mirror to see Barker standing by his gate, the cake in his hands as he watched her drive away.

For Barker's sake, Julia was going to get to the bottom of the wreath before it turned into anything else. She had no idea who had placed the order at Pretty Petals, but she did know she could find out why Jeffrey Taylor had come to Peridale.

CHAPTER 4

By the time Julia got back to the café, word of the wreath had spread around the village, no doubt thanks to their disastrous visit to Pretty Petals. When she locked the door after an unusually busy Monday afternoon, she was even more determined to get to the bottom of the strange mystery. Leaving her car parked in between her café and the post office, she sent Jessie home and set off walking across the village.

Evelyn's B&B sat on the corner of Peridale's main street, just past The Plough, and across from the small police station. It curved along the corner of the road in an L-shape, with an overgrown and wildly colourful garden at its heart, which still looked beautiful despite the dark grey sky above. Julia stood at the gate and looked up at the many windows scattered across the old cottage's frontage, knowing it was deceptively larger inside than it appeared. Despite this, a small sign poking out from a rose bush, which was in desperate need of pruning, let her know there were no rooms available.

Julia unclipped the gate and walked up to the front door holding a cardboard box containing two scones packed with cream and jam. Instead of a traditional doorbell, there was a metal chain, which Julia was instructed to pull by a small, hand-painted sign in swirling handwriting.

After Julia had pulled on the chain, which sent a melodic tune chiming throughout the cottage, the door shot open dramatically to reveal Evelyn in a loose lilac caftan with a turban secured around her head to match. A glittery diamond brooch held the turban in place, staring out into the world like a third eye.

"*Julia*!" Evelyn exclaimed. "*Come in*! Come in! Are those scones? The universe foretold that I would have an unexpected visitor. Would you mind taking off your shoes? I've only just finished shampooing the carpets this morning."

Julia obliged and kicked off her shoes. She followed Evelyn through her eccentrically decorated B&B and into the small sitting room overlooking the beautiful garden. When the B&B was closed for the long winter months, Evelyn travelled the world alone, picking up unusual trinkets and strange artefacts, which were displayed throughout her home as her own personal museum. Dot had always called the collection '*tacky*' because it wasn't the usual style in Peridale, but Julia liked Evelyn's taste in décor. It was chaotic and cluttered, but it made perfect sense for Evelyn, whose mind was similarly disordered and jumbled.

"Would you like a tarot reading, my dear?" Evelyn asked as she unclipped a small wooden box on the table. "I never had you down as a believer of tarot cards, but we're all full of surprises, aren't we?"

"No, thank you," Julia said with a polite smile as she pushed the scones onto the table. "Maybe another time. Been anywhere nice recently?"

"I spent the winter in Morocco," Evelyn said proudly, adjusting her turban. "I picked up a rather beautiful collection of Moroccan tea glasses there. Can I make you a cup? It will go lovely with these scones of yours!"

Before Julia responded, Evelyn scooped up the scones and floated off to the kitchen, her caftan fluttering behind her. Julia hadn't known how she was going to approach the subject of Jeffrey Taylor, but she knew a cup of tea was a good place to start.

"It's Maghrebi mint tea," Evelyn announced when she returned with a steel tray containing an oddly shaped teapot with small coloured glasses, and the scones on two plates. "I know you like your peppermint, so I'm sure you'll love this."

After pouring the tea, Evelyn scooped up one of the glasses in the palms of her hands and inhaled deeply. Her eyes flickered behind her lids, a content smile washing over her. Julia copied Evelyn's actions, surprised by the minty sweetness of the murky liquid. It calmed the nerves she had about the true nature of her visit.

"Do I detect spearmint?" Julia asked.

"Your baker's nose never fails you!" Evelyn exclaimed. "A young man who went by the name Amine introduced me to it. Amine means '*faithful and trustworthy*', although I would disagree after finding out he had a wife. Alas, I was twice the boy's age, but isn't that what travel is for?"

Julia choked on her tea but attempted to pass it off as a cough. She held it in her throat, a respectful smile on her lips as her face burned bright red. Evelyn was a decade Julia's senior, but was better travelled than any other person in Peridale, and had the stories to prove it.

"It is very delicious," Julia agreed as she placed the cup back on the tray. "I'll have to see if I can buy some online."

"I brought back plenty!" she cried, waving her hand. "I'll give you a bag before you leave."

"That's very kind of you."

"Not a problem at all, my dear." Evelyn drained her cup and placed it back on the tray. "If you didn't come for a reading, and I guess you're not here for a room, not that I have any left, may I ask the purpose of your visit today? It's nice to see you, but I'm just more accustomed to seeing you in your café."

Evelyn reached out for a scone and immediately plucked it from the plate to take a large bite. With cream and jam on her lips, she chewed silently, her eyes closed once more, and an even wider grin taking over her face. Julia was happy to see her scone having the desired effect.

"I actually wanted to ask you about -,"

Before Julia could finish her sentence, the lamps flickered and turned off entirely. They sat in darkness for a moment looking up at the lights in the ceiling, but when they didn't turn back on, Evelyn sighed, ditched her scone, and forced herself up off the sofa.

"Those fuses!" she cried out. "Been on the blink ever since I got back!"

Evelyn scurried into the hall, leaving Julia alone in the sitting room. She peered out of the window as shadowy clouds rolled over Peridale, pushing the room into even further darkness. From the hallway, she heard a small bang, followed by Evelyn crying out. Julia pulled her phone out of her bag and flicked on the bright flashlight before following the B&B owner.

"Evelyn?" she called out. "Are you okay?"

"Down here," her voice echoed through an open door. "I can't see a darn thing!"

Julia pulled on the door and shone the light down into the dark cellar. Using the wall to guide her, she descended down the stone steps, every flicker of warmth leaving her body. Nerves flooded Julia's system as she realised she was surrounded by darkness in the same building as a man who had been sent to prison for murder. When she reached the bottom, she shone the light in front of her, the shadows shifting and shaping before her eyes. When the light caught Evelyn's glittery brooch, she hurried to her, glancing over her shoulder as the blackness consumed the space around her.

"I can never figure this thing out," Evelyn whispered as she flicked various switches on the fuse box. "All the labels have worn off."

Julia shone her light over the different switches, pausing on two large red ones, which were both pointing down. She forced them back up and was relieved when light flooded into the cellar from the open door at the top of the stairs.

"Happens whenever I've got a full house," Evelyn said as she adjusted her turban. "Everybody has everything plugged in at all times these days. What happened to a good book, or a conversation?"

They headed to the stairs, both of them pausing and letting out small gasps when they saw a shadowy figure standing at the top, the light illuminating only the outline. Julia shone her flashlight up to the figure, sheer fright spreading through her when she saw an almost skeletal man's face staring down at her. Tattoos crept up his arms, only stopping at his sharp jawline, darkening his presence even more.

"Jeffrey?" Evelyn cried out with a small chuckle. "You startled me!"

Julia held back and let Evelyn lead the way up the stone steps, unable to look directly at the man. She could feel his eyes trained on her, forcing the hairs on her arms to stand on end.

"Oh, *Jeffrey!*" Evelyn cried when she reached the top of the stairs. "What have I told you about taking your shoes off after you get back from your run? I've only just finished shampooing the carpets!"

Julia looked down the hall, where large muddy footprints led all the way to Jeffrey. Mud was splattered up his calves, which were saturated in tattoos, just like his arms and neck. Julia was sure every inch of his slender body was smothered in ink. She landed on his gaunt face, unsettled by his icy eyes, which felt like they were staring deep into her soul. Her stomach knotted when she noticed that the man was missing the top half of his left ear, which jutted out at an unnatural angle.

"Sorry," Jeffrey said flatly as he kicked off his shoes.

Evelyn shook her head and rolled her eyes as she leant over to pick them up. She opened the front door and placed them on the doorstep. Heavy droplets of rain beat down on

Evelyn's garden from the gloomy sky above.

"I *foresaw* rain!" Evelyn cried proudly out into her garden. "The man on the TV said differently, but I could feel it coming."

She closed the door behind her, a satisfied smile on her face. Julia looked to Jeffrey to see his reaction, but she was surprised by his complete lack of expression. He suddenly reached out, and Julia flinched out of the way. When he closed the cellar door behind her, her cheeks flushed with embarrassment. She caught the letters '*I N N O*' tattooed thinly on his right knuckles, but she couldn't see the completed word on his left hand.

"There was a draft," he stated, not directing it at either of them. "I'm going up to my room."

They both watched Jeffrey climb the staircase, each step creaking under his weight as he ascended slowly. Julia didn't realise she had stopped breathing until he turned onto the landing.

"He's not a man of many words," Evelyn muttered as she tapped her chin. "But the cards see his kind soul beneath that exterior."

"Is he a guest?" Julia asked, not wanting to admit he was the reason behind her visit.

"Of sorts," Evelyn said as she floated back into the sitting room. "He's here for three months. Of course, I gave him a discount for such a lengthy stay."

"Three months? That's a long time."

"He's looking for a home in the village, but you know what the Peridale property market is like. It's hard to find cottages up for sale here. Nobody ever leaves. You were lucky to get such a good deal with your cottage when you did."

"Do you know where he came from?"

"Hull," Evelyn said, her brows pinched together. "I think he's here to start a quiet new life. I foresee him opening up soon. A man with that many tattoos must have many stories to tell."

Julia nodded her agreement as she scooped up her handbag, somehow feeling Jeffrey's eyes staring at her through the ceiling. She thought about telling Evelyn where her new guest had come from but decided it wasn't her place to out Jeffrey's time in prison.

"Thanks for the tea. It was lovely."

"You're going already?" Evelyn asked as she settled into the sofa and poured herself another cup. "What was it you wanted to ask me?"

Julia glanced up at the ceiling as she heard movement in the room directly above them. She considered asking Evelyn more about her strange new guest, but she stopped herself, unsure of what she thought her visit would achieve.

"I just wanted to see how you were," Julia lied with a smile. "I had some scones left over, and I know how much you like them."

Luckily for Julia, Evelyn didn't seem suspicious of her kindness, which immediately made her feel guilty. Evelyn scurried off to the kitchen and returned with a small bag of green tea leaves, which she thrust into Julia's hands.

"They're best when you leave them to steep for a long time," Evelyn said with a wink. "Don't be a stranger, my dear."

Julia thanked her for the tea leaves and stepped out of the B&B, looking down at the muddy running shoes on the doorstep. She hurried down the garden path, the torrential rain soaking her through in seconds. Before she unclipped the gate, she looked back at the cottage. Through the sitting room window, she saw Evelyn settling into her sofa and inhaling a fresh cup of the Moroccan tea. Julia's eyes wandered up to the window above it, sure she had just seen movement behind the sheer curtains.

Pulling up her collar, she turned on her heels and opened the gate, feeling no closer to figuring out who had ordered the wreath. What she did now understand was why Barker was so unsettled by Peridale's newest resident. As she hurried through the rain, she still felt his icy eyes burning into her skin.

"*Julia*!" a familiar voice cried out through the darkness. "Julia! Over here!"

She squinted in the rain to see Barker huddled in the doorway of The Plough, the light above the sign casting down on his face. She hurried across the road and joined him in the shelter.

"What are you doing here?" she asked as she forced her wet hair out of her eyes.

"Went to the station, but there still wasn't any news about my job, so I thought I would come and drown my sorrows," Barker said, the stench of beer strong on his breath. "What are you doing up here?"

"I just went for a walk to clear my head," Julia lied, peering through the heavy rain to the B&B at the same time a lamp flicked on in the window above Evelyn's sitting room. "Didn't expect to get caught in a shower."

"I'm waiting for it to calm down before I walk home," Barker said, edging forward to peer up at the dark sky. "Doesn't look like it will be anytime soon."

"Well, I'm already soaked through. You could join me on my walk home?"

Barker looked at the rain bouncing off the road, and then to Julia. He wrapped his hand around hers and pulled her out into the shower with a playful smirk. Hand in hand, they hurried through the village, defying the murky clouds circling above. Julia almost led him to her car that was parked in its usual spot next to her café, but she decided she didn't want to soak her seats through, so they set off up the winding lane. As they approached Barker's cottage, the torrential downpour suddenly slowed down, and the clouds cleared a little, allowing the last light of the evening to peek through in scattered rays.

"Typical!" Barker yelled up at the sky, his hair flat over his eyes. "Just *typical*!"

"Are you going to invite me in?" Julia asked as she wrapped her arms around her shivering body. "A cup of hot cocoa would go down perfectly right now."

"You always have the best ideas," Barker said as he unclipped his gate. "A cup of -,"

They both stopped in their tracks at the bottom of the garden path, their eyes landing on the same thing. Something else had been left on Barker's doorstep, but this time it was something far more dangerous than a wreath; it was a body.

They slowly approached the facedown figure as though not to startle him. The rain stopped completely, allowing fresh blood to pour from the back of the man's skull, dripping down his short brown hair to mix in with the moss on Barker's doorstep.

"Call the police," Barker whispered darkly, holding a hand back to stop Julia getting any closer. "And an ambulance, although I think it's too late for that."

Julia nodded and unclipped her handbag, her fingers

scrambling for her phone. As she pushed the device against her ear, she stepped back and watched as Barker carefully rolled the man over. He jumped back, both hands gripping his mouth as he stared down at the wide-eyed, pale-faced man gazing loose-jawed at the clearing sky.

"It's Jim Austen," Barker mumbled through his fingers. "It's the Chief Inspector. He's my boss."

CHAPTER 5

Julia watched the sun rise over her garden from her kitchen window as she hugged a hot cup of Evelyn's Moroccan tea. Mowgli jumped up onto the counter and stepped over the sink and gently nudged her. She tickled under his chin, and he purred rhythmically, his fluffy tail standing on end and flicking against the spider plant on the windowsill.

"You always know when something is wrong, don't you, boy?" Julia whispered as she set her cup down so she could pick him up. "Are you hungry?"

Mowgli clung to her robe, his claws digging through the fabric and gently pushing into her shoulder. She squeezed him tightly before setting him down by his food bowl. She glanced at the cat clock on the wall, with its swishing tail and darting eyes. It wasn't even six in the morning yet, but she emptied a pouch of cat food into his bowl all the same.

She stomped on the pedal of the bin, catching her reflection in the shiny stainless steel lid. Dark blotches circled her eyes, giving away that she hadn't been able to sleep. Every time she had tried, she had seen the glassy, lifeless eyes of Chief Inspector Austen staring up at her.

The moment she returned to her tea, a soft knock rattled the frosted pane of glass in her front door. She hurried from the kitchen and past the sitting room, where Barker was snoring soundly in the chair by the dying fire. She pulled her robe together and opened the door, relieved to see DS Forbes.

"Sorry it's so early, Julia," Bradley said, his plump red cheeks burning brightly in the early morning cold. "Is Barker still here? The forensics team has finished at his cottage."

"He's here. Please, come in."

Bradley bowed his head and stepped inside. He walked into the sitting room and cleared his throat. Barker sat up straight, his eyes springing open. He stared around the room after rubbing them, before landing on Bradley with a startled look.

"DS Forbes," Barker croaked as he ran his hands down his face. "Any news?"

Bradley sat on the couch, so Julia perched on the edge of Barker's armchair so she could rest a hand on his back. She rubbed gently, and he smiled appreciatively up at her.

"Jim's wife, Pauline, hasn't taken it too well," Bradley cooed, his voice catching. "He was due to retire next year.

Their first grandchild is on the way too."

Barker dropped his face into his hands and let out a small groan. Julia gripped his shoulders to let him know that she was still there, but it didn't appear to make a difference.

"This is all my fault," Barker whispered through his fingers. "He would never have died if it wasn't for me."

"He was struck with a rock, which appeared to have killed him quite quickly," Bradley said, reading aloud from a small notepad. "They're estimating that the time of death was between half past five and six in the evening, which means he hadn't been dead long when you found him. The rain has washed away most trace evidence, so there wasn't much forensics could pick up, but they spent all night trying anyway. Jim is – I mean - he *was* a good man. They're doing the best they can for him. So far, it's looking like a mugging gone wrong. His pockets were completely empty, and nobody has been able to find his phone. We've put a trace out for it, but if it's not used, it's not going to be easy to track down."

"This wasn't random," Barker muttered, lifting his head from his hands for the first time since Bradley had started talking. "This was about me."

"It's just a coincidence," Julia whispered, clenching his shoulder again. "There's no way you could have known."

Barker shrugged Julia off and started pacing back and forth across the hearthrug, his hands firmly clenched in his hair.

"This is connected to the wreath," Barker stated. "It's so obvious. Whoever killed Jim thought they were killing me. People always used to joke that we looked the same from behind. We got our hair cut by the same person, and we were the same height. He was coming to see me, and whoever left that wreath was waiting for me to get home, and they struck, but they got the wrong man."

"You never officially reported the wreath," Bradley reminded him. "It's better that it comes from you, rather than me. I don't want to land me in trouble too."

Bradley attempted to chuckle, but it came out flatly, leaving behind a thick silence in its wake. Barker walked over to the window and stared out at the fields ahead with his hands pressed up against the thin glass.

"This was personal," Barker said. "Somebody wanted to kill me."

"Julia's right, it could just be a coincidence," Bradley said, his tone low. "Although I have to admit, it does look suspicious. You'll both be expected to give official statements at the station later today, but you already know that."

"I suppose you want our alibis?" Barker asked coldly without turning around.

"You know it's just routine, boss."

"I was in the pub from three until six," Barker said. "Half a dozen people saw me there, including Shelby and Bob. I was outside of the pub waiting for the rain to stop for approximately two minutes when Julia walked by. We then walked home together and – *well* – you know the rest."

"And Julia?" Bradley murmured after he finished scribbling down what Barker had just told him. "Where were you before you met up with Barker?"

Julia moved from the chair arm to the seat, shifting uncomfortably as she stared at the back of Barker's head. She didn't want to admit that she had lied to him, even if it was before they had found the poor man's body. Now wasn't the time to continue that lie.

"I was visiting Evelyn's B&B," Julia said as she stared down at her hands in her lap. "I left my café at half past five, which my lodger can account for. I then walked up to the B&B, which took around two minutes. Evelyn will be able to tell you my exact time of arrival. I wasn't sure of the time I left, but it was less than a minute before I saw Barker."

"The important thing is you're both accounted for at the time of the death, and long before it," Bradley said, snapping his pad shut after scribbling more notes. "It will make it easy to eliminate both of you really quickly so we can find the monster that did this to Jim."

Julia smiled her thanks, even if she could feel the tension radiating from Barker after learning the truth of where she had really been after finishing work.

"Can I make you a cup of tea?" Julia asked, sensing the awkward silence that was growing between them. "Or perhaps make you something to eat? You must be starving after working all night."

"I should get going," Bradley said with an apologetic smile as he pushed himself off the sofa, his large stomach hanging low over his belt. "Barker, I know people at the station would like to hear from you. They're all pretty shook up about this."

Barker nodded, but he still didn't turn around. Clutching her robe together, Julia showed Bradley to the door and thanked him for stopping by. She waited until he was at the bottom of her garden path so she could wave him off, before turning and walking slowly back into the sitting room, where the tension was almost palpable.

"Why didn't you tell me you went to check up on Jeffrey Taylor?" Barker asked as he finally turned around.

"It wasn't like that."

"What was it like then, Julia?" The sudden increase in tone took her by surprise. "Because it seems like you enjoy sneaking around behind people's backs."

"I didn't know *this* was going to happen!" she snapped back, her arms folding firmly across her chest. "I just wanted to see Jeffrey for myself, and maybe ask him straight if he sent the wreath to scare you. I didn't even get a chance. He's intense, and I didn't speak two words to the man."

"I could have told you that," Barker mumbled as he brushed past her, grabbing his jacket off the back of the couch. "I told you about the Jeffrey Taylor case to *stop* you looking for information. You have *no* right sniffing around in my past, but you just can't help yourself."

Julia watched as he stormed towards the door, confused at what had just happened. She chased after him, catching the door before it slammed in the frame.

"Where are you going?" she called out as he hurried down the lane.

"To give my statement."

She stood on her doorstep, watching open-mouthed until Barker finally disappeared around the bend towards his cottage. Her closest neighbour, Emily Burns, was already in her garden, although her eyes were glued on Julia. She didn't doubt news of their argument would spread around the village before noon. When she finally turned around, she wasn't surprised to see Jessie standing in her bedroom doorway in her black pyjamas.

"Lovers' tiff?" Jessie asked sympathetically.

"To be honest with you, I don't know what that was,"

Julia said, shaking her head. "Sit down, and I'll make you some breakfast."

She closed the front door, and they both walked through to the kitchen arm in arm. Julia pulled eggs from the fridge, cracking them one by one into a bowl. She added salt, pepper, and a splash of milk, then poured them into a hot frying pan. As she scrambled the eggs with a fork, Jeffrey Taylor's dirty running shoes flashed into her mind, and she realised he was likely out and about in the village at the same time Jim Austen was murdered. She wished she had remembered that during Barker's outburst because it might have helped her case.

CHAPTER 6

After a nap and a shower, Julia pottered around her cottage, unable to rest because all she could think about was Barker. She hovered over his number on her phone more than once but stopped herself from pressing the green call button. He needed space and he would talk to her when he was ready.

Instead, she did the only thing she knew to do in times of trouble; she baked. She poured her frustration and guilt into a new version of the chocolate cake, this time substituting the cow's milk for chocolate oat milk to create an even richer taste. When she finished glazing the cake in glossy icing, she dropped a glacé black cherry on top.

She took a step back from the cake to assess her work,

wishing Barker were there to taste the first slice. During her baking, she had come to the conclusion that she owed Barker a big apology for going behind his back. She realised that figuring out life's jigsaw puzzles meant nothing if she didn't put those she loved before her urge to discover the truth.

With Jessie looking after the café and Mowgli chasing birds around the garden, Julia boxed up the cake and decided to turn to the one person who had always been there for her in times of need.

Cake in hand, Julia set off walking into the village. When she reached Barker's cottage, she paused to stare at the doorstep, the body still fresh in her mind. She looked into Barker's sitting room window, but he didn't appear to be home. She checked the silver watch on her wrist, wondering if he could still possibly be giving his statement.

When she reached her gran's cottage, it felt like coming home. It was a place she had found solace many times in her life. It had been there for her during her mother's death when she was a little girl, and then two decades later after her husband, Jerrad, had kicked her out of their London apartment, and it was there for her today when she needed somebody to lean on. Of course, she knew it was really her gran, and not the building that provided the deep-rooted feeling of home, but it was comforting seeing the cottage almost completely unchanged from her childhood.

Julia walked through to the sitting room and was immediately startled to see her gran on the ground, crammed between the television and the coffee table. For a moment, she thought she might have fallen, until she saw her gran's leg shoot up in the air as she lay on her side, her eyes glued to the black and white screen.

"Gran," Julia announced herself. "Are you – *okay*?"

"Get down here and join me," Dot panted. "It's a Jane Fonda. Found it in a box of tapes in the attic. Still works."

As though to prove otherwise, the videotape crackled, sending wobbly lines up and down the screen. Julia had offered to buy her gran a newer TV on more than one occasion, but Dot didn't see the point. Julia noticed the smart watch flashing her heart rate on her wrist, and she let out a small laugh at her gran's hypocrisy. She was sure if her gran somehow started a television club, she would want the biggest and latest model.

"Why is it on mute?"

"Can't stand the woman's voice," Dot exclaimed as she stood up and started to jump side to side, copying the women on the screen, who looked like they were wearing clothes of a similar neon hue to her gran's, even though they were in black and white. "You know how I feel about American accents, love. Like nails down a chalkboard. What's that?"

Dot stopped to wipe the sweat from her face with a bright green towel as she glared down at the cake. With everything else that had been going on, Julia had forgotten all about her gran's new healthy living obsession, or she had at least subconsciously hoped she would have been bored of it by now.

"It's a salad," Julia said hopefully. "It's just trapped inside a chocolate cake. You can only get to it by eating the outside first."

"I'll get *one* plate," Dot said coolly as she shuffled past Julia towards the kitchen. "I'll have a *single* bite of yours. I thought I told you not to bring contaminants into my house?"

Julia put the cake box on top of a copy of *Senior Fitness Weekly* and picked up the remote control to pause the video. Jane stopped mid jumping jack, her arms and legs floating in the air behind the crackly static.

"Where are the rest of the girls?" Julia asked when Dot returned with the single plate and two forks. "Isn't the whole point of a club to do something with other people?"

"They're too weak," Dot said bitterly, her wrinkled lips pursing tightly. "They can't keep up with me!"

"Don't you think you might be being a bit hard on them? Not everybody has your – how shall I put this – *zest* for life?"

"Somebody has to be hard on those old biddies, or else we all rot and die! You need to stay sharp and active, especially at my age, Julia. You should watch that documentary I told you about. It will make you see things *very* differently."

Julia was sure it would, but getting fit and losing weight were the last things on her mind. She pulled the cake out of the box and instead of cutting a slice, she dropped it onto the plate and started digging from the middle.

"I suppose you heard of the murder outside of Barker's cottage?" Julia asked through a mouthful of the milky cake.

"Emily Burns called first thing this morning when she saw all of the police. I went to the café the second it opened and Jessie – *well*, she told me what happened between you and Barker, so I thought you might like some time alone. I knew you'd come when you were ready."

"That's what I'm hoping happens with Barker," Julia said, glancing at the clock as it ticked past three in the afternoon. "He said I couldn't help sticking my nose into things."

"He's *not* wrong," Dot murmured as she dug her fork into the middle of the cake. "The difference is, you're not an idle gossip. You only stick your nose into the worthy causes. I don't doubt that whatever you did was because you thought it was the right thing to do."

"I did, at the time."

"Then that's all that matters."

"How do you know if somebody is keeping something from you?" Julia asked as she stared down at the cake on the end of her fork. "I don't think I know Barker as well as I want to believe that I do."

"Why do you say that?"

"The way he reacted this morning, it felt like something more. He told me not to go digging in his past, but I only went looking for something based on what he had said to me."

"What did you do?"

Before Julia could answer, she was interrupted by the roaring sound of a lawn mower engine starting up. She looked out of the window to the village green, expecting to see somebody trimming the neat grass, but there was nobody there.

"I've got a gardener in the back," Dot explained. "I've let it get out of hand. So, what did you do?"

Julia tried to think of what she had done, but the spluttering of the lawn mower working through the long grass was too distracting. She crammed the chocolate cake into her mouth, her brows furrowing tightly.

"I thought you fired your garden guy for accidentally cutting the heads off your tulips?"

"I got someone new," Dot said, waving a hand dismissively. "Evelyn recommended him. Does it matter?"

"No," Julia said with a shake of her head. "I thought you didn't like Evelyn? I thought she was too '*wacky*' for you?"

"Oh, she is. When she caught me looking at the ads in the post office window, she said she *foresaw* that I needed help. What a load of old *codswallop*! If that woman has the sight, then she needs her eyes tested. The man she recommended was charging a fair price, and quite frankly, I'm on a budget after buying this gizmo on my wrist."

Julia crammed another forkful of cake into her mouth, unable to shake the uneasy feeling in her stomach. Instead of ruminating, or asking her gran more questions, she ditched the fork and the cake, and walked through to the dining room, where she saw Jeffrey Taylor forcing a lawn mower through the overgrown grass.

"Julia? What has gotten into you?" Dot cried as she chased after her. "It's all that sugar and fat in the cake! It's pushing you over the edge!"

"I'm all right, Gran," Julia insisted, shaking her gran's hands off her. "Your new gardener is the reason Barker is mad at me."

"Julia, please tell me you didn't -,"

"*Gran*!" Julia cried, cutting her off before she could finish her sentence. "Barker knows Jeffrey. He sent him to prison."

"Jeffrey sent Barker to prison?"

"Barker sent *Jeffrey* to prison," Julia said with a sigh. "He was sentenced to life on a serial murder charge."

"There's a murderer in my garden?" Dot muttered, her hand clasping over her mouth. "Call the *police*! Call the *army*! Call *somebody*! He's in possession of a dangerous weapon right this second! Do you know how fast those blades travel? Fast enough to chop off my poor head!"

"Calm down, Gran," Julia said, grabbing her by the shoulders to give her a good shake. "He was released because they found that he had been wrongly convicted."

"So he's innocent?"

"Maybe."

"*Maybe* isn't good enough, my dear!"

"In the eyes of the courts, he is," Julia said, narrowing her eyes on Jeffrey as he rammed the lawn mower over a tough patch of grass. "I'm not so sure. He makes me feel uneasy."

"Why is he in Peridale, anyway?"

"Starting a new life, apparently," Julia whispered as her gran joined her to stare out of the window. "That's what Evelyn said."

"Evelyn talks a lot of *tosh*! She probably foresaw it and skipped asking him," Dot snapped with a roll of her eyes. "Oh, it's quite exciting though, isn't it? A convicted serial killer here in Peridale? Certainly beats any other gossip I've heard this week. Well, aside from the murder, of course. Do you think he was the one who bashed Jim's head in with the rock?"

"*Gran!*"

"*What?*" Dot cried, waving her hands in the air. "You young 'uns are too sensitive. Can't call a spade a spade these days without you getting on your FaceTweet and SnapBook, or whatever they're called. Not everything needs a petition you know, sweetheart! I'm going to make him a cup of tea. He might have some juicy prison stories."

Dot hurried off to the kitchen, leaving Julia to watch him work. He pushed the mower towards the end of the garden, the spluttering noise growing further away. When he reached the bottom of the long stretch of grass, he pulled his grey, sweat-stained T-shirt over his head to wipe down his face. In the jumble of dark tattoos covering the length and breadth of his body, a skull and crossbones between his shoulder blades jumped out at her, sending a shiver down her spine. She stared into the shadowy, soulless eyes of the inked drawing, unable to look away. Through the heat lines of the afternoon, she was sure she saw its mouth smirking at her.

Jeffrey suddenly looked over his shoulder, his icy blue eyes piercing across the garden and staring deep into Julia's, as though he had known she had been standing there watching him the entire time. She took a step back into the darkness of the dining room, turning her attention to the kitchen while her gran poured milk into a cup of tea.

"I'll take that out," Julia said, putting her hands on the cup.

"You will *not*!"

Julia firmly pulled the cup from out of her gran's hands and hurried out of the open back door, closing it behind her. She glanced through the kitchen window, where her gran was glaring at her with her mouth ajar. Julia had more important things to extract from the mysterious newcomer than prison stories.

"I've brought you a cup of tea," Julia said, applying her friendliest smile. "Thought you might be thirsty."

Jeffrey took the cup from her, ignoring the handle and grabbing it around the middle as though it wasn't hot. Without blowing, he took a deep gulp of the tea, finishing half of it in one go. He tossed the other half into the grass before passing the cup back to Julia. She stared down at the dregs of sugar at the bottom of the cup, unsure of what to say.

"We met yesterday," Julia offered, smiling even wider. "Remember? At Evelyn's?"

"I remember," he replied flatly.

"I didn't realise you were a gardener."

"I'm not."

"Oh," Julia mumbled, her smile wavering. "Well, you're doing a great job. I hope my gran is paying you well. You have to be pretty fit to push a mower through this grass. I'm sure it grows twice as thick as the rest of the grass in Peridale, but I'm sure you're more than fit enough, what with your running."

Jeffrey's expression didn't waver, his piercing eyes not looking away from hers. She was sure she hadn't seen him blink yet. She waited for him to speak, but nothing left his lips.

"My gran is suddenly into fitness. I'm thinking of joining her for a jog, but I never know where to go. Where do you go running?"

Julia almost wanted to take the words back. It was painfully obvious that her embarrassing attempt to extract information from the man wasn't going to work. When she finally noticed him blink, she eased a little.

"Around," he said. "I should get on with this."

"Of course," Julia said with a nod, almost glad of a reason to step back. "Good luck with the rest of it."

She turned around and hurried back to the cottage, her face scrunched up in humiliation. She almost wished she had just let her gran take out the tea to badger him about his time in prison. Before both of her encounters with Jeffrey, she had gone in with a clear idea of what she had wanted to find out, but he was so peculiar, it scrambled her brain and turned her into a nervous wreck.

"I know who you are," he called across the garden, stopping her dead in her tracks.

"I'm sorry?" she replied, turning around.

"I know who you are," he repeated as he rubbed his T-shirt across his tattooed chest. "You're Brown's girlfriend."

Julia's heart stopped, and her cheeks burned brighter than they ever had before. She opened her mouth to defend herself, but no words rolled off her tongue. She felt like she stood there for hours, staring wide-eyed across the garden at the tattooed stranger, unable to form a single sentence in her mind. It wasn't until he turned and continued mowing the grass that she summoned the strength to run back into her gran's cottage.

"Well?" Dot demanded. "What did he say?"

"Nothing."

"*Nothing?*" Dot cried. "You're useless, my dear! Nobody knows about our new criminal resident yet, and I want first dibs on the gossip. Give me that cup. I'm trying again!"

Julia handed over the cup and walked through to the sitting room to grab the rest of her chocolate cake. She looked down at it, but it just reminded her too much of Barker, so she left it behind. She knew it would probably find its way into her gran's bin, but she had no other use for it right now.

Leaving her gran to badger the gardener, she stepped out into the daylight. She looked across the village green, considering helping Jessie close the café for the day, but the thought of having to face the people who had heard she was the one who had found Jim's body put her off. Instead, she headed off to the station to give her statement, knowing the sooner she could put the whole event behind her, the better.

CHAPTER 7

After a long and chaotic shift at the café, Julia was more than pleased to see Barker sitting on her garden wall when she pulled up outside her cottage. She could barely contain her smile as she climbed out of the car.

"I'll leave you two to it," Jessie mumbled, pulling her house keys from her pocket. "Try not to bite each other's heads off again."

Barker chuckled softly and dropped his head. When he looked up and met Julia's eyes, she knew everything was going to be okay between them. She looked down at the plaster on her hand where she had almost sliced off a finger cutting a slice of toast because she hadn't been able to concentrate all day.

"I was just sitting in The Plough staring into a pint, wondering why I wasn't here with you," he whispered, reaching out and grabbing Julia's hand. "I owe you an apology."

"So do I."

"You were just trying to help," he said with a quick wink. "I should never have talked to you like I did. To say the last couple of days have been stressful is an understatement."

"Do you want to come inside? There's a slice of chocolate cake with your name on it."

"I was wondering if you wanted to come with me to the Fern Moore Estate?" Barker asked as he pushed away from the wall. "DS Forbes kindly informed me that Billy Matthews was caught trying to sell a phone he claimed to have found in a bush. I'll give you one guess to figure out whose phone it was."

"Jim's?"

"*Bingo.*"

"They arrested him? Is it safe to talk to him now?" Julia asked cautiously. "I don't want you to get in any more trouble."

"At this rate, I'll be lucky to get my job back now. Jim was the only person who was really in my corner. I owe it to him to at least try and piece this together."

Julia didn't need to hear any more. In minutes, they were driving out of the village and towards Fern Moore. She turned to Barker and couldn't help but smile. They might have only been giving each other the silent treatment for one day, but it only confirmed the love she felt for him even more. There was nowhere she would rather be than by his side.

Fern Moore Estate was just outside of Peridale, but very separate. If you asked any villagers if Fern Moore was part of Peridale, they would deny it until they were blue in the face. The estate had always had a troublesome reputation. As a teenager, Julia and her school friends were advised to stay away if they didn't want to get into any fights. As an adult, she drove past it on the A roads, happy to look in the other direction. Their search for Billy Matthews was her first official visit to the area.

The estate consisted of two large U-shaped buildings looking over two courtyards, which had been built in the early 1980s and housed hundreds of families in small flats. External walkways ran along the fronts of the flats, acting as makeshift balconies. The courtyards appeared to be a meeting place for the residents, not unlike Peridale's village green. Instead of regularly trimmed pristine grass, Fern Moore's common area housed an out-of-date, vandalised, and graffiti-covered children's play-park, which didn't look safe for any child to be playing on. Julia wasn't surprised to see the gate padlocked, and the park empty and full of beer cans.

"Billy Matthews is up there," Barker whispered, pointing to a flat at the end of one of the walkways on the second floor. "Let's not stick around too long."

Julia nodded and hurried to keep up with Barker as they walked towards a narrow stairway, passing a lift that looked like it hadn't been in use for years. Just like the park, graffiti covered so much of the stairwell that it was almost impossible to recognise the original wall colour underneath.

Their heels clicked on the concrete walkway as they

passed all of the flats, each of them with a single-paned window and a blue front door, which didn't look much thicker than plywood. Julia heard snippets of conversations, arguments, and television programmes as they rushed towards the last flat, neither of them wanting to linger for too long. Some of the flats looked more well kept than others, with clean curtains in the windows, and flower baskets decorating the frontage, but most looked as rundown as the dated complex felt. Julia loved her wide-open countryside too much to imagine ever living in such a confined space.

"I'm here so often they should cut me a key," Barker mumbled as he rapped his knuckles loudly on the door. "Billy Matthews wouldn't know how to stay out of trouble if his life depended on it."

A woman screeched behind the door, her voice seeming to bounce and echo into every corner of the estate. The door cracked open, a chain stopping it from opening more than a couple of inches. A cloud of cigarette smoke greeted them, and Julia tried her best not to cough. When it cleared, they saw the squinting face of a woman in her late-thirties, clutching a cigarette between her lips, smoking it hands-free while she balanced a white-haired toddler on her hip. The woman was wearing a stained nightgown, which Julia guessed she had been wearing since that morning, rather than having just changed into it.

"What?" she barked through a hoarse cough. "What do you want?"

"We're looking for Billy, Sandra," Barker said, stepping forward as he glanced awkwardly to Julia. "I'm Barker Brown. We've met several times."

"Whatever he's done, he's not here," she cried over the

sound of the TV, rolling her eyes heavily before looking over her shoulder. "*Turn that racket down!*"

Julia peered into the messy living room, spotting a young teenage girl with bright red hair sitting on the couch, a remote control clasped in her hands. Instead of turning the TV volume down, she cranked it up.

"Do you have any idea where Billy is?" Julia asked over the noise, applying her friendliest smile.

"Even if I knew, love, I wouldn't tell you," Sandra said with a smirk. "We don't snitch on our own 'round here, especially not to the police."

"We're not here on official business," Barker said, not seeming to want to admit he was no longer an active DI. "We just wanted to ask him some questions about his arrest earlier today."

"What arrest?" Sandra snapped as she puffed smoke expertly out of her nose like a dragon.

"Do you have any idea what time Billy will be back?" Barker asked, avoiding her question.

"If you're not police, clear off."

With that, Sandra slammed the door shut and disappeared back into her flat. The TV suddenly turned off, followed by loud shouting, and then a girl crying. They lingered for a moment, but it was evident they weren't going to find the information they had wanted from Billy's mother.

"She's not the most – *cooperative* mother," Barker said tactfully.

"You could say that."

They shared a smile before heading back towards the stairwell. Julia felt like they were on a wild goose chase, following breadcrumbs into the dark. She knew there was every chance Jim's death was the mugging gone wrong that DS Forbes suspected, but she also knew it was likely to be something more personal. If somebody had thought they were murdering Barker, she knew it would only be a matter of time before that person tried to finish what they had started.

"What now?" Julia asked as they reached the bottom of the stairs.

"I don't know," Barker said as they emerged from the stairwell. "*Hey*! Get away from that car!"

Barker darted towards a gang of boys who had gathered around Julia's Ford Anglia. Her heart stopped when she noticed one of them trying the door handles. Startled by Barker, most of them scattered, apart from three, who stepped back with dangerous smirks on their faces. The boy who appeared to be the leader of the group was wearing a black cap, a blue matching tracksuit with three white stripes running down either side, and bright white trainers. Under the shadow of the hat, Julia recognised the boy's face.

"I should have known it would be you," Billy snorted as he slurped beer out of a can from the side of his mouth. "PC Plod and his sidekick, coming to save the day."

Julia found herself clutching her handbag closer to her body as she approached the gang. Billy caught her eyes and smirked, his brows darting up and down. With the clothes and the can of beer, it was easy to forget he was still a child.

"Just the boy I was looking for," Barker said smugly, stuffing his hands into his trouser pockets. "Would you mind stepping away from the lady's car, Billy?"

"It's crap anyway." Billy swigged from his beer can and spat the beer across Julia's windshield. "I've seen tins of beans more advanced than this hunk of junk."

Julia bit her tongue, knowing it wasn't the right time to jump in and defend her beloved vintage vehicle. She looked to Barker, who stepped forward to stand between the boys and the car.

"Heard you were arrested yesterday, Billy," Barker said firmly, his arms folded protectively across his chest. "Trying to sell a dead man's phone? That's low, even for you."

"I was framed, wasn't I, lads?"

Both of his friends grumbled their agreement, their arms and chests puffed out, despite all being on the thin side. They stayed two steps behind Billy, apparently knowing their place behind their leader.

"That's always the story with you, Billy," Barker said with a small laugh. "You never just own up to anything, do you?"

"That's because pigs like you always blame me for everything," Billy said, glugging the last of the beer before crunching the can in his hand and tossing it into the ruined park. "You lot like to pin things on lads like us."

"And what are '*lads like you*'?" Barker asked.

"Street lads. You think because we dress like this we're criminals."

"But you *are* criminals," Barker said flatly. "You alone have a criminal record longer than my arm, and that's not even including your scrawny henchmen."

The two boys took a step forward, their arms puffing out even more as they glared under their caps at Barker. Julia found their appearance more amusing than menacing, even if she wouldn't want to cross them in a dark alley.

"Is this your bird?" Billy scoffed, stepping forward and walking around Julia. "Bit fat, isn't she?"

"*She* has a name," Julia snapped as she straightened out

her pale blue dress. "Would you speak to your mother like that?"

"Probably," Billy said, which caused a snicker among his friends. "I found the phone, alright? I didn't know whose it was. Some pig caught me trying to flog it down the Marley Street Market. I wasn't to know it was a dead man's."

"I heard you found the phone in a bush," Barker said firmly, cocking his head back to stare down at the boy. "Sure you didn't take it from his body after you hit him over the head with a rock?"

"Why would I want to do that?" Billy snorted. "Didn't even know the poor bugger."

"Because you thought he was me."

"Don't flatter yourself, PC Plod."

"That's DI Brown, to you."

"Not from what I heard," Billy said, walking behind his two friends and slapping them both on the shoulders. "The streets have been talking about you getting sacked. Best news we've heard all year!"

Barker gritted his jaw, his cheeks burning bright red, just as they had when Harriet had called him out on his suspension. Julia stepped forward and rested her arm on his shoulder, but he shook it off to start circling the boys.

"The thing is, Billy, you *are* a criminal," Barker said coldly, making sure to look in the kid's eyes at all times. "It's only a matter of time before you do something that's going to land you behind bars for good, and when that day comes, the streets will be a safer place."

"Yeah, well, until then, I'll just keep doing what I do with my lads."

The two boys mumbled their agreement as they

watched Barker circle them once more.

"It's no life, is it, Billy?"

"So what? Nothing else to do."

"Where did you get the phone?"

"I told you, I found it."

"But where?"

"In a bush at the bus station," Billy said, holding back his laughter. "What does it even matter? They let me go. They have CCTV footage of me finding the phone. I didn't kill that pig, even if it is one less of you on the streets."

Barker suddenly stopped in his tracks, the whites of his eyes shining brightly. Julia was sure he was about to lay his hands on the kid, so she jumped in between them and rested her hands on Barker's face. He looked through her for a moment, before finally meeting her eyes. She shook her head and pulled him towards the car.

"Wish it would have been you that had taken a brick to the head," Billy said before spitting at Barker's feet. "After what you did, it's the least you deserve. C'mon, lads. These two losers aren't worth our time. I heard there's a party at Trisha's flat."

With that, the trio headed towards the nearest stairwell and disappeared, not before turning and smirking at Barker one last time. Julia rested her hand on his chest, letting him know they weren't worth it.

"I'm all right," Barker said after shaking his head. "He's usually even worse than that."

Julia pulled him over to a green steel bench outside of the closed park. The paint had worn away where people had scratched their names in more than one place to reveal the rusting metal underneath. They both perched on the edge of the bench, looking up at the sky as pale pink leaked into the horizon.

"What did Billy mean when he said '*after what you did*'?" Julia asked, resting a hand on his.

"How long have you got?" Barker whispered with a small laugh. "I've arrested that kid a dozen times since moving to Peridale. I think the boys at the station had given up on him, but I wasn't going to let things slide."

"Do you think he murdered Jim?"

"I don't know," Barker said with a sigh as he stared up at the fading sky. "I can't believe this is happening. When I first came to this village, a lot of people at the station weren't happy about me coming in from the city. They thought they should have promoted from within the station, but Jim championed me. He was behind me the whole way, even when he had to suspend me. He was probably just coming to see how I was doing that night. That's the type of guy he was. He would give you the clothes off his back if you asked him. He didn't deserve to go out like that. That should have been me."

Julia bowed her head. She felt selfish for being glad that it wasn't Barker who had died, but she didn't want to tell him that. She couldn't imagine how she would have reacted if it had been Barker that she had found blood soaked on the doorstep that night.

"When I went to Evelyn's B&B to talk to Jeffrey, he wasn't there," Julia said.

"You don't have to explain."

"Just listen," Julia interrupted him. "He wasn't there at first, but he came back around six, just before it started raining. His shoes were all muddy. Evelyn said he had been out for a run, and even though he didn't correct her, he didn't say anything to the contrary."

"You think he was in the village at the time of the murder?"

"I'm almost sure of it," Julia said, edging closer to him. "He was at my gran's yesterday doing her gardening, and I tried to talk to him to establish an alibi, but he didn't give me anything. He did, however, know that you and I were connected. He called me '*Brown's girlfriend*.'"

"He always called me '*Brown*'," Barker muttered. "Just talking about Jeffrey is bringing back so many bad memories. I thought he was firmly in my past with the rest of it, but here he is, swanning around the village like he owns the place."

"The rest of it?" Julia asked.

Barker looked at her before looking up to the sky again as dusk set in. He stood up and held his hand out for her.

"A story for another day," he said. "Have you told anyone about Jeffrey's ill-timed run?"

"I told the police everything in my statement yesterday."

"Good," Barker said with a firm nod. "We have to trust they know what they're doing because right now, all I want to do is go back to the village, grab a bottle of wine from the shop, and curl up on the couch with you and a DVD."

Julia rested her head on his shoulder as they walked back to the car under the setting sun. Barker's proposition sounded like the best thing she had heard all week, and for one night, she was going to forget all about the wreath, Jim's murder, and Jeffrey Taylor.

"Can I pick the DVD?" Julia asked as she unlocked the car.

"Yes, but I'm not watching *Breakfast at Tiffany's* again."

"But it's my favourite film."

"And *Die Hard* is mine," Barker said as he climbed into the car. "But we haven't watched that three times, have we?"

"As long as I'm with you, Barker, I'll watch *Die Hard* one hundred times."

"I'm going to hold you to that," Barker said with a wink as he pulled his seatbelt across his chest. "Did you mention something about chocolate cake earlier? I'm starving."

CHAPTER 8

I t was a rare occasion that Julia took a lunch break and an even rarer one that she left the café and went somewhere else to eat. Her lunch usually consisted of a hurriedly made sandwich, which she would eat in small bites in the kitchen in between serving customers, but she had been given a lunch invite that she couldn't refuse.

Still in her apron and covered in flour, she ran across the street to The Plough where Barker was already perched on a bench waiting for her. She glanced back to the café, hoping Jessie would be okay on her own despite the sudden lunchtime rush.

"I can't stay long," Julia said, glancing at the door. "Is he here?"

"You've got flour in your hair," Barker said as he reached out to brush it away. "He's already inside."

They walked into the old pub, the musky smell of old wood and beer hitting Julia. To her surprise, it was already quite busy, but she didn't recognise many of the faces, so she guessed they were tourists passing through for the day, unlike her café, which was filled with regular faces today. The one face she did recognise was that of DS Forbes, who was already tucking into a meat and potato pie, which he had drowned in gravy.

"Sit down!" Bradley exclaimed, standing up a little, his large stomach hitting the table. "I hope you don't mind, but I already ordered. I was starving! They've got me working double time since – *well*, you know."

Bradley scooped up a large forkful of the pie filling and crammed it into his mouth. A blob of gravy trickled down his chin, landing on the paper napkin he had tucked in his collar to protect his white shirt. Julia found the man comical, but she wasn't confident of his inspector skills. She had been more than a little intrigued when he had called Barker and asked them out to lunch to inform them of the latest developments.

"I'll have whatever Bradley has," Barker said to Shelby when she came over to take their orders. "And a pint of whatever craft beer you have at the moment."

"I'll have the same, but make my drink orange juice," Julia said without looking at the menu. "I need to go back to work with a clear head."

"I need a pint to take the edge off," Bradley said after sipping his beer, which he also spilt down his front. "The stress of this case is making me lose my hair!"

Julia looked up to his balding head, which shone

brightly under the light, wondering if it was possible to notice if the little hair he had left at the sides was thinning.

"Have you heard about Jim's funeral?" Bradley asked. "Happening on Sunday. They released his body last night."

"So soon?" Barker muttered, glancing awkwardly to Julia.

"They didn't have much to discover in the post-mortem, did they?" Bradley said with a small shrug, his voice catching a little. "Pauline wants us all there in our uniforms for his send-off. It's what Jim would have wanted."

"These developments?" Barker asked, eager to shift the course of the conversation. "Must be pretty good if you wanted to meet us here."

"It is need-to-know information," he mumbled through a mouthful of the pie as he tapped the side of his nose. "But I trust you both understand what I'm telling you doesn't leave this pub."

"Of course," Barker said.

"Absolutely," Julia added.

"Good." Bradley took another deep gulp of his pint, followed by another mouthful of pie, before speaking again. "Billy Matthews' alibi has fallen apart. He said he was with his two cronies, but we've arrested them for nicking a car without him on the night of the murder. Shilpa from the post office came forward with her CCTV recordings this morning when she heard about the murder. Her security camera reaches out to the bottom of the lane leading up to your cottage. Caught Billy Matthews heading up that way at about half past five, putting him there at Jim's death."

"Have you arrested him?" Barker asked, edging forward.

Shelby returned with the plates of food, followed by the drinks. Barker followed Bradley's lead and drowned his pie in gravy, but Julia much preferred to taste her food, so she decided to go without. She pricked the thick crust to let a little of the steam escape as Bradley took the pause in conversation to wolf down more of his pie.

"It's all circumstantial so far," Bradley said. "You know how it is, boss. Billy was caught trying to flog Jim's phone down at the market, but CCTV proved his story about finding it in a bush at the bus station. Then he's caught near the crime scene around the time of the murder, but he wasn't the only one. We don't have anything we can pin to him quite yet."

"Did you look into Jeffrey Taylor?" Barker asked, his voice lowering to a whisper.

"Ah," Bradley said, finally finishing his pie and wiping his mouth with the napkin tucked in his shirt. "Your old friend. He's a fascinating character with a real motive, but it's difficult to pin this on him too. I checked into what you said about Jeffrey being out and about in the village during the rain, and it seemed he ran past every CCTV camera that we've checked in the village. He did run up your lane at around quarter to, but he was not seen again until he passed the station camera around six and headed into the B&B. He must have run up by Peridale Farm and circled the long way. I checked in with Peridale Farm, but they're living in the dark ages and don't have any cameras. Here, I have a video on my phone."

Bradley wiped his gravy-covered fingers on his trousers before pulling his phone from his pocket. He flicked through his files before turning the screen around and pressing the play button. A grainy video started to play, and it took Julia a second to recognise it as the perspective of the village from the post office. It pointed out at the village green, her gran's cottage, and the small lane leading up to their cottages. First, a man in a red tracksuit and black cap, who was unmistakably Billy Matthews, walked up the road while looking down at his phone. He disappeared from view, and then the footage jumped to Jeffrey Taylor jogging across the village green and towards the lane as he checked his watch. Neither man looked like they were on their way to commit murder, but Julia knew it was possible they hadn't headed in that direction with the intention of killing Jim, rather taking the opportunity when they thought they saw Barker alone on his doorstep.

"And the wreath?" Julia asked, not wanting to let them forget about it. "Did you find out who ordered that?"

"I found out about your little visit, but of course, that was before you officially reported it, and before – *ya'know* – Jim's death. I got a description of the girl who placed the order, but aside from that, we haven't been able to identify her yet."

"Are you still suspecting that it's connected?"

"Honestly? No," Bradley said as he pushed his plate away and rested a hand on his stomach. "We're looking into the angle of a random attack. We found Jim's wallet in the bush where Billy found the phone, and they had taken his cash and cards."

"Why ditch the phone?" Julia asked.

"Phones are traceable," Barker said. "Usually when there is a mugging, the victim can walk away to tell the tale, so tracing the phone isn't necessary. When it turns into a murder case, it's one of the first things the police do, so the murderer is likely to dump the phone the first chance they get."

"Did you check the bus station CCTV?" Julia asked.

"We did," Bradley said with a nod as he dabbed at his hot, bright red cheeks. "It was dark and raining on and off that night. We're looking into a couple of suspicious people who were around that area at that time, but again, it's proving difficult to pin down. This isn't the first attack of its kind recently though. There have been a spate of muggings and break-ins across the Cotswolds in the last couple of weeks, so we're looking into those cases to see if we find anything in common."

"You won't find anything," Julia said firmly, not realising she had spoken the words at the same time she had thought them. "This wasn't random. Murder doesn't happen on your doorstep for the sake of a mobile phone and a wallet. Surely if they wanted something of value they would have broken into the cottage after killing Jim? Was anything taken, Barker?"

"Not that I know of."

"This wasn't random," Julia confirmed. "Somebody wanted to kill Barker, and they hit the wrong man, which means Barker's life is still at risk."

"Has anybody threatened your life since, boss?" Bradley asked, turning to Barker.

"No," Barker said uneasily. "Not yet."

"Then there's no reason to suspect they will, right?" Bradley replied, nodding resolutely. "We're looking into many interesting lines of inquiry, so I'm sure we'll crack the case in no time!"

It took everything in Julia's power not to sigh with exasperation. Bradley seemed like a lovely man, and she was sure in any other circumstance she would enjoy his company, but in the capacity of acting Detective Inspector, she found him infuriating. He felt more like a comedy character plucked from a detective show, than a man capable of solving a real murder case.

When the conversation turned to football and beer, Julia knew Bradley had told them everything he knew. She had expected to hear some grand revelation, but she was left hungry for more information, and also full from too much meat and potato pie. She wasn't surprised Billy's alibi had fallen through, nor was she surprised Jeffrey was in the area, but Bradley was right about the evidence so far being purely circumstantial. Until she discovered a real clue, it was going to be difficult to prove if either man was truly involved in the murder.

She finished her orange juice and excused herself. She thanked Bradley for the invite, and he stood up, knocking the table with his stomach once more. Barker walked her to the front door, his hand on the small of her back.

"He's better at his job than he comes across," Barker whispered to her, having sensed her apparent reservations of his abilities. "You just need to get to know him. He's one of the better ones we have. It just takes him a little longer to funnel his energy. He'll get there."

"I'm sure he will," Julia said, forcing a smile. "Go and finish your pint. I need to get back to work anyway."

"I'm going to ask if he's heard anything about my job," Barker said after kissing her on the cheek. "I feel like I should have heard something after Jim."

"I'm sure it will be any day now," she said as encouragingly as she could. "Will I see you at my cottage tonight?"

"Only if I'm invited."

"You're always invited," Julia leant in and kissed him on the lips. "See you later."

Barker winked at her and walked back to the table. Julia stepped out into the daylight, shielding her eyes from the bright sun. She dusted a little flour off her apron as she walked past a group of tourists drinking beer at one of the outside tables. She smiled at them before heading to the edge of the road. Traffic in Peridale was usually quiet, but she looked both ways as she always did. When she looked in the direction of the B&B, she saw a familiar shade of red moving amongst the tall flowers in Evelyn's garden. If it hadn't been for the CCTV footage she had just seen, she might not have thought anything of it, but she had Billy Matthews fresh on her mind.

Julia crossed the road so that she was opposite the B&B, not wanting to arouse suspicion. She walked past the police station, smiling to a young constable she recognised from around the village. When the constable jumped into a police car and pulled out of the small station car park, she took her opportunity to cross the road without being seen.

Ducking under the B&B wall, she peered over the 'NO VACANCIES SIGN' to see Billy creeping around the side of the cottage, glancing over his shoulder as he did. Julia followed him around the building, staying as low to the ground as she could, but sure that her curls were darting up and down; she just hoped the flowers were enough to hide them.

Luckily for Julia, the cottage was on the street corner so she could see directly into its entire garden. She saw Billy knock on the backdoor as he skittishly made sure nobody was watching him. He looked in Julia's direction, forcing her to duck out of view. She heard the door open, but she didn't dare look.

As it turned out, she didn't need to see the person on the other side of the door to know who it was. In the peace and quiet of the sleepy village afternoon, she heard a very clear voice say something very familiar.

"I foresaw you would come, Billy," she heard Evelyn say. "Come in. Did anybody see you?"

The door closed, stopping Julia from hearing the rest of the conversation, not that she needed to. She tried to think of an innocent reason Billy would be visiting Evelyn, but he didn't seem like the type of person who would enjoy a cup of Moroccan tea and a tarot reading. Julia didn't want to think Evelyn was capable of anything other than friendly conversation, but her mind was taking her to dark places.

Before she could dwell on them any longer, somebody tapped on her shoulder, causing her to jump up. She was relieved to see it was just her gran, who was wearing her brightest neon workout clothes yet.

"Dare I ask what you are doing?" Dot asked as she marched on the spot, looking at the ground where Julia had been.

"Tying my shoelaces," Julia said quickly, glancing to the cottage and hoping that nobody was looking out of the windows. "Must dash. Need to get back to the café."

Julia kissed her gran on the cheek as she hurried down the road and back to her café. She kept her head down, unsure of who she was hiding from, but feeling like she needed to. It wasn't until she was walking through her café that she noticed her ballerina flats didn't even have laces.

"You took your time," Jessie said as she juggled making an espresso and a cup of tea. "Where have you been?"

"It doesn't matter," Julia whispered, taking over the

making of the espresso. "But I think Evelyn is connected to this mess revolving around Barker, I just don't know how."

CHAPTER 9

The morning of Jim's funeral came around quicker than Julia would have liked. She had hoped she would have landed on something vital to crack the case so she could look Jim's family in the eye without being consumed with guilt, but luck had evaded her.

She had kept one eye firmly trained on Evelyn and another on Jeffrey, and despite neither of them appearing to slip up, it had been easier than she had expected to play spy. Evelyn had been visiting her café every day for tea and a scone. At first, Julia had suspected Evelyn had known about her over-the-wall peeking, but if she did know, she was a better actress than Julia had thought. Jeffrey, on the other hand, had been popping up in people's gardens all over the village, no doubt thanks to Dot's glowing recommendation and the juicy titbit about his criminal past. The sound of lawn mowers had been echoing around the village so much, Julia had wondered if she had developed tinnitus on more than one occasion.

She assessed herself in the mirror and attempted to brush Mowgli's cat hairs off her black dress for the fourth time. She picked up her mother's pearls, the only jewellery she had inherited after her death, and held them up to her neck. Squinting, she stepped back, deciding about the jewellery.

"Are you sure you don't want me to come with you?" Jessie asked, appearing in the mirror behind Julia.

"You stay home and enjoy your day off," Julia said as she turned to brush cat hairs off her backside. "You've earned it this week covering for me."

"I don't mind," Jessie said with a shrug as she sat on the edge of the bed. "I've enjoyed it. If you dropped dead tomorrow, I think I could slip into your shoes, although not those shoes. I don't do heels."

Julia looked down at the black heels, wondering if they were too much. She could hear her sister's voice in the back of her mind telling her they were the only shoes that would go with the dress, even if they did make her calves burn on the few occasions she had worn them.

"Are they inappropriate?" Julia asked as she wobbled on her six-inch stilts. "They're not me, are they?"

"Yes and no," Jessie said, rolling onto the bed to stroke Mowgli, who was curled on top of Julia's pillow. "But who cares? Did you even know the guy?"

"Not really," Julia said. "I knew him as Barker's boss. I

only saw him a couple of times, but I want to be there to support Barker. We did find the body as well. I feel like I need to pay my respects to his family."

"Speaking of Barker, he's in the living room."

"How long has he been here?"

"Ten minutes?" Jessie muttered, more interested in Mowgli. "Maybe half an hour."

"Why didn't you tell me?"

"You told me to enjoy my relaxing Sunday."

Julia left Jessie stroking the cat and hurried through to the sitting room, where Barker was fiddling with his tie in the mirror above the fireplace. Julia stepped in front of him and pushed his hands down. She unwrapped the tie and started again, carefully wrapping and looping the fabric. When she was satisfied, she brushed lint off Barker's jacket and kissed him on the cheek.

"I did my father's tie on the morning of my mother's funeral," Julia said as she stood behind him and met his eyes in the mirror. "I was only twelve. That was my first funeral."

"I guess I was lucky. My first one wasn't until I was thirty."

"Somebody close?"

Barker suddenly looked away and started fiddling with his cufflinks. Just when she thought he might answer her question, he walked towards the window and stared up at the sky.

"Looks like it's going to rain," he mumbled.

If it weren't for today's funeral, Julia might have pushed it. It hadn't gone unnoticed to her that his first funeral when he was thirty must have been around the same time as Jeffrey's sentencing. She wondered if this was the tragic event from his past that he had hinted at. He had said it was a story for another day, but it was obvious today wasn't that day.

Julia had attended her fair share of funerals at St. Peter's Church, but never one as busy as Jim Austen's. By the time they arrived, which was still twenty minutes early, the church grounds were fully packed. If Julia had to guess, she would say there were over one hundred people there, a lot of whom were in official police uniform. She had encouraged Barker to wear his uniform, but he had thought it would be insensitive considering his current job status, so he opted for a simple black suit, which he still looked handsome in, but didn't quite feel right for his Chief Inspector's funeral.

When the hearse pulled slowly into the village and circled the green, followed by two black cars, all of the uniformed officers removed their hats and bowed their heads. She spotted Bradley wiping under his eyes with a tissue. She looked to Barker and was surprised when she saw him crying too. She pulled her handkerchief from her bag and discreetly pushed it into his hand.

"Great man," Barker said firmly as he dabbed at his eyes. "Great man."

Julia looped her fingers through his and squeezed as tightly as she could. He squeezed back to let her know that he appreciated her being there. She had done the same for her father on the day of her mother's funeral in the very same church over two decades ago. Her father hadn't squeezed back.

When the hearse pulled up outside of the church, a group of uniformed men stepped out of the second car and put the coffin on their shoulders. Julia felt a lump rise in her throat when she noticed the police hat on top. A group of weeping mourners got out of the first car, Julia's eyes instantly landing on a grey-haired woman who was sobbing silently into a silk handkerchief. She guessed this was Jim's wife, Pauline, and the young pregnant woman who was comforting her was their daughter, carrying their first grandchild. She looked away, her mind jumping back to that night they had found his body. When she looked back, she was sure she caught the woman scowling in their direction.

The service was a long one, detailing every achievement of Jim's long police career, as well as his large family, and his many hobbies. Julia learned that he had three children, who she could see standing next to their mother at the front of the church. He had started out in the police force as a cleaner and had been inspired to join when he met his wife, who was a constable at the time. He also enjoyed fishing and Italian cooking. It had been easier for Julia to cope not knowing much about the man she had discovered dead, but the reality of the situation was hitting her, and she was even more determined to uncover the truth.

When the priest delivered his final words, the curtains around the coffin closed and John Lennon's *'Imagine'* played through the crackly speakers. Julia and Barker were two of the first to leave the church, having stayed at the back. Julia had told Barker to join his colleagues at the front, but he had insisted on staying where he was.

"Boss," a young constable said to Barker with a nod of her hat. "Good to see you."

"You too, Sarah."

"Shame it's not under better circumstances," she said,

taking off her hat and holding it against her chest. "Jim would be proud of the turnout."

"He was a popular man," Barker said. "And a good friend."

"That he was," Sarah said, resting her hand on Barker's arm. "See you at the wake?"

"I don't think so," Barker said with a small shake of his head. "Not my scene."

"Mine neither, but I think Pauline needs all of the support she can get right now. I'll see you tomorrow."

"Tomorrow?"

Sarah narrowed her eyes and stared at Barker, appearing unsure of what to say. She waited for him to figure out what she was talking about, but when he didn't, she lifted a hand to her mouth and blinked slowly.

"Nobody has told you, have they?" She whispered, looking over her shoulder at her fellow officers as they filed slowly out of the church. "You didn't hear this from me, okay?"

"Hear what?" Barker asked, glancing to Julia, puzzlement evident on his face.

"On the night Jim was murdered he was coming to tell you about your investigatory meeting, which is happening tomorrow. I'm surprised nobody has told you."

Barker gritted his jaw and flared his nostrils as he looked into the faces of his colleagues as they passed him without paying him attention.

"Me too," he replied sternly. "Thank you, Sarah. Your name won't be brought up."

She thanked him with a smile and walked away, leaving Barker and Julia to retreat to the shade of the large oak tree. Julia tried to think of something reassuring or positive to say, but she knew nothing would make a difference.

"What *is* an investigatory meeting?" Julia asked after a moment's silence.

"It's bad news," Barker said, a shake in his voice. "It means they've reviewed all of the evidence and they want to hear my side of the story."

"Isn't that a good thing?"

"It doesn't usually get to this unless they've found something they don't like," he said, looking darkly into her eyes. "I never thought it would get this far. I've never heard of one of these things going well."

"Surely if you can explain what happened, everything will be okay?"

"I have to plead for my life in front of the Chief Superintendent and whoever has replaced Jim as Chief Inspector, as well as the men in suits from the Independent Police Complaints Commission."

"This is all my fault," she mumbled under her breath. "Barker, I'm so – I'm *so* sorry."

"It's not your fault," he said, cupping her cheek in his palm. "Whatever happens, I'll get through this."

"*We'll* get through this," she corrected him.

Barker smiled so genuinely, it warmed Julia to her core, almost making her forget where she was. When she caught that they were being watched out of the corner of her eye, that warmth vanished. She turned to look at Pauline, who was standing alone on the path, her pale eyes red and swollen.

"This is *your* doing," she said, pointing a finger at Barker. "My husband would still be here if it wasn't for *you*."

"Pauline, I'm -,"

"I *don't* want to hear it," she snapped, holding up her hand, which was clinging onto her handkerchief. "Just *go!*"

Her children walked towards her and moved her down the path. Only one of them smiled an apology to Barker, with the others appearing to share their mother's sentiment. Julia turned to Barker, completely stunned by her accusation, but he didn't look as shocked.

"Let's go," he said. "I've done what I came here to do."

Julia nodded and wrapped her hand around Barker's once more. She almost couldn't believe Jim's wife was placing the blame for his death on Barker, and not on the person who had killed him. It only renewed Julia's urgency to discover the truth.

As they walked out of the church grounds hand-in-hand, Julia spotted Harriet Barnes from Pretty Petals lingering by the gate. When their eyes met, it became apparent to Julia that she was there to see her.

"Julia," Harriet said as she hurried forward while scratching at the pencils holding her messy grey bun together. "I was hoping I would see you here. I put together the flowers for this poor man's funeral, but I hung back to speak to you."

"You did a beautiful job," Julia said with a soft smile, hoping it would serve as a form of apology for their awkward meeting in the florists exactly a week ago.

"Thank you," she said, the sincerity in her voice letting Julia know there was nothing to forgive. "I need to apologise for the way I acted when you came to visit me. I didn't realise the seriousness of the situation."

"It's not you who needs to apologise."

"A man is dead, and I feel like I could have stopped

that from happening if I had taken the wreath more seriously. I swear, I thought it was only a prank."

"So did I," Barker said reassuringly. "Don't blame yourself."

"It's hard not to," she mumbled as she put on her glasses, while pulling a piece of paper out of her pocket. "I tracked down the girl who ordered the wreath. It was entirely by accident. I was shopping in the supermarket out of town, and I spotted her getting into a taxi. I did something idiotic, and I followed her all the way home, to the Fern Moore Estate. Here, I wrote down the address of the flat she went into."

She handed over a scrap of paper to Julia with shaking hands, who read it before immediately giving it to Barker.

"That's Billy Matthews' address," Barker whispered.

"It was a young girl with bright red hair," Harriet said. "That's all I know, I swear. I hope this goes some way to helping, even if it is too late."

"It's not too late," Julia said, resting a hand on Harriet's shoulder. "This is great, thank you."

Harriet smiled her appreciation of Julia's thanks before hurrying off to her small white van, which had her shop's logo printed on its side. Julia made a mental note to make sure to bake that fruitcake for Harriet after all.

"Is she talking about Billy's sister?" Julia asked. "I saw a girl with red hair in the flat when we visited."

"Mercedes-Mae Matthews," Barker muttered as he closed his fist around the piece of paper. "I should have known."

As they walked towards the lane leading up to her cottage, Julia was already planning the trip she was going to make alone to Fern Moore while Barker was at his investigatory meeting.

CHAPTER 10

In the café the next morning, Julia lined Barker's stomach with a full English breakfast along with multiple cups of coffee, but despite her best efforts to calm him, he was still obviously nervous.

"You'll be fine," Julia reassured him as she topped up his coffee. "Just tell the truth."

"What if the truth isn't good enough?"

"Then at least you've been honest, and you can hold your head high," she said, resting a hand on his shoulder. "Can I get you anything else? A brownie? Or a slice of chocolate cake? I was working on a new version last night with chopped up brownies added into the mix, and I think you're going to really like this one."

"I don't think a chocolate cake will fix this, I'm afraid," Barker said with a sigh before he stood up. "How do I look?"

"Like a man who is going to get his job back," she said as she brushed a piece of white fluff off his shoulder. "You're going to be all right, Barker. I believe in you."

Jessie snorted behind her back, but Julia pretended not to hear. She kissed and hugged Barker one last time and waved him out of the café, watching him walk up to the street until he disappeared from view.

"What are you going to do if he doesn't get his job back?" Jessie asked as she sprayed the front of the cake display cabinet with window cleaner. "You'll have an unemployed boyfriend."

"That's not going to happen."

"But what if it does?"

Julia closed her eyes and tried to smile, wanting to remain positive so she could be there for Barker, no matter the outcome.

"When you're finished with that, I need you to start on the stock-check," Julia said as she pulled her apron over her head. "I need to ask a girl about a wreath."

"Huh?"

"I'm going to Fern Moore," Julia explained as she pulled on her pale pink peacoat. "I found the address of the girl who ordered Barker's wreath, so that's at least something I can get to the bottom of today. If I figure out whose idea the wreath was, I will be one step closer to discovering the truth."

"You're going to Fern Moore alone?" Jessie asked with a smirk. "You're feeling brave, aren't you? Even I wouldn't go there alone, and I spent six months sleeping on the streets."

"It's not so bad," Julia said, unsure of who she was trying to convince.

"Your funeral."

Julia grabbed her car keys and headed for the door. She remembered what had happened last time she had taken her car to the estate, so she dropped her keys into her bag, pulled out her phone, and called a taxi.

The taxi pulled up in front of the closed play-park, and Julia paid the driver. She was sure he drove away quicker than he would have done if he had been dropping her off anywhere else. She pushed her hands into her pockets and looked up to the flat she remembered as Billy's, the distant sound of a police siren tickling her eardrums. Something rattled behind her, so she spun around, only to see an empty beer can rolling along the street in the breeze.

Knowing it was wise to do what she needed to and leave as quickly as she could, she hurried to the stairwell she remembered taking with Barker and made her way to the second floor.

When she reached it, she hurried along the outdoor walkway. She was sure it seemed scarier than when Barker had been by her side. She looked down at the courtyard, her heart skipping a beat when she didn't spot her comforting Ford Anglia, only to remember the taxi seconds later. In the far corner of the estate, she noticed a large gang of boys heading for the park, cans of beer crammed firmly against their lips. Gulping hard, Julia turned back to the end of the walkway and headed straight for the last flat.

She knocked on the door and waited for Sandra's shrieking voice to yell over the sound of the loud TV.

When it didn't, she wondered if she had come all this way only to find that nobody was home. She remembered it was mid-morning on a weekday, and she suddenly felt foolish for expecting to talk to the redheaded teenage girl. Julia turned back to the courtyard and watched as the boys climbed over the fence and into the restricted park. She only spun around again when she heard the chain rattling behind the door.

A flash of red hair and freckled skin caught her attention through the gap, and she felt relieved that her trip hadn't been in vain. She stepped forward, smiling down at the girl, who didn't look much older than thirteen-years-old.

"What?" the girl snapped, her voice quieter than her mother's. "Mum's not in. Come back later."

"I'm here to see *you*, Mercedes," Julia said.

"It's Mercedes-*Mae*."

"Sorry, Mercedes-*Mae*," Julia said, her smile growing. "I wondered if I could ask you a question?"

"No you can't," Mercedes-Mae mumbled, already closing the door. "Go away."

"It's about the wreath," Julia called through the door, turning her ear to the wood. "I'm not going anywhere until you tell me who put you up to that."

Julia stood and listened for almost a minute, but she heard nothing, other than the TV volume rising. She dropped to her knees and pulled on the letterbox, which was surprisingly loose. She peered into the flat, where she could see the young girl staring at the TV, a baby in her lap. The flat was scarcely decorated and looked in need of a good tidy up.

"I can tell the police what I know," Julia called into the

flat. "I'm not sure they'll be as understanding as me."

"You are the police," she cried back without looking away from the TV. "Mum said I'm not to talk to the pigs."

"I'm not the police. I'm a baker. I own a café."

Mercedes-Mae turned and looked at Julia through the tiny slot in the door, her red eyebrows pinching curiously. Julia smiled once more, forgetting her hidden mouth. She wished she had brought one of her cakes to illustrate the fact. She was almost surprised she hadn't thought of that, seeing as her cakes seem to have many uses when it came to discovering information.

To her surprise, Mercedes-Mae put the white haired toddler on the floor and walked over to the door. The chain rattled and the thin door opened before Julia could get up to her feet. Mercedes-Mae walked back into the flat and resumed her seat in front of the large flat screen TV. Julia took the invitation and welcomed herself in, closing the door behind her.

The flat smelled of stale cigarettes and spilt beer. Julia tried not to be too judgemental of the girl's home, which she seemed comfortable in, but she couldn't help but feel like she wanted to start cleaning.

"Can I sit down?" Julia asked.

"Free country."

Julia took that as a yes and sat next to the girl. The toddler, who she realised was a boy, looked up at her as he crammed the corner of the remote control into his mouth. He frowned a little, wary of the stranger in his house.

"You know why I'm here, don't you?" Julia asked politely over the racket of the TV. "To ask about the wreath?"

"I'm not telling you anything," the girl said. "I got fifty

quid out of it."

"A man has died."

"I guessed," she said, arching a brow. "That's what wreaths are for, ain't they?"

"A man died *after* the wreath was delivered. *Murdered.* The wreath appeared to be a warning."

Mercedes-Mae turned to Julia, her eyes distrusting. Julia wasn't sure if she seemed truthful to the girl, even though she had nothing to gain from lying to her. She guessed the girl wasn't trusting of many people.

"Why aren't you at school?" Julia asked, deciding to take a different approach.

"Didn't wanna go."

"Why not?"

"Don't like it."

"Doesn't your mother mind?"

Mercedes-Mae shrugged, letting Julia know that her mother didn't care either way. Her heart twitched, but she tried to stay as detached as she could. She reminded herself why she was there and shifted in her seat.

"Don't your friends miss you?"

"Don't got any," she said bluntly. "*Leo*, get off that!"

She snatched the remote control from the baby on the floor, who automatically started howling at the top of his lungs. Instead of comforting her brother, the girl just cranked the TV volume up even more, to the point where Julia could feel the vibrations rattling through the couch and into her body. For a moment, she just sat and observed the situation, but she couldn't just sit there and watch the poor baby cry. Reaching out, she scooped him up and sat him on her knee. He immediately stopped crying and stared at her with his bright blue eyes.

"Hello, Leo," she whispered. "Are you going to be a good boy?"

"He can't understand you," Mercedes-Mae snapped. "He's a baby."

Julia bit her tongue through a smile, wondering how a thirteen-year-old girl could already be so jaded. At her age, Julia had lived a year without her mother, and even she had been more opportunistic and hopeful about life.

"The wreath," Julia continued. "Are you going to tell me who paid you to order it?"

"Some guy," she said casually, her eyes glued to the TV. "I dunno who he was. Came 'round to the estate, gave me the note and fifty quid, and told me where to drop it off. Easy. Got myself these new kicks."

She lifted her feet up, and Julia realised her '*new kicks*' were a pair of brand new pink and yellow trainers, from a brand she recognised on the high street as being from the expensive side. She wondered if the girl's mother even questioned how she had obtained the new shoes, or if she had even noticed.

"What did the man look like?" Julia asked, feeling like she was on the edge of a discovery.

"How am I supposed to know, lady?" she cried, turning the TV up even more as she squinted at the screen. "Had a funny ear."

"Funny ear?" Julia asked, her heart fluttering. "And tattoos?"

"So you already know him?" she asked suspiciously, suddenly turning the TV off. "Is this a trap? Are you the police? I'm calling my brother."

"It's not a trap," Julia said, trying to contain her nerves behind a smile. "Thank you. You've told me everything I need to know."

Julia kissed Leo on the top of his soft, white hair before passing him over to Mercedes-Mae, who reluctantly took him, before dumping him on the floor again. Julia showed herself out, immediately hearing the chain being locked the second she closed the door behind her.

Feeling like a bundle of nervous energy, Julia forgot her earlier fear and pulled her phone out of her handbag and called for a taxi. She waited by the park, scanning the faces of the young boys as they all stared suspiciously at her, some of them throwing insults that landed on deaf ears. At that moment, Julia could take all of the insults in the world because she felt like she had finally made a breakthrough, and that was all that mattered. She searched for Billy's face in the crowd, but she wasn't surprised when she didn't see him. She suspected he would be at the B&B, which was where Julia told the taxi driver to take her.

When the taxi pulled up outside the B&B, she paid the driver and jumped out. She unhooked the gate and ran down the garden path, only stopping when her hand hovered over the chain doorbell. She took a step back and glanced back at the police station, remembering that it was her habit of running into situations before informing the police that had gotten Barker into the exact situation he was in. Just imagining him in the station, tugging at his collar as he tried to explain why he had let a civilian dictate a murder investigation was enough to make her think twice. She doubled back down the garden path, turning once more to the B&B before opening the gate again.

A shiver of panic rattled down her spine when she saw Billy standing in the living room window, his phone to his ear and his eyes trained on her in the shadow of his cap. She began to shake and fear tore through her insides when she noticed Jeffrey standing behind him, his hand resting on Billy's shoulder.

It took all of Julia's energy to turn and unclip the gate. Across the road, she spotted Evelyn climbing off the bus with hands full of shopping bags. Evelyn smiled at her, but Julia couldn't return it. Feeling pale and sick, she dropped her head and headed straight to the police station to tell them what she now knew.

CHAPTER 11

J ulia could remember precise moments in her life when she had felt like her body wasn't her own. The first time she remembered that happening was when she was a twelve-year-old girl, walking through the school corridors after being told her mother's cancer had won. Another time was when she had walked through the streets of London, clutching all of her possessions in four black bags after her husband had changed the locks and left her a note informing her that their marriage was over. As Julia walked towards the desk in Peridale's police station, she knew she was having one of those moments.

"Can I help you, love?" asked the kindly desk sergeant. "You look as white as a ghost."

Julia heard the words, but all she could do was stare. She could still feel Billy and Jeffrey's eyes trained on her through the walls.

"Barker," was all she could say.

As though fate was shining down on her at that moment, Barker walked through a door, tugging off his tie. He looked as beaten down as Julia felt. When their eyes met, she felt her mind return to her body.

"They haven't come to a decision," Barker said with a defeated smile. "They're going to review everything I told them and get back to me. You should have heard the way they were talking to me. It was like I was a criminal, and the new Chief Inspector is a total -,"

"I know who sent the wreath," Julia blurted out. "I went to Fern Moore and spoke to the girl Harriet told us about, Billy's sister."

"You went without me?"

"That doesn't matter," Julia said, waving a hand dismissively. "I didn't need you charging in doing your Detective Inspector routine, no offence."

The door opened behind Barker, and a group of uniformed officers walked through, laughing at a joke one of them had just told. Barker grabbed Julia and pulled her to the side and out of earshot.

"Well?" he asked, his eyes wide. "Who was it?"

"Oh, Barker," Julia whispered. "She said a man with a *'funny ear'* paid her to place the order."

It took Barker a moment to piece things together, but when he realised whom the man with the funny ear was, his eyes widened, and he looked around the station, his face suddenly pale. It was obvious to Julia that he was experiencing the same out-of-body experience she had only just shaken off.

"Jeffrey," he whispered. "*Jeffrey* killed Jim."

"It gets worse."

"How can this get worse?"

"Billy is in on it somehow." Julia couldn't believe the words that were leaving her mouth, and by the looks of it, neither could Barker. "And I think Evelyn is involved too."

"*Evelyn?*" Barker muttered, almost laughing. "The crazy tarot lady? What have I ever done to her?"

"I don't know, but they're all over at the B&B right now, and I think they know that I know."

Barker ran his hands down his face as he looked around the station where he no longer held authority. They both looked at the desk, and then to each other, seeming to both realise they had no concrete evidence, aside from a thirteen-year-old girl's testimonial, which she likely wouldn't repeat in the presence of an actual officer of the law.

"What are we waiting for?" Barker asked. "Let's go and finish this once and for all."

"Are you sure?" Julia asked, glancing to the door, still unable to shake off their piercing eyes. "This is what got you into trouble in the first place."

"I need to hear it from his lips, Julia," he whispered, resting a hand heavily on her shoulder. "That man has been haunting me long before he came to Peridale. Besides, we're not going alone."

Barker reached into the inside pocket of his jacket and pulled out his mobile phone. He scrolled through his contacts, hitting the most recent one before pushing it to his ear. With a hand firmly planted on his hip, he looked around the station as he willed the person on the other end to pick up.

"DS Forbes? Bradley? It's Barker. Where are you?"

"Right here."

Julia was surprised to hear the answer come from behind her. They both turned to see Bradley holding open the door of the station with his foot as he bit into a bagel, the phone balanced between his shoulder and ear. A blob of cream cheese fell from the rim of the bagel and down his shirt, but he didn't seem to notice. Julia and Barker both looked to each other, sharing the same grin.

"We know who sent the wreath," Barker said as he pulled Bradley out of the station and into the car park. "It was Jeffrey Taylor."

"The ex-con?" Bradley mumbled through a mouthful of the bagel, as he looked to the B&B. "Are you sure?"

"I tracked down the girl who ordered the wreath," Julia repeated, feeling like time was suddenly running out. "She gave me a description of Jeffrey, mainly his *'funny ear'*."

"He's missing half an ear," Bradley said with a nod, his hand drifting up to his left ear, leaving behind a trace of cream cheese. "If he sent the wreath, he must have killed Jim too?"

"A leopard doesn't change its spots," Barker said, glancing to the B&B. "He's across the road right now. It's your call, DS Forbes."

Bradley finished his bagel and tossed the wrapper to the ground. He turned from the station door to the B&B, his plump cheeks turning a painful shade of maroon.

"Let's go and see if we can make him confess," Bradley said as he wiped his fingers down the front of his white shirt. "That's what a real Inspector would do, isn't that right, boss?"

"I'm proud of you," Barker said, slapping Bradley on

the shoulders. "They'll make a DI out of you yet."

Bradley led the way across the street, a grin spreading from ear-to-ear. He unclipped the gate and scurried down the path to the front door. Julia was pleased to see a pair of handcuffs attached to his belt, but she wasn't sure just one pair would be enough. Bradley looked around for the doorbell, ignoring the sign on the wall instructing visitors to yank on the chain. He opted for knocking on the door. Julia reached around him and pulled on the chain, pointing out the sign to him. He nodded appreciatively.

As they waited for the door to open, Julia could sense Barker's apprehension. She felt she was at an advantage having come face to face with Jeffrey on more than one occasion, but Barker hadn't been so lucky. Despite his face popping up in every garden around Peridale, they hadn't managed to cross each other's paths. Julia did not know if that was purposeful or not.

Through the frosted stained glass panel in the door, Julia saw Evelyn float down the hallway in one of her caftans. She paused halfway and turned to adjust her turban in the mirror. If Julia didn't know better, she would have said the B&B owner was stalling. When the door opened, the smile plastered on her face came across as being obviously false. She didn't look surprised, or shocked to see the three of them there.

"Julia," she cooed, her eyes wide and bright. "Brought me some more of those delicious scones?"

"Drop the act, Evelyn," Bradley said firmly, as though he had just wandered off the set of a 1970s police television show. "Where's Jeffrey? We know he's here."

To Julia's surprise, Bradley's faux-forcefulness cracked Evelyn's façade in seconds. Every muscle in her body seemed to soften as her face dropped. Julia was surprised she didn't press the back of her hand against her turban and faint into a ball on her cream carpet.

"I foresaw this day would come," she mumbled, her face turning a fresh shade of green. "You better come in. Do you mind taking off your shoes? I've just shampooed the carpets."

The unlikely trio kicked off their shoes at the door as they sent unsure glances to each other. Julia hadn't expected a Wild West-style shootout, or for Evelyn to make a run for it, but she hadn't expected a defeated invitation inside. From the curious expression on Barker's face, it appeared he hadn't either. Bradley, on the other hand, looked suspiciously around the hallway as though every trinket and ornament were a crucial piece of evidence.

"Can I get you some Moroccan tea?" she offered as she floated into her sitting room. "I have the most beautiful tea set that I picked up in a souk in -,"

"We didn't come for tea, Evelyn," Bradley said, cutting her off midsentence. "Where's Jeffrey?"

Almost fulfilling Julia's expectations, Evelyn collapsed dramatically into her stylish sofa. She rested the back of her hand against her cheek as she stared off dramatically into the corner of the room. Bradley turned and joined her in staring into the corner as though expecting Jeffrey to mystically appear. Julia arched a brow at Barker, but he sent her a look that read as *give him a chance*. Julia almost regretted involving the police on this one occasion. She knew she could get to the point quicker and more successfully, which was why she had gone alone to Fern Moore. She knew her unassuming café-owner exterior was a lot less threatening than two men in suits.

"Before you arrest me, I need you to know why I did it," Evelyn said calmly as she sat up and adjusted the position of her caftan. "I need *my* story to be heard first."

Bradley sat opposite her and pulled a notepad from his pocket. He licked the end of a pencil, flicked to a fresh page, and stared expectantly at her. Julia held in a frustrated sigh. She could almost hear Jeffrey and Billy laughing all the way out of Peridale as they stood there and played along with Evelyn's performance.

"Start at the beginning," Bradley said, his pencil hovering over the paper. "Tell me everything you know."

"I started writing to Jeffrey in prison a year ago," Evelyn said, the creases in her caftan consuming her attention. "I was meditating one day at the bottom of my garden when I heard a call to help those in need. When I came back into the house, one of the guests had left a newspaper open on an article about a program for prisoners who didn't get visitors. It broke my heart. Imagine being locked up like that and not having somebody to talk with? It was *fate*! A sign from the divine creator to help those society had turned its back on. I visited many men and women before I met Jeffrey. I would listen to their stories, and in return, they would listen to tales of my travels. People assume I can't be lonely because I trot around the globe and always have a home full of guests, but sometimes you find the most isolated people in the busiest crowds."

"Was this a – *erm* – sexual relationship between you and Mr. Taylor?"

"Oh, heavens *no!*" Evelyn exclaimed, laughing at the suggestion. "It was merely mentor and student. When I first met Jeffrey, I was taken by his claims of innocence. Of course, everybody I spoke to claimed to be innocent, but his story resonated with me. I believed him."

"He always was manipulative," Barker muttered under his breath. "Did he tell you how he killed six women? How his DNA was on one of the women, and how they found him at the scene of the last murder?"

"Purely accidental, *Detective Inspector!*" Evelyn suddenly sat up and tilted her head to Barker. "Jeffrey was their drug provider, not their murderer. The victims were all women of the night, were they not?"

Julia was surprised by Evelyn's blunt tone. She turned to Barker to gauge his reaction. The grit in his jaw and the silence of his tongue confirmed what Evelyn had asked.

"The whole case, headed by you, Mr. Brown, was a mess. The real killer confessed all when new evidence cleared Jeffrey's name!" Evelyn reached out and picked up the wooden box on the coffee table. She pulled back the engraved lid and dragged out a deck of tarot cards, which she started to shuffle in her hands. "I always trusted Jeffrey's honesty. The cards told of his innocence every time I have given him a reading."

"The cards tell you what you want to hear," Barker said, shaking his head and pinching between his eyes. "It's hocus-pocus nonsense."

"I once had a reading that told me I would be a firefighter," Bradley mumbled as he stared off into space. "I suppose they weren't far off."

"We all have many paths," Evelyn said, tapping the top of the deck. "Not all of them come true."

"Sounds like a get out of jail free card to me," Barker mumbled.

"Draw your destiny, Detective Inspector."

Barker looked down at the cards, smirking in disbelief.

He looked to Julia for guidance, but all she could do was offer a small shrug. She didn't believe in the cards any more than he did, but she knew that Evelyn believed in them, and that was enough for her. To her surprise, Barker relented and drew a card. He turned it over to show a young man sitting under a tree, his arms crossed and his expression stern. A disembodied arm floating in a cloud next to the boy offered a gold chalice, despite him already having three identical cups in front of him.

"*Four of Cups!*" Evelyn exclaimed, taking the card from Barker. "Just as I suspected. It has many meanings. This card proves you are stubborn, Detective Inspector. You are unable to look out of your world to see new offerings. You think you have all of the facts, therefore you will not accept new information, but you are wrong. Jeffrey is innocent, and you are just too stubborn to see it."

Barker shifted on the spot, his cheeks burning brightly. It seemed as though Evelyn had hit a nerve, sending him into silence. In some ways, Julia understood what Evelyn was trying to say, even if she did think it was a coincidence that Barker would pick that card. She was sure Evelyn could have spun any of the cards to tell a story about Barker and his faults.

"This is all well and good, Evelyn, but what about Jeffrey?" Bradley asked, taking the conversation back to their original reason for being there. "How has he come to be in your B&B?"

"When he told me of his release, I insisted he come here," she said as she slotted the cards neatly back into their box. "He was paid handsomely for his false imprisonment, and I recommended he try and find a place to buy in Peridale."

"You told me he had moved from Hull," Julia said.

"I didn't lie to you, Julia."

"You just didn't tell me the whole truth."

"Technically, not a lie."

"But a deception, all the same," Bradley jumped in. "But I suppose if the courts say he is innocent, who are we to argue?"

"Are we forgetting why we came here?" Barker asked, cocking his head suggestively to Bradley. "The wreath?"

"*Quite right!*" Bradley said, repositioning his pencil over the page. "What is your involvement in the wreath that was left on Barker's doorstep?"

"What wreath?" Evelyn asked, her brows pinching tightly together. "I know nothing of a wreath."

"Cut the act, Evelyn!" Bradley demanded.

Evelyn's face disappeared into her neck as she stared at Bradley, her nostrils flared and her eyes filled with confusion. For the first time since they had entered her B&B, Julia felt this was Evelyn being her true self.

"I saw you sneak Billy in here," Julia said, sitting next to Evelyn and resting a hand on her knee.

"Ah, Billy," Evelyn said, nodding her head. "I suspect he is the reason you are here."

"Well, yes," Julia said.

"Restraining orders are unlawful, in my opinion," Evelyn said with a heavy exhale. "Especially between father and son."

As Evelyn stared down at her fingers in her lap, Julia, Barker, and Bradley all looked to each other. Bradley and Barker both shook their head, before training their eyes on Evelyn.

"Jeffrey Taylor is Billy Matthews' *father*?" Barker asked

loudly. "You've got to be kidding me."

"Well, *of course*," Evelyn muttered, looking awkwardly to Julia. "I assume that is why you are here? I facilitated a meeting place for them to breach the restraining order. When I heard Jeffrey's story about how he was being blocked from seeing his son, it touched my heart, especially when I learned the son didn't live far from Peridale. Jeffrey only heard that he had a child days before his false imprisonment, and despite numerous attempts to contact the child's mother, she blocked him at every turn. I was the one who told Billy who his father was, and I brought him here to meet him. It was a beautiful thing. A perfect bond that nobody can explain."

"They do have a lot in common," Barker said faintly.

"Which is why I brought Jeffrey to Peridale," Evelyn said, not picking up on Barker's sarcasm. "It was essential for Jeffrey to build a relationship with his son, even if we had to do it in secret. You never know who is watching. I suppose it wasn't going to last forever."

"Do you realise what you've done?" Barker cried. "You were the catalyst those two criminals needed to cook up a murder plot against me!"

"*Murder?*" Evelyn cried, matching Barker's tone and suddenly standing up. "They are *kind* men, Barker Brown! Sweet, *innocent* people."

"Billy Matthews is *anything* but innocent," Bradley whispered as he struggled to keep up with his note taking. "Please, do continue."

Evelyn appeared to grow to match Barker's height somehow, her eyes trained on his. Julia was sure Evelyn was cooking up some spell that she had picked up on one of her travels. She waited for either of them to talk, but when they didn't, she stood up and stepped between them, pushing Evelyn back down to the sofa.

"The thing is, Evelyn, we have proof," she said, sitting next to her and resting her hand on Evelyn's. "Jeffrey paid a young girl, Billy's sister, to order a wreath to leave on Barker's doorstep. One day later, Chief Inspector Jim Austen turned up dead on that same doorstep, in an act that we suspect was meant for Barker. You must be able to see how suspicious this looks?"

"I didn't murder that man," a voice called from the doorway.

They all turned to see Jeffrey Taylor standing in the door, with his tattoo-covered arms folded casually across his chest. Billy appeared behind him, his nostrils flared, and his arms wide and ready to fight.

"Are you confessing to sending the wreath?" Bradley demanded, jumping up and pocketing his notepad.

"I didn't kill that man," Jeffrey repeated, his eyes darting to Barker, a wicked smirk prickling the edges of his lips. "I *did* want to scare you though. I think it worked."

Julia noticed Barker's fists clench by his side. She jumped up and looped her fingers around his to stop him from doing something he might later regret. Jeffrey darted his brows up and down, begging Barker to do something, but Julia had her hand firmly gripped around his.

"Jeffrey Taylor, you're under arrest for causing a threat by means of intimidation," Bradley said as he pulled the handcuffs from his belt. "You are also under arrest for the murder of Jim Austen. You do not have to say anything. But, it may harm your defence if you do not mention when questioned something, which you later rely on in court. Anything you do say may be given in evidence. Did you get all of that?"

"Here we go again," Jeffrey said coolly, the smirk growing as he turned around, his hands behind his back ready for cuffing. "Billy, get out of here."

Billy stared into his father's eyes with horror, his head shaking ever so slightly. Jeffrey appeared to nod as Bradley tightened the cuffs around his wrists. Billy turned his attention to Barker. He ran his thumb across his neck before doubling back and heading for the door, which slammed behind him. Julia felt Barker about to run after him, but she tugged him back, remembering what had happened last time they had attempted to chase the teenager through the village.

"This way," Bradley said as he tugged his prisoner towards the door. "Don't try anything funny."

To Julia's surprise, Jeffrey went without question. He didn't protest his innocence, nor did he fight his arrest. His lack of objection and complete silence sent an eerie shiver running through the B&B. Barker followed after him, but Julia hung back and looked down at Evelyn who had sunk into the sofa and was wafting herself with a paddle fan.

"I'll put some Moroccan tea on," Julia said.

"Good idea."

CHAPTER 12

The oven beeped, signalling that the Shepherd's Pie was ready. Julia finished lighting the candles, the flame of the match dancing up to her fingers. She shook the small stick, killing the flame.

"*Alright!*" she called to the oven. "*I'm coming!*"

She took a step back and assessed her beautifully set table. It was perfect for the relaxing evening she had planned out for her and Barker to enjoy after two weeks of madness. She dimmed the lights, then ran through to the kitchen and turned off the alarm. A quick glance at the cat clock above her fridge let her know that Barker was five minutes late.

Using her red and white polka dot oven gloves, she

pulled the Shepherd's Pie out of the oven, delighted with how beautifully golden the mashed potato had turned. She rested the dish on her cooling rack, yanked off the gloves, and grabbed the white wine from the fridge. She checked the label, unsure of what she was even looking for. Her sister, Sue, insisted it was the best wine at the supermarket, and that had to be good enough for Julia.

"Hurry up, Barker," she mumbled to herself as she poured the wine into two glasses. "Where are you?"

Mowgli jumped up onto the counter and nudged her. She tickled under his chin, but the Shepherd's Pie appeared to be more interesting. He padded along to it, gave it one quick sniff, before jumping off and sauntering over to his cat biscuits.

Julia took the two wine glasses through to the dining room, where the vanilla-scented candles were already infusing the air with their sweet fragrance. She heard a key rattle in the door and smiled to herself as she realigned the forks.

"Great timing," she called through as she dusted down the front of her dress and tossed her hair over her shoulders. "The Shepherd's Pie has just -,"

Julia's voice trailed off as she walked through to the hallway. She was surprised to see Jessie, and doubly surprised to see Barker draped over her shoulder, blood dripping from his eyebrow, and a bunch of squashed flowers in his hand.

"I know I said I'd stay at Dot's tonight, but I didn't want him walking here on his own," Jessie said apologetically as she slumped Barker onto the couch.

"What happened?" Julia asked, rushing to his side.

"Billy Matthews happened," Barker said. "He followed

me to Pretty Petals. I got you these."

Barker held up the flowers. They were barely holding together behind their plastic wrapping, but Julia accepted them all the same. She took them through to the kitchen and put them on the counter next to the Shepherd's Pie, which was suddenly lower down on her list of priorities. She soaked a cloth under the cold tap, grabbed a bag of frozen peas from the freezer, and hurried back into the sitting room.

"It looks worse than it is," Barker said with a small laugh as he danced his finger around the bloody cut running through his eyebrow. "I always wanted a scar there. I'll look quite distinguished, don't you think?"

"He only got one punch in," Jessie said from her position on the arm of the couch. "Barker was lucky I was coming back from the shop when I was. I scared him off."

She flexed her knuckles and Julia gasped when she saw they were just as bloody as Barker's eyebrow. She noticed Julia looking, so she pulled her sleeve over them and shook her head to let Julia know she was fine. When Julia had finished cleaning up Barker's cut, she ran back into the kitchen, rinsed the cloth, then cleaned up Jessie's knuckles. She was relieved to only see small grazes underneath the blood.

"Are you going to the police?" Julia asked, turning her attention back to Barker, who winced as he pressed the bag of peas against his brow.

"There's no point," Barker mumbled through the grimacing. "I can't really blame him. Once again, it's down to me that his father is behind bars. They officially charged Jeffrey with Jim's murder this afternoon."

Julia was surprised that Barker didn't seem pleased to

be saying that. Even though she had her own doubts about the strangeness of what had happened at the B&B, she couldn't logically pin the murder on anyone else.

"I'll leave you two alone," Jessie said, already pulling up her hood. "Dot will wonder where I am. I only went out to buy some food. She's trying to feed me something called quinoa and I don't trust it. See ya."

When they were alone, Julia sat next to Barker and rested her head on his shoulder. He smiled down at her to tell her he would be fine, but it didn't ease her concerns.

"He's just angry that he's lost his dad," Barker said, almost apologetically for Billy. "That, or -,"

Barker didn't finish his sentence. He pulled the bag away and tossed it onto the table. The cut looked deep, and it looked like it needed stitches. Julia ran into her bathroom and grabbed her first aid kit from under the sink. She pulled out a small row of butterfly stitches and antiseptic spray.

"Or what?" Julia asked as she sprayed Barker's brow.

"*Ow!*" he cried out. "What was that?"

"Or what?" Julia asked again, a small grin forming on her lips as she carefully applied the stitches around Barker's brow. "Do you need some painkillers?"

"I'll be okay," he said with a shake of his head. "What would I do without you, eh?"

"You'd cope."

"That's just the thing," he said, a soft smile on his lips. "I don't think I would. You've been my rock this last month, Julia. I really mean that."

Julia was touched. She sat next to him, her fingers dancing up into the back of his hair.

"Or what?" she repeated for a third time.

"I just can't help thinking that Jeffrey is going along

with all of this too easily," Barker said. "What if he's covering for somebody?"

"Billy?"

"It's the most obvious choice."

"It is," Julia agreed. "It's crossed my mind too."

"Or, he really did do it, and he's just accepting that he's going back to prison."

"Did you believe Evelyn's story about him being innocent?"

"Not one word," Barker exclaimed, shaking his head heavily. "Did you?"

Julia didn't answer immediately. She thought about her response for a moment. Evelyn had sounded pretty convinced, and she had put across a strong argument for his innocence. The fact somebody else had confessed to Jeffrey's original crimes was a major sticking point for her.

"I don't know," she admitted. "Mistakes do happen."

"Let me tell you something about Jeffrey Taylor. He's manipulative. He's got Evelyn wrapped around his little finger. Whoever this new person charged with those murders is, I wouldn't be surprised if Jeffrey had someone stitch them up from inside. That little story Evelyn told about Jeffrey being those women's 'drug provider' was a load of nonsense. He singlehandedly ruled the underground drug scene in Hull. Getting him off the streets was one of the best things I ever did."

"Even if it wasn't for the right crime?"

"He did it, Julia," Barker said stubbornly. "I know he did. Just like he killed Jim Austen. I slept better than I had in weeks last night knowing that monster was behind bars again. I just don't want the charges to be dropped on another technicality. I want the evidence to be so concrete that he can't wriggle out of it. Bradley is rushing ahead, all excited that he's caught Jim's killer, but if this is going to stick, they're going to need more than a wreath and a tiny clip of CCTV footage putting him in the vague area at the time of the murder. If he gets away with this and he stays in Peridale, he's going to be a ghost from my past that I would rather live without."

Julia walked through to the kitchen and plated up the Shepherd's Pie. On her way back to the sitting room, she blew out the candles in the dining room. Leaving the wine behind, she put a pillow on Barker's knee and balanced the plate on top of it.

"So much for a romantic night," Barker said sarcastically. "This looks delicious."

"It's just something I tossed together."

"Certainly looks better than something I would toss together."

As they tucked into their food, Mowgli strolled into the sitting room and jumped up onto the armchair next to them. He circled the same spot for a couple of seconds before curling into a tight ball and falling straight to sleep.

"Wouldn't you just love to be a cat?" Barker remarked as he cleared his plate. "Napping whenever you please, and only worrying about when the next meal is going to be put down. It's an easier life, isn't it?"

"Who wants an easy life?" Julia asked, pushing her food around her plate. "It's the struggles that make us stronger."

"I'm going to end this year stronger than ever then."

"You've clearly been through struggles before," Julia said as she put her plate on top of Barker's and pushed it onto the coffee table. "You mentioned there was a story you were saving for another time, and I was wondering when that time was going to come."

"Ah," Barker said firmly, dropping his head. "You don't forget a thing, do you Julia?"

"It's a blessing and a curse," she said, tucking her legs underneath her and hugging a pillow as she turned to Barker. "You don't have to tell me anything you don't want to."

"It's not about *wanting* to tell you," Barker said quietly, turning his head and resting it on the back of the couch so that he was looking into her eyes in the low light. "Some things just aren't easy to talk about."

Julia nodded, knowing exactly what he meant. It hadn't gone unnoticed to her that she still hadn't told Barker about her recent divorce. It wasn't that she didn't want to tell him, she just didn't want the shadow of her past staining their still very fresh relationship. She enjoyed being Julia without the baggage of being a divorcee at thirty-seven.

"I was engaged," Barker said, his eyes suddenly darting down. "Eight years ago. It was around the same time I was working on the Jeffrey Taylor case."

"Oh," Julia said, unsure of what she was expecting to hear. "Did it not work out?"

"She died," Barker said, looking back up into her eyes. "When the trial finished, I was being hailed a hero for putting Jeffrey behind bars. I was on cloud nine. I had always dreamed of being a Detective Inspector, and there I was, living that dream. Do you know how many people crack a serial murder case when they're fresh out of their inspector exams? It rarely happens. The night Jeffrey was sentenced, we all went out to celebrate. Everybody was buying me drinks, and even though I had Jeffrey's threat from earlier that day rattling around my brain, I felt like we had done good work. I've already told you about the doubts I had during the trial, but they all vanished that night. It was over, and I was glad of it. I met Vanessa when I first moved to Hull. She was a constable and we worked together a lot. They warned me about mixing business and pleasure, but we fell in love. It all happened pretty quickly, but it was love. I proposed to her that night and she said yes. I didn't even have a ring. I was drunk, if I'm honest with you, but I didn't regret it in the morning.

"We were only engaged for three days when she died. She was shot. It was a random attack. Some lunatic called the police to his house telling them he wanted to report a burglary, and when he invited them in, he shot them both in cold blood. He had been arrested for drunk driving the month before and they had taken his licence off him. That was his little revenge plan. Pathetic, wasn't it? Just like that, she was gone. The other officer pulled through. I went from a career high to the lowest point of my life.

"I tried to get back to normal, but it was impossible. I couldn't walk around the station, or the town, without seeing her everywhere. I transferred to London, and that's where I stayed until I transferred to Peridale."

Julia wiped the tears from her cheek as quickly as they appeared. She tried to speak, to offer Barker her condolences, but she couldn't say anything. With her tear-soaked hand, she grabbed his and squeezed. He smiled his appreciation, the pain of that time alive in eyes.

"Jeffrey being here brought my past crashing into the present. It was a shock. It brought everything about the trial, and Vanessa flooding back. I felt like I had put enough distance between then and now, but it was like no time had passed."

"A broken heart never fully heals."

"But the place it breaks can sometimes be the strongest part," Barker said, smiling through his sadness. "You're the first woman I've loved since Vanessa. I dated, but nobody ever stuck. You, however, are my silver lining."

"Why didn't you tell me any of this before?" she asked.

"I didn't want you to think I was weak," he whispered. "I didn't want you to think my love for you was any less real because of my past."

Warmth radiated from Julia's chest and flooded through her body. She thought about telling Barker about her divorce, but it felt so insignificant compared to what had just been shared. Clutching his hand and staring deep into his eyes, she felt like she was starting to see the real Barker, and it only made her love him more.

She tried to think of a way she could put those feelings into words, but she knew she could never do them justice. Instead, she cupped his face in her hands and pulled him into a kiss. He fell on top of her, their foreheads banging together. They giggled through their pressed lips, and Julia knew that Barker's heart was singing just as loudly as hers.

CHAPTER 13

The next day in Julia's café, things started to feel more normal again. Every customer talked about the strange newcomer being charged with Jim's murder, thanks to the '*RELEASED MURDERER STRIKES PERIDALE!*' headline on the front page of *The Peridale Post*. After the chaos of the last two weeks, hearing the villagers gossiping again reminded her that she was home.

"I'm honestly surprised it took them so long," Emily Burns exclaimed, barely pausing after taking a sip of tea. "He mowed my lawn four days ago! He could have killed *me*!"

"And *me*!" Amy Clark chipped in, mumbling through a

mouthful of angel cake. "He pruned my roses. Do you know how sharp those sheers are? I'm surprised he didn't cut my head clean off!"

"He only killed Jim because he thought it was Barker," Jessie mumbled under her breath as she cleared away the tables.

Jessie's tolerance for idle village gossip was a lot lower than Julia's, but she wasn't surprised. It seemed that only Peridale natives really understood how things worked. They would talk about the topic until they had discussed and speculated every minuscule detail, and then something new would come along and the cycle would begin again. Luckily for Julia, her customers didn't know her involvement in the solving of the case so her name was left completely out of the story. It was information she was more than happy to keep to herself because she knew if she corrected anybody on their facts, she would become part of the story, and by the time it worked its way around the village, it would have been changed and chopped so much, it would be a completely fictional version of events by the time it made its way back to her.

When the lunchtime rush was over, Dot marched into the café, in her usual new uniform of neon workout clothes. Today she was wearing luminous pink Lycra leggings, a toxic shade of green tracksuit jacket zipped up to her chin, with a matching sweatband covering her forehead. Today, however, she didn't have the usual steely glare of determination she usually had when she was wearing her uniform. She looked completely rundown.

"Cup of tea when you're ready," Dot mumbled as she collapsed into the chair nearest the counter, sweat dripping down her red face. "What's that brown cake in the display?"

"My latest chocolate cake creation," Julia said. "Want a slice?"

"Contaminants," Dot mumbled like a parrot that had swallowed a fitness dictionary. "*Calories*."

Julia dropped a teabag into a small teapot. As she filled it up with hot water, she looked at her gran, who was staring at the cake display case like a zombie staring at fresh brains. Her tongue poked out of her mouth and ran along her thin lips. Julia glanced to Jessie, who was also watching. Jessie rolled her eyes and opened the display case, pulling out the large cake.

"Are you sure you don't want some, Dot?" Jessie asked, waving the cake under her nose. "It's Julia's best work yet. A milk chocolate sponge with chocolate fudge buttercream, topped off with flaked chocolate that just melts in your mouth."

"Get it away from me!" she cried, fear rushing across her face.

Jessie rolled her eyes and placed the cake onto the counter. She grabbed the teapot Julia had just made up and positioned it in front of Dot, along with a teacup, a pot of milk, and sugar. Dot added the milk, but ignored her usual three sugar cubes.

"Why won't this thing stop vibrating?" Dot cried, shaking her wrist against her ear. "All night and all day. Beeping and booping at me! Telling me to breathe, and stand, and walk, and measuring my heart rate like a demonic doctor obsessed with my blood pressure."

"Just take it off," Julia offered.

"I *can't*!" Dot said with a shake of her head. "Do you know how much this thing cost? A whole month's pension, that's how much!"

"You're crazy," Jessie whispered. "Absolutely nuts."

Dot lifted the cup of tea to her lips with shaking fingers, but her eyes were firmly honed in on the chocolate cake. Julia had made the new version that morning to surprise Barker with, but she had decided to put it up for sale in the café first, and she was only taking home the leftovers so that Barker couldn't complain that she was trying to fatten him up.

"Here it goes again!" Dot cried as her watch beeped. "It's telling me to breathe! *I am breathing*! Does it think I'm dead? Tell it to stop, Julia!"

"Leave my gran alone," Julia teased, pointing a finger at the watch. "Or else."

"Do you think this is a joke?" Dot yelled, scratching at her skin under the watch. "It's taken over!"

"Isn't the whole point of a club that you spend time with people you like and do something fun?" Julia asked. "This doesn't look much fun, Gran. You're sitting here on your own shouting at a watch."

"But what about my steps?" Dot cried as she shook the watch against her ear again. "If I don't complete my steps goal, I don't get the little medal on the screen. I haven't missed a day!"

"You know if you shake your arm, it clocks up the steps?" Jessie offered as she walked by.

"But that's pointless."

"It works," she said with a shrug. "You're the sucker who's letting a watch control your life."

Before Dot could launch into an impassioned rant about why the watch was the best thing she had ever bought, the bell above the café rang out, and Shilpa Ahmed from the post office next door walked in.

"Afternoon, all," she said. "We appear to be matching today, Dot."

Shilpa motioned to her green sari, which was a similar shade of green as Dot's sweatband, but somehow looked much more delicate with its embroidered white floral pattern and flowing design. Dot didn't seem to take the compliment well. She tore off her sweatband, ripped off the watch, and tossed them both to the floor. Using her heel as a weapon, she stomped down on the watch, cracking the screen. As a final act of defiance, it beeped back at her, causing her to stomp down until she was looking at a pile of grass and microchips.

"*Are you happy now?*" she screamed at the top of her lungs at the mess on the floor. "Will you leave me alone?"

"Is it something I said?" Shilpa whispered to Julia.

Julia shook her head as she cut a large slice of the cake. Before she could stab a fork into it, Dot snatched the cake from the plate with her fingers and crammed it into her mouth. Her eyes rolled back into her head and for the first time since starting her fanatical health kick, she looked peaceful.

"You're free now," Jessie said as she massaged Dot's shoulders. "Congratulations."

"S'good cake," she mumbled through half-closed lids as the sugar surged through her body. "S'good."

Julia chuckled at her gran, glad that she was back. She had always thought her gran's stiff white blouses, held under her chin with a brooch, and pleated calf-length skirts were a little old fashioned, but she was looking forward to getting them back if it meant she never had to see her gran decked out in neon ever again.

"What can I get you, Shilpa?" Julia asked. "I have some

of those red velvet cupcakes you like."

"You know how to spoil me," she said as she glanced through the cake display case. "I'll take two. One for now, and one for later."

"Good idea," Dot said wisely, wagging her finger at Shilpa. "I like your style."

Julia reached down to pluck the two cupcakes out of the counter display. As her fingers closed around the first cupcake, something burst through her café's window, sending shattered glass flying through the air. Dot and Shilpa both let out wild screams as a chunk of Cotswold stone rolled across the floor, stopping when it snagged on Dot's sweatband. They all peered through the fresh hole in the window and onto the village green, where Billy Matthews was standing in his red tracksuit, his hands firmly in his pockets.

"I'm gonna kill him!" Jessie yelled as she ran for the door.

Billy set off running but Jessie was hot on his heels. As the pair disappeared from view, Julia pulled her phone from her bag under the counter, her hands shaking out of control. Staring down at her screen, she wondered if she should call the glaziers or the police first.

"Is everybody okay?" Julia asked, looking up from her phone as she dialled '999'.

"I'm fine," Dot said as she resumed her cake, which was much more important to her at that moment. "Honestly, that boy is nothing but a menace."

"I'm surprised he's walking around the streets, considering he was one of those three people on that security footage I gave to the police," Shilpa added.

Julia pressed the phone against her ear and listened to

the dial tone. Somebody answered, asking what emergency service she wanted, but all she could do was stare at Shilpa, unsure of what she was even supposed to be saying to the operator on the other end.

"Wrong number," Julia mumbled into the handset before tossing it on the counter and looking directly at Shilpa. "Did you say *three* people?"

"Well, yes," she said, almost unsure of herself. "How do you know about that?"

"I was shown the footage. I saw Jeffrey, and I saw Billy."

"And the third person," Shilpa said, nodding surely. "The third person dressed all in white."

Julia's heart stopped. She looked through the broken window, suddenly feeling the world grinding to a halt around her. In her mind's eye, she could see Barker alone, and probably still asleep in bed.

"Do you still have that footage?" Julia asked, already grabbing her coat from the hook in the kitchen.

"Of course," Shilpa said. "We keep all security footage for thirty days. I merely gave the police a copy. Is it important?"

"Very. I think it might just prove who *really* killed Jim Austen."

Leaving her gran in charge of the café, Julia followed Shilpa into the post office next door. Her son, Haaken, was behind the counter, but when he saw his mum return, he grabbed his coat and headed for the door.

"Don't forget it's your uncle's birthday tonight!" Shilpa called after him. Haaken waved his hand over his head, his headphones already in his ears.

After Shilpa punched in the code to unlock the door, they both walked behind the counter and towards a small computer crammed between a tall filing cabinet and a basket full of parcels.

"Let me see if I can remember how this thing works," she muttered to herself as she hovered over the keys. "It was a Monday, wasn't it?"

"The day after the beer festival."

"Ah, yes," Shilpa said with a nod. "I remember, not that I drink. I think this is it."

Shilpa clicked a file and a video jumped up on screen. She pressed the play button and started fast-forwarding through the clip. Julia watched as the sunny morning turned into the dull afternoon. When the storm clouds appeared and prematurely darkened the village, Shilpa slowed the footage down to normal speed.

Julia saw Billy Matthews, just as she had before. He walked up the lane, staring down at his phone, and only looking up when he was outside of Barker's cottage. She realised the footage she had seen had been cropped so that Barker's cottage had been cut entirely out of view.

"Here's the next one," Shilpa said, tapping her finger on the screen.

Jeffrey Taylor came into shot, running across the village green. He turned onto the lane, only slowing down when he reached Billy. They hugged and then turned in the direction of Barker's cottage. Julia's heart stopped, but to her surprise, they climbed over the wall and disappeared into the fields surrounding their cottages.

Seconds later, a car pulled up outside of Barker's cottage and a man jumped out. He locked the car over his shoulder and walked towards Barker's front door.

"This is when it started raining," Shilpa said just as the rain began to fall. "Gets a little trickier to see, but if you look closely, you can see the white figure."

Julia leaned into the screen, the distance of Barker's cottage already difficult to see without the added difficulty of the rain blurring the footage. Just when she thought she wasn't able to see whatever Shilpa thought she had seen, something large and white stepped out from the side of Barker's cottage.

"I thought it was a ghost," Shilpa whispered. "Creepy, isn't it?"

Julia squinted, her nose practically touching the screen. Through the blurry pixels, she watched the ghostly figure walk to the door, and then suddenly walk away and hop over the same wall Billy and Jeffrey had. She pulled back when she realised she had just witnessed Jim's murder through the blur of the rain. If she hadn't have known what had happened, she would never have been able to tell what she was looking at, but because she had been able to think about nothing else since that dreadful night, something in her brain suddenly clicked and the door blocking her logical mind from truly figuring things out unexpectedly burst open.

"That's not a ghost," Julia whispered, taking a step back from the screen. "It's a forensics suit. I need to go. Thank you, Shilpa."

Before Shilpa could ask her any questions, Julia ran out of the post office, ignoring the small crowd that had formed around her café's broken window. With Barker's life more at stake than ever, shattered glass was the last thing on her mind.

She set off towards Barker's cottage, relieved when she

saw DS Forbes out of the corner of her eye drinking a pint outside of the The Plough.

"Julia!" he beamed over his pint, froth in his moustache. "Join me for a pint?"

"It's you who I need to join me, DS Forbes," she said hurriedly. "There's not a lot of time to explain, but we need to get to Barker's cottage right now. His life might be in grave danger and I don't trust anybody else other than you right now."

"Grave danger, you say?" Bradley asked, a brow arching curiously as he stood up. "Lead the way, young lady!"

Thankful that she didn't have to explain herself any more, she set off towards Barker's cottage with Bradley hot on her heels.

CHAPTER 14

B radley banged on the door, calling out for Barker through the wood. They both listened, but they couldn't hear a thing. Julia stepped over Barker's weed-infested flowerbed, and then cupped her hands up against the sitting room window.

"I can't see him," Julia whispered.

"Maybe he's not home?"

"Or maybe we're too late." Julia climbed back over the flowerbed and dove into the hanging basket next to the door, her fingers closing around something cold and metal. "For emergencies."

She shook the dirt off the key and crammed it into the lock. To her relief, the door opened with ease. They both looked at each other before stepping into the dark cottage.

"Barker?" Bradley called out. "You home?"

"I'll check the bathroom," she said. "He sometimes likes to take bubble baths with the radio on. You look in the bedroom."

"Gotcha."

When they had both finished checking the rooms, they met in the hallway, neither of them having found Barker. Julia pushed her fingers up into her hair and turned on the spot.

"Why do you think he's in danger?" Bradley asked.

"Somebody tried to kill him, and it wasn't Jeffrey," Julia said as she pulled her phone from her handbag. "Jeffrey might have left the wreath, but he didn't commit murder. I'm going to try and call Barker."

Julia tapped a couple of buttons on her screen and put the phone to her ear. She waited a moment before tossing the phone down onto the side table.

"He's not picking up," she said as she clipped her handbag shut. "Maybe we should just wait for him to get back?"

"How do you know Jeffrey isn't the murderer?" Bradley asked, looking as confused as ever. "We charged him yesterday morning."

"Has he confessed?"

"Well, no, but murderers don't tend to when they don't want to go back to prison."

"I have proof Jeffrey didn't kill Jim. Somebody tampered with Shilpa's security footage, cutting out a crucial piece of evidence. In its entirety, it proves Jeffrey and Billy's innocence. Why did you crop yourself out of the video, DS Forbes?"

Silence fell on the cottage, perhaps the whole village, and Julia was sure she could hear a pin drop. She dropped her smile, tilted her head forward and stared at Bradley from under her brows.

"*Excuse me?*" he spluttered, forcing a laugh through his reddening face. "Are you insinuating that *I* tampered with evidence?"

"I'm implying that you *murdered* Jim Austen and you went to great lengths to conceal your tracks." Julia's heart pounded as she glanced down at the phone. She felt every detail of the last two weeks flooding to the forefront of her mind. She couldn't believe it had taken her so long to figure it out. "You never wanted to kill Jim, did you, DS Forbes? Your tears at his funeral were real, but they weren't tears of grief, they were tears of guilt."

Bradley's expression darkened as he glared at Julia, the air around them turning cold as gloomy clouds rolled over Peridale, casting out the little afternoon daylight that was reaching them in Barker's hallway. With his back to the front door, dark shadows cast down Bradley's face, his plump cheeks forcing his eyes deep into his skull.

"Why would I kill Jim Austen?" he mumbled, droplets of sweat forming on his brow. "He was the best Chief Inspector this town has seen."

"Because you thought he was Barker," she said, the veins in her temples throbbing. "All of your little comments about taking Barker's job and becoming a DI weren't jokes, were they? You wanted his job so badly that you would kill for it. Barker told me people in the station resented him for moving into the village and filling the position. You might not have been vocal about it, but you resented him more than most."

"I've worked my backside off in that station!" Bradley cried, spit flying from his mouth as his usually squeaky voice deepened. "I have given them forty-one years of my life! I've worked in that station since I was eighteen-years-old and I've been held back at *every* turn! Every man in my family for generations has been an inspector, and they've kept me stuck as a sergeant doing the grunt work. Do you know how *embarrassing* that is for me? I thought I was getting that job! I figured it was finally *my* time to go through my inspector's exams and prove everybody wrong! I retire in seven years. I'm running out of time! I have to go home and look my wife in the eyes every day and tell her '*not today, but maybe tomorrow*'. I thought my tomorrow had come, and then Barker Brown moved to the village and snatched *my* chance from under my nose!"

"It's not Barker's fault you didn't get promoted."

"But Barker is so perfect!" Bradley cried as he started to pace from side to side. "He's handsome, slender, has a full head of hair, a beautiful girlfriend, a lovely home, a great salary, and he's twenty years younger than me! I've put in *my* work. What has *he* done to get here? He's coasted through! His suspension was *my* time to shine! It was *my* day!"

"Why not just wait for the outcome of his investigatory hearing?" Julia asked, squinting into the dark as the clouds thickened. "There was a chance he wasn't even going to keep the job."

"Jim was pushing him through," Bradley sneered through gritted teeth as he slammed his fist into his palm. "Jim was a good man, but he was *blind*. He thought Barker was the fresh breath of air this village needed. *Ha*! What's wrong with the old ways? What's wrong with helping out your own? Before Jim came here that night, he told me he was coming to let Barker know about his hearing, and that he was going to try his best to get Barker his job back. *Why? He* didn't deserve it! *I* deserved it."

"So you thought you would stop Barker before he even had a chance to hear what Jim had to say?"

"The timing was just too perfect!" Bradley cried, a sinister laugh forcing its way through his lips. "Do you know who the most successful criminals of all time are? The ones who strike when the timing is *right*! The wreath was *too* perfect. Murder had never even crossed my mind until then, but it was an opportunity I had to take!"

"So you took a forensics suit and waited behind his cottage for him to come home," Julia offered. "You know better than anyone how easy it is to leave behind trace evidence. You waited for Barker, and you hit him with a rock from his garden, except it wasn't Barker."

"It was dark!" he snapped, suddenly standing still and pointing a finger in Julia's face. "People always used to say they looked the same from behind. I never saw it until -,"

"Until you saw Jim's face."

"I tried to save him," he cried, his voice cracking. "He was dead in seconds."

"You took his wallet and phone to make it look like a mugging gone wrong, and you dumped them somewhere obvious so somebody would find them and strengthen your plan."

"Billy finding the phone was a stroke of pure luck! I knew I could get away with it. When Shilpa handed me that security footage, I thought I had been caught. Turns out she didn't know what she was looking at. Who knew cropping a video could be done on a phone? I never even submitted that evidence, but I knew you were sticking your nose in, so I showed it to you so you would push yourself towards Jeffrey and Billy. I knew *you* of all people wouldn't be able to keep your nose out, and if anybody was going to help me frame them, it was Julia South, baker extraordinaire!"

"And it almost worked," Julia agreed with a nod. "Everything I found did lead me to Jeffrey and Billy, except one thing."

"What's that?"

"My gut instinct," Julia said, taking a step towards the man in the dark. "I assumed Jeffrey was guilty because I wanted to believe Barker was safe with him out of the picture, but something didn't sit right with me. Looking back now, it's so obvious. You couldn't help but keep slipping in how much you wanted to be an inspector. Your ego let you down."

Bradley continued to pace back and forth, his eyes trained on the ground. He darted his fingers up to his head and rubbed the bald patch, disrupting the faint strands of hair that remained. He mumbled to himself, nodding his head and laughing sinisterly under his breath.

"Too bad nobody will believe you," Bradley said as he tapped his finger on his chin. "You've already caused enough trouble. Nobody is going to take the word of a baker over a Detective Sergeant, and soon to be inspector! There's no way Barker is getting his job back now, and after I arrested Jeffrey, they have to let me take the exams."

"And you'll let an innocent man spend the rest of his life in prison for a crime he didn't commit?"

"He's done it once!" Bradley cried. "What's another life sentence? He has no life here. He's going to rot behind bars, and I'm going to get away with this! It's the *perfect* crime!"

"Maybe nobody will believe *me*," Julia said as she stepped forward to pick up her phone. "But maybe they will believe *you*. I recorded this entire conversation. I knew Barker wasn't here. He's not been back here since the murder. He's asleep in my cottage as we speak, I just knew I needed to let you think I trusted you. The thing is, DS Forbes, men like you are so desperate to be acknowledged that you'll confess to a crime because you think you got away with it so well. Maybe you should have listened to your *own* gut?"

Bradley's nostrils flared, and his cheeks burned the deepest shade of maroon she had seen as he stared down at his protruding stomach. Just at that moment, the heavens opened, and rain pelted down on the cottage's roof, echoing around the corners of the dark hallway. The open door rattled in its frame, the hinges screeching out for oil. They watched each other through the dim light like two alley cats waiting for the other to make the first move. A bolt of purple lightning cracked through the sky, illuminating the handcuffs strapped to his belt.

"You know I can't let you leave?" Bradley whispered as he took a step forward, his hand reaching out for the phone. "You should have just stuck to your baking. I'm going to miss your lemon drizzle cake."

Julia looked down at her phone, and then down to the handcuffs. A gust of wind forced the door open, startling both of them. It bounced into the room and back into its frame, the small glass panel shattering in an instant. They both looked at it for a second, but nothing was going to stop Bradley. He turned back to Julia, fury filling his beady eyes.

He took his moment and dove forward, his fingers grazing against the edge of the phone. Julia darted to the side and with all of her force, she pushed the round man towards the hallway side table. He tried to catch his balance, but he was too heavy and gravity was too strong. He reached out for air as he stumbled backwards into the radiator before crashing down onto the small oak table, which buckled under the weight. Julia dropped the phone and struck, ripping the handcuffs from his belt. She wrapped one end around his chunky wrist and the other to the radiator pipe. At the moment he realised what was happening, she jumped back and watched as he struggled to stand.

"You're going to pay for this!" he cried as he rattled his hand against the pipe.

Another crack of lightning flashed through the hallway, its purple hue catching the glass screen of her phone, which was still recording every word. They both spotted it at the same time, but Julia's hands closed around it first. As she attempted to move away, Bradley reached out and wrapped his fingers around her brown curls and yanked her head back. Burning pain soared through her scalp, and she was sure he was about to rip her hair right out. She yelled out in agony, but the rumbling thunder drowned her.

Julia cried out for help, but she knew it was in vain. He wrapped her hair around his fist and yanked even harder as he tried to grab the phone with his cuffed hand. She reached up to her head and tried to pull his fingers away, but they were fused so tightly, she wasn't going to be able to do it with one hand. Despite this, she didn't let go of the phone.

"Let go!" he yelled as he jerked her hair. "Let go right

now!"

Another bolt of lightning cracked through the sky and the pressure around her hair released. She paused for a moment, unsure of what was happening. When she realised he had let go, she scrambled to the bathroom door and out of his reach, clutching the phone in both hands.

Through her tears, she saw Bradley slump against the radiator. What she first thought was an unfortunate well-timed bolt of lightning striking the cottage and travelling through the pipes revealed itself to be a hooded figure standing in the doorway.

"I think I've split my knuckles this time," she heard Jessie say.

Julia wiped her tears away and let herself breathe. She looked down at the blurry phone screen and finally ended the recording. She saved a copy to her phone and sent it to Barker, just to be safe.

"Your timing is impeccable as ever," Julia whispered as Jessie helped her up off the ground.

"I was heading back to the cottage to find you. I managed to catch Billy, and they arrested him for smashing your window. I saw Barker's open door, so I thought I'd be a good neighbour and close it, but of course, you're here, and there's a fat man handcuffed to the radiator. Do I want to know where this was going?"

They both looked down at Bradley as he rolled his head around his shoulders, letting out a deep groan as his face clenched up. Julia wrapped her arm around Jessie's shoulder and pulled her into a hug. For the first time since the appearance of the wreath, she relaxed, and all she could do was force out a relieved laugh.

CHAPTER 15

The rain continued through the night, but the sun rose brighter than ever in the morning, pushing every last cloud out of the sky to reveal nothing but crystal blue clearness for miles in every direction. Julia woke refreshed knowing that Barker was safe once more. Sitting up in bed with the sheets wrapped around her, she looked down on him and smiled. One of the butterfly stitches on his brow had popped up during the night, so she gently pressed it back down.

"It's weird to watch people when they're asleep," he mumbled through the side of his mouth, his eyes still closed. "I was having the strangest dream."

"Was it about me making you breakfast in bed?"

"No, it was about Bradley. I still can't believe I thought we were friends. It's already slipped away now, but I'm sure he was trying to kill me – *again*."

Julia pulled on her pale pink robe and walked through to the kitchen, feeling light without the weight of an unsolved murder on her shoulders. Her heart still ached for Jim, but it brought her some comfort knowing his family now knew the truth. She hoped they would find it in their hearts not to blame Barker for Bradley's illogical actions.

After feeding Mowgli, Julia set out three plates and got to work making breakfast. When she finished, she placed the fried eggs, sausages, bacon, baked beans, toast, and black pudding on the plates. She put two of them on one tray, and the third on another.

"It's just me," Julia whispered through Jessie's door as she knocked softly. "I've made breakfast."

Julia pushed the door, and it opened with ease. Jessie was already sitting up and at her dressing table, staring into the mirror with something silver pressed against her lips. She dropped whatever was in her hand and looked down. Julia met her eyes in the mirror, and she was surprised to see Jessie playing with her lipstick.

"Looks better on you than me," she said as she placed the tray on the edge of the bed. "You can keep it."

"Doesn't matter," Jessie said as she wiped the subtle berry shade off her lips with the back of her hand. "Looks stupid."

"You're fine just the way you are," Julia said with a small wink. "You don't have to wear makeup to impress anyone."

"Who said I was trying to impress someone?" she snapped, looking down her nose at Julia through the reflection, the berry stain smudged across her chin.

Julia kissed Jessie on the top of the head and backed out of the room, leaving her to her breakfast. She picked up the second tray and walked through to the bedroom, where Barker was sat up in bed, his phone pressed against his ear, and a smile firmly on his lips.

"Thank you very much, sir," Barker said with a nod. "I'll be in later today. Again, I can't thank you enough. I'll see you soon."

Julia placed the tray in between them and crawled up the bed and back under the covers. She scooped up some of the beans with her toast and crammed it into her mouth.

"Who was that?" Julia mumbled through her food.

"That was my new Chief Inspector," Barker said as he tapped his phone against his palm with a smile. "He just wanted to let me know that in light of recent events, they're dropping their investigation into my conduct and reinstating me with immediate effect."

"Barker, that's amazing!" Julia beamed, wiping baked bean sauce off her chin as it drizzled from the toast. "I'm so proud of you."

"It was all you, Julia," he said. "You're a better DI than I'll ever be, even if I am the best detective in the country when you compare me to a crazed killer desperate for a promotion."

"Perhaps," Julia said with a nod as she mopped the toast around the beans. "But I promise I will leave all detective inspecting to you from now on."

"Why does that sound like a lie?"

Julia's cheeks blushed as she dunked the crust of her toast into the runny egg yolk before tossing it into her mouth. She occupied herself with eating until Barker did the same, and she was glad when he didn't push her to admit she might have stretched the truth a little. She decided she wouldn't actively go searching for any more murderers unless she needed to. With Barker back where he belonged, she was confident that Peridale was in safe hands once more.

After breakfast, they all walked down to the café, where Julia was surprised to see Dot organising two men as they fitted a new pane of glass in her café's empty window frame.

"Gran!" Julia cried. "You did all of this?"

"It's the least I could do, love," she said, without taking her eyes away from the glaziers. "Little higher on the left there boys."

Both of the men looked at each other, and it was apparent to Julia that Dot had been bossing them around since they had arrived. She turned to the village green and inhaled the fresh spring air, glad of the normalcy once more. She knew the moment her café opened, all people would want to talk about was Bradley Forbes' arrest, but if it was any other way, it wouldn't feel like home. It would only be a matter of time before something else occupied the gossipers' attention.

"Here comes trouble," Barker whispered into Julia's ear as he nodded up the road. "Maybe I should go."

Julia looked towards Evelyn's B&B to see Jeffrey and Billy walking side by side towards them. Julia wrapped her fingers around Barker's hand to let him know that she was there. It was inevitable that they would bump into each other eventually. In Julia's eyes, the sooner they got it out of the way, the better.

Jeffrey and Billy whispered back and forth as they approached. Julia prepared herself for an all out war, and she could feel Jessie doing the same. Her fists clenched tightly by her side, so Julia did what she had done to Barker, and she held her hand. With Barker and Jessie with her, Julia held her head held high as Jeffrey and Billy walked up to them, stopping only inches away.

With his head cocked back, Jeffrey stared down at Barker, his lips tight and his jaw tense. Julia expected Jeffrey to try and plant a fist on the end of Barker's nose, so she was more than surprised when he outstretched a hand.

"Truce," Jeffrey said calmly. "There's no point going around in circles."

Barker looked to Julia and then down at the hand. She was worried he would be stubborn and refuse to take it, but to her relief, he slapped his hand into Jeffrey's, and they shook firmly. A small smirk, kinder than the one she had previously seen from him, tickled Jeffrey's lips. She looked down at his hand as he let go of Barker's, noticing that the tattoos on his left knuckles spelt out 'C E N T'. Combined with his other hand she had seen when she first met him, she realised his knuckles read 'I N N O C E N T'.

"I'm sorry for the wreath," Jeffrey said as he pushed his hands into his baggy jeans pockets. "I was surprised to see you here. I wanted to scare you, and that was wrong of me."

"Right, yeah," Barker mumbled, clearly taken aback by the apology. "And I'm sorry for everything too."

"Apology accepted," Jeffrey said before nudging Billy firmly in the shoulder. "Is there something you want to say, son?"

Billy sighed and rolled his eyes. He looked down at the ground and circled his white trainers around in the dust. For the first time since encountering the young criminal, Julia saw him as the child that he was.

"Sorry for hitting you," he mumbled to Barker. "Sorry for smashing your window."

"And the rest," Jeffrey demanded.

"Sorry for trying to nick your bag, but I already apologised for that one."

"Yeah, not good enough," Jessie growled, letting go of Julia's hand. "Truce or no truce, I'll still kick your backside if you try anything again."

"I don't doubt it," Billy said with a small smirk, sending a wink in Jessie's direction.

Jessie blushed and suddenly dropped her dark hair over her face. Julia wondered if this was whom the attempted lipstick application had been for.

"I need to set a better example for my son," Jeffrey said as he slapped his hand down on Billy's shoulder. "It's a fresh start for all of us. You're going to stay out of trouble, aren't you kid? And you're going to pay this lady back for the window."

"Suppose so," Billy mumbled with a shrug.

"Well, I appreciate that," Barker said awkwardly. "Now that I have my job back, I'll hold you to it."

Billy narrowed his eyes on Barker before rolling them and turning around. Jeffrey smiled one last time before spinning on his heels and following his son back towards the B&B. They continued to whisper back and forth until they suddenly stopped outside of The Plough. Billy turned and ran back towards them, and Julia almost thought the truce was over already. Instead of running towards Barker, he ran towards Jessie.

"Call me," he said as he passed a small piece of paper with a phone number scribbled on it to her. "I like a girl who can keep up with me."

Jessie stared down her nose at the piece of paper, seemingly unable to look him in the eyes. Julia almost expected her to screw it up and toss it back at him, but she slyly pocketed it in her hoody.

"Yeah, whatever," she mumbled. "Loser."

Billy shook his head and laughed as he turned and jogged back to his dad. Jeffrey slapped him on the back, and they continued walking up to the B&B, ready for their fresh start. Julia smiled and shielded her eyes from the sun when she saw Evelyn welcoming them inside.

"What now?" Julia asked Barker as they turned back to the café arm in arm with Jessie trailing behind, no doubt looking at the phone number.

"I guess we go back to normal," Barker said, holding the café door open for Julia as the workmen wiped down the fresh pane of glass. "Is there any of that chocolate cake left?"

SHORTBREAD AND SORROW

BOOK 5

CHAPTER I

J ulia inhaled the sweet icing as she finished piping Jessie's name onto the smooth surface of the birthday cake. She stepped back and assessed her work, unhappy with how wobbly the '*J*' looked. Mowgli, her grey Maine Coon, jumped up onto the counter and looked down disapprovingly at the cake before turning and sashaying to his food dish.

"You've missed a candle," Sue, Julia's sister, whispered over her shoulder. "There should be seventeen, and you've only put sixteen."

Julia quickly counted the candles. Her sister was right. She let out a soft chuckle, plucked a seventeenth candle from the large bag, and slotted it in a free space around the edge of the cake. Being the best baker in the small Cotswold village of Peridale meant she was often called upon late at night to quickly whip up birthday cakes for residents who didn't want to admit they had forgotten a loved one's special day. She always did her best to meet their deadlines, but when it came to family and friends, she always put a little extra love and care into the baking. She had been mentally planning Jessie's cake for weeks.

"Smells delicious," Sue said as she hovered over the cake. "Is that vanilla?"

"Just a dash," Julia said, slapping Sue's hand away before she swiped her finger along the edge. "Dot and Jessie should be back by now."

They both looked at the cat clock above the fridge as its tail and eyes darted from side to side. It was a little after midday, but it didn't surprise Julia that their gran was late. Dot worked to her own clock, which rarely synced up with anybody else's.

Julia placed the cake in the fridge and quickly wiped away the spilled flour. She dumped the dishes and whisk in the sink for washing later, and dusted the dried icing off her caramel-coloured flared dress.

"Have you got anything sweet to eat?" Sue asked as she poked through Julia's fridge. "I've been craving chocolate all week."

"Top shelf," Julia said with a soft smile as she reached around Sue to grab a plastic tub. "Plenty of chocolate cake left over. I know it's Barker's favourite, but I think I've made it so much that he's sick to death of it."

As though he had heard his name, a key rattled in the front door, and Barker hurried into the cottage, still in his work suit. He dropped his briefcase by the door, hung his sand-coloured trench coat on the hat stand, and checked his reflection in the hallway mirror, tweaking his dark hair slightly. Sue and Julia looked at each other and smirked.

"You've given him a key?" Sue mumbled through a mouthful of cake. "You two must be getting serious."

Julia blushed. Barker had moved to the village nearly four months ago to fill the vacant Detective Inspector position at the local police station. They hadn't started out on the best terms, but they had been dating for over three months now, and they were very much in love. The exchanging of front door keys had happened two weeks ago, and at the time, Julia had not thought it was a big step, mainly because they were both getting tired of having to knock on each other's doors whenever they wanted to see each other. From the amused look on her sister's face, she was beginning to wonder if she had missed a relationship milestone that was a big deal to other people. Julia promptly dismissed the thought. Ever since their first meeting, her relationship with Barker had been anything but conventional.

"Am I late?" Barker asked as he kissed Julia softly on the cheek, his greying stubble brushing against her soft skin and his spicy cologne tickling her nostrils. "Is that *my* chocolate cake you're eating, Sue?"

"You can have some if you like," Sue said as she took another bite, cake flying from her mouth. "I've been craving chocolate."

Another key rattled in the door, signalling the arrival of Jessie and Dot, both of whom also had their own keys to Julia's cottage. She was pleased to see it was Jessie, her lodger, who was unlocking the door, and not her Gran, who had a habit of letting herself in whenever she felt like it, day or night.

"It's only us," Dot announced, just like she did every other time she entered. "I know we're late! *I know, I know*! But there was a tractor driving up the lane, and the taxi couldn't get through. Hello, girls."

"Hello, Gran," Julia and Sue replied in unison.

"Barker," Dot said with a curt nod, dropping her shopping bags by the door before adjusting the brooch holding her white collar under her chin, using the same mirror Barker had used to play with his hair. "Aren't you supposed to be at work fighting crime and not scoffing cake?"

"It's my lunch break," Barker mumbled through some of the cake Sue had shared with him.

Julia looked down at the shopping bags Jessie was holding. She had a huge grin on her face, and Julia was surprised to see she was still wearing the '*Seventeen Today!*' badge that Dot had insisted she put on before she took her out for a birthday shopping spree.

"I don't remember getting that much stuff on my seventeenth birthday," Sue murmured in Julia's ear.

"Times have *changed*!" Dot exclaimed as she waved her hands around, her hearing as robust as ever. "The kids these days want all sorts of things that I can't quite wrap my head around. What's the point in those Apple Pad *whatchamacall them* things if you can't write on them! Not like any pad *I've* ever known."

"They have apps on them," Jessie said, reaching into one of the bags to pull out the latest model of a tablet. "And the internet, and stuff."

"That couldn't have come cheap," Barker said after an intake of breath.

"Never you mind!" Dot said, extending a finger and wagging it in Barker's face as she pushed past him. "Julia, where's your radio?"

Julia watched as Jessie sat at the counter and eagerly unwrapped the plastic off her new gadget. It warmed Julia to see the look of joy on Jessie's face, especially because she would like people to think she was just another surly-faced teenager. After a lifetime of foster care, and six months sleeping on the streets before Julia had taken her in, she knew the gifts meant much more to Jessie than she would admit. Julia had gone to great lengths to ensure every part of her first birthday in Peridale was the best she had ever had. She hadn't even minded dipping into her little pot of savings to give Dot money to buy Jessie the tablet she had been eyeing up online for weeks.

"*Radio?*" Dot exclaimed. "*Where* is it? Tony Bridges' program is coming up on *Classic Radio* any second!"

"What do you want to listen to that for, Gran?" Sue asked, arching a brow at Julia, who could only shrug back. "Tony Bridges is *ancient!* He was on the radio back when I was a kid and he was old then."

"And me," Barker added.

"None of your business!" Dot mumbled as she ducked under the sink and rummaged through the cleaning products.

Julia reached up and grabbed the radio from the top of the fridge. She brushed off a layer of dust and handed it to Dot, who snatched it up to her face. She twiddled with the dials and buttons, lifting it up to her ear to give it a hard shake until she found the station she wanted.

"*And that was the smooth sound of Barry Manilow,*" Tony Bridges, the radio presenter, announced as the music faded out. "Coming up next we have a little Stevie Wonder, and *then* it's our daily *Music Quiz* at half past the hour!"

Dot glanced at the clock as she rested the radio on the counter, nodding her head as she counted the tiny markings on the clock. They all exchanged glances, confused and amused by her strange behaviour. Julia had never thought her gran was much of a music fan, but she knew her gran was a fickle woman who could change her habits and interests at the drop of a hat.

Remembering what she had been waiting to do all morning, Julia nudged Sue and nodded to the light switch. Sue tapped the side of her nose and scooted across the room as Julia pulled the birthday cake out of the fridge. Jessie was so distracted by her new purchase, she didn't notice Julia striking a match to quickly light all seventeen candles. Julia winked to Sue, who flicked off the lights, sending her bright kitchen into partial darkness thanks to the lingering grey clouds outside.

Julia enthusiastically led a chorus of '*Happy Birthday*' over Stevie Wonder, which grew louder and louder as Dot crammed her ear up to the speaker and cranked up the volume. Jessie blushed, pretending to be transfixed by the screen, but she was unable to contain the smirk prickling the sides of her lips.

"Make a wish," Julia announced as she set the cake on the counter.

Jessie rolled her eyes, but her smile broke free when she looked down and saw her name iced onto the cake's surface. She clenched her eyes, thought for a minute, and then blew out the candles with one swift breath. They gave her a little round of applause, which only caused Dot to turn up the radio even louder.

"What did you wish for?" Barker asked as he glared over his shoulder at Dot.

"I wished that you'd turn into a donkey," Jessie said with a small shrug. "Because you're always making an a-,"

"I *guess* you won't want this then," Barker jumped in, pulling a small envelope out of his inside pocket.

He waved it in front of Jessie's face for a second before she snatched it out of his hands and ripped it open. Instead of a birthday card, or even money, an application form fell out. Julia recognised it as a learner driver provisional license application form, although it had changed a lot since she had applied for hers at Jessie's age.

"I thought I could teach you to drive," Barker said coolly, his cheeks reddening a little. "I'll put you on my insurance once you have your provisional. In my car, of course. No offence, Julia, but I don't think I would trust your old banger to get to the end of the road with anybody else driving it but you."

Julia was too touched to be offended. Barker hated her vintage aqua blue Ford Anglia, but she would keep driving it until the wheels fell off and the engine finally died.

"You'd do that?" Jessie mumbled, dropping her hair over her face. "Thanks."

"I like you sometimes," Barker said with a wink as he ruffled Jessie's hair. "Only *sometimes* though."

"Yeah, well it's a good job I don't like you most of the time." Jessie slapped his hand away and ducked out of the way, a small smirk on her lips.

Julia laughed, even though Sue looked a little confused by their exchange. Julia treated Jessie like she would her own daughter, and even though she was dating Barker, he was more of a brother than a father figure. They bickered and fought like siblings, but she knew they cared about each other, maybe even liked each other, not that they would admit it.

Just as Julia sliced into the cake after taking out the candles, which she would put back into her collection ready for use on another birthday cake, Dot whizzed past her, grabbing the house phone off the wall as she did. She ran across to the bathroom and slammed the door, the spiral cord on the phone almost entirely stretched out. A small laugh of disbelief escaped Julia's lips.

"She's nuts," Jessie said. "She bought me new Doc Martens too. I told her she didn't have to."

Julia smiled because she knew they had been bought with Dot's own money. She sat next to Jessie and watched as she tapped away on the tablet, installing various apps and games.

"What's she doing in there?" Sue whispered, glancing over at the bathroom door.

"Do you really want to know?" Barker asked.

They both stared at each other for a moment before snickering like naughty school children. Julia picked up a piece of the sliced cake and took a small bite. Just as she suspected, the sponge was light and fluffy, and the icing was delicate and sweet. Even by her impossibly high standards, it was almost perfect.

"There's something I want to tell you when Gran gets back," Sue murmured, chewing the inside of her lip.

"*Oh?*" Julia asked, a brow arching.

Sue opened her mouth to speak as she looked down at her fumbling fingers, but before any words came out, Dot's voice filled the kitchen.

"*Hello? Am I on?*"

Julia turned to the bathroom door, as did Jessie, but Sue and Barker turned to the radio on the counter.

"*You're through to Tony Bridges' music quiz*, where *you* can win a holiday for *you* and *two* of your friends, granted that *you* get the answer right!" Tony exclaimed jollily through the speakers. "Tell us your name and where you're from."

"Oh my God, I'm *actually* through," Dot cried through the phone, loud enough that Julia could hear her on both ends. "Do you know how many times I've tried to get on this stupid show? *Every day* for two *whole* weeks! *Two*! I was about to give up!"

There was an awkward pause on the radio and in the room. Sue hurried over and turned up the volume as she cast a curious look over her shoulder to Julia.

"Yeah, well, *a lot* of people try to get on the air," Tony said with an uncomfortable laugh. "My producer tells me your name is *Dorothy* and you're from Peri – Perimale?"

"It's *Dot*," she snapped harshly. "And it's *Peridale*. What's the question? I don't have time for niceties. I want to win the holiday!"

There was another awkward silence as Sue and Julia both cringed. Julia was unable to even look at the radio. She could practically see the bemused grin of the DJ in the studio as he motioned to his producer to find out who had let the crazy old woman on air.

"Well, it seems we have ourselves a firecracker here, ladies and gents," Tony joked. "It's a good job I like them lively. *Okay*, folks, I'm going to get straight into this one. It's an easy one today. Are you ready Dot?"

"Of course I'm ready! I phoned in!"

Tony coughed and took a large intake of breath before

deciding to speak.

"Okay, *here we go*! The Police spent three weeks at number one with their classic hit '*Message in a Bottle*', but in what year and month? I need *both answers* for you to win the holiday."

"She'll never get that," Sue whispered. "She doesn't know anything about pop culture."

"I think it was 1981," Barker mumbled.

"What's *The Police*?" Jessie asked.

They all turned to the seventeen-year-old and scowled, which caused Jessie to scowl right back.

"I remember hearing that song as a kid," Julia said. "But it could have been anytime in the early 1980s."

Dot cleared her throat, forcing them into silence. They turned back to the radio and listened attentively through bated breaths. She grumbled for a moment, whispering nonsensically under her breath. Julia was sure she was about to say something completely out of the blue, maybe even hang up entirely.

"I need an answer, Dorothy."

"It's *Dot,*" she said through gritted teeth. "I know it. I know it. I think it was *September* in 1979. *Yes*. That's right. I'm *sure* of it."

There was another long dramatic pause before congratulatory trumpets crackled through the speakers, surprisingly them all.

"Well I don't believe it folks, but it seems Dot has pulled this one out of the bag! That's absolutely correct. How did you know?"

"It was number one when my first granddaughter, Julia, was born," Dot said, her tone softening a little. "I remember because it was playing in the delivery room and I told one of the nurses to shut it off. Total nonsense if you ask me. Not what I'd call music."

"Well, you've won the holiday!" Tony cried as the trumpets faded out. "Would you like to find out where that nonsense is taking you?"

There was a drumroll, which echoed loudly around the small kitchen. Sue turned to Julia, an excited grin on her face as she clenched her hands against her mouth. Julia almost couldn't believe what was happening, but it was her gran, so she had stopped trying to second-guess her thought processes a long time ago.

"You've won an all-inclusive five-night stay in a luxury spa hotel on the banks of the gorgeous Loch Lomond in Scotland!"

"*Scotland*?" Dot cried. "Bloody *Scotland*? The woman yesterday won a three-week cruise around the Bahamas. This is an *outrage*! I want to speak to your -,"

Before Dot could continue with her rant, Tony cut her off, and in turn, Sue clicked off the radio. They all turned to the bathroom door and watched as Dot shuffled out, a defeated look on her face as she mumbled bitterly to herself.

"*Scotland*!" she cried again. "Well, I suppose it's better than a kick in the teeth."

"I can't believe you just won a radio competition!" Sue squealed, pulling her gran into a tight hug. "All thanks to Julia's birth."

"Me and the girls have been trying all month! They've been calling it their *May-Cation Bonanza*! I guess they ran out of the decent holidays in the first week! The questions are *too* easy. That's their problem. And you better believe it, young lady." Dot wriggled out of the hug and adjusted her roller-set curls. "Because you're coming with me. You too,

Julia."

Julia looked to Barker, and then to Jessie, and finally to her gran. Just from the look on Dot's face, it didn't seem that Julia had any choice in the matter.

"Gran, I can't," she protested. "I have the café, and the -,"

"I'll watch the café," Jessie jumped in. "I've done it before."

"And I'll make sure she doesn't burn it down," Barker added, to which Jessie stuck her tongue out at him. "I can start teaching her to drive too. It'll be fun."

"I wouldn't exactly call it *fun*," Jessie grumbled.

Julia stared at Sue, who already looked like she had her heart set on it. Julia looked down at the cake, trying to remember the last time she had been on holiday, Scotland or not. It had been a long time before she had opened her café, and that was more than two years ago. She exhaled, and her mind wandered to the list of spa treatments that would be on offer. She could feel Sue's eager eyes pleading with her to say yes, and she wasn't sure she had the heart to say no to her sister.

"I'll be able to juggle my shifts around at the hospital," Sue said as she pushed into Julia's side and rested their heads together. "*Please*, big sis. We need some girl time. It'll be fun."

"You had me at *spa*," Julia said with a defeated smile. "When do you think we should go? Next month?"

"Well it's Sunday today, and we get five nights, so we'll go to the spa on Wednesday. I'll get it all sorted on the phone, so you don't have to worry about a thing! He did say all-inclusive." Dot shuffled over to the door and picked up her shopping bags. "I must dash. I'm going to have to buy some new boots and a thick coat. Scotland is hardly the Bahamas, but that doesn't mean we can't make the most of it. Enjoy the rest of your birthday, Jessie."

Dot waved a hand and disappeared out of the door like the whirlwind she was. In her absence, they all sat in baffled silence, staring absently at the birthday cake.

"I guess we're going to Scotland," Sue laughed, shaking her head. "The home of shortbread and kilts!"

"You know they don't wear underwear under those things," Jessie mumbled through a mouthful of cake with a small shudder. "What did you want to tell us?"

Sue looked awkwardly around the kitchen, her cheeks blushing. She looked Julia dead in the eyes, and Julia could feel the fear consuming her sister. When she blinked, she appeared to push it away in an instant, glazing a fake smile over the top. She shook her curls, which would have been identical to Julia's own chocolaty curls if she didn't insist on her monthly blonde highlights. She frowned and looked down at the ground, before looking up and staring absently out of the window and into Julia's garden, just as the clouds started to clear and the sun began to peek through.

"You know what, it's slipped my mind," Sue said faintly, snapping her fingers together. "Couldn't have been important. I think I'm going to follow Gran out. Shopping is in order, and I need to make sure Neil is going to be okay by himself. You know what men are like. Enjoy the cake!"

Barely a minute after Dot had left, Sue hurried out of the cottage. Jessie and Barker didn't seem to have noticed the strange look in Sue's eye, but Julia had, and she knew for certain that whatever it had been, had been important, despite her claims of forgetting.

"Scotland," Barker whispered under his breath. "That

sounds lovely. Let's all go out for lunch at The Comfy Corner. My treat. I want to spend as much time with you as I can before Dot whisks you away."

He pulled Julia in and kissed her on the side of the head. She realised she was going to miss Barker while she was away, even if it was only for five nights. Despite that, she knew Sue was right. It had been too long since they had enjoyed quality sister time together. Julia was embarrassed to say it had been months since she had really had an in-depth girls' chat with her little sister. All it would take was a glass of wine and Julia would be able to get to the bottom of her stumbled announcement.

CHAPTER 2

Relief surged through Julia when she saw a sign for the *McLaughlin Spa and Hotel*. Even though they had been driving in her tiny luggage-packed Ford Anglia for seven hours, it felt like she had been trapped in a tin can for days, no thanks to her gran's sudden and unwavering enthusiasm for her radio competition prize.

"Did I mention the hotel overlooked Loch Lomond, which is the largest loch in Scotland by surface area?" Dot repeated again like a parrot that had swallowed an encyclopaedia. "Says in this book that it was formed ten thousand years ago at the end of the last ice age."

Julia and Sue both glimpsed at each other in the front seat. If they weren't so exhausted, they probably would have laughed at hearing the fact for the third time. She eased her car into second gear and slowed to a crawl as they entered a small village which looked like it could be Peridale's twin.

"This is Aberfoyle," Dot exclaimed enthusiastically. "It's the nearest village to the spa. According to this book, there were only eight hundred residents during the census in 2010. Do you know how many residents Peridale has, Julia?"

"I don't, Gran," Julia said, forcing a smile as she glanced at her in the rear-view mirror. "We're not far away."

"I'm going to need a spa after this drive," Sue mumbled out of the corner of her mouth. "Or maybe a nice long nap."

The thought of a nap enticed Julia. She had been in such a rush to leave that morning, she hadn't had time to enjoy her usual peppermint and liquorice tea, nor eat any breakfast. Her stomach rumbled when she looked out of the window as they passed a small café, not unlike her own. The dry sandwich at the last service station hadn't even touched the sides.

Despite her exhaustion and hunger coupled with the temptation of cake and tea, the dropping miles on her sat-nav encouraged her forward. Even if she hadn't been completely sold on the idea of a spa break at first, it was all she had been able to think about since. She had never been great at relaxing, especially when she knew there was always something that needed to be done at the café, but with Jessie taking care of things and Barker watching over her, she was ready to forget all about Peridale and spend the next couple of days with an empty mind.

They drove out of Aberfoyle and followed a small

winding road up a steep grassy hill. Her poor car groaned, so she shifted gears, slammed her foot down on the accelerator, and willed it to make it over the top. When the road eventually flattened out, she knew it had been worth it.

"*Wow*," Dot whispered. "Would you look at that?"

"It's *beautiful*," Sue agreed.

The view completely stole Julia's breath. It took all of her strength to keep her eyes on the road, and not on the sprawling green hills and misshapen loch. Small islands dotted through the water, as though they had just drifted downstream and decided they were going to settle where they were. Beautiful swathes of grey, blue, and green all mixed together, bringing to mind a murky watercolour painting where the artist had forgotten to clean their water.

"I see the hotel!" Dot cried, jumping forward and cramming her finger between the two of them. "It's *there!*"

Sue and Julia both looked to where she was pointing. Their eyes landed on a large, imposing medieval castle on one of the larger islands nearer the bank. Its pale gold stone almost blended in with the colours of the landscape, and if it wasn't for the blue and white Scottish flag flying proudly at its entrance, Julia might not have noticed it out of the corner of her eye.

"Are you sure that's it, Gran?" Julia asked as she checked the tiny map on the screen, which wasn't showing her anything beyond the winding road ahead.

"Of course I'm sure!" she snapped. "I've done my research on the place. It dates all the way back to the 13th century."

"They had spas back then?" Sue asked with a wrinkled nose.

"Of course not!" she snapped again, rolling her eyes at

Julia in the rear-view mirror. "The spa was a recent addition in the last twenty years, but the castle, official title Seirbigh Castle, has been with the McLaughlin family since the 1930s. It was nothing more than a couple of ruins on an island when they bought it, but they fully restored it and gave it a purpose."

Julia spotted another sign for the hotel and almost couldn't believe her gran was right. The road took a sharp right turn, and the castle appeared in front of her. She turned to her sister, who was sharing the same look of disbelief. Julia let out a small laugh as she looked up at the grand structure. She hadn't expected much, considering it was a radio competition prize, but Seirbigh Castle had blown those low expectations right out of the water.

"This is going to be the best five days of our lives," Sue said as she took in the incredible vista. "Look at this place!"

The road narrowed, forcing Julia to slow to a snail's pace. Her car rocked as they transitioned onto the stone bridge that connected the land to the island. Dot hurriedly wound down her window and crammed her head through the gap.

"We're driving over the loch," she cried into the breeze.

"Somebody has changed their tune," Sue whispered to Julia. "I thought she wanted the Bahamas?"

"If I'd have known Scotland was so beautiful, I wouldn't have complained," Dot snapped back, her hearing not failing her once again. "The TV makes it look like an awful dreary place. If they showed more of this, people might actually want to come here."

Julia and Sue both shook their heads in unison as they dismounted the bridge and drove towards the castle. The gravel crunched under the tyres below as the crisp loch air drifted in through the open window. She inhaled, and a feeling of calm washed over her, forcing her to sink a little lower into her seat as she pulled her car into one of four empty spaces at the base of the castle entrance.

Before Julia had finished unbuckling her belt, Dot jumped out of the car and ran to the edge of the small island. She whipped a small disposable camera out of her handbag, wound it along, crammed it to her eye and started snapping the breath-taking view. Julia was sure an entire roll of film wouldn't be enough to capture the true beauty of the place.

Julia and Sue unloaded the car while their gran scuttled from spot to spot to get different angles. Julia had managed to fit all of her luggage into a single weekend bag, but her sister and gran had taken a more liberal approach to their packing, each bringing what appeared to be the entire contents of their wardrobes.

"A hat box?" Julia asked as she reached out for the oval case, arching a brow.

"I didn't know what the weather was going to be like," Sue said, snatching it out of her hand. "I bought it when me and Neil went to Moscow, and I've been trying to find an excuse to use it. I thought it would be snowing."

"It's spring."

"It's *Scotland*."

Julia laughed and shook her head. She shut the boot and locked the car before picking up as many of the bags as she could. Between them, they managed to grab everything, leaving their gran to continue her photo shoot. Before they set off up the slope towards the castle's entrance, Julia looked out at the dark loch once more, which stretched out for miles in either direction. She inhaled again as the wind licked her hair, the air moist and floral.

"*Heather*," she said to Sue, pointing to the purple flower covering the bank around them. "It smells beautiful."

"Your baker's nose never fails you," Sue said, before turning to their gran, who was halfway back along the bridge and snapping the water below. "*Gran*! We can't check in without you."

Dot reluctantly dragged herself away and dropped her camera into her bag, not without snapping a picture of Julia and Sue first. Without offering to take any of the bags, she shuffled past them and up the slope, which wound around the side of the castle.

The entrance, which was signposted as '*McLaughlin Spa and Hotel Retreat*' in bold gold lettering, looked like any other traditional castle entrance Julia had seen. It was doorless, and tall, double any of their heights. The castle appeared to be divided into three separate buildings, all joined together like a mismatched jigsaw. Julia wasn't much of a history buff, but she was sure if she had a look at her gran's guidebook, she would read that parts of the castle were older than others, with different invasions and families adding on their own sections. The entrance, which was the simplest part of the building, appeared to also be the oldest.

Led by Dot, they walked in through the entrance, which took them to a large ajar mahogany door. The first sign of modern civilisation was a table containing tourist leaflets next to the door. Dot picked up one of each, before yanking on the gold handle. The door creaked open, and she slipped through, letting it slam shut again. Julia shook her head, and Sue let out a long sigh. Julia dropped her bags and opened the door for Sue, who slipped in, and in turn she dropped hers and held it open for Julia.

Julia walked along the embroidered red carpet into the grand entrance hall. A matching mahogany staircase swept up the left side of the space, ending at a landing, which led off to many doors. The walls were exposed in some parts, and wood-lined in others, with heavy-framed oil paintings cluttering them in equal quantities. A large reception desk, with the spa's logo, sat at the far side of the room, with a door directly behind it leading off to what appeared to be an office. The desk was unmanned, but that didn't stop Dot from hurrying over and enthusiastically slapping the small metal bell. It rang out through the entrance hall, echoing into the corners. Julia slowly sauntered over as she attempted to take in every detail. She dropped her bags by the desk and turned to face the roaring fire that burned in the fireplace, which was as tall, if not taller, than her. It put her cottage's fireplace to shame.

Just from her first glimpse of the spa, Julia was sure she was going to enjoy it very much. She could already feel herself relaxing, and it was a feeling that she enjoyed, even if it was foreign to her. Peridale felt all of the three hundred and sixty miles away that it was, and even though she loved her little village, she was surprised how glad she was to be away.

Unfortunately for Julia, that tranquillity didn't last long. A door slammed, casting out any peaceful thoughts from her mind. She stepped back and looked up at the landing where the noise had come from. To her surprise, a black bag flew towards her, and she barely darted out of the way before it landed on the ground and split open. The plastic bag burst on impact and women's clothes, in a size much smaller and much more expensive looking than Julia's, spewed across the stone floor.

"I've told you once, and I'll tell you again!" a man's deep voice bellowed, his Scottish accent the strongest Julia had heard. "We're *over*!"

The man appeared from the door the clothes had flown out of, dragging a woman by the arm. He seemed to be in his early sixties, but slight in frame and very short. His head was completely bald and shiny and looked as though it was barely balancing on his narrow shoulders. His sharp cheekbones and sunken sockets created two shadows where his eyes should have been. The woman, on the other hand, was curvaceous and looked to be in her mid-forties. She struggled against the man's grip, but he was clearly much stronger than her despite his weak appearance. The hairs on Julia's neck instantly raised and every instinct in her body told her to help the woman.

"Please, Henry!" the woman begged. "You're *hurting* me!"

The woman's pleas fell on deaf ears. He dragged her towards the stairs, her long jet-black hair flying over her face. Julia stood and watched, completely numb, but fully expecting the man to fling her down the stairs.

"Our marriage is *over*, Mary," he yelled, tossing the woman to the floor at the top of the stairs. "It's been over for a long time. I've had enough of you digging your claws into my fortune."

He hurried back into the room, and two more black bags flew over the balcony, landing with the others. Julia and Sue jumped back, both of them looking at the woman who was sobbing at the top of the stairs.

"Henry, let's talk about this," Mary pleaded, her accent distinctly English against Henry's. "I love you."

"You wouldn't know love if it hit you in the *face*!" he

180

cried again, appearing at the top of the stairs with a suitcase in his hands. "You've got an hour to get out before I call the police."

He opened the case and projected the clothes into the air. Before they even had time to flutter to the ground, he launched the suitcase after it. It cracked and split into two halves on impact.

"*Dad!*" a voice called from behind the reception desk. "*Guests!*"

Henry glared down at Julia and Sue, before turning and disappearing back into the room, slamming the door behind him once more.

Julia turned to the young woman behind the counter, unsure of what to do. She looked to Sue, who shrugged as Mary's sobs echoed around the grand hall.

"Is she okay?" Julia asked, looking down at the woman's name badge, which read '*Charlotte McLaughlin*'. "She seems quite upset."

"Leave her," Charlotte snapped, her tone cold. "She brought this on herself. Total gold-digger, just like the last three. I'm sorry you had to witness that, but it's been a long time coming."

"It's a good job we're not paying, or I'd ask for some discount!" Dot cried, her face red and eyes wide. "Quite *unacceptable*, young lady!"

"I can only apologise," Charlotte said through almost gritted teeth. "So, you must be the competition winners. Welcome to Seirbigh Castle. I hope you had a pleasant drive through our beautiful corner of the world."

Despite her friendly smile and soft Scottish accent, Julia could tell the girl was reading the lines from a mental script she had recited hundreds of times. She was strikingly beautiful, with large doe eyes and thick lashes, and soft auburn hair, which cascaded over her shoulders, only stopping in the small of her back. Faint freckles scattered her nose and cheeks, which only made her pale green eyes even more striking. Just like the beautiful landscape outside, it looked as though the woman had been painted by a skilled artist's brush.

"Let me show you to your rooms," Charlotte said as she pulled two keys off the board behind her. "I've got you down in one double and a twin room."

Before they could debate who got what, Dot snatched the double bed key out of Charlotte's hand and smiled unapologetically at her granddaughters. Julia couldn't begrudge her gran the bigger bed; it was her competition prize after all.

Sue picked up the bags once more and headed awkwardly towards the foot of the stairs, stepping over the large pile of clothes and broken suitcase. Mary was still sobbing at the top.

"*This* way," Charlotte called over, stopping Sue before her foot even touched the bottom step. "That's staff quarters. Out of bounds to guests."

Sue frowned and turned on her heels before stepping back over the clothes. Julia scooped up the rest of the bags, grateful that Dot had at least grabbed one of the lighter ones this time. They followed Charlotte through a door, and along a narrow stone corridor, with windows on either side looking out onto the loch, which wasn't any less striking on second viewing. They entered one of the other parts of the castle, which appeared to be the largest and most recently built, although still centuries old.

"The spa and pool are through there," Charlotte said,

directing a finger towards the end of the corridor as they walked to a less grand, but still stunning, sweeping staircase. "Breakfast is served at eight sharp every morning. You'll find the dining room by going back towards reception and through the double doors to the left of the office. Lunch and dinner are served at twelve and seven respectively. Since you're the only guests, try not to be late."

"*Only* guests?" Dot asked, a faint brow arching high.

"We've been quiet recently," Charlotte replied quickly, her customer service smile still plastered across her face, but something else entirely twinkling in her eyes. "Rest assured, you will still be getting the *best* treatment. We're running with a skeleton staff at the moment, but the spa is still fully functional."

"As it *should* be," Dot said with a stern nod.

They reached the top of the stairs and walked along another long corridor. Charlotte paused outside of one of the doors and took the key from Dot. She unlocked it and swung the door open. Julia felt her jaw drop before she realised she was doing it.

"Since we're empty, I thought I'd make use of our bridal suite," she said, glancing smugly to Dot. "I think you'll be quite comfortable in here."

Dot swallowed down a lump in her throat and nodded as she walked into the room. She walked straight over to the four-poster bed and looked to the large windows overlooking the loch. Julia knew it was a tactic as old as time, and one she had used herself in the café more than once. Always give the tricky customers something special because they're less likely to complain.

"I think I will," Dot said with a nod as she laid back on the bed and closed her eyes. "Put my things on the dresser,

Julia."

Julia shuffled in and dropped her gran's bag, gazing at the beautifully decorated room, which looked bigger than her whole cottage combined. Elaborate tapestries covered the wood lined walls, with ornate mahogany furniture filling the space. Through an open door, Julia could see an ink-green tiled bathroom with a freestanding bath with gold feet. She would be happy if her bedroom were only half as beautiful as this one.

"You ladies are next door," Charlotte said, sounding eager to move them along. "There's an adjoining door if you would like me to unlock it?"

Sue glanced at their gran's room and shook her head. "It's okay. Keep it locked. I came here to relax."

Julia smirked as they carried their bags to the next door. She was relieved to see an equally beautiful smaller room, which was similarly decorated, with two wooden single beds next to each other.

"If you need anything, the phone on the bedside connects straight through to reception," Charlotte said as she bowed out of the room, her hand already on the door handle. "I hope you enjoy your stay."

"I'm sure we will," Sue said as she jumped onto the bed. "Thanks."

Unlike her gran's room, their room was on the corner of the building, so they had two windows. One was overlooking the loch, and the other looked over the rest of the castle. From this height, Julia could see her Ford Anglia parked in the shadows. Her eyes wandered to a figure sitting on the stumpy wall of the bridge with a pile of clothes at her feet. She realised it was Mary. She a packet of cigarettes from her pocket and with shaking hands, put one between her lips and lit it with a match.

"I wonder if she's going to be okay," Julia whispered.

"Who?" Sue mumbled through a content and calm smile. "The wife? Well, soon to be ex-wife. Who cares? It's not *our* problem. We're here to relax. Speaking of which, I think we should hit the spa *right now*."

Sue grabbed Julia's hand and dragged her towards the door. She looked back at her bed, wishing she could curl up and have a nap, but she knew that wasn't why she had agreed to come on the trip. She had come for quality sister time, and even though face masks and massages were more Sue's style, she was sure she was going to enjoy every second of it with her little sister by her side.

CHAPTER 3

J ulia woke with a smile five minutes before her alarm the next morning. Her skin felt soft with the floral scent of the massage oil still lingering. Her muscles felt relaxed and loose, and her mind was clear and at peace. She looked over to Sue, who was snoring soundly, a glistening trail of dribble across her cheek. She snorted and rolled over, pulling the covers over her head, as though she knew it was nearly time to wake up for breakfast.

After a quick shower in the freestanding bath, Julia quickly dressed in a simple dark grey knitted jumper, fitted black jeans, and trainers. She hadn't brought any of her typical 1940s style dresses with her because hadn't been sure the weather would call for it, but as she looked out of the window and down at the tranquil loch, she knew she had majorly misjudged the retreat.

Sue woke with her alarm, which had been set to go off at ten to eight. She groaned and rolled over, before sitting up in bed, her highlighted hair matted and sticking up. She looked around the room, her eyes landing on Julia in the dark, who was half hiding behind one of the curtains as she looked down at the loch.

"Morning, sleeping beauty," Julia exclaimed as she tossed back the heavy silk drapes. "Sleep well?"

Sue shielded her eyes and groaned even louder. Julia was sure she was about to try and go back to sleep, but she suddenly darted out of bed and hurried into the bathroom in her nightie. She slammed the door behind her and by the sounds of it, buried her head in the toilet.

"Are you okay in there?" Julia called through the wood with a wince.

"Must have been the beef last night," she groaned back. "I feel fine."

"You know I have a dodgy stomach."

Julia tried to remember if she knew that, but she couldn't recall that being a known fact about her sister. She remembered one time when they were kids that their friend, Roxy Carter, had pierced her own ear with a hot needle and a piece of apple, and Sue had thrown her guts up on the village green, but that was the only thing that sprung to mind.

Leaving her sister to get ready, Julia thought about calling Jessie or Barker to check how they were getting on. She got as far as hovering over the green call button, but hesitated, knowing they probably didn't need checking up on. She trusted them not to kill each other, or run her café into the ground.

She tossed her phone onto her bed and turned to look out of the other window and down at the rest of the castle. She immediately spotted Charlotte's striking auburn hair, which glistened brightly under the piercing morning sun. She was walking along the bridge where Mary had been sitting and crying with her clothes and cigarette the afternoon before. A tall redheaded man in a business suit was by her side. They appeared to laugh at something, not that Julia could hear it. She was sure if they looked up, they wouldn't see anything other than a shadow. When they reached the end of the bridge, they hugged and parted ways, with Charlotte walking up the slope towards the entrance, and the suited man disappearing around the side of the castle and out of view.

"What are you looking at?" Sue mumbled as she came out of the bathroom, wiping her mouth with the back of her hand and scratching her head with the other.

"Just taking in the view," Julia muttered as she watched Charlotte walk through the castle entrance. "We better get going. Gran won't miss a free breakfast for anything."

Just as Julia suspected, Dot was already waiting outside her room, obsessively checking her watch. With Sue trailing behind, they hurried down the staircase, along the corridor overlooking the loch, and into the entrance hall. Dot headed straight for the double doors by the reception desk, but Julia hung back to hold open the door for Sue, who had turned a ghostly shade of white.

"Why don't you go back to bed?" Julia suggested.

"I'll pass," Sue said with a shake of her head. "I'm already starting to feel better."

Julia smiled as supportively as she could, but her sister

looked anything but '*better*', in fact, she looked worse than she had when she had stumbled out of the bathroom. When Sue walked through and headed towards the double doors, Julia let go of the door and turned to follow. A man had appeared at the reception desk, and for a moment, Julia wondered if he was the same man she had seen out on the bridge with Charlotte, but she immediately noticed he was much older. He was wearing a weighty brown overcoat, which had been patched up in many places. His sparse hair was wiry and coarse, sprouting out of the sides of his head without any style. He turned to Julia, a dark shadow of stubble covering the lower side of his face, and a definite smell of whisky on his breath.

"You my replacement?" he barked, his accent the thickest yet. "Cannae believe they've picked a lass to take over my job."

"Excuse me?"

"*You're* the new groundskeeper?"

"I'm a *guest*," Julia said with a small laugh. "But I'm sure if I *were* the new groundskeeper, I could do the job *just* as well as any man, thank you very much."

The man scowled and grunted. He shook his head and lumbered past her, the scent of moss and heather following him, hinting at a lifetime spent outdoors in the same jacket.

When the man vanished, Julia laughed in disbelief to herself and headed for the double doors. She walked down another corridor to a different part of the castle, and she came out into a long hallway lined with framed portraits. At the end, there was what looked like a glass sunroom overlooking the water. She guessed that was a more modern addition. An arrow on the wall pointed her to the dining hall, which was on the left through a wide stone arch opposite a room marked '*Drawing Room*'.

Dot and Sue were already sitting at a table in the middle of the empty dining room. There was a canteen style buffet, but the lights weren't turned on, and there was no food on display. Ceiling high windows looked out over the hills, flooding the room with light, but the cavernous room still looked dark and gloomy somehow.

"Sit down," Dot said, offering a chair to Julia. "Doesn't look like we're going to get served anytime soon. This place is run like a sinking ship!"

At that very moment, a flustered young woman with rosy cheeks pushed through a door on the far side of the room. Her frizzy mousy hair flew free of the bun on top of her head, and her baggy apron was stained in flour and various sauces. It was a look Julia knew all too well.

"Sorry," she mumbled, her accent English, like Mary's. "I'm not used to serving. Orange juice and coffee?"

"*Tea*," Dot snapped, not seeming to notice the girl's stress. "And it better not be the *cheap* stuff!"

The girl dropped four tea bags into an already filled teapot, and placed it in the middle of the table with shaky hands. Julia attempted to give the young girl a smile, but it was either unwanted or unnoticed. Knowing how stressful a kitchen could be without the proper support, she hoped it was the latter. She could remember many times in her café's early days when she had been so overwhelmed that she had regretted ever opening.

The girl pulled out a notepad and scribbled down their breakfast orders. Dot ordered a full Scottish breakfast, making sure to mention the tattie scone and sautéed mushrooms specifically. The girl seemed relieved when Sue asked for corn flakes and Julia asked for poached eggs on toast. The sound of a full Scottish breakfast intrigued her, but she decided she would leave that for a day when she wasn't likely to cause the girl, who didn't look a day over nineteen, a breakdown.

"It's a good job we haven't paid for this," Dot whispered under her breath as the girl walked away. "Could you *imagine*?"

"Give her a break, Gran," Julia replied. "It's not easy doing it on your own. Charlotte said it was a skeleton staff at the moment, remember?"

"*Skeleton* staff?" Dot cried, craning her neck to look at the girl before she vanished back through the doors with her trolley. "She looks very much *alive* to me, sweetheart."

"It means they have the bare minimum working," Sue added, a little colour returning to her cheeks after a sip of tea. "It's what we do at the hospital during the late shifts and on days like Christmas."

"Well if this is the skeleton, I'd hate to see the ghost staff," Dot said through pursed lips. "Although, the lady in the spa is a miracle worker. I feel twenty-five again!"

To demonstrate, Dot cracked her neck and stretched out her arms. Julia laughed and glanced at the large windows, the view taking her breath away once more. She didn't care about the skeleton staff or the empty dining room, or even the ruckus that had welcomed them yesterday. Nothing could ruin the next five days of total relaxation.

There was a loud bang, and the doors opened again, making them all jump. The cook hurried back with their food, along with a rack of golden toast and a dish of yellow butter. When Julia smiled at her this time, she seemed to notice and smiled back, appearing relieved that breakfast was over for the morning.

"Thank you," Julia made an effort to say while their eyes briefly met.

"You're very welcome, miss," she said with a small nod before hurrying back through the doors again.

The doors banged again, causing Dot to slop baked beans down the front of her white blouse. She pursed her lips tightly and let out a long sigh through her flared nostrils as she dabbed at the stain with a napkin. Julia and Sue caught each other's eyes and shared a little grin.

Julia's eggs were poached to perfection, and Dot didn't complain once about her breakfast, which both sisters knew was a good sign. Sue barely touched her corn flakes, instead choosing to move them around the bowl while staring at them with a curled lip as though she was looking into a bowl of rotten eggs.

A third bang made them all jump, so much so that Julia spilt her tea in her lap. She dabbed up the tea with a napkin as she looked to the door, but the young cook didn't appear, and the doors were still in their frame.

"What was that?" Julia asked as she dried her jeans.

"Sounded like a gunshot," Sue whispered.

"Deer hunting is *very* popular around Loch Lomond," Dot exclaimed before reaching into her bag to pull out her guidebook. "Let me find the chapter. It's a fascinating read."

Julia glanced out of the window, but she couldn't see anybody on the bank ahead, despite the gunshot, if that's even what it was, sounding relatively close.

"I didn't know they had deer in Scotland," Sue said as she pushed her mushy cereal away. "I think the pool is calling this morning."

"That sounds like a good idea," Julia agreed as she screwed up the tea-soaked napkin and tossed it onto her plate. "Let's stack these up. Make the poor girl's job a little easier."

As Julia and Sue made the breakfast dishes as neat as possible, Dot flicked through the pages of her tiny book, clicking her fingers together when she landed on the section about deer hunting.

"Ah, *here* it is!" she exclaimed, straightening her back before reading aloud. "*'Red deer hunting is a very popular sport in Scotland, particularly in the months of August and September'*."

"But it's only the end of May," Sue said.

Her gran opened her mouth to continue reading, but a piercing woman's scream echoed through the empty dining room. Dot turned to look at the doors to the kitchen, but Julia was sure it had come from the opposite direction.

"What was that?" Dot cried. "This place is a *shambles*! I'm going to be sure to call Tony Bridges and let him know -,"

"*Quiet, Gran,*" Julia whispered, holding up her hand. "I can hear a woman crying."

Julia stood up and followed the sound through the dining room and back along the corridor that had taken her there in the first place. The sobbing grew louder and louder, pulling her back towards the entrance hall. Julia hurried along the corridor, and burst through the heavy doors with Sue and Dot hot on her heels.

Julia's hand drifted up to her mouth when she saw Mary crouching over Henry, who was lying in a pool of blood and shattered pieces of wood. He was in the same place Mary's clothes had been the day before. Julia hurried forward and rested her hands on the woman's shoulders as she looked up at the landing. Just as she suspected, there was a huge chunk of the mahogany bannister missing where the man had fallen. Julia looked down at the man's body. When she noticed the blood pouring from his chest, she knew she had just discovered the source of the mysterious bang.

"He's been *shot!*" Mary wailed. "I was looking for him at the reception desk, and he just flew over and landed right here. *He's dead!*"

"Did you see who did it?" Julia whispered urgently. "Is there another way to get downstairs without being seen?"

"This is the only way," she sobbed. "*Oh, Henry!*"

At that moment, Charlotte appeared through the doors that led to the part of the castle where their sleeping quarters were. She walked in, her eyes instantly landing on her father. Instead of screaming out, she stared down at the body, before hurrying over to the reception desk to pick up the phone.

"*Police,*" she said quickly down the handset as she held it to her face, her eyes wide as she continued to stare at her father. "Please, come quickly."

Julia left Mary's side and tiptoed up the sweeping staircase. She looked at the broken bannister, and then through the open door into what she assumed was Henry's bedroom. There was no murder weapon, and nobody else in sight. She took a step into the room and checked behind the door, making sure not to touch anything, but it was in vain; the room was empty.

Edging as close to the broken bannister as she dared, she stared down at Henry's body, wondering how the murderer had managed to flee without passing Mary. She had to stop herself from checking all of the other closed doors along the hall, deciding that was a job best left to the police. Knowing there was nothing else she could do yet, she pulled Mary away from her husband's body and comforted her at the bottom of the staircase.

While the grief-stricken woman sobbed against her shoulder, Julia pulled her in close and listened for the sirens.

CHAPTER 4

J ulia stared out of the window of the sunroom as the sun set on the loch. She attempted to focus on a man and child fishing in the distance, but the image of Henry's body was still fresh on her mind.

"How long are they going to keep us in here?" Dot moaned as she paced back and forth. "It's been *hours*!"

"They're going to interview everybody in the house," Julia explained calmly. "Including us."

"But we didn't *do* anything!"

"Then you'll have nothing to worry about," Sue added. "I don't see why they couldn't have made us stay in the spa or the pool room. It's an entire day of our trip wasted."

Julia looked sympathetically at her sister and smiled

reassuringly, not sure how to tell her that the owner's murder was likely to put an end to their free trip. She decided it was better if she came to that conclusion on her own. She looked out at the water as pink and orange stained the horizon. It was beautiful, but it was a sunset she couldn't enjoy.

The shy young cook, who Julia had learned was called Blair, appeared in the doorway holding a fresh tray of tea and cakes. Julia gratefully took the tray from her, replacing the one she had brought in two hours ago.

"Do you know what's happening?" Dot asked, a little kinder than she had spoken to her earlier in the day. "I feel like they're not going to let us leave."

"I've just been interviewed," she said nervously, her fingers fumbling with the strings on her apron. "Told them I was in the kitchen the whole time. Men in white coats have been crawling all over the castle."

"Forensics," Julia mumbled, almost to herself. "Have they taken his body?"

"I think so, miss," Blair said with a quick nod.

"I've told you, it's *Julia*," she said with a kind smile. "Did you bake these? They look delicious."

"Lemon drizzle cupcakes, miss – *I mean* – Julia," she said, her voice soft and cheeks flushing at her own correction. "I've never seen a dead body before, but I walked past it when I took a tin of shortbread up to Charlotte. It's her favourite and I thought it might cheer her up. I think the poor woman is in shock. She hasn't said a word."

"Death can do that," Julia whispered, again to herself. "Although I did find it peculiar that she didn't call for an ambulance as well as the police. It was like she just assumed her father was already dead."

"Did you see the poor fella?" Dot mumbled through a mouthful of cake. "Oh, *Julia*! This girl might rival you. *Delicious*, Blair. Where was I? *Oh, yes*! The man was *clearly* dead. He had a huge chunk missing out of his -,"

Blair sniffled, and a flow of silent tears delicately streamed down her youthful cheeks. Julia wrapped a hand around her shoulders and pulled her into a little hug. It hadn't struck her that the girl had just lost her employer. From what Julia had seen of Henry, she hadn't very much liked the man herself, but she knew everybody had different sides to them.

"Why don't you sit down and enjoy your cakes?" Julia offered. "You've been rushed off your feet all day."

"No can do," Blair said quietly, quickly wiping her tears away as though they were forbidden. "I've got to clean the kitchen for Charlotte and Rory's dinner."

"Rory?" Julia asked.

"Charlotte's brother and Henry's – *his* son," she choked on the words before turning and hurrying off.

"Poor mite," Dot said as she plucked another cake from the tray. "She's a fragile one. She'll toughen up with age, but I can't imagine it's very pleasant seeing any man like that. *Oh*! This one has a *jam* filling!"

Dot tore open the cupcake and strawberry jam dribbled down her fingers. Dot licked it up and tossed the second cake into her mouth without a second thought. Julia was sure they were lovely, but her stomach wouldn't settle long enough to eat. She began to pace back and forth by the window as the light faded from the sky forcing the sconces to do their job. She was itching to know what was going on, and she desperately wanted to know what had happened.

"You've got *that* look in your eyes, Julia," Sue said sternly with a shake of her head. "I don't like *that* look."

"What look?"

"The look you get right before you wade into something," Dot replied for her. "It's like when a bull sees red."

"It's the waving of the flag that entices the bull, not the colour," Julia corrected her as she continued to pace. "Bulls are actually colour-blind. It could be a green flag or a red flag, and the bull would still charge."

"Well, murder is *your* flag," Dot said as she poured herself a cup of tea. "And this castle is waving it in front of you!"

Julia wanted to deny it, but her gran was right. She had been trying to piece things together ever since the police officers had chaperoned them into the sunroom and told them not to leave. Who had hated Henry so much that they would want to shoot him? Where did they get the gun? Why now?

"*Evening*, ladies."

Julia stopped in her tracks and turned to see a fresh-faced young man standing in the doorway. He had sandy blonde hair, which was slicked back off his smooth and shiny forehead. His overpowering sweet aftershave filled the room, turning Julia's stomach further. Just from his demeanour and suit, she knew he was with the police.

"Detective Inspector Fletcher," the man said as he flashed a badge, his Scottish accent soft and barely noticeable. "Jay Fletcher. May I have a seat?"

Julia motioned to the seat she had been sitting in earlier. She crossed her arms tightly over her chest and stared down at the man, waiting for some grand revelation.

Instead, he frowned down at the cakes, and then up at Dot, who was grinning like a Cheshire cat as she bit into another cake. Jam dribbled down her chin and onto her already stained blouse.

"I know you ladies were together in the dining room when Henry McLaughlin died so this won't take long," he said as he pulled a pad from his jacket pocket. "I just want to know your account of things, in your own words."

"Aren't you a little young to be a DI?" Dot said. "You're fresh out of Pampers."

The handsome young man smirked and shook his head. It was clear it wasn't the first time he had heard that. Julia wouldn't have guessed the man had even passed his thirtieth birthday yet.

"I assure you, I'm more than competent," he said sternly, his charismatic smile still plastered across his face. "Who wants to go first?"

"We were eating breakfast in the dining room alone," Julia started, taking a step forward. "Blair, the cook, was coming in and out, serving us. We heard the gunshot, and we thought it might be deer hunters, but we realised it was out of season. Then, I heard Mary scream and I followed the sound of her crying to the entrance hall. We stayed by her side until the police arrived. Do you know who murdered Henry?"

"It's my job to ask the questions," he said with a small laugh. "I didn't catch your name."

"Julia South," she said quickly. "This is my gran, Dot, and my sister, Sue. But it was murder, right? He was shot in the chest. I can't see that being an accident."

"We're not ruling anything out."

"A wound like that must have been from a pretty

powerful gun," Julia said, her eyes glazing over as she stared down at the cakes in the dim light. "It didn't sound like a handgun. There was too much echo. Too much of a bang. Besides, if deer hunting is popular here, you would expect people to have rifles of some kind. Unless you have very long arms, it's almost impossible to shoot yourself in the chest with a rifle, unless you cut the end off, but don't most people go for the head if they want to end their own life? No point prolonging it, and doing it so publically where you can possibly fall and break through a bannister."

Julia met the DI's eyes, and he stared at her, a mixture of disbelief and suspicion filling his young face. She suddenly remembered she wasn't in Peridale anymore, and this wasn't Barker.

"You seem to know a lot, Miss South."

"She's an *astute* woman," Dot exclaimed proudly. "Assisted on many murder cases back home."

"And where is home?" he asked, his pen hovering over his paper.

"Peridale," Sue said. "The Cotswolds. Beautiful little village."

"*Peridale?*" he echoed, tapping the pen on his chin. "Sounds familiar. Think I heard about a DI down there who was suspended for letting some baker run his murder investigation. Funny how quickly those kinds of silly things get around. Wouldn't know anything about that, would you Julia?"

"No," she lied.

"We all had a good laugh about that up here," he said, shaking his head with a smirk. "Wouldn't get that happening up in Scotland, I'll tell you that."

Julia's cheeks burned brightly, and she looked down at

the floor, avoiding his eyes. She turned and stared through the windows, but the sun had completely fallen out of the sky, so all she could see was her own reflection looking back at her in the glass. Behind her, she noticed the DI standing up, taking one of the cakes as he did.

"Since you're checked in until Monday morning, I'd like you to stick around," he said as he peeled the wrapper off the small cake. "I'm satisfied that you've told me all you know, for now, but I can't have you leaving the country, can I?"

"They're keeping the spa open?" Julia asked, quickly turning around.

"Charlotte thinks it is for the best," he replied. "We can only advise. They have *paying* guests checking in before the weekend, and they can't afford to lose the business. Call me if you think of anything else, ladies."

He passed Julia a business card, popped the cake into his mouth, looked each of them in the eyes, and then turned and sauntered slowly down the hallway and through the double doors at the end.

"He doesn't know a thing," Julia said quickly as she turned the card over in her hands before pocketing it. "If he suspects the three women with concrete alibis, he's grasping at straws."

"You shouldn't have let him know so much," Sue said, her eyes strained with concern. "You made it sound like you were involved, or even guilty."

"I was just piecing together the obvious," Julia said, shrugging dismissively and turning back to the window. "I didn't tell him anything he shouldn't have already figured out hours ago."

"Do we have to stay here all night?" Dot asked as she

unpeeled her fourth cupcake.

"I would expect we were the last on his list of suspects to interview," Julia said, already heading for the door. "After this amount of time, I'd say forensics are likely to have everything they need."

Dot stuffed her handbag with the rest of the cakes, sipped the last of the tea, and hurried through the door and down the corridor. Sue was more hesitant, not taking her eyes away from Julia as she walked towards her.

"You're up to something," Sue whispered when they were face to face. "I know you."

"I'll follow you up in ten minutes," Julia said, nodding for her to follow their gran. "I want to offer my services to Blair. If we're here for the next five days, I don't want to sit around getting pampered now that a man has died."

Sue nodded that she understood, but Julia could see the disappointment flickering in her eyes. Julia gave her a quick kiss on the cheek and a hug.

"We'll still have sister time," Julia reassured her.

Sue smiled and dropped her head before hurrying along the corridor towards the double doors, where Dot was waiting for her. Julia smiled and waited until they had left, before turning to the dark dining room and darting in between the tables towards the door at the end of the room.

Without hesitation, she pushed through the doors and into another dark room. When her eyes adjusted, she noticed a large dumbwaiter elevator, which told her the kitchen was in the basement. She spotted a narrow stone staircase, and hurried towards it, not wanting to waste a second.

The steps were steep and cold, and they wound in a spiral, leading her deep into the island. When she reached the bottom, she pushed on a small door, fluorescent lights instantly blinding her.

Blair was by the sink, washing the dishes while the radio played pop music next to her. Julia looked around the kitchen, surprised by how modern it was. Some serious money had gone into the equipment, and it made her a little jealous that her café's kitchen wasn't anywhere near as well stocked. She took a couple of steps forward before clearing her throat.

It wasn't her intention to startle Blair, but she understood why she did. The girl spun around, and a white plate slid from her pink rubber gloved hands and shattered against the exposed stone floor.

"*Sorry*," Julia said, hurrying over and picking up the biggest shards of porcelain. "I didn't mean to scare you."

"It's okay," Blair said with a small laugh as she rested her hand on her chest. "I'm just not used to people coming down here. It's been pretty quiet 'round here recently."

Julia spotted a dustpan and brush next to a mop bucket in the corner, so she swept up the mess she had caused so Blair could carry on with her job. The girl smiled gratefully down at her.

"Your accent doesn't fit in here," Julia said as she tossed the shards into the bin. "English?"

"Blackpool," she said with a nod. "Moved up here for this job. There wasn't much going on back home, and I couldn't resist the idea of working in a spa."

"Have you baked long?"

"My whole life," she said, her cheeks flushing. "It's the only thing I'm good at. My mum taught me."

"Mine too," Julia said. "She died when I was a little girl, but she passed on a lot of her knowledge."

"Oh, I'm sorry," Blair whispered, dropping her face. "You bake?"

"I own a café."

"A *café?*" Blair remarked, smiling shyly through her stray strands of hair. "That's my dream."

Julia returned the girl's smile. She had sensed they were similar, but she hadn't realised how much they really had in common.

"That's part of the reason I came down here," Julia said, stepping forward and leaning against the counter. "To offer my services."

"Services?"

"Free of charge, of course," Julia said with a curt nod. "DI Jobs-Worth up there wants me to stick around until Monday, and I'm not really one for spas and pampering. I feel most comfortable in a kitchen, and I'm itching to get stuck into some baking. You seemed pretty rushed off your feet this morning."

"Oh, that's very kind of you," Blair said, shaking her head as she focussed on the dishes. "But, I don't think Charlotte will like that."

"Does she ever come down here?"

"Well, *no*, but -,"

"Then nobody has to know," Julia urged, nudging her with her shoulder. "I'll even share my secret recipes with you, and I'll tell you all about how I opened my own café."

The offer of knowledge from a more experienced baker made Blair's eyes light up, just as Julia had hoped. Her heart pounded in her chest, and she almost felt guilty for using it as a bribe against the girl, but she knew it was the only way she was going to have access to the people and information she needed.

"Until Monday?" Blair asked, her eyes squinting.

"And then I'll be gone."

Blair appeared to think about it for a moment before nodding and facing Julia with a soft smile.

"It would be nice to bake with somebody for once," Blair admitted.

"Then it's settled," Julia said, holding out a hand for Blair to shake. "I'll be here bright and early in the morning."

Blair reached out to shake her hand with the pink rubber glove, but stopped herself and ripped it off before accepting Julia's hand. Her skin was soft, and her grip was weak. She reminded Julia so much of her younger self. She could almost sense the same fear of the future that had consumed Julia at that age.

"It will be fun," Blair said, a smile taking over soft features.

"It will be," Julia agreed, before feigning a yawn. "I should follow my sister up to bed for now. It's been a long day."

Julia rested a hand softly on Blair's shoulder, and she nodded her understanding. Leaving her to finish the washing up, Julia walked swiftly towards the door and back up the spiralling staircase, knowing she had just discovered her key to unlocking the secrets that Seirbigh castle held.

CHAPTER 5

J ulia woke with the sunrise and was showered, dressed, and out of the bedroom before Sue had even had a chance to stir. She had spent most of the previous evening trying to convince Julia to stay out of things and take advantage of the treatments on offer, but Julia would rather put her mind to good use instead of pretending to be a piece of sushi in a seaweed wrap.

As she walked along the stone corridor joining the bedrooms and the entrance hall, she paused and looked out over the loch. The sky was still pale and grey, and the water completely still. She closed her eyes and inhaled the crisp morning air. There wasn't a sound for miles. It reminded her of the early mornings in Peridale when she could sit in her garden and enjoy the quiet of the countryside before the village woke and started their daily gossiping.

She reluctantly tore herself away from the view and walked through to the entrance hall. She hadn't been expecting to see anybody, so she stopped in her tracks and jumped a little when she saw Mary standing behind the desk in a navy blue pantsuit, her black hair scraped back into a neat ponytail, and a professional smile on her red-stained lips.

"Somebody is up early," she remarked, smiling effortlessly at Julia. "Off for a quiet dip before the others rise?"

Julia looked down at the floor to where the woman's husband had been lying dead less than twenty-four hours ago. She craned her neck to get a good look at the bannister, which had been patched up with bright yellow caution tape, and then back at Mary. Julia attempted to return the smile, but her bafflement restrained her cheeks from moving more than a couple of millimetres.

"I'm actually going down to the kitchen to give Blair a helping hand with breakfast," Julia said, casting a finger absently towards the double doors. "I run a café, so I thought I would make myself useful."

"That's very kind of you but quite unnecessary," Mary said, her smile unwavering. "You're a *guest* here, and Blair can more than cope."

"I honestly don't mind," Julia insisted, forcing her smile a little wider. "I like keeping my hands busy."

"Well, in that case, I'm sure she'll appreciate the help."

Julia nodded her agreement and hurried towards the doors. She didn't realise she had stopped breathing until she was on the other side of the double doors. As she rushed through the silent and shadowy dining room, she couldn't believe she had just come face to face with the same sobbing woman she had held at the foot of the stairs only the day before.

"Morning," Julia said, pushing Mary to the back of her mind as she walked into the kitchen. "Something smells good."

"I'm making Charlotte and Rory's breakfast," Blair said. "Charlotte is an early riser, so I thought I would try and keep things as normal as I could for her."

"Does Rory live here too?" Julia asked as she took one of the frying pans Blair was trying to juggle. "I don't think I've met him."

"He lives in Aberfoyle. He's a lawyer," Blair said as she flipped the bacon. "He's here a lot. They usually don't tell me when he's here for meals, so I have to go out and look to see if his car is there."

"And what about Mary?" Julia asked, unable to shake the woman from her mind. "What's her role here?"

"She's the manager," Blair said as she flipped the bacon once more. "Can you put some toast under the grill? The bread is in that bin there."

Julia nodded and assisted the girl as she wished. She was so used to being the one juggling the pans and the dishes that it was surprisingly enjoyable to take the backseat role and carry out the orders.

"I'm surprised she's here," Julia said. "When I arrived yesterday, Henry was throwing her out."

"That happens a lot," Blair said, glancing awkwardly at Julia out of the corner of her eyes. "She's his *fourth* wife, but from what I've heard, she's the one who has stuck around for the longest, aside from the first one."

"How long?"

"Three years."

"So not very long at all," Julia whispered under her breath. "And the first wife? I guess that is Charlotte and Rory's mother?"

"Henry's one true love, or so they *say*. Sandra died during childbirth when Charlotte was born. People say Charlotte is like her mother's twin."

"And what was Charlotte's relationship like with her father?"

Blair gave Julia a curious look as she spun around and started serving up the breakfasts. Julia busied herself with cutting the toast into triangles and slotting them neatly into the silver toast rack. She decided it was better to wait for Blair to speak voluntarily instead of bombarding her with more questions.

"It is – *I mean* – it *was* frosty," Blair whispered, glancing over to the door as though Charlotte was going to burst through at any moment. "Charlotte's *official* role is customer services. She deals with bookings and checking in the guests, but everybody knows she wants to manage this place. She resents working under her stepmother. The story goes that anyone who marries Henry becomes the manager."

"Is Mary a good manager?"

Blair blushed and dropped her face a little as she poured the baked beans onto the plates. Her silence spoke more than a thousand words.

"She's inexperienced," Blair said tactfully. "She thinks I'm enough to cook and serve during the quiet times, but we've got two couples checking in for the weekend, and she still thinks I'm going to be able to do it all on my own.

There was another girl here, but she was fired a week after I arrived two months ago. I was thinking about it last night, and I'm so grateful that you're here because I was worried about juggling everything. On top of that, the McLaughlin's use me as their personal chef. Rory is the worst for it, and he doesn't even work here. He'll call down when I'm in the middle of preparing dinner and tell me he's bringing five friends 'round for a hot tub party and he'll order the most complicated things. A lot of the time, I don't even have the food here, so I have to send somebody into the village."

"He sounds lovely," Julia joked with a wink.

"Between you and me, he gives me the creeps," Blair whispered back. "Can you grab the jug of orange juice from the fridge? I squeezed it fresh an hour ago, so it should be cold enough now. I'll make up a pot of tea, and then I'm ready to serve."

Julia fetched the jug while Blair prepared the tea. She looked down at the trolley, but couldn't figure out where to put the jug with the plates, toast, butter dish, and cutlery. When Blair returned, she was pushing a separate trolley with the teapot, two cups and saucers, a dish with sugar cubes, and a jug of milk. Julia set the jug onto that trolley and grabbed two small glasses from the display on the wall. Blair smiled, plucked up the glasses and replaced them with two different ones. Julia chuckled apologetically.

"And you manage this on your own?"

"I have the dumbwaiter," Blair said, hooking her thumb over her shoulder to the elevator next to the door. "I have to carry the trolleys one by one up the stairs though."

"On your own?"

"I make two trips."

"I'll help you," Julia offered, closing her hands around the food trolley as Blair set two domed silver cloches over the plates. "It's far too much to carry on your own."

"You should stay down here."

Julia hurried over to the wall and plucked an apron off one of the coat hooks. She took her hair out of the ponytail and crafted her curls into a bun that matched Blair's.

"If they say anything, I'll take the blame," Julia said as she pushed the trolley into the dumbwaiter. "Besides, they've got more important things to worry about today."

Blair reluctantly pushed the second trolley into the dumbwaiter, closed it and pressed some buttons on the panel. The lift shuddered into life and sent the food up to the next floor.

"You can wait outside the bedroom," Blair whispered as she held the door open for Julia, a mischievous smile taking over her usually shy expression.

They met the trolleys on the next floor and pushed them quickly through the dining room and back towards the entrance hall. Blair seemed grateful to have Julia if only to hold the doors open for her. They whizzed past the reception desk, where Mary was talking on the phone. Julia noticed a young man in a green Barbour jacket she hadn't seen before crouching over the fireplace and stacking up logs of freshly chopped wood to start a fire. He glanced over his shoulder when he heard the rattling trolleys and smiled at Blair. She smiled back, blushing a little, before picking up the trolley and hurrying up the stairs. Before Julia had time to think of the best way to do it, she hoisted up the trolley under her arms and hurried up the stairs, hoping gravity and her thirty-seven-year-old knees would spare her the embarrassment this time. When she reached the top step, she let out a relieved sigh.

"It looks so much higher from up here," Julia panted as she cast her attention to the broken bannister.

Blair nodded, but she didn't say anything. She couldn't bring herself to look at the wood. Julia couldn't blame the girl. She was almost glad the family were keeping Blair so busy, so she didn't have to linger and think about what had actually happened here. Julia, on the other hand, could think of nothing else.

"*Oh no!*" Blair exclaimed, stopping in her tracks. "I've forgotten the ketchup. Rory insists on smothering everything in the stuff. He's like a child."

"I can go back," Julia offered, looking back down the stairs.

"It's easier if I do," Blair said, already hurrying past Julia. "I'll be quicker, and I know where it is. Just wait here and don't go inside."

Julia nodded her promise that she wouldn't. She looked to the door that Blair had been heading towards and waited until the girl was hurrying back through the double doors and towards the kitchen. She pushed the trolleys towards the door, which was slightly ajar. A picture on the wall caught her eye. It depicted a man, who she instantly recognised as Henry McLaughlin, with a small boy and girl a couple of steps in front of him. They were standing tall on the bridge in front of the castle, with their chins pushed forward with smile-less expressions. It wasn't the type of family picture that Julia would have hung on display. In the shadows of the castle walls, she pushed her hands into her apron and bowed her head, all while tilting her ear towards the gap.

"They *know* it was Father's gun from the mantelpiece

in the drawing room," she heard a man say. "You *know* he kept that thing loaded."

"*Everyone* knew it," she heard Charlotte whisper back. "He did it to scare people. Just relax."

"Jokes on him now," the man returned with a soft laugh. "You didn't tell the police I was here yesterday, did you?"

"Of course not!" she replied. "Can you imagine how that would look?"

Silence fell, and Julia held her breath, sure she was about to be caught in the act of eavesdropping. When she saw Blair scuttling back towards her holding a bottle of ketchup, red-faced and breaking out in a sweat, she let out a relieved sigh.

"Wait here," Blair instructed as she backed up and pushed herself against the door with the trolleys trailing behind.

Blair entered the room, and Julia did as she was told. She hung back, but she took her opportunity to look inside. She caught a glimpse of Charlotte sitting up in bed in a silk robe, with a similarly redheaded man in a business suit lying across the bottom of her bed while reading a broadsheet. Neither of them looked particularly grief-stricken or heartbroken that their father had been murdered just down the hall the day before. Before the door slammed shut, the man turned to look at her, but when he saw her apron, he looked back at his newspaper. Julia couldn't be certain, but she was fairly sure he was the same redheaded man she had seen Charlotte talking with and hugging on the bridge the morning of Henry's murder.

Julia was broken from her train of thought when she heard the unmistakable sound of two plates, two full

Scottish breakfasts, and two domed metal cloches clattering against the wooden floor. Despite her strict instructions to stay outside, Julia was bursting through the door and hurrying over to help before she even realised what she was doing.

"You *stupid* girl!" Charlotte cried furiously, sitting up sternly in bed. "Are you *trying* to get yourself *fired?*"

Blair shook her head, tears already rolling down her face. Julia dipped down and dropped her head away from Charlotte as she helped Blair gather up the mess into the two metal cloches.

"*S-s-sorry*, miss," Blair stuttered. "I'll make you fresh ones right away, *m-m-miss.*"

"As you should," Rory, the brother, exclaimed, nodding firmly at both of them. "I tell you, sis, you can't get the staff these days."

Blair and Julia cleaned up as much of the mess as they could before putting it on one of the trolleys and hurrying out of the room. The second they were outside, Blair broke down and fell into Julia's arms.

"I'm sorry, Julia," she stumbled through her tears. "I just can't shake the image of Henry's body from my mind. It haunted my dreams all night."

"I understand," Julia whispered as she stroked the back of the girl's hair. "I've been there myself more times than I would like to admit."

"You've seen dead bodies?"

"My fair share."

"Does it get easier?"

"Sure it does," Julia said, hoping the shake in her voice didn't reveal the lie. "Let's go down to the kitchen and make you a nice cup of hot tea. Have you ever tried peppermint and liquorice? I have a couple of teabags in my room."

* * *

JULIA INHALED HER FAVOURITE TEA, AND she instantly felt at home. She thought about Mowgli, Jessie, and Barker, and suddenly she found herself missing Peridale. She turned to Blair as she took her first sip, and was pleased when she didn't recoil in horror.

"It's delicious," Blair said as she wiped the tears from her cheeks. "Do you serve this in your café?"

"It's on the menu, although I think I'm the only person who drinks it."

"Do you have a lot of cakes on your menu?"

"The majority is cakes," Julia said with a small chuckle. "Sometimes I think I'm the only person in the village people trust to bake them anything. It's a burden I enjoy."

"And you do it all alone?"

"I have Jessie," Julia said before taking another deep sip of the hot tea. "I took her in off the streets. She was homeless, but now she's my apprentice and my lodger. She's not much younger than you."

"You must be a kind woman," Blair said, her smile soft, but noticeably sad. "She's a lucky girl."

The door to the kitchen squeaked open, but Blair didn't act as startled as she had when Julia had crept in, nor did she look surprised to see the handsome man who had been lighting the fire in the entrance hall. The lower half of his face was taken up with a short beard, but his line-free eyes and low hairline told Julia the man wasn't much older than Blair.

"I thought I heard you crying," he said as he hurried over, the scent of heather and moss lingering on his green overcoat. "Are you alright?"

"I dropped Charlotte and Rory's breakfasts," Blair said with a stifled laugh. "Right in front of them."

"Oh, sis," the man said as he wrapped his arm around her shoulders. "Mam always said you were born with two left hands and two right feet."

The young man looked at Julia and smiled kindly at her as he comforted his sister. Julia was relieved to learn that Blair wasn't alone in the large castle, especially considering what had happened.

"This is my brother, Benjamin," Blair said. "Ben, this is Julia. She's a guest, but she's helping me out. She owns a café."

"A café?" Benjamin exclaimed as he reached out to awkwardly shake Julia's hand with his left arm, catching her off guard and forcing her to quickly switch hands. "That's my sister's dream, isn't it Blair? It's nice to meet you."

"You too," Julia said as she let go of the young man's hand. "Did you move up here together?"

"I came up first," Blair said. "When Henry fired Andrew McCracken, I put in a good word for Ben."

"There aren't many jobs back home," Benjamin explained. "Not since the recession. Tourism isn't what it was, and I didn't fancy working behind a bar. I've always been an outdoors kind of guy, so the groundskeeper job suited me perfectly."

"So *you're* the new groundskeeper," Julia said with a nod. "I think somebody mistook me for you yesterday. There was a man at reception who asked if I was the new groundskeeper. Quite rude, actually."

Benjamin took a sharp intake of breath and pushed his hands behind his coat to rest them on his slender hips. He nodded his understanding and rolled his eyes a little, reminding Julia of Jessie.

"I guess you've met Andrew," he said. "I only arrived a few weeks ago, but he's been up here quite a lot. Probably trying to get his job back. I've avoided meeting the fella so far, but I can't see it happening much longer."

"He's a drunk," Blair explained with a whisper. "Not a very nice man."

Julia opened her mouth to speak, but she suddenly stopped herself. She realised that she had seen Andrew on the morning Henry was murdered, meaning he was in the castle right before it had happened. The cogs in her mind started to crank slowly as the pieces slotted into place.

"Does Andrew live quite close?" Julia asked.

"Last I heard, he was staying above a pub in Aberfoyle," Blair said.

"Do you know which pub?"

"Is it significant?"

Julia thought for a moment, smiling as not to give away her genuine motives.

"I wanted to go into the village with my sister, and I wondered if it was a good pub," she said, hoping the first thing that sprung to her mind was good enough.

It appeared to be. Neither sibling looked too suspiciously at her.

"The Red Deer Inn," Blair said. "Although it's not the nicest place to eat. You might be better trying one of the little tearooms or cafés on the backstreets. We should get on with remaking Charlotte and Rory's breakfasts before we need to start on your gran and sister's."

While Blair gathered the ingredients from the fridge, Julia pulled her notepad out of her handbag, flicked past a recipe for a double chocolate fudge cake, and scribbled down '*Andrew McCracken - The Red Deer Inn*'. If the former groundskeeper who had been fired by the victim only two weeks previously was lurking around the castle on the morning of Henry's murder, Julia wanted to speak to him.

CHAPTER 6

J ust after lunch, Julia and Sue drove into Aberfoyle village, leaving their gran to enjoy the spa. Julia had intentionally waited until the masseuse had carefully placed the cucumber slices on Dot's eyes before grabbing Sue and dragging her out of the castle.

"You've got flour in your hair," Sue said as they drove slowly through the village as the afternoon sun beat down on them. "Why do you think this man will be able to tell you something, anyway?"

"Because he was there the morning Henry was murdered," Julia said as she tried to look around the car in front to see what was causing the holdup. "Even if he can't tell us anything about that morning, he might be able to paint a picture of Henry so I can try and figure out who would want to murder him."

"Well, there's only so many people it could be," Sue said with a sigh. "I was thinking about this while Maria was giving me a deep tissue massage. Aside from us, the only people in the castle when Henry was shot were Charlotte and Blair, so it must have been one of those two."

"Blair was down in the kitchen, and from what I can see, there was only one door out of that room, and it led to the dining room. We would have seen her."

"Don't these old castles have secret tunnels?"

Julia almost laughed off the suggestion, until she realised it wasn't entirely ridiculous. If Charlotte had been the one to shoot her father with the gun she had known was sitting loaded in the drawing room, it would explain how she had come to be on the other side of the castle right before she had seen him. Julia still hadn't been able to shake the cold and distant look in Charlotte's eyes when she had seen her father's corpse.

"I suppose," Julia agreed with a nod as they turned down a small cobbled backstreet. "But they weren't the only two in the castle, were they? Mary was there too. She found his body."

"But she couldn't have done it," Sue said with a small laugh of disbelief. "Those tears were *real*."

"Or very well acted," Julia mumbled. "You should have seen her this morning, Sue. She was behind the reception desk in a pantsuit ready for a day of work like nothing had happened. She didn't look like a woman who had just lost her husband."

"Let's not forget the man had thrown her out the day before," Sue added. "I wonder why she came back when she found his body."

"Maybe to reason with him?"

"Probably."

"Or maybe to kill him?"

"*Or* that," Sue said with a roll of her eyes. "Although I don't believe she did. Either way, she's a lucky woman. She died the man's wife, so I guess that means she keeps his fortune. Another couple of months and a divorce later, and she wouldn't have been entitled to a penny."

"You sound just like Gran."

"Well, it's true," Sue whispered. "You have to think about these things. Maybe she was chipper this morning because she realised she had landed on her feet. A castle like that would be worth more than a few quid."

"From what I heard from Blair, Charlotte isn't going to stand by and let her stepmother take over the running of the castle. Blair thinks Mary only got the job as manager because she was married to the king of the castle."

"It would explain why the place was so quiet," Sue said with another heavy sigh. "It's a beautiful spa, but it would be nicer if there were more guests to talk to. In fact, it would be nice if I had my *sister* by my side to relax with me. Gran is already driving me up the wall!"

Julia smiled apologetically to her sister as she pulled into the car park in front of The Red Deer Inn. She looked up at it, and it lacked all of the charms of The Plough pub in the heart of Peridale. It was a nondescript building that Julia wouldn't have even recognised as a pub if it weren't for the giant red sign and the lopsided parasols jutting out of the plastic tables cluttering the entrance.

"He couldn't have lived above a quaint tearoom?" Sue groaned as she got out of the car. "Or a nice little jewellery shop?"

The two sisters linked arms as they walked towards the pub. Burly men in white vests exposing their bulked-up and tattoo covered arms glanced at the two women. Julia stiffened her back a little and tried her best not to make eye contact with the men, who she was sure were trying everything to do just that.

"It stinks of beer," Sue said with a gag as they stepped into the dark and musty pub. "I'm so glad my Neil isn't a drinker. It's making me feel sick."

Julia couldn't disagree with her sister. As they walked towards the bar, she tried her best to take short intakes of breath through her mouth. The dank pub stank of stale cigarette smoke worked into the wood decades before the smoking ban, spilt stale ale soaked into the carpets, and greasy peanuts, which were scattered across the cluttered bar.

An old man looked from under his hat at the two women, groaned and returned to his pint. Sue clung even tighter onto Julia's arm.

"I think we should order a drink," Julia whispered. "To blend in."

"I'll have an orange juice," Sue replied. "And make sure to ask for a *clean* glass."

Julia nodded and decided an orange juice was a good idea, especially since they had to drive back down the winding lanes to the castle. She leant over the bar and caught the attention of the only other woman she had seen since entering.

"You lost?" the woman barked in her thick Scottish accent, her tone clearly condescending. "We dinnae do afternoon tea."

The woman was a few years older than Julia, but she looked like she had lived a harder life. Her wiry peroxide blonde hair was scraped up into a loosely pinned roll at the back of her head. A large black beauty spot balanced on her top lip, which bounced up and down as she spoke. Her leopard print blouse left little to the imagination.

"Two orange juices please," Julia said, trying her best to smile, not that she thought it was going to help.

"English too?" the woman scoffed, shaking her head as she collected two glasses from above her. "Dinnae get your kind 'round these parts too often. Sure yer nae lost, lassie?"

"We're actually looking for somebody," Julia said as she swallowed hard and smiled even wider. "A Mr McCracken? We heard he rents a room here?"

"What's it to you?" she snapped.

Julia took her lack of denial as confirmation that she was at least in the right place. She wriggled her arm free of Sue's and pulled her purse from her small bag. She pulled out a Scottish ten-pound note that she had changed at the post office before leaving Peridale, and pushed it across the bar.

"Keep the change," Julia said. "We just wanted to ask him some questions. A man has been murdered at Seirbigh Castle, and we thought he ought to know."

"Are you the polis?"

"Do you mean '*police*'?" Sue asked, arching a brow and glancing at Julia.

"*That's* what I *said*," the woman replied flatly as she poured orange juice from a carton and into the two glasses. "*Polis*."

"No," Julia answered, giving her sister a look that she hoped read as '*leave the talking to me*'. "We're just friends.

We just wanted to let him know since it was his former employer."

"Henry McLaughlin, yer say?" she asked, suddenly frowning as she picked up the money from the bar. "He's been morrdered?"

"*Huh?*" Sue jumped in.

"Done in," the woman barked, glaring at Sue. "Killed. *Murdered.*"

"Yes, he's been murdered," Julia said quickly before her sister could speak again. "Mr McCracken?"

The barmaid looked down at the drinks, then to the money in her hand, then to Julia, and then more disdainfully to Sue. She nodded silently into the corner of the room before turning her back on them and putting the money in the till. With her orange juice in hand, Julia turned and saw the man she had seen in the reception area on the morning of Henry's murder. She suddenly felt foolish for not scoping out the place first before asking the unfriendly locals.

Andrew McCraken was staring into a dark pint of bitter ale, still in his musty overcoat. The grey stubble on his face had grown even longer, and his thin hair looked even more out of place. He was sitting beneath a dreary oil painting of what appeared to be Loch Lomond with Seirbigh Castle in the distance. It didn't do the true beauty any justice. Julia and Sue walked over to his table, but he didn't look up.

"Excuse me? Andrew?" Julia asked politely. "You might not remember me, but we met two days ago at the castle?"

The man grunted and frowned, looking up from his pint as though Julia had just interrupted a deep and important thought that he hadn't been able to keep hold of.

"*What?*" he slurred. "Can't a man enjoy his pint in *peace* anymore?"

Sue gave Julia a look that screamed '*please make this quick because I'm scared and I want to leave*', but Julia dismissed it and sat uninvited across the table from Andrew. She knew she wouldn't find out what she wanted to know if she was shy about it. Sue decided to stay hovering, like an unsure bumblebee buzzing over a dandelion.

"We met at the castle two days ago," Julia repeated, looking under Andrew's low and furrowed brow and into his eyes. "Do you remember me?"

The man shrugged and picked up his pint. He glugged half of it down, slammed it onto the table, and smeared his mouth with the sleeve of his jacket. From the brown stains cluttering his sleeve, this seemed like normal behaviour.

"If *she's* sent you down here to try and convince me, you can get away wi' yer," he barked, pointing a long and dirty fingernail in Julia's face. "A've had it with that place."

"Nobody sent us," Julia said, glancing up to Sue who looked just as confused. "I've come to ask you why you were at the castle on the morning Henry McLaughlin was shot down and murdered in his own home."

The man met her eyes, a flicker of anger crinkling them at the sides. He didn't seem surprised to hear that Henry was dead, which made Julia suspect he already knew. She wasn't sure if Aberfoyle was anything like Peridale, but news as exciting as a murder didn't stay quiet for long, even if the barmaid hadn't found out yet.

"Charlotte called me up there asking me to take my old job back," Henry mumbled, staring into the depths of his pint. "But I told her what I told her today! The man sacked me for being a drunk! *I'm no drunk*! I just like a drink.

There's a difference *y'know*!"

"Charlotte came down here today?"

"Left ten minutes before you arrived to poke yer nose in," he grunted with a small laugh. "Practically begged me. I worked for that family for twenty-five years. *Twenty-five*! I served in the Falklands, y'know. Then Henry gets all high and mighty and shows me the door for drinking on the job. He couldn't keep hold of his staff, but I thought I was the exception until he gave me the boot two weeks ago. Wanted my job back at first but realised I was well shot of that place. I hope he rots in hell."

Andrew lifted his pint to the ceiling before gulping down the remaining contents. Julia edged forward, eager to hear more.

"Henry liked to fire people?"

"It was his favourite thing to do, lassie," Andrew said with a dark chuckle. "Gave the wee man power. He hardly cleared five feet in height. Napoleon complex right enough! Girls never last more than six months in that kitchen."

"And the family?" Julia asked, her heart racing. "What are they like?"

"A nightmare," he grunted, shaking his head heavily as he leant back in his chair to rest his head on the chunky frame of the oil painting. "That Charlotte is the worst, but she does have nerve, I'll give the lassie that. She stands her ground, but she's spoiled. Her brother is worse."

"And Mary?"

"The latest *Mrs McLaughlin*?" he snorted. "I've been there long enough to remember the *original Mrs McLaughlin*. She was the only one up to the job. The rest haven't held a candle to Sandra. Mary is running that place into the ground. I've never seen the place so quiet.

Charlotte has been gunning for the lassie's job since Henry got rid of the last wife. What was her name again? *Claire? Bridget?* It's hard to keep track. Now if you don't mind, I'm getting another drink, and I'd like it if you weren't here when I got back."

Andrew shuffled away from the table and towards the bar. Julia sat for a moment, absorbing the information she had just heard. She turned to Sue, and then to the bar. Andrew and the barmaid were both staring bitterly at them, and she knew they had overstayed their welcome.

"Why would Charlotte try so hard to give Andrew his job back?" she thought aloud. "And why on *that* morning? Why call him up there so early?"

"I don't know, and quite frankly, I don't care," Sue mumbled, linking arms with Julia and dragging her towards the exit. "I want a pedicure, a facial, and a nice long nap."

Julia didn't argue. Andrew had given her more than enough to think about, and as time ticked on, she found her attention directed more and more towards Charlotte McLaughlin.

CHAPTER 7

As the sun set on Seirbigh Castle, Julia found herself in her kitchen apron once more and pushing a trolley down the corridor towards the entrance hall. She glanced over her shoulder, where she could hear her gran loudly placing her dinner order with Blair. Looking down at the silver cloche, which contained haggis, neeps and tatties on the plate beneath it, she almost couldn't believe she had convinced Blair to let her take the food up to Charlotte alone.

She pushed through into the entrance hall, which aside from the roaring fire in the giant fireplace, was dark and deserted. She looked behind the reception desk and through to the office, but it was completely empty. She almost walked right by the fireplace and to the foot of the stairs, but something white fluttering on the stone slab in front of the flames caught her eye.

Leaving the trolley by the desk, she tiptoed over, glancing over her shoulder to make sure she was truly alone. She knew it was possible that somebody would be there any moment to turn on the lights, but her intrigue drove her forward.

She crouched down and stared at the corner of a white piece of paper that was charred and smouldering at the edges. She patted it with her hand and blew off the excess ash before lifting it up to her eyes. It appeared to be an official looking letter, but the only thing that was still visible was an address in Aberfoyle. Julia looked into the fire where she was sure she could see the ash remnants of a large stack of paperwork that had been dumped onto the flames. She knew it could be nothing, but she pocketed the piece of paper anyway.

With the trolley in hand, she made her way up to the landing and towards Charlotte's bedroom. She glanced at the miserable family portrait again and wondered if the little girl with the sad face could actually shoot her own father.

Julia knocked softly and waited a few seconds for Charlotte to summon her inside, before pushing carefully on the door, keeping her head bowed as she entered. She was relieved to see Charlotte sitting up in bed alone, in almost complete darkness aside from her bedside lamp. The heavy drapes were drawn, blocking out the last of the day's sunlight. Charlotte was wearing a pale pink silk robe, and her auburn hair was flowing down her chest, almost hitting the paperwork she was reading.

"I thought it was you I saw in here this morning," she

said with a smile, the angry tone from earlier completely gone, and back to the welcoming one that had greeted her at check-in. "What are you doing in that apron?"

"I'm giving Blair a helping hand," Julia said with a smile as she pushed the trolley into the bedroom. "DI Fletcher wants us to stick around, so I thought I would help out."

"Oh," Charlotte said with a smile, a slight furrow in her brow. "Well, I guess I should thank you then."

Julia waved her hand to tell her that wasn't necessary. She pulled the cloche off the plate and looked down at the steaming slices of haggis, her stomach turning a little. Charlotte had insisted Blair cook it especially for her because it was her favourite meal, and even though it had taken Blair a trip into the village and nearly a full day of preparation, she had been too polite to refuse.

"Reading anything fun?" Julia asked, casting her gaze to the paperwork covering the sheets as she placed the plate on the nightstand.

"Just accounts," Charlotte said quickly before gathering them and dropping them into a cardboard box, which she swiftly shut. "Boring stuff."

Julia nodded and smiled, not wanting to admit to Charlotte that she knew what accounts looked like, and they weren't them. For a start, Julia didn't spot any numbers, just reams and reams of tiny letters covering many pages. If she hadn't spent the last two years wrapping her head around her own accounts for the café, Charlotte's lie might have washed over her.

"How are you feeling?" Julia asked as she poured a glass of water from the metal jug on the tray. "You've been through a lot these last couple of days."

As though a reminder that she should be grieving, Charlotte's expression suddenly dropped, and she looked into her lap, her hair falling over her face. She stared up at the ceiling as though to stop herself from crying, but no tears came forward. She scooped her long hair around one side, her robe slipping off her right shoulder. She wasn't wearing anything underneath, and Julia wouldn't have stared if it weren't for the dark black and purple bruise just below her right shoulder. When Charlotte caught her looking, she quickly pulled her robe together and grabbed the plate.

"That looks painful," Julia said as she passed Charlotte a knife and fork. "My gran swears by putting raw meat on a bruise, but I'm not sure if I quite believe that."

Charlotte forced a small laugh as she stared down at her haggis, her knife and fork clasped in one hand.

"I hit it on a door," she said quickly without missing a beat. "It looks worse than it feels. Why don't you take a seat, Julia?"

Charlotte motioned to the end of the bed as she cut into her haggis. Cooked mince and spices filled the room, turning Julia's stomach even more; eating was the last thing she wanted to do right now. She looked warily at the edge of the bed, and then to the door. She had promised Blair she would be back in a matter of minutes, but an invitation to talk to Charlotte, even if it was an unexpected one, fascinated Julia too much to turn it down. She perched on the edge of the bed.

"Tell me about yourself," Charlotte said. "You're from down south, right?"

"Peridale," Julia said. "It's a beautiful little village in the Cotswolds. I run a café there."

"A café?" she remarked, arching a brow before she put a forkful of the food into her mouth. "On your own?"

"I have help with the day-to-day side of things, but I run the business on my own."

"Not an easy thing to do," Charlotte said, glancing to the box. "I'm sure I have a lot to learn."

Julia followed her eye line to the box, dying to know what information the paperwork contained. She thought about the charred slip of paper in the front pocket of her apron and wondered if this box was next for burning.

"So you're going to be running things around here?" Julia asked, looking around the vast space. "It's a big castle for one woman. I thought Mary was the manager?"

"*She* thinks that too," she said with a devious smile. "She has no claim to this place. She might have been my father's wife, but she wouldn't have been for much longer. The lawyers have the relevant paperwork to prove the divorce was all but final. She's being *dealt* with."

Julia's stomach dropped. The sinister look in Charlotte's eyes as she took another mouthful of haggis unsettled her. Julia turned her attention to the window. Through the gap in the heavy drapes, the sun was setting on Scotland for another day. She had never felt further from home.

"Have you managed to get out and about?" Julia asked, making sure to gauge Charlotte's reaction. "The weather has been lovely. The fresh air might do you good."

Charlotte slowly chewed her food, her expression unwavering. There was a little glimmer in her eyes that told her that Charlotte knew she had been to the village to speak to Andrew. Julia forced her soft smile to remain while her heart trembled in her chest.

"I went into the village this morning," she replied flatly. "To speak to our ex-groundskeeper. I offered Andrew his old job back, but he was reluctant to take it."

"I thought his position had been filled by Blair's brother?" Julia asked. "I met him this morning. He seems like a nice man."

"That position is soon to become vacant," Charlotte said through a strained smile. "I'll let you go. You shouldn't spend your trip cooped up in that kitchen. Enjoy what we have to offer."

"I'm sure I'll have a chance before I leave," Julia said softly as she stood up. "Enjoy your dinner."

She closed her hands around the trolley and walked as quickly as she could out of the dark room. When she closed the door behind her, she realised she had stopped breathing entirely. Taking in a deep lungful of the musty castle air, she stared at the portrait on the wall again. Once more, she wondered if that little girl could be capable of murdering her father, and this time, her conclusion was less optimistic.

* * *

WHEN SHE WAS BACK IN THE DEPTHS OF the castle, Julia was relieved to see that Blair had finished serving Dot and Sue's dinner and was drinking a cup of tea while flicking through a gossip magazine. It was comforting to see her doing something normal for once.

"I thought you'd gotten lost," Blair exclaimed as she looked up from her magazine. "I was about to come looking for you."

"I had a little chat with Charlotte," Julia said, trying not to give away anything on her face. "I just think she's lonely."

Blair frowned a little, but to Julia's surprise, she didn't question her further, and she returned to her magazine.

Julia decided to take advantage of the quiet time to retrieve her phone from her bag. She pulled the slip of paper out of her pocket and opened up the internet browser. She hovered over the search bar, blankly looking down at the address. With a shake of her head, she put the slip of paper into her bag, closed down the browser, and did something more important.

"*Barker*?" Julia whispered into the phone as she pressed it against her ear. "It's Julia."

"*Julia*!" Barker exclaimed, the joy in his voice soothing her in an instant. "Enjoying the spa? I've wanted to call you all day, but I didn't want to ruin your relaxing time. How's Dot and Sue?"

"They're good," Julia said, pushing forward a smile as she pinched between her eyes. "How are things there?"

"Everything is fine," he said. "We've just finished eating dinner. Jessie made us fish and chips."

"How's the café?"

"It's all fine," he said with a small chuckle. "You don't have to worry about a thing. Jessie has really stepped up to the plate. She's taking it all in her stride."

"And Mowgli?"

"He's on my knee right now."

An easy smile spread across Julia's face. She closed her eyes, and she could picture the scene as clear as day. Barker would be sitting in the seat nearest the fire, with the heat licking at his feet because he didn't like to wear socks in the house. Mowgli would be snoring softly, popping his head up every time Barker fidgeted. Jessie would be sitting at the opposite end of the room, her face buried in her new tablet, with a cup of peppermint and liquorice tea balanced dangerously on the chair arm. She would take a couple of sips, but she wouldn't finish the cup; she never did.

Sadness swept over Julia like a heavy tide she couldn't fight. She wanted nothing more than to be there with them.

"*Julia?*" Barker mumbled. "Are you still there?"

"I'm still here," she whispered. "Signal isn't great."

"I said that I'm taking Jessie on her first driving lesson tomorrow," Barker whispered down the handset. "I've upgraded my insurance premiums to cover everything."

She heard Jessie call out something in the background. It was no doubt a sarcastic remark about how she was going to be an excellent driver. Julia laughed to herself.

"Thank you for being there for her," Julia said, her heart fluttering. "I really appreciate it, and I know she does too."

"She's growing on me," Barker said, loud enough so that Jessie could hear him. "Like a bad rash."

Jessie called back something that Julia heard, but wouldn't repeat in the presence of Blair. She chuckled and looked over her shoulder, but she was still engrossed in her magazine.

"I'll let you get back to your relaxing week," Barker said, making Julia wish the conversation didn't have to end. "I miss you."

"I miss you too."

When she finally hung up, Julia stared down at her phone for what felt like a lifetime. Being away from Barker and Jessie made her realise how much she loved them both. Nothing tied any of them together aside from their desire to be there, and she knew that's what made them a family, dysfunctional or not.

The door to the kitchen opened, tearing her from her thoughts. She slipped her phone into her bag and was relieved to see Blair's brother, Benjamin, the very man she had wanted to talk to next.

"Evening, ladies," Benjamin said. "Anything tasty to eat, sis? I'm starving."

Blair closed her magazine and grabbed the shortbread that Julia and she had prepared in the gap between lunch and dinner. Julia and Benjamin pulled up a seat on either side of Blair at the counter while Blair teased the lid off the metal tartan tin. Benjamin didn't wait to grab a piece of the buttery and crumbly shortbread.

"Anyone would think you were Scottish," he mumbled through a mouthful, his eyes closed and content. "Delicious as ever."

"Julia can take the credit for that," Blair said proudly as she smiled at Julia. "She suggested a drop of vanilla extract, and it really punches through, don't you think?"

"Genius," Benjamin said with a nod. "You're quite the inventive baker, Julia."

Julia blushed as she reached out for a piece of shortbread. The room fell silent as they all enjoyed the baking. Julia swallowed quickly, deciding it was the perfect time to ask Benjamin the questions that had formed in her mind after speaking with Charlotte.

"What are your roles as a groundskeeper, Ben?" Julia asked casually. "There isn't much ground on this tiny island."

"It's a bit of a vanity title," he admitted with a smirk. "I have a little hut around the back of the castle where I work, but I'm more a maintenance guy. I fix up the castle best I can, light the fires, chop the firewood. That sort of thing. I make sure the castle is looking neat for when guests arrive. The family owns a little land beyond the bridge for the hunting, so I keep that in order too. It doesn't sound like a lot, but a castle this old takes a lot to keep it together."

"I don't doubt it's a difficult job," Julia said as she brushed the crumbs off her fingers. "I heard hunting is popular here? Do you get a lot of guests interested in that?"

"I haven't worked the hunting season yet, but I hear this place will be full of hunters in the coming months. Almost exclusively, according to Mary."

"Do you know much about hunting?"

"A little," he admitted. "I've been out and about with the rifle getting in some practice."

"I thought it was out of season?"

"For deer, yes," Benjamin said as he plucked another piece of shortbread from the tin. "But there are plenty of other animals scurrying around out there. Shrews, badgers, foxes, voles. Even the odd moose if you're lucky, but they rarely come this far south. I don't think I'll ever get used to shooting them down though, but Charlotte insisted I get used to it before the season starts. I'm not even sure if it's legal this time of year."

"Charlotte is a hunter?"

"She's more a mad woman with a gun," Benjamin said with a chuckle. "Shot at every shadow and piece of heather blowing in the breeze. She was trying to teach me, but her technique was so sloppy, I learned more by watching videos online."

"I bet that can cause some nasty injuries," Julia suggested casually as she played with a stray curl that had fallen from her bun. "I heard that guns like that can have some serious kickback."

Benjamin nodded as he looked down at the piece of shortbread in his left hand. He tossed it into his mouth before turning back to Julia.

"Are you thinking of giving it a go?" he mumbled through a mouthful. "I can take you out if you want."

"Thank you, but no thank you," Julia said, waving her hands in front of her. "I couldn't imagine shooting down an animal like that."

"Me neither," Blair agreed. "It's barbaric."

"It's *nature*," Benjamin said with a laugh. "The circle of life. *Hakuna Matata* and all that stuff."

"That's not what that means." Blair rolled her eyes and slapped his hand away from the tartan tin. She secured the lid, and much to her brother's dismay she put it back on the shelf with the other similar tartan tins. "I'm going to bed before Rory shows up and starts putting in crazy orders."

"Good idea," Julia agreed as she let out a yawn. "It's been a long day."

Julia slid off the stool and took off her apron. She paused and turned as Benjamin grabbed at the magazine. It slid out of his buttery fingers and off the table. He let out a groan before bending over to pick it up.

"Are you sticking around at Seirbigh Castle, Benjamin?" Julia asked, suddenly remembering what Charlotte had said about his position soon becoming vacant.

"I have no plans to leave," he said as he clumsily opened the magazine. "Why do you ask?"

"No reason," Julia lied, deciding it was best not to let the poor man know that he was likely to be fired from his job in favour of his predecessor if Charlotte had her way.

"Goodnight."

Julia grabbed her bag and made her way up the winding stone stairs, through the empty dining room, and back towards the entrance hall. She stopped in her tracks when she spotted DI Fletcher slapping his hand repeatedly on the reception bell.

Julia dropped her head and attempted to hurry past him, but he stepped into her path, his hands in his pockets, and his youthful face filled with a smug expression.

"Off to bed so soon?" he asked, a well-groomed brow arching up his smooth forehead. "Or are you going back to the village to badger more of my witnesses?"

"I don't know what you mean," Julia said, looking him dead in the eyes. "*Excuse me*, DI Fletcher."

The young man stared down at her for the longest moment before finally relenting and stepping to the side. Julia rolled her eyes and pressed forward, ready to crawl into bed.

"Stay out of my investigation," he called after her as she pulled on the door leading to the second part of the castle. "A baker should know her place."

Julia glanced over her shoulder, her cheeks burning brightly. She could think of one hundred and one things she could say to the little boy in a man's suit at that moment. She shook her head, deciding it wasn't worth it. Letting the door swing in its frame, she hurried along the dark corridor, ready for her bed. If she had money in her pocket, she wouldn't have bet on Detective Inspector Jay Fletcher solving the case before she left the castle.

"Don't count me out just yet," she whispered to herself in the dark as she made her way up to her bedroom. "Don't count me out."

CHAPTER 8

J ulia wandered around the castle in the dark, the scent of heather and moss deep in her nostrils. She tried to wiggle her nose to get rid of the smell, but she couldn't quite feel her face.

Something banged in the dark. Julia spun around, but the castle walls shifted around her. Ancient bricks crumbled away, dust and debris falling from every angle. She ran for her bedroom door, but it fell away with the rubble. Skidding to a halt, she looked beneath her as the floor fell away. She could see the loch below, rippling and moving, and completely black. It was inviting her in, but she knew she had to stay away.

A woman's shriek pierced through the dark. She

crammed her hands up to her ears as she looked for a way out, but the floor continued to fall away. She stepped back and leant against the castle wall, but it betrayed her. As she fell towards the dark loch below, the sky swirling above her, the shrieking grew louder and louder, distracting her from her impending death.

Before she hit the loch, Julia bolted up in bed, sweat pouring down her burning face. As she panted for breath, she looked towards the piercing strip of sunlight seeping in through the heavy drapes. She realised it had just been a nightmare. She looked down at her bedroom floor, and it was still well and truly intact.

What was real, however, was the shrieking. Sue bolted up in bed, her hair matted and sticking up on one side. She looked around the room before landing on Julia.

"Was that you?" Sue whispered. "What time is it?"

Julia squinted at the small clock on her nightstand. It was only a little after six. The woman shrieked again, forcing them both out of bed and straight over to the far window.

Julia tore back the drapes, the bright morning sun blinding them both. She forced her eyes to stay open and adjust so she could see the commotion that was happening below. Squinting into the light, she saw a flash of red hair and a flash of black. She realised she was watching Rory attempting to drag Mary out of the castle.

"You have *no* right being here!" Rory cried as he hauled Mary towards the bridge. "Ex-wives don't have rights!"

"But I'm *not* an ex-wife," she screamed, thrashing against him unsuccessfully. "Henry was my husband!"

With his arms around her waist, Rory picked Mary up like she weighed no more than a bag of flour and carried her over to the bridge. For a moment, Julia thought he was going to throw her over the edge and into the murky loch below.

"It was a clever trick trying to destroy the divorce papers, but my father wasn't stupid enough to only have one copy," Rory cried, his Scottish accent growing thicker the louder he became. "You're not getting a penny of his fortune or a single brick of this castle!"

Julia was about to suggest they go down and help her, but a loud and persistent knock at the door startled them both. Sue hurried over and let Dot in. Julia wasn't surprised to see her.

"What's that racket?" she cried, her hair a mess, and her eyes still half closed as she stumbled forward in her floor-length white nightie. "I can't see from my window."

"Rory is trying to kick Mary out," Sue whispered as Dot wrestled her way through the drapes to push in front of Julia.

"Didn't Henry already try that?" Dot exclaimed as she pushed her nose up against the glass. "She bounced right back like a boomerang and then a man turned up dead. If I were him, I wouldn't mess with her. She's *obviously* cursed."

"*Gran!*" Julia cried with a sigh. "Now isn't the time."

Rory dropped Mary on the edge of the bridge and pushed her in the direction of the cars parked on the other side. He said something to her that they couldn't hear, which elicited even more shrieking. Mary charged at him like an angry bull, but Rory was twice her size and built like a rugby player, even if he was wearing a sharp business suit.

"Just *go!*" he yelled, pushing her to the ground. "Nobody wants you here. Don't you get that?"

Mary let out a sob and melted into the ground. Rory

hovered over her for a moment, before tossing something at her feet and turning on his heels with a shake of his head. As though nothing had happened, he adjusted his cufflinks and set off back towards the castle. As he walked, he glanced in the direction of Julia's window, and all three of them jumped back. She couldn't have been sure from her distance, but Julia was somehow certain he knew they had been watching.

Julia ran across the room and tore open her bag. She dug around for the slip of paper, and when she found it, she grabbed her phone and pulled up the internet browser once more. She quickly typed in the address, and she wasn't surprised to discover that the address belonged to a solicitor's office that specialised in divorces. It brought back memories of her own divorce, and her heart ached for Mary. Still in her nightgown, she hurried out of the room and made her way through the castle.

* * *

THE CLOUDS ABOVE WERE THICK AND pale, and fog had consumed the loch, blocking off the beautiful view and closing them in completely. Julia hurried through the castle entrance, the gravel underfoot scratching at her soles.

Hitching up her pale pink nightie, she walked as quickly as she could to where she had seen Mary, but she needn't have bothered. Mary hadn't moved an inch and was still slumped against the wall, sobbing into her hands. Julia hung back for a moment, clearing her throat to announce her presence.

Mary looked up at Julia, her brows tight and her eyes swollen. Her face was bare of any makeup, and she looked as though she hadn't been awake for long. Julia wouldn't have been surprised if Rory had dragged her out of bed intentionally in the early hours of the morning for maximum impact.

"*What?*" Mary barked, her voice coarse. "Come to gloat?"

"Not at all," Julia said softly, hurrying forward and crouching down. "Can I sit down?"

"Do what you want," Mary snapped, a little less harshly this time. "It's not like I own the place."

She let out a small bitter laugh before another flood of tears consumed her. Julia sat on the cold ground next to her and leant against the cold stone wall. She looked up in the direction of her bedroom, sure she could make out the shadows of Dot and Sue twitching at the drapes. She was almost certain they were talking about how she should have stayed out of things, but that wasn't Julia's style. She couldn't stand by and watch another woman cry; not after already doing that on her first day in the castle.

"I'm divorced," Julia whispered, nudging Mary's shoulder. "Only recently too. We separated well over two years ago, but I dragged out signing the papers for as long as I could. I didn't want the man back. I was happy to be rid of him, but I couldn't get past the notion of being a divorcee before I had even turned forty. Then I realised that was an old-fashioned way of thinking, and I've even met a great man who is ten times the man my husband was."

"I'm not divorced," she said as she wiped the tears from her cheeks. "I'm *widowed*. We might have worked things out."

Mary's sobs restarted, letting Julia know that Mary didn't believe that any more than she did. Julia slid her arm around her shoulders and pulled her in. To her surprise, Mary melted into her side like a child against its mother, despite Julia being the younger one.

"There's still life out there for you," Julia said, squeezing hard. "Beyond this castle."

"So you're saying I should just give it up?" she snorted, tucking her hair behind her ears. "It's *rightfully* mine. The divorce was never finalised. Like you, I was dragging my heels, but Henry had had enough. He threw me out, and then – and then he was *murdered*. I loved him."

"There are kinder men to love."

Mary sniffled and looked hopefully at Julia. For the first time since she had arrived, Mary smiled at her, and it felt genuine. Julia immediately discounted any involvement in Henry's murder. She felt foolish for even doubting the sincerity of the poor woman's tears.

"I thought I was different," Mary said with a small laugh. "I knew I was *number four*, but I thought he was a good man."

"Doesn't it always start out that way?" Julia asked as she rested her head on the wall and looked up at the milky sky. "Mine packed all of my things into black bags, put them on the doorstep, changed the locks, and informed me with a note that we were over. He didn't even write it. It was his secretary's handwriting. That's who he left me for. She was ten years younger than me, and twenty pounds lighter. Blonde, too."

"Maybe all men aren't so different," Mary said with a small laugh. "I didn't want to believe the rumours, but the castle walls talk. I kept hearing that he was going behind my back with the guests and even the staff, but I didn't want to believe it. It was easier to pretend everything was okay and ignore the obvious, just to keep up the charade."

Julia knew that feeling all too well. Now that she had some distance from her own marriage, she knew she had been sucked in by his charm and wit, but the rest had been nothing more than a sham. She had happily played along if only to say she was in a happy marriage. She almost couldn't believe she had ever been that woman.

"What are you going to do now?" Julia asked carefully, glancing up to her bedroom window where they were still being watched.

"I'm going to fight," she said sternly as she wiped her nose with the back of her hand. "That man owes me that much, doesn't he?"

Julia didn't say anything. She hadn't asked for a penny during the divorce, even though Jerrad had more than a large pot of savings. She had wanted to get out with her hands clean and only take what she had earned for herself. Years of working in the cake production factory had given her just enough savings to set up her café and a little left over to put down a deposit on a mortgage for her cottage. She looked up at the castle, wondering if she would have acted any differently if the stakes were higher. She would like to think it wouldn't have made a difference, but she knew it was easy to say that on the other side.

"What about Charlotte and Rory?" Julia asked. "They're not going to give this up easily."

"They've wanted to get their grubby hands on this place for years," Mary said, suddenly sitting up straight and shaking off Julia's hand. "I need to see my lawyer. I'm not vanishing like they want. If those brats want a war, it's a war they've got."

Mary stumbled to her feet and turned to the castle. She

inhaled the fresh morning air and closed her eyes as she tucked her long black hair behind her ears once more. She straightened out her black silk pyjamas and picked up a set of car keys that were on the ground, no doubt tossed at her by Rory.

"Why don't you come down to the kitchen for a cup of tea?" Julia suggested as she struggled up to her feet. "They never go down there. I'll even cook up some breakfast."

"I need to go," Mary said, looking to the end of the bridge where three cars were parked. "Those two are going to be doing everything they can to freeze me out. I need to catch up. I thought doing my job and acting like everything was normal might have been enough, but they're sneakier than that. I even tried burning the evidence of the impending divorce, but of course, they have copies! Henry was a clever man, but I'm clever too. They were letting me think I was safe here so they could pull the rug from under my feet, but the joke is going to be on them. The man was *my* husband. *I* was his next of kin."

"Didn't he have a will?"

"I was his *fourth* wife," Mary said as though it was evident. "I doubt that man has changed his will since his *precious* Sandra died. We were all just stand-ins on his arm, and I was one of the unlucky idiots to fall for it. Thank you, Julia. You've really given me some perspective."

Mary quickly hugged Julia before hurrying along the narrow bridge to the cars at the bottom. She jumped into a silver one and sped off into the distance, her tyres screeching and sending gravel flying as she did. Julia watched as she zoomed around the corner and disappeared into the hills. Turning back to the castle, she looked up to her bedroom window and sighed. She had a feeling in the pit of her stomach that she had made things worse, not better.

* * *

AFTER RETURNING TO HER ROOM AND explaining what had happened to Dot and Sue, Julia quickly dressed and set off towards the kitchen to help Blair with preparing the breakfast. On her way, she was surprised to see Charlotte behind the counter, looking as void of personality as she had on the day they had arrived, and even more surprised when Charlotte looked to Julia as though she had been expecting to see her.

"Ah, Julia," Charlotte said after quickly swallowing her tea and placing her mug under the counter. "If you're on your way down to the kitchen, you'll have to stop I'm afraid. I haven't been myself these last couple of days, and I didn't pause to think that you're not insured to work here. If anything happens, we'd be liable, and a lawsuit is the last thing we need right now. There's so much paperwork to sort out, and a funeral to plan."

"I'm a very careful cook," Julia insisted. "And suing people isn't my style. Honestly, I actually enjoy helping out."

"Even so, I can't take the risk," Charlotte said as she flicked through a book under the counter. "I'm going to have to insist you don't go anywhere near the kitchen, or I'm afraid I'll have to take some kind of action. I'd hate to see your gran and sister suffer for your actions."

Charlotte suddenly looked up at Julia, their eyes connecting for a brief second. Despite the reception friendly smile, Julia was in no doubt that Charlotte had just threatened her. Deciding against arguing, Julia turned back on her heels and headed back towards the door she had just come through. She couldn't help but think Charlotte was trying to stop Julia from speaking to Blair, and she didn't know why, but it only made her want to speak to her more.

"Oh, and Julia?" Charlotte called after her as she yanked on the door. "We're having a celebratory dinner tomorrow night in our private drawing room. It's a tradition my father was very keen on doing for our guests every Sunday night, and I would like to continue it, especially since we had new arrivals last night. I hope to see you and your family there at seven."

"I wouldn't miss it," Julia said without a second thought.

Julia yanked on the door and hurried along the corridor and towards the sweeping staircase up to her bedroom. She couldn't believe any daughter grieving for her father would be throwing a celebratory dinner only days after his murder. She was beginning to wonder if Charlotte had any human emotions after all.

"Where are you going?" Dot exclaimed when they met in the corridor on the floor of their bedrooms, a towel draped over her shoulder. "I thought you were helping Mary Poppins down in the cellar?"

"Charlotte has just informed me that I'm forbidden from going down there," Julia said with a sigh as she scratched the back of her head. "Something to do with insurance, but it sounded like an excuse to me. She's up to something."

"Well if she is, let it go!" Dot cried as she hooked her arm around Julia's. "We only have the weekend to enjoy the spa before we're back in Peridale and then we never have to think about this place again. I'm not taking no for an answer, young lady."

"Where's Sue?"

"Honking her guts up," Dot said with a roll of her eyes. "Food poisoning by the sounds of it. It turns out that your little friend isn't such a good cook after all. I've already called down and told them to count us out for breakfast. Turns out two couples checked in last night, so she'll have plenty more victims to poison with her cooking. Maybe it's best you stay away from her. I don't want her shoddy standards rubbing off on you. Sue said she'll join us when she's feeling better."

Julia glanced over her shoulder to her bedroom door as her gran dragged her down the corridor towards the staircase. Spending a day in the spa was the last thing she wanted to do, but she knew she didn't have much choice. She could try and sneak down into the kitchen to talk to Blair, but she was sure Charlotte and Rory would be keeping a watchful eye on the young girl all day.

She let her gran drag her down to the ground floor where the spa and pool were situated. Once on a bed, Julia picked a face sheet mask at random and allowed the kind woman to apply it. Thankfully for Julia, she didn't try to make small talk, which allowed her mind to really think.

She stared up at the wooden ceiling and tried to think of reasons Charlotte would want to keep her away from Blair. She wondered if her conversation with Mary had been seen by either of the siblings and if that was a possible reason, but she couldn't make a connection between the wife and the cook. She knew she could be clutching at straws, and the insurance could be a legitimate reason for keeping her out of the kitchen, but it didn't sit right with Julia. Charlotte might have had a pretty face and a sweet smile, but Julia was sure if she lightly scratched beneath the surface, she would uncover the young woman's dark insides very quickly.

Within a matter of minutes, Dot was already snoring under her slices of cucumber. Julia wondered if she was too harsh on Charlotte. She had, after all, just been orphaned, even if her relationship with her father didn't seem all that close. Julia wasn't particularly close to her own father, and her own mother had died when she was a little girl, but she couldn't empathise with Charlotte despite their similarities. She knew it was very possible for people to hide their pain from the world, but Julia didn't feel anything from Charlotte, other than coldness.

Before she could delve any deeper, Sue shuffled into the spa, her face a pale shade of green. She gratefully accepted a white robe and took the bed next to Julia. Without saying a word, she tossed her head back and inhaled deeply.

"Food poisoning?" Julia asked.

"Something like that," Sue mumbled. "I can't wait to be out of this place. What are you doing here, anyway?"

"It's a long story," Julia whispered, sitting up and turning to Sue. "I've been banned from the kitchen, but I need to figure out a way to get down there. I'm pretty sure Charlotte and Rory are going to be keeping watch."

"What's that got to do with me?" Sue groaned.

"I need to get a message to Blair so she can meet me," she continued quietly as she flung her legs around the side of the bed, letting her sheet mask slide off her face. "I think she knows something crucial to cracking this case, even if she doesn't realise it. I'll look less suspicious if you're with me."

AGATHA FROST

"You'll look less suspicious if you just stay here and let them pamper you," Sue whined, her eyes clenching and her bottom lip protruding.

"Fine," Julia said as she tugged off her robe and tossed it over the bed. "I'll just go on my own. I just thought it would be fun to have some sister time that wasn't spent horizontal in a coma with gunk on our faces."

Julia turned on her heels and walked towards the entrance. Out of the corner of her eye, she spotted a notepad and a pen on the glass reception desk. She tore off a piece and quickly scribbled down a note before pocketing it. As she headed to the door, she was surprised to see Sue quickly tearing off her robe.

"You know emotional blackmail is below the belt," Sue whispered as they both quickly headed down the corridor and towards the entrance hall. "What did you have in mind?"

"Let's just take a stroll around the island and see where it takes us."

CHAPTER 9

The moment they stepped out of the castle, Sue gasped and grabbed Julia's hand. They took a careful step forward, but the fog had rolled in from the loch, meaning she could barely see more than a couple of steps ahead of them.

"Maybe we should go back," Sue begged, tugging on Julia. "It doesn't look *safe*."

"It'll be fine," Julia said, pulling Sue forward. "We just need to watch our step."

"What are we even doing out here?"

"Looking for someone."

They carefully walked down the gravel slope towards the bridge, taking small baby steps as the cool fog consumed them. Julia looked back at the castle, but it was nothing more than a dark smudge in a chalky sea of white.

Instead of taking the bridge across the loch, they stepped down onto a small winding path that circled the edge of the tiny island. Julia gulped hard as she looked down into the murky surface of the water, which would swallow her up without a second thought if she took one wrong step. The bank sloped up towards the base of the castle, heather and lumpy rock covering its surface. The earthy tones of the spiky plant didn't smell as delightful since her dream.

"I don't like this," Sue whispered, her fingers tightening around Julia's. "I don't like this *one bit.*"

The path curved and Julia suspected they were walking around the back of the castle. She looked up at the bank and kept her eyes peeled for a hut, but she wasn't sure she would see it even if it was right in front of her. She looked back, but the bridge had vanished from sight.

The path suddenly took a sharp incline away from the water, relaxing Julia a little. Through the fog, she could see that they were walking back towards the castle. When the ground levelled out, the path suddenly cut off, joining in with the bumpy land. Despite Sue dragging her heels, Julia pressed forward, heading towards the blur of the castle. When they finally reached it, she pressed her hands against the cool stone, reassured that she was going the right way.

They followed the castle walls and came to the dining room. Julia peered through the windows, but it was dark and empty. She had hoped Blair was there so she could somehow call her over so they didn't have to go any further.

They hurried past the tall windows and followed the building around. A thumping sound pierced through the fog like a cracking whip, startling them both. Sue pulled back, but Julia pulled her towards the sound. She was surprised when she came out into a clear stone courtyard. They stepped inside, turning back to watch as the thick fog rolled by.

She let out a thankful breath when she saw Benjamin chopping logs of firewood against an old tree stump. Despite the chilly morning, he had forgone a shirt so that his sweat-glistening and lightly haired chest was on display. To Julia's surprise, he was chopping the logs of wood with the sheer force of his left arm, his right tucked neatly behind his back.

"*Wow*," Sue whispered. "That's *strength*."

Benjamin looked up, the axe swinging and missing the log. It buried into the tree stump. He wiped the sweat from his forehead before picking up his shirt and pulling it on.

"It's sweaty work," he said with a twinkling smile. "You ladies are braver than me to venture into that fog. I'm waiting for it to clear."

Sue gave Julia an '*I told you so*' look, but Julia pursed her lips, telling her not to bother saying anything. She let go of her sister's hand and walked towards Benjamin, looking up at the castle as she did. Tall walls rose high on all sides, the different parts of the castle joining together. Julia tried to work out where she was in relation to the rest of the building, but she couldn't quite figure out where they had walked in the fog. At the end of the courtyard, she spotted the stone hut Benjamin had told her about.

"We were actually coming to find you," Julia said with a soft smile. "I hope we're not interrupting."

"Not at all," he said as he swung the axe down again. "This is my last log. What can I do for you?"

"I was wondering if you could pass a message on to Blair?" Julia asked as she retrieved the handwritten note from her pocket. "I've been banished from the kitchen, and I really wanted to talk to her."

"Couldn't you just wait for one of her breaks?"

"I want to talk to her *away* from the castle," Julia whispered, looking around, suddenly becoming aware of all of the windows. "I think she knows something that might help unlock the secret to Henry's murder, and I think Charlotte knows that and she's trying to keep us apart."

Benjamin took the note and opened it, his brows curiously pinching together. He quickly read the note that asked Blair to meet Julia in a café in Aberfoyle after she had finished for the day, along with Julia's phone number.

"I thought you were a baker?" he asked with a little smirk as he pocketed the paper. "You're acting like some kind of detective."

"She *is* a baker," Sue said, joining Julia by her side. "She just seems to *forget* that every time a murder happens near her, which is happening increasingly more often than I would like to admit. Gran thinks she's the harbinger of death."

"She does?" Julia exclaimed, turning to her sister.

"Well, she's not going to say that to your *face*, is she?" Sue mumbled with a shrug.

"I'll pass on the note," he said with a wink. "You don't think my sister is in danger, do you?"

"I don't know," Julia admitted, not wanting to lie to the man. "But Charlotte appears to think it's crucial to keep us apart."

"*Or* it is just the insurance?" Sue whispered.

"Or that," Julia said with a sigh. "But it's all just a little suspicious."

"I'll keep an eye on her and an ear to the ground," Benjamin said as he started tossing the logs into a wheelbarrow. "If you want to get back into the castle, there's a door that leads to the drawing room. It's not really for guests, but I'm sure I can make an exception with the fog. I wouldn't feel right letting you walk along that path. It's not safe at the best of times."

Sue rolled her eyes and pouted before linking arms with Julia and following Benjamin across the courtyard. Julia looked up at the many windows to her right, suddenly realising they were part of the family's quarters above the entrance hall. She gulped, hoping she had been quiet enough to not betray herself.

Benjamin walked them to a stone wall, forcing Julia and Sue to look questioningly at each other. To their equal surprise, Benjamin pulled on the bricks, and a piece of the wall the exact size of a door opened onto a dark corridor.

"Follow that down to the bottom, and you'll come out in the drawing room," he said as he held the heavy stone door open.

"A secret passageway?" Sue asked, her face lighting up. "I *knew* it!"

"The castle is full of them," Benjamin said with a smirk. "Makes my job a lot easier. There's a peephole in the door at the other side. Just make sure nobody is watching when you slip through."

Sue clenched her hand around Julia's once more, and they stepped into the dark. With one final goodbye, Benjamin pushed the door shut, concealing them within the walls of the castle. Just like when walking through the fog, she took tiny steps through the stuffy and narrow corridor.

Mildew and decay tickled her nostrils.

"This is *so* cool," Sue whispered. "I *told* you there would be secret passages."

"Explains how Charlotte managed to get across the castle so quickly if she *did* kill her father."

"*If?*" Sue mumbled. "I thought you were certain it was her?"

"I'm certain of nothing until I have all of the facts," she whispered back, turning pointlessly to her sister in the pitch black. "It's just a hunch."

A narrow stream of light illuminated the dusty air, letting them know they had reached the door into the drawing room. Julia let go of Sue's hand and pushed her eye up against the tiny circle in the wall.

She saw an explosion of mahogany through the tiny gap. A grand banqueting table stretched out down the centre of the room, a crystal chandelier as big as Julia's car dangling over it. The walls were lined high with dark bookshelves, which were crammed with thick leather-bound volumes. On the other side of the room, she spotted the giant ornate doors, which would lead them back to the safety of the castle.

"Looks clear," she whispered back to Sue. "Try to be quiet."

Julia pushed carefully on the door. It felt heavy under her hands, but it eased forward, flooding the darkness with light. She held it open enough for Sue to slip through, before squeezing through herself. She closed the door, surprised to see it was a bookshelf on the other side. She smiled to herself, feeling like she was fulfilling some kind of childhood fantasy to have her own bookcase door that led to a secret room.

"*Get down*," Sue whispered, yanking Julia to the ground and behind a red Chesterfield sofa. "*We're not alone*."

She pointed over the top of the sofa to the large bay window looking out over the loch. Julia peered over the edge, instantly bobbing back down when she saw a flash of red hair over the top of a high-backed leather armchair pointed in the direction of the foggy view.

"*Charlotte*," Julia mouthed to Sue. "*Stay here*."

Julia wriggled free of Sue's grasp and crawled out from behind the couch. On her hands and knees, she scurried forward like a cat, pausing behind a side table. She peered around the corner of the mahogany unit, instantly ducking back when she saw the profile of the person sitting in the other chair. Julia looked around and spotted another Chesterfield sofa positioned behind them. Without a second thought, she hurried forward and pushed her back up against the hard sofa. She strained her ears, but she needn't have bothered. Charlotte wasn't concealing her conversation behind a whisper.

"I need you to get *rid* of her," she said firmly, no doubt staring out into the fog. "She's *trouble*."

"I'm done wi' this," the thick Scottish accent of Andrew replied. "I've done yer dirty work, lassie. Find somebody else to *use*."

"Don't act like you're not being paid for your services, Mr McCracken," Charlotte said, the chair creaking under her. "Seirbigh Castle will be mine in a matter of days if you have done what you said, and you will get what was promised to you."

"'Course I did what I said," he growled back. "But you told me that was the last thing."

"You've come this far, Mr McCracken," Charlotte replied as she stood up. "Don't stumble at the final hurdle. The girl is trouble and you know it's going to be difficult to legally fire her considering the circumstances. Besides, she knows too much. She could speak out. I want her out of Seirbigh Castle before all of the paperwork is official. Now that Mary is gone, *she's* the final thorn in my side. Do what you have to do, Mr McCracken, and welcome back to the family. You should never have been disposed of in the first place."

Footsteps clicked on the polished wood floors, sending Julia scurrying back behind the side table. She caught Sue's eyes, who was desperately waving for Julia to come back. Julia waited until she heard the door close before dashing back to her sister.

"Have you gone *crazy*?" Sue whispered angrily. "I hope that was worth it."

"It was," Julia replied. "Let's get out of here."

Julia grabbed Sue's hand and still keeping low to the ground, they hurried towards the doors on the other side of the room. Before she reached it, she glanced over to Andrew as he reached around the side of the chair to top up his whisky from the glass decanter.

They slipped through the door, coming out facing the dining room. It was still dark and empty, but Rory was now sitting at the closest table with his back to them, hunched over something. Julia stopped in her tracks and tried to peer around him to see what he was doing, but all she could conclude was that he was writing something.

"Ah! There you are!" the voice of DI Fletcher made them both spin around. "I've been looking for you everywhere. Can you gather in the entrance hall with the other guests, please?"

"Why?" Julia asked as Rory turned to see what was happening.

"*Now*, Miss South," he ordered as he stepped to the side and motioned towards the double doors leading through to the reception area. "Rory, do you know where your sister is? I need to speak with you both in private."

Julia reluctantly let Sue drag her down the corridor, without taking her eyes away from DI Fletcher. Just from the look on his face, she could tell he wasn't gathering them to give them good news. She wondered if he could have possibly cracked the case and have a suspect in custody. It seemed unlikely, but it would be a relief to put an end to the whole affair.

They joined their gran by the reception desk, where she was staring sternly at the new guests, still in her white robe and bright green facemask.

"Where have you two been?" she snapped when she noticed them.

"We went for a walk," Julia said, hoping the truthful part of that statement made up for the fact she was keeping quiet about the outcome of that walk. "What's going on?"

"I don't know," she said with a sigh. "But it's keeping me from my depleting spa time. DI CryBaby gathered us all here to tell us something important. I wonder if he's just got his first chest hair and wants to share the news."

The two new couples both snickered at Dot's joke, but she stared at them sternly, letting them know they didn't have permission. Julia smiled reassuringly at the two young couples. Just from their confusion and lack of interest in the collapsed bannister above them, she could tell they had no idea that they were standing directly on the scene of a man's murder.

The double doors opened, and DI Fletcher walked in, followed by Rory and Charlotte. Charlotte was sobbing heavily, her face buried in her brother's chest, and Rory was trying his best to comfort her, his expression solemn and his eyes vacant. Julia's stomach turned uncomfortably.

"A car was found crashed an hour ago on the road to Aberfoyle," DI Fletcher announced. "The driver, Mary McLaughlin, the manager of this hotel, was found dead behind the wheel."

A gasp ricocheted through the small crowd, but Charlotte's increased sobs drowned it out. Rory wrapped his arms around his sister and pulled her in.

"I saw her drive away this morning!" one of the new men explained. "She was screeching outside. It woke us up!"

"*Me too*!" the woman in the other couple said with a nod. "Drove off like a *madwoman*."

"We saw her too," Dot volunteered. "Didn't we girls? Julia even went down and spoke to her."

Guilt consumed Julia. She looked down at the ground, unable to look the young DI in the eyes. Why hadn't she tried harder to stop Mary from driving off? She tried to think of what could have caused the woman to crash, but Charlotte's cries were distracting her.

"I'm going to need to take statements from each of you," he said, already pulling a notepad out of his pocket. "Since you can't seem to stay out of things, why don't we start with *you*, Miss South?"

CHAPTER 10

J ulia followed DI Fletcher back into the dining room. He pulled up a seat at the table Rory had been sitting at, but the paperwork he had been working on had already vanished.

"You know they're faking that grief?" Julia asked as she sat uninvited across the table from DI Fletcher. "Neither of them showed that much emotion when their own father was shot down. Find the gun yet?"

"We're doing our best to find the murder weapon," he said as he flicked through his notepad to a fresh page. "Why don't you start at the beginning?"

"Your best isn't good enough." Julia clung onto the edge of the table, leant through the dim light, and looked the DI dead in the eyes. "A woman has *unnecessarily* died."

The DI arched a brow, a slight smirk pricking the corners of his lips. He pulled the lid off his pen, but he didn't write anything down. Instead, he just continued to stare at Julia as though he was a mixture of amused and irritated by her behaviour. It reminded her of the way Barker had looked at her when they had first met, but she doubted the young DI in front of her contained any of the same humility when he clocked off at the end of the day. Her chest tightened just thinking of Barker; she wanted nothing more than to see his face at that moment.

"We have no reason to believe it was anything but a tragic accident," he said, turning the pen upside down to tap furiously on the table surface. "Those roads are dangerous at the best of times without the added difficulty of driving through fog. Mary McLaughlin wouldn't be the first woman to succumb to those roads."

"*Woman*?"

"Turn of phrase, Miss South," he replied through a strained smile. "I assure you I meant *nothing* by it, but the point still stands. Mary skidded off the road on a tricky turn and crashed through the barrier wall."

"If you analyse the car, I'm sure you'll find some tampering," Julia said firmly as she sat up and turned to the thick fog outside. "Cut brakes, perhaps?"

"There wasn't much left of the car," he said as he tugged at his collar. "Or of Mary. On a road that quiet, there's no telling how long the fire raged for."

Julia closed her eyes and forced back the tears. Why hadn't she insisted Mary stay behind? She tried to reassure herself that she couldn't have known this would happen, but after everything she had heard so far today, a second murder wasn't as surprising as she would have liked to have believed.

"Charlotte *is* involved," Julia said. "I heard her talking to the ex-groundskeeper, Andrew McCracken, moments before we bumped into you. If fact, I'm sure Andrew is still there. I haven't seen him leave yet, have you?"

Julia jumped up and hurried across the dining hall to the drawing room. She pushed confidently on the heavy double doors, but she didn't need to take a step into the room to know the chair was empty. She rushed over, but the only evidence Andrew had even been there was the drained whisky tumbler and the almost empty decanter.

"I can't see anybody, Miss South," he said as he followed her into the room, wincing as he scratched at the side of his head with his pen. "Why don't you sit down and tell me about this conversation?"

"Charlotte was asking Andrew to get rid of somebody, and she alluded to the fact he had already done it once. She mentioned Mary was now gone to leave her to take control of the castle." Julia turned to the bookcase she had slipped through, and a light bulb sparked above her head. "*The secret passage!*"

The DI walked over to the armchair and picked up the decanter. He lifted off the lid and gave it a sniff, but Julia was already running across the room. She stared at the bookcase she was sure concealed the hidden door.

"Secret passage?" he called after her as he weaved in and out of the furniture to catch up. "Do you realise how ridiculous you sound right now?"

"It's true," Julia said, scrambling at the books for a secret lever or switch. "It's *right* here. It leads out into the courtyard. He could be halfway back to the village by now."

"Who?"

"*Andrew!*"

"What does Andrew McCracken have to do with Mary McLaughlin's death?" he asked with an exasperated sigh. "Please, Miss South, try to stay on topic."

"Aren't you listening to me?" she cried, turning away from the bookcase and back at the DI. "Charlotte is pulling all of the strings. She shot her father and had Mary killed. She's desperate to run this castle. Her very words were *'whatever it takes'*. She's ruthless."

"Do you have any evidence, aside from a conversation you claim to have overheard?"

"I *did* overhear it," she snapped. "Sue was there. She'll account for the secret passage too. Benjamin, the new groundskeeper, told me the castle was full of them. I suppose that's how Charlotte managed to be in the opposite part of the castle when her father was discovered. She must have slipped away and waited until witnesses could see her walking onto the scene."

"You're not making any sense."

"I'm making *perfect* sense!" she cried, her hands disappearing up into her curls. "Why aren't you writing any of this down?"

He sighed and pinched between his brows as he took a seat on the red Chesterfield Julia and Sue had been hiding behind not that long ago.

"Just tell me what happened when Mary drove away from this castle?" he asked, opening his notepad again. "And *please* stick to the *facts.*"

Julia reluctantly sat next to him. She ran through the story of being awakened by the shrieking and seeing Rory pushing her out of the castle. She told him all about their conversation, and how Mary had insisted on going to see her lawyer. When she was finished, she looked down at the polished floor, Mary's tears ringing through her ears.

"Thank you, Miss South," he said as he slapped the notepad shut. "You've been very helpful."

"Have I?" she mumbled with a strained laugh. "I could hand you the killer with a stack of evidence and you would instantly dismiss me."

"If you hand me the killer with a stack of evidence, I'll owe you a drink, Miss South," he said with a wink as he stood up. "But until then, your witness statements are more than enough."

The DI turned on his heels and strode confidently out of the drawing room, his black trench coat fluttering behind him. She turned back to the bookshelf, wondering how things had turned so peculiar so quickly. Standing up, she walked over to the window and stared out at the loch through the fog. It was growing thicker by the second, keeping them from the rest of the world. Seven hour drive or not, it was more than tempting to jump into her trusty Ford Anglia and drive back to Peridale.

Deciding she was going to have a lie down in her bedroom while DI Fletcher spoke to Dot, Sue, and the others, Julia abandoned the drawing room, but not without looking back at the bookshelf once again. Her stomach squirmed uncomfortably at the thought of the peephole staring directly at her within the mass of leather-bound books. All of a sudden, she had the unnerving feeling she was being watched, and perhaps had been the whole time.

Shaking out her curls, she pulled on one of the ornate doors, stepping out into the corridor just as DI Fletcher appeared with Sue behind him. Before the door closed, she spotted Charlotte and Rory sitting at the bottom of the stairs, still putting on a performance for the rest of the guests. One of the new women was even trying her best to comfort them.

DI Fletcher and Sue walked past her, both giving her very different looks. DI Fletcher's said *'go away'*, and Sue's said *'please stay'*. They both slipped into the drawing room, no doubt walking to the seats by the window to prevent eavesdropping. Turning to the empty dining hall, Julia had a better idea than listening in on the interview. With Charlotte and Rory otherwise occupied, she set off weaving between the tables and towards the kitchen.

* * *

JULIA CREPT DOWN THE WINDING STONE steps, her fingers dragging along the cold wall to steady her. She checked her watch, surprised that it was still only a little after nine. So much had happened since being awoken by Mary at six that morning, it felt like she had fit an entire day into just a few short hours.

Forcing herself not to think about Mary's crash, she reached the bottom of the stairs and peered through the round window in the door. She was relieved to see Blair alone in the kitchen, leaning over the stove as she moved bacon around in a pan with one hand, while she stirred baked beans with the other. She took a step back and wiped sweat from her rosy forehead, her eyes clenched tightly shut. Julia didn't know how anybody could expect this young girl to juggle the cooking for an entire castle on her own.

She was about to push on the door to help Blair finish preparing breakfast, but she stopped herself when Blair tore off her apron and tossed it on the table. She was wearing a khaki green wool jumper underneath it, rolled up at the sleeves. She dragged the sleeves down and began pulling it over her head. As she did, her white T-shirt slid up with it. Julia let out a small gasp when she saw the small, yet definite bump protruding out of Blair's stomach.

Almost out of sheer shock, she hurried into the kitchen, startling Blair as she pulled the jumper over her face. She tossed it onto the table and quickly yanked her shirt down, turning away from Julia as she loosely tied her apron around her waist, just as it had been every other time Julia had seen her.

"You're pregnant?" Julia asked, her voice barely above a whisper.

"You shouldn't be down here," Blair mumbled, her cheeks burning brightly as she flipped the bacon. "Charlotte has forbidden it. You're going to get me in trouble."

"You're *pregnant*!" Julia repeated, taking a step forward.

Blair turned to face Julia, hovering over the frying pan with the metal spatula in her hand. They stared at each other for what felt like an eternity, neither of them knowing what to say. The stare was only broken when Blair yelped and tossed the burning hot spatula into the pan. Clutching her burnt hand tightly, she stepped back and immediately began crying. Julia hurried forward and turned off the stove. She took the young girl into her arms, who wrapped her arms around her shoulders, clutching onto her tightly. Through the apron, Julia could feel the tiny life pushing up against her.

"It's going to be okay," Julia whispered as she stroked the back of Blair's head.

"You can't tell anyone," she said as she pulled away

271

from the hug, her pale cheeks tear-stained and her nose glistening. "Please, miss. *Promise* me you won't say anything."

"I promise."

"I haven't even told Ben yet," she said as she tried to suppress her sobs. "They'll fire me if they find out. They've done it before. I can't afford to lose this job. We both send money to our mam back home. She wouldn't survive without it."

Blair walked over to the sink, cramming one hand under the cold tap as she wiped her tears with the other. Julia did the only thing she knew what to do. She flicked on the kettle, grabbed two cups, and pulled two peppermint and liquorice tea bags from the box she had given to Blair.

When the kettle boiled, she filled the cups and placed them on the counter. Blair gratefully accepted the tea. Staring into space, she hugged it tight to her chest as the weight of the world pushed down on her. Julia had to remind herself the girl was only nineteen.

"I need to finish breakfast," Blair said without moving, her eyes still wide. "Charlotte always eats later on a Saturday because she likes to sleep in on the weekends. I had the four new guests this morning, so I'm already running late."

"I don't think she's going to be thinking about breakfast," Julia said carefully. "Mary died this morning."

"*Died?*" Blair furrowed her brow tightly, suddenly turning in her seat. "How?"

"She crashed her car driving away from the castle this morning. I spoke to her just before it happened. The police seem to think it was an accident."

"You don't?"

"Do you?" Julia asked, arching a brow. "Considering

what happened to Henry, I don't think there are any accidents around here anymore. Everything has been happening very deliberately and when it's supposed to."

"I'm not sure what you mean," Blair whispered as she lifted the cup to her lips.

"I think you do," Julia replied, putting her cup down. "Or you don't realise you do. I overheard Charlotte talking earlier today, and I didn't understand what she meant at the time, but I think I do now. I think she knows you're pregnant. She asked Andrew to get rid of you."

"Get *rid* of me?" Blair echoed, the shake in her voice obvious. "What does that mean?"

"I don't know, but she wants this castle, and she is doing whatever she can to get it. She got rid of Mary, and I think you're next. She seems to think you know something that could derail her plans."

Blair looked down into her cup without blinking. Julia knew Blair knew exactly what she was talking about.

"I don't know anything," Blair mumbled, placing the cup on the table and hurrying back over to the stove. "I really need to get on with this before Charlotte calls down."

"Didn't you just hear what I said?"

"This has *nothing* to do with you," Blair snapped bitterly, casting an angry look over her shoulder at Julia. "You're just a guest here. You get to go back to your café in two days, and I have to stay here. If Charlotte is going to fire me, I need to work as hard as I can to try and change her mind. I can't bring my baby into this world without a penny to my name."

She placed her hand momentarily on her stomach, outlining the shape of the tiny barely-there bump. Julia could feel every part of Blair's frustration and anger radiating from every pore in her body, but despite her warning, she felt there was nothing she could actually do to improve the girl's situation.

"Just be careful," Julia whispered as she passed, resting a hand on Blair's shoulder. "This family is dangerous."

Blair shrugged off her hand and focussed on cooking Charlotte's breakfast as though nothing had sunk in. Sighing to herself, Julia reluctantly pulled on the kitchen door. She cast an eye through the tiny round window before she set off up the winding staircase. Blair lifted her hands up to her eyes and sobbed silently for a moment before shaking her head, picking up the spatula, and flipping the bacon once more.

"Julia?" a voice from the dark startled her.

Julia spun around to see Benjamin. She let out a relieved laugh, glad it wasn't Charlotte or Rory.

"I was just about to give your note to Blair," he said, pulling the letter from his pocket. "Is everything okay?"

"There's no need." Julia grabbed the note from Ben. "I've spoken to her. Can you just keep an eye on her for me? I don't think she appreciates me sticking my nose in, but I'm worried about her."

"Of course," he said quickly. "I always do. She's my little sister."

Julia thanked him with a smile before stepping around him. She hurried up the winding staircase and back through to the dining room. The fog had started to clear, but only to be replaced with a miserable grey sky.

Wondering if Sue was finished with her interview, she pushed her ear up to the door. She strained her hearing, but it was in vain. She looked ahead to the sunroom, where Charlotte and Rory were standing by the window and looking out at the clearing fog. They were both talking in whispers, the amateur dramatic tears from earlier having stopped entirely.

As she walked back to the entrance hall, Julia felt the sands of time slipping away. She had less than two days to get to the bottom of this mystery before she could head home to Peridale with a clear conscience.

CHAPTER 11

The next morning at breakfast, Julia wasn't surprised when Blair ignored her entirely, only nodding when Julia put in her order for poached eggs on toast. Dot and Sue didn't seem to notice, so she decided against letting them in on Blair's secret. She had promised after all, even if that promise didn't make much difference in the grand scheme of things anymore.

After breakfast, Julia let Sue drag her to the spa one last time, if only to use the quiet time to properly think about everything. No matter how many different theories she pieced together about what had really happened to Henry and Mary McLaughlin, something didn't sit right every time. Her mind kept landing back on Charlotte, but her vision was clouded, and she knew she was missing vital clues concerning the reasoning behind the murders.

After her facial and shoulder massage, which she had enjoyed more than she had expected to, she wasn't surprised to see DI Fletcher sniffing around the castle once more. She was, however, surprised to see Andrew McCracken stacking the fire with logs a little before lunch, as though he had never been fired in the first place. When he walked past her, Julia tried her best to make eye contact with the man to see his true intentions, but he appeared to be avoiding her at all costs.

Above Andrew's apparent return to work, Julia was even more surprised to learn from one of the other guests that the dinner in the drawing room was still happening as scheduled that night, despite what had happened to Mary. Even though she wouldn't put anything past Charlotte at this point, she didn't quite understand how she could transition from grieving stepdaughter to gracious host in the space of a day.

"I haven't seen a single man in a kilt yet," Dot complained as she settled into a chair in the sunroom with a cup of tea. "I wanted to check Jessie's theory about the underwear. Despite that, this trip has been rather lovely."

"Ignoring the two deaths," Sue whispered as she peeled the wrapper off one of the cupcakes Blair had brought them.

"Everybody dies, sweetheart!" Dot exclaimed loudly, turning the heads of the couple who were enjoying the view on the other side of the room. "It doesn't mean I can't *relax*! I've had at least one of every facial and massage on the menu, and I feel remarkable for it. Feel how soft my skin is."

Dot crammed her hand in front of Sue's face, who recoiled before reluctantly giving it a stroke.

"Like a newborn's behind," Sue mumbled.

"We need to do this more often," Dot said, sighing contently as she turned back to look out at the clear loch. "I've really enjoyed this time alone with my two favourite granddaughters."

"We're your *only* granddaughters," Sue said.

"And that's why you're my favourites," she teased with a wink. "Are you okay, Julia? You look distant."

Julia broke her gaze from the bank across the loch and turned to her gran, forcing a smile. She nodded, unsure if she had the energy to deny it. The truth was, she was distant, and she didn't know how her gran was so oblivious to what was going on in the castle. Every fibre of her being was telling her something bad was going to happen very soon, like an orchestra rising to its final crescendo.

"I think she's just missing Barker," Sue answered for her when she noticed Julia's lack of response. "I know I'm missing my Neil. Do you think we'll be able to drive into the village on the way home and pick up some souvenirs? I promised I'd bring him something."

"Sure," Julia replied, souvenirs the last thing on her mind. "Is that Benjamin?"

She stood up and walked over to the window, squinting at the mossy bank ahead. Benjamin was walking amongst the heather in his usual green Barbour jacket. With Andrew apparently being back she had assumed Benjamin had already been given his marching orders. She had even tried to put Blair's distance down to that, and not what had transpired yesterday in the kitchen.

"Looks like him," Sue said.

"Who's Benjamin?" Dot asked. "Whoever he is, he looks like a fine specimen of a man."

"He is," Sue said, blushing a little, no doubt remembering him with his shirt off the morning before. "He's the cook's brother."

"I wonder if he's as miserable as her," Dot exclaimed, catching the attention of the couple again. "My stomach hasn't felt right all week!"

"I thought you said you'd been relaxed?" Julia mumbled over her shoulder, her defence of Blair automatic by this point, despite being blanked that morning. "Why have *two* groundskeepers?"

"*Huh*?" Dot replied, arching a brow. "Why does it matter?"

"Because we're in a castle that has been running with a skeleton staff since we arrived. Why rehire the old groundskeeper and keep his replacement around?"

"Maybe because there's a lot of ground?" Dot suggested with a roll of her eyes. "Honestly, Julia, I don't know why you care so much about these things."

"Because somebody has to," she said before pulling her phone from her pocket and walking out of the sunroom.

As she scrolled to Barker's number, she walked past the dining hall and straight through the open doors to the drawing room. She was relieved to see it empty. She pushed the phone against her ear, closed her eyes, and waited. Barker picked up on the last ring.

"*Hello*?" he called down the phone. "*Julia*?"

"It's me," she said, a smile flooding her face. "I just wanted to hear your voice."

"*What? I can't hear you? Jessie!* Take that turn! *Slow down!*"

Julia heard what she thought was the screeching of tyres as somebody slammed on the brakes and turned.

"Are you driving?" Julia asked.

"Jessie is," Barker called back. "If you can call it that. Can I call you back?"

"Yeah, sure," she whispered, opening her eyes. "No problem."

"Are you okay?" he asked, seeming to pick up on the sadness in her voice. "You sound – *Jessie*! You have to stop at zebra crossings! Julia, I have to go. I'll call you back later."

Barker hung up, leaving her alone in the drawing room once more. She twirled the phone in-between her fingers, turning her attention to the banquet table, which had already been set for the meal ahead. Two larger, almost throne-like chairs had been brought in and placed at either end of the long table, no doubt for the two siblings to take centre stage. Julia shook her head, unsure why she was still surprised by Charlotte and Rory's behaviour.

"Can I help you?"

Julia spun around, her heart stopping when she saw Charlotte standing in the doorway of the drawing room, her auburn hair flowing freely down her front, concealing the sides of her pale face. Despite the young woman's impossibly tall heels, Julia hadn't heard her creep up on her.

"I was just admiring your table setting," Julia said quickly, pushing forward a smile. "It's very beautiful."

"The silver has been in our family for three generations," she replied flatly, returning the fake smile.

Julia looked to the silver cutlery and goblets, nodding her appreciation of their beauty. When she turned back to Charlotte, it was obvious neither of them cared for the forced small talk.

"If you need any help with tonight, I'd be more than happy to step in," Julia offered, already knowing the answer.

"That's a very kind offer, but it's quite alright," Charlotte said as she walked past Julia towards the two large armchairs facing out towards the window. "Now, if you'll excuse me, I have a little work to be getting on with."

Julia watched as Charlotte settled into the same armchair she had sat in the day before. Julia looked back to the secret door, and she suddenly had the strangest feeling that Charlotte knew exactly what Julia had done and what she had overheard. Her heart fluttered when she realised it was more than likely that DI Fletcher had presented Julia's madcap theory to her. Not wanting to stay in the woman's frosty presence any longer, she turned back to the open doors, stopping in her tracks when she saw Andrew watching her in the doorway.

The overpowering scent of whisky mixed in with the heather uncomfortably turned Julia's stomach. He stared down at her with puffy glassy eyes, the stubble thicker than ever, and his little wisps of hair practically standing on end. She was unsure if he was even looking at her, or just through her. Not wanting to stick around to find out, she walked around the looming man, only turning back when she was in the safety of the corridor. Andrew walked over to the other armchair, where a full decanter of whisky and a clean crystal tumbler were waiting for him. Julia would have given every penny she owned to listen in on their conversation, but she knew it wasn't safe, even if she did crawl around on her hands and knees and hide behind furniture again.

Her gran and sister had left the sunroom, and they were waiting for Julia by the reception desk in the entrance hall. When Julia caught up with them, Rory appeared from the office, a professional yet unsettling smile on his smug face.

"Remember your check-out is at ten tomorrow morning, ladies," Rory said through his smile, his eyes trained on Julia. "I hope you've enjoyed your stay here."

Dot opened her mouth to reply, but Julia looped her arm around her gran's and pulled her towards the door. They set off towards their bedrooms to prepare for that evening's dinner, leaving Rory hanging.

"He doesn't even work here," Sue whispered to Julia as they walked up the steps towards their bedroom. "I thought he was a lawyer?"

"I think what this castle needs more than ever is a lawyer," Julia whispered back, careful not to catch Dot's attention. "I think I might have a theory about what is going on here."

"Let me guess, you're not going to tell me?" Sue asked, suddenly stopping in her tracks.

"I need proof. But don't worry, we're going to get it."

"*We?*" Sue mumbled as she pinched between her brows. "So an afternoon nap is out of the question?"

"You can nap back in Peridale," Julia replied as they set off back up the stairs to catch up with their gran. "You've slept like a cat on this trip. I didn't realise relaxing was so exhausting."

"Well, it is."

With a large yawn, Dot retreated into her bedroom with a promise to meet them in two hours to head down to the drawing room together. When they were alone in their bedroom, Julia explained her theory to Sue, whose jaw dropped further and further with each sentence.

"You're insane, Julia," Sue whispered, shaking her head as she slammed herself down onto her bed. "I really hope you're right about this."

"Me too," Julia whispered, her chest pounding.

Sue looked as though she was going to add something else, but her eyes fluttered, and as though she couldn't control it, she drifted off to sleep and was snoring in seconds. Julia let out a small yawn herself as she walked over to the window looking out over the castle.

She looked down at the bridge where she had shared Mary's final moments. Despite her reservations, she owed it to Mary to uncover the truth, whatever the cost. She turned back to her sister as she curled up like a tiny baby on top of her sheets. She looked so peaceful and comfortable. The thought of a nap tempted Julia more than it ever had, but she was scared of her thoughts slipping away from her.

CHAPTER 12

"*reathe in*!" Sue demanded as she attempted to zip up the dress she had insisted Julia wear. "I can't believe you didn't bring any gowns!"

"I can't believe you brought *six*!"

"You never know when the occasion calls for an outfit change." She hoisted up a leg and crammed it against the small of Julia's back as she forced her into the wall.

The zipper travelled all the way up to Julia's neck. She attempted to relax, but it appeared she was not going to be breathing for the rest of the night.

"It's too tight," Julia wheezed, resting her hand on her stomach.

"It's meant to be," Sue whispered as she pushed her in

front of the floor length mirror. "Stop complaining and be a girl for once."

Julia's reflection caught her off guard. Back home, she usually wore simple and comfortable dresses that stopped at her shoulders and exactly at her knees. While in Scotland, she had been wearing comfortable jeans and jumpers. Neither of those outfits stared back at Julia in the mirror.

"I look -,"

"*Beautiful*," Sue interrupted as she picked up Julia's hair and held it up at the back of her head. "I think we should put your hair up."

Julia looked down at the scarlet dress, which ran from her wrists, up to her shoulders, and then down to the floor. It cut across her chest in a sweetheart neckline, making her décolletage pop in a way she had never seen before. Under her bust, the dress ran tight against her body, nipping in at the knees before flaring out into a subtle mermaid tail. Gold embroidery ran up her sleeves, along the shoulders, and down the sides of the dress, contouring her body in a way that she had never seen before. Even though her sister was a size smaller than her, and it felt uncomfortable, Julia couldn't believe how well the dress hugged her body in a way she would have usually hated.

"Why do I have to wear the tight one?" Julia asked when she looked at Sue's black chiffon Grecian dress, which floated down her front in a complementary empire line. "Will I even be able to sit down?"

"Who cares?" Sue mumbled through a mouthful of hair grips as she twisted and pinned strands of Julia's hair against her scalp. "You look like a movie star. Do you remember when we raided Mum's wardrobe and played dress up?"

Julia nodded, the memory a fond one. Julia had been ten, and Sue had been five. They had paraded around their mum's bedroom, climbing in and out of her dresses while painting their faces in lipstick. When their mum had caught them, instead of being angry, she had joined in and played along. Julia hadn't known it at the time, but her mum had already been given the cancer diagnosis that would kill her two years later. She had often looked back on that day and wondered if their mum had played along so enthusiastically because she had known her days with her daughters were numbered. It was a memory Sue had asked Julia to recite to her so many times that she wasn't sure if Sue even remembered the actual day, or just Julia's account of it.

"Mum would be proud of you, you know," Julia said, catching her sister's smoky eyes in the mirror. "You've got a great job at the hospital, you're married to a lovely man, and you're going to make a great mother one day."

Sue smiled, her eyes filled with an unexpected sadness. Julia knew those few extra years she had had with their mother used to cause friction between them when they were both teenagers, but she knew that resentment hadn't followed them into adulthood, but in that moment, she was sure she saw a flicker of something that reminded her of those arguments they used to have.

"Come on," Sue said as she crammed the final hair grip into Julia's hair. "You're done. You said we don't have long to get this evidence."

Julia examined her hair in the mirror, pulling down a couple of strands to make it look less put-together. She looked nothing like herself, but she couldn't deny that Sue had an eye for fashion. She grabbed Sue's red lipstick from her makeup bag and quickly applied it to her lips. She puckered them together before turning back to her sister, who was smirking at her with two arched brows.

"*What?*" Julia mumbled as she tossed the lipstick back into the makeup bag. "Tonight's a big night. I might as well look the part."

"You look like her," Sue said as they walked towards the door. "Everybody says so."

"And everybody says you look like me, so you do too," she whispered back, squeezing her shoulder reassuringly.

Arm in arm, they tiptoed past their gran's bedroom and back down the stairs. Julia's heart fluttered in her chest, and it wasn't from the tightness of the dress. She knew she had one shot to uncover something concrete so she could put an end to things tonight, and if she didn't, she wasn't sure everybody would make it past sunrise.

* * *

AS THE BLUE SKY TURNED PINK AND orange, they hurried along the path circling the island. Julia figured out that if she pulled the dress up so that the tightest part was just above her knees, she could almost jog.

"It really is beautiful," Sue whispered, squinting as the last of the orange sun reflected off the cool surface of the water. "We'll have to come back to Scotland and actually enjoy it properly sometime."

"What's not to enjoy about solving a murder?" Julia whispered.

"I can't tell if you're being sarcastic or not."

Julia decided against answering. She hitched her dress up even further as they made their way up the slope and back towards the castle. Even though it was awful that two people had died, she couldn't ignore the adrenaline she felt pumping through her system whenever she was piecing something together. It was a thrill she never felt when she was putting together a cake recipe or serving a customer in her café.

They hurried into the courtyard and towards the secret door that led them through to the drawing room. Benjamin popped his head out of his work hut as their heels clicked against the stone cobbles, a screwdriver in his left hand and a piece of circuit board in his right.

"Evening, ladies," Benjamin said with a tip of his head. "You look very nice."

"It's for the dinner in the drawing room tonight."

"Is it Sunday already?" he asked, blinking heavily and shaking his head. "This week has been a strange one. I'm surprised it's still happening."

"I'm glad you're here, actually," Julia said as she dabbed at the sweat breaking out on her forehead. "Can you open that secret door again?"

"Don't want to chip a nail," Sue said with a shrug as she showed off her freshly painted black nails.

Benjamin turned and tossed the screwdriver and the circuit board into the hut. There was a small clatter and the screwdriver rolled straight back out again, but he ignored it and yanked on the door.

"You know there are easier ways to get to the drawing room," he said through tight lips as he dragged it open.

"We're not going *into* the drawing room," Julia said as she stepped in, hitching up her dress once more so that it didn't brush against the dusty floor. "If everything goes to plan, we'll be coming back through very soon. You can leave it open."

Benjamin saluted, a curious smile tickling his lips. He returned to his hut and left the ladies to their sleuthing. To Julia's surprise, Sue was right by her side as they hurried along the corridor. She didn't complain about the dust or the dampness, nor did she try to suggest they do something else. Her sister's silence was confirmation she felt that same thrill too, and she enjoyed it.

When they reached the door, Julia crammed her eye against the peephole, and peered into the drawing room. To her surprise, Charlotte had hired a team of servers, who were all running about like headless chickens organising the table setting and cleaning up the room.

Just as expected, Charlotte hurried in after a couple of minutes of spying. She was wearing a floor-length black dress, with red and blue tartan panels running down the side. Her auburn hair had been styled so perfectly it looked as though it had been professionally done. It swept away from her fresh face and waved down her shoulders, all the way down to her waist.

"Let's go," Julia whispered. "She's there."

Not wanting to waste a second, they both turned around and hurried back down the corridor. They walked through the open door, just as the sun drifted over the horizon in the far distance.

"Can you make sure you're in the drawing room after the main course?" Julia asked Benjamin when he popped his head out once more. "I'd appreciate it if you found Andrew and brought him along too. I suspect he's lurking around the castle somewhere."

"I guess so," he said with a small shrug as he tinkered with the circuit board. "What if he won't come? He's been avoiding me since he was rehired yesterday."

"Oh, he'll come," Julia called over her shoulder as she hurried out of the courtyard. "He won't want to miss this."

They hurried back along the path, and by the time they reached the entrance hall, darkness had completely consumed the castle.

"How did you know she'd already be there?" Sue asked.

"She wants to present herself as the gracious host," Julia whispered as she yanked on the heavy entrance door. "She's like a robot who adjusts herself perfectly to every situation. She cries when she needs to look like she's grieving, she's sweet when she's dealing with customers, and she's prompt and organised when she's hosting a dinner party for her guests."

They both slipped through the door, instantly stopping in their tracks when they saw Rory standing in the entrance to the office behind the desk. He was wearing a kilt that matched the red and blue tartan running down Charlotte's dress, and he was so consumed with the piece of paper he was looking over, he didn't notice that he was no longer alone. Julia glanced to the grand sweeping staircase, each second painfully slipping away. Her window of opportunity wasn't going to be open for much longer, but she couldn't risk attracting Rory's attention.

"I need a distraction," Julia whispered to Sue as Rory turned his back to them and walked back to the office.

"What kind of distraction?" Sue asked, looking confused at Julia.

"I don't know," Julia said with a shrug as she pushed Sue forward. "You'll think of something."

Sue stumbled forward, glancing awkwardly over her shoulder at Julia. She looked around the entrance hall as she tiptoed closer to Rory. Julia crept up the first couple of steps, keeping close to the wall. When she looked back over, Sue was reaching up to the top of the giant mantelpiece, the bottom of her chiffon dress fluttering dangerously close to the amber flames of the roaring fire. With the edge of her fingertips, she picked up a white and blue china vase and lifted it above her head. With the same force of Benjamin chopping wood with his one hand, she sent the vase flying into the ground near the reception desk. It shattered into a million pieces with a clatter, and Rory instantly appeared in the doorway.

"What was that?" he cried.

"That vase just *flew* off the mantelpiece!" Sue cried dramatically, waving her arms above her head. "It could have *hit* me!"

"What vase? Oh, *God*. That's a *priceless* family heirloom! What have you done, you *stupid* woman?"

"It was like a poltergeist or something," Sue cried desperately before glancing to Julia and giving her a fleeting unsure grin. "I'm going to *sue* you! Sue *will* sue!"

Rory walked around the reception desk and stared down at the vase with his hands in his red hair. Julia took her moment and crept silently up the stairs, sticking to the wall so as not to disrupt the ancient wood. When she reached the landing, she let out a giant sigh of relief.

Julia gave Sue a thumbs up over the broken section of the bannister before slipping completely out of view. She walked straight to Charlotte's bedroom door at the end of the wood-lined hall. She paused and stared at the family portrait once more, looking into the dull and lifeless eyes of the redheaded little girl staring back at her. She dreaded to think what the photographs that didn't make their way into frames and onto the walls looked like.

Without bothering to knock, Julia opened the door. She knew it was very possible that Charlotte had retreated to her bedroom in the time it had taken them to make their way around the castle, but she hoped for the best and stepped inside. The bedroom was empty.

Unsure of what she was specifically looking for, Julia looked around the enormous bedroom, hoping something obvious would jump out at her. The only light in the room was coming from a lamp on the antique desk on the far side of the room. Julia decided it was as good a place to start as any, so she hurried across the bedroom, stepping over Charlotte's clothes from earlier, which were strewn across the wooden floor.

The surface of the desk lacked a handwritten confession or anything else incriminating. The only thing that was out of place was a single pen, which sat in the centre of the mahogany desk. Julia tried the drawers, but they were locked.

She turned around and looked to the bed, but the box of paperwork she had seen during her brief visit was no longer there. Charlotte was a clever woman; she wasn't going to leave anything of interest on display for somebody to find. She wouldn't put it past Charlotte to intentionally clean up after herself in case someone did go snooping.

She set off towards the bed, hoping to find something in one of the nightstands, but stopped in her tracks when the door handle creaked and the door edged open. Fear fired up in her heart as she looked around the bedroom for a quick place to hide, but she was in the middle of wide open space.

Facing the door in the dim light, she accepted that she

had been caught and that it was all over.

CHAPTER 13

"*Julia*?" she heard her sister whisper. "Is this the right room?"

Sue slipped inside, closing the door softly behind her. Julia's heart steadied in her chest, and she let out a thankful laugh. She continued to the nightstand and pulled open the drawer, her heart still pounding hard. She arched a brow when she saw an eye mask, a pack of over-the-counter painkillers, a book, and a pair of tweezers. They were perfectly arranged as though they were part of a show home, and not actually items that were ever used.

"What are we looking for?" Sue whispered, looking around the room as she tucked her caramel curls behind her ears.

"I'm not sure," Julia whispered back, turning back to the desk. "Those drawers are locked, which makes me think there is something in there, but the key could be anywhere."

Sue walked over and yanked on them just to make sure. She looked in the pot of pens and pencils on the desk, instantly pulling out a tiny silver key.

"Anywhere, you said?" Sue said with a smirk and a wink. "You give the woman too much credit."

Sue wriggled the key in the top drawer. The lock clicked, and she stepped to the side to let Julia open it up. Heart banging behind the tight dress, Julia quickly slid open the drawer. Her eyes lit up when she saw a single brown manila envelope. She lifted it out with shaky fingers and pulled out a thick stack of stapled paper. Deciding it wouldn't make a difference if they were caught at that moment, she sat down and began flicking through the paper.

"It looks like a contract of some kind," Sue whispered as she looked over Julia's shoulder. "What's it for?"

"I think it's the deeds to the castle," Julia whispered as she flicked through the legal jargon. "It's hard to tell."

She landed on the final page, and her eyes wandered to the three signatures at the bottom. One was Henry's, one was Charlotte's, and the other Rory's. In the bottom right-hand corner, a date had been scribbled in the same handwriting as Henry's signature.

"This is from a *month* ago," Julia said, the surprise obvious in her voice.

"Why would he sign his castle over to his kids a month ago?" Sue asked, taking the contract from Julia. "That makes no sense. I thought Charlotte hated her father."

"I think she did, but she wanted this castle more than anything."

"So she forced him to sign over the castle and then killed him?" Sue theorised out loud as she scratched at the side of her head. "That doesn't sound right. Why wait a month, and why shoot him like that? There are easier ways to kill a person, too. Why make it so obvious?"

Julia didn't know. She had seen Rory and Charlotte reading through and signing so much paperwork recently, she had expected to find something suspicious to pin to them. She wasn't a lawyer, but the contract appeared to be legitimate.

"Rory is just a co-signer," Sue said, pointing out the small print under his signature. "This is a straight swap from Henry to Charlotte."

"He's their lawyer," Julia said as she put the paperwork back where she had found it, locked the drawer, and dropped the key back into the pot. "This isn't what we're looking for, but it helps."

"But what *are* we looking for?"

"I'm not sure, but I don't think we'll find it in here. We need to go next door."

They crept out of Charlotte's bedroom and back along the hall. Julia didn't dare look over the edge of the broken bannister, but she could hear that Rory was sweeping up the vase and talking to somebody under his breath. Knowing she didn't have much time before dinner, Julia pulled Sue into the room where it had all started on the day of their arrival.

"This is weird," Sue said as they crept into Henry's dark bedroom. "Do you believe in ghosts?"

"No," Julia said bluntly. "Start looking. There must be

some more paperwork in here to explain why he was signing things over to his daughter."

Julia hurried over to Henry's desk. It was cluttered in accounts, which Julia cast a quick eye over. She didn't need to consult her accountant to spot that the castle had been losing money every month. It looked like the business account savings were propping up everything and quickly depleting every month, which explained the skeleton staff. She tried the drawers, and to her surprise, they were all unlocked but also filled with more accounts and receipts. The disorganisation made her feel queasy. She spent an afternoon every month getting her own accounts neatly into order before sending them off to her accountant. She dug amongst the papers, but she was sure she wasn't going to find what she needed to piece together everything she knew.

Sue dropped to her hands and knees and peered under the bed. She pulled out an old sock and a book, but nothing else of interest. Julia rested the back of her hand against her forehead, wondering if she was barking up the wrong tree entirely. In her mind, this should have been easier, and she should have already been back in her room with Sue discussing what they had found.

Julia dug through Henry's bin, recoiling when she touched a rotten banana skin. She wiped her fingers on the heavy silk drapes, the moonlight twinkling through as she did. She peered out of the window into the dark, which looked down onto the stone courtyard. Sue tried a door on the opposite side of the room and walked through to the bathroom.

"I doubt you'll find anything in there," Julia called after her as loudly as she dared. "Maybe the contract is enough?"

"For DI BabyFace?" Sue called back. "You either hand over two signed confessions or you might as well put on your own handcuffs for trespassing and wasting police time."

Sue flicked on the bathroom light and began grabbing at the bottles on the counter. Julia tried Henry's nightstand, hoping it would be a little more revealing than Charlotte's had been. To her surprise, it was stuffed full of various bottles and boxes. She began pulling them out and laying them on the man's unmade bed. There was a bottle of hand sanitizer, a tube of hand cream, dissolvable tablets for a dry mouth, a pink bottle of *Pepto-Bismol*, and a get well soon card.

"He was taking opiate-based painkillers," Sue said, appearing in the bathroom door with a handful of bottles. "*Oramorph, oxycodone, tramadol* – doctors don't prescribe these lightly."

"Look at this," Julia said, calling Sue over. "Remember when mum was dying and she constantly had a dry mouth and dry skin?"

"I don't want to think about that," Sue mumbled as she placed the bottles on the bed.

"Just *look*," Julia said. "What do you see?"

Sue looked down at the items in front of her. It took her a moment to piece together what Julia had only just figured out, but when she did, her eyes opened, and her jaw loosened.

"He was *bald*," Sue whispered. "And *ghostly* white."

"He had cancer," Julia whispered back, taking in the items again. "He was *dying*. That's why he signed over his castle when he did. That's why he was divorcing Mary. He wanted to hand Seirbigh Castle down to a McLaughlin, not his fourth stand-in wife. Charlotte said the silver in the drawing room had been passed down three generations. Gran said the family bought this place in the nineteen-thirties."

"Why Charlotte?" Sue asked. "Surely Rory would be the most obvious choice. He's oldest, and he's a man."

"Charlotte wanted it, and that mattered to Henry," Julia whispered as she picked up the card. "*'Get well soon, mate. Andrew'*, brief, but he *was* part of the family according to Charlotte."

"What does all of this mean?" Sue asked as she walked over to the door and stood exactly where the murderer would have been standing. "She would have been *right* here when she shot her father."

Sue held an invisible rifle, and shot it, her shoulder motioning the pushback that would have caused Charlotte's bruise. Julia's eyes opened wide, and she suddenly realised how wrong she had gotten everything.

"Because *she* didn't," Julia said as she stuffed the items back in the drawer. "We need to go. It's nearly time."

"*What*? I thought you said she murdered her father and then Mary to clean up the transfer of the castle?"

"I was wrong," Julia said with a heavy shake of her head. "I know who killed Henry, even if I don't know how they managed to get out of here without being seen."

Julia straightened out the sheets, flicked off the bathroom light, and then the desk lamp. She hurried back to the door, but her heart stopped when she heard the doorknob rattling in the dark. She looked at Sue, who was standing inches away from the door with her hand outstretched, but nowhere near. Without another word, she dragged Sue into the walk-in closet and carefully closed the door just as the bedroom door opened and light flooded in from the hall.

Pressing her finger against her lips, Julia stared through the slats in the door as a shadowy figure stepped into the bedroom, closing the door behind them. She was sure the pounding of her heart would give them away, even if she were barely breathing. In the faint light of the moon, she noticed the figure walk over to the desk. They flicked through the papers before they began screwing up each of them and tossing them into the bin. They peeked through the drapes, and in the silver streak of the moonlight, Julia saw the long and flowing auburn hair.

Charlotte opened a bag and pulled out a variety of different items and laid them on the desk. When she was finished, she began throwing something from a bottle around the room. Before Julia could try and figure out what it was, she smelt the petrol, her hand clenching her nose and mouth.

A match crunched across a piece of sandpaper, and a flame illuminated her soft pale face. She looked down blankly at the bin before dropping the flame. It landed on the soaked paper and immediately engulfed itself. Charlotte stared down into the flickering yellow light for a moment before turning on her heels, tossing the empty petrol bottle on the bed, and walking out of the bedroom.

The second she heard the door close, Julia burst out of the closet and ran into the bathroom. She looked around for something to fill with water, landing on a copper bedpan, which was attached to the wall like a piece of art. She yanked it off and instantly filled it. With the pan of water, she ran back into the bedroom as the flames started to lick at the drapes. She tossed the water, and with a sizzle, darkness swallowed the room again.

"What the -," she heard Sue cry, followed by the screeching of coat hangers, and a heavy thud.

Julia dropped the bedpan with a clang and ran over to the closet. Through the dim light, she could just make out the shape of Sue on the floor. It took Julia a moment to realise what was wrong with where Sue was placed in the pile of clothes until she realised she was too far back.

"*Another* secret door," Julia exclaimed as she helped Sue up off the floor. "Oh, Sue, you're a *genius*! That's how they got away."

"I didn't do anything," Sue cried as she accepted Julia's hand. "I tripped over the train of my dress. Maybe you're right about heels being dangerous."

Julia pushed back the clothes and they both stood side by side looking beyond the secret wooden panel and down into the dark winding stone staircase. A cold draft licked at their faces as they clung to each other, neither of them saying a word.

"Shall we see where it leads?" Sue whispered, her voice shaking. "You go first."

"I think I know where it leads," Julia whispered back. "C'mon, we have a dinner to attend."

"Are you joking?" Sue cried as they both stepped out of the closet. "That *madwoman* just tried to set fire to us!"

"She didn't know we were in here," Julia said as she walked over to the desk and pulled back the drapes. "*Here,* look at this."

The items Charlotte had put on the desk were a whisky decanter, a crystal tumbler, an old mobile phone, and a pair of wire cutters.

"I don't get it," Sue mumbled as she squinted into the

dark. "It's just random stuff."

"No, it points to one person," Julia said as she pressed a button on the phone to light up the screen. "Andrew McCracken. *Look*, a picture of the castle as the background wallpaper. Andrew loves this place more than anybody, even if he wouldn't admit it. Charlotte is trying to frame him for burning it down."

"Why would she want to do that?" Sue asked, shaking her head. "I thought Charlotte loved this place?"

"Charlotte *wanted* this place," Julia corrected her. "Now that she's got it, she can do what she wants with it."

"Like burning it to the ground?" Sue mumbled as she rested the back of her hand on her forehead. "I feel dizzy."

"It's the petrol fumes," Julia said. "We should get out of here. Gran will be wondering where we are."

"Julia," Sue said, grabbing her hand. "Remember that thing I wanted to tell you before we came to Scotland. God, it feels so long ago now."

"You're choosing *right now* to tell me?"

Sue stumbled back a little and reached out for Julia. She rested her hand on her stomach as she inhaled deeply.

"*Sue?*" Julia said as she dragged her through to the dark bathroom. "What's wrong?"

Julia flicked on the light, and Sue perched on the edge of the white freestanding bathtub. Sue's dress ruffled up, collecting around her stomach. She went to smooth it down, but the dress didn't entirely flatten under her hand.

"My life flashed before my eyes when I saw those flames," Sue whispered as she looked down at her stomach. "If we had died then, I couldn't have lived with myself for not telling you."

"*You're pregnant,*" Julia mumbled for the second time

that day.

Sue nodded, tears collecting in the corner of her eyes as a smile spread from cheek to cheek.

"I wanted to tell you, I just didn't know how," Sue said with a laugh as she burst into tears. "You know me and Neil have been trying for years, and I didn't want to jinx it. It's only early days, but I have the tiniest bump, and it's going to start showing soon."

Julia wrapped her hands around Sue and pulled her into the tightest hug of their lives. She felt their heartbeats sync up with the life between them, the emotion of it overwhelming her.

"That's amazing," Julia whispered into her sister's ear. "I'm so happy for you. I love you."

"I love you too, *Auntie* Julia."

They both laughed for a moment before pulling away from the hug. They wiped their mascara streaks with tissue paper, before joining hands and walking back through the bedroom with their hands over their mouths and noses.

"A baby is the beginning of all things," Julia said as they walked back towards Henry's door. "Not just for you."

"*Huh?*"

"I'll explain on the way," Julia said as they slipped out into the hall. "Can I borrow your phone first? I need to make a call."

CHAPTER 14

Julia, Dot, and Sue were sat on one side of the table, with the four new guests on the other side, flickering candles and mountains of food separating them. Julia made sure to sit right in the middle so that she was directly between Charlotte and Rory, both of whom kept glancing awkwardly at the ornate doors every time they opened.

Julia, on the other hand, found herself checking the bookcase where she now knew the peephole was, hoping her hastily made plan had come together in time. After a starter of tomato soup and a full roast dinner for the main course, her stomach was almost as full as her mind.

"This is all very delicious," Dot remarked to Charlotte,

who was sitting right by her. "It's been too long since I've had a really good three-course meal."

"*Four* courses," Charlotte corrected her. "Well, that's if you count the cheeseboard and wine at the end, which *I* do."

Charlotte smiled politely before taking a sip of her wine. Her eyes darted to Julia, but they didn't stay for long before landing on her brother. They both shared a small grin for a moment, before glancing to the doors in unison.

The waiters, including Blair, hurried in to clear the table before the dessert was served. Blair appeared to be still ignoring Julia, but that could have been because she was rushed off her feet trying to prepare and serve nine people four courses, even if she did have help.

"I'd like to make a toast," Charlotte exclaimed as she tapped her fork against her wine glass. "As you all know, this week has been testing, to say the least. Our family has been to hell and back, but sometimes you need to go to hell to realise what is important to you."

Julia and Sue rolled their eyes at each other, while the guests across the table seemed to be lapping it up. One of the women even dabbed at the corner of her eye with a napkin.

"Seirbigh Castle will fight to see another day," Charlotte said, raising her glass in the air. "*To Seirbigh*."

"And to Seirbigh's *new* owner," Rory said with a wink as he tipped his glass in his sister's direction. "*Cheers*."

Charlotte returned the wink as she tipped her glass back to him. Julia sipped her wine, wondering if their behaviour was only obvious to her because she had been the one to put out the fire.

"*When?*" Sue whispered quietly into Julia's ear as the

conversation started up again around the table.

"*Soon,*" she replied, leaning in. "We're waiting for two more guests."

Sue nodded and began tearing up the edges of her napkin, something she had done since she was a child whenever she was nervous. Julia was glad she was the only one who knew this, or else it would be a giveaway sign of what was to come.

"I think you're all going to enjoy the Cranachan for dessert," Charlotte exclaimed loudly, her Scottish accent rolling the '*r*'. "It's a traditional dessert made from whipped cream, whisky, honey, and fresh raspberries, with toasted whisky-soaked oats sprinkled on top. *Ah*, here it is!"

At that moment, the doors opened again, and they all turned to see Blair pushing one of her trolleys into the room with nine of the desserts in small glass bowls on top. Through the open door, Julia caught a glimpse of Benjamin talking with Andrew in the hallway. Her stomach flipped, and she realised her time had come.

Blair started serving the desserts with Rory, before making her way down the table. When she put Julia's on the plate, she was sure it was hastier than the others. She reached Charlotte, and her hands began to visibly shake as she lifted the dessert from the trolley. As though in slow motion, it slipped from her fingers and landed with a splat in Charlotte's lap. A gasp shuddered across the table as she jumped up and recoiled in horror, cream and oats staining her black and tartan dress. She turned to Blair and raised her hand above her head, ready to strike the child down. Blair cowered like a puppy about to be punished, but Charlotte dropped her hand and forced a smile.

"Easy mistake," she said through a strained laugh as she

picked up a napkin and began to dab at the dress. "I wasn't that hungry anyway."

Despite Charlotte's backtrack, it didn't stop Blair bursting into tears. She clutched her mouth, her eyes wide as she watched Charlotte attempt to wipe her dress clean. Charlotte struggled to laugh it off, but the poor girl's eyes were filled with such obvious fear, it sent a cold shiver running through the room.

A small yelp forced through her fingers as the tears rolled down her face, causing Benjamin to run into the room. He wrapped his hands around his sister's arm, but she didn't move, nor did she look away from the stain on Charlotte's dress.

"What's wrong with her?" one of the women asked.

"She's in shock," Julia said, standing up and sitting Blair in her seat. "Blair, just *breathe*. It's not good for you to get worked up."

Blair's eyes met Julia's, and she dropped her hand, nodding her head as she forced back the tears. Julia recognised that fear. She had seen it in her sister only an hour ago in Henry's bedroom.

"Honestly, it's *fine!*" Charlotte called out jovially. "I wasn't going to hit her. It was just a reaction."

From the looks of the faces on the guests, it was obvious they were no longer lapping up Charlotte's façade. Julia took this moment, turning to face Charlotte with a stern look in her eyes.

"I wouldn't put it past you to hit a *pregnant* woman, Charlotte," Julia called out, turning back to Blair as she did. "I'm sorry, Blair, but your secret isn't as safe as you thought."

Charlotte shuffled uncomfortably in her chair and

tossed her long hair over her shoulder. The edge of her bruise peeked out ever so slightly from the edge of her dress.

"What are you talking about?" Charlotte demanded. "I've had quite enough of your comments! You didn't even *pay* for this trip!"

"You know full well what I'm talking about, Charlotte," Julia said confidently, forcing her shaky voice to steady. "I've put it together, even if nobody else has yet. I overheard you talking with Andrew. You wanted to get rid of Blair, but you didn't want to fire her because she is pregnant and that could reflect badly on you. Of course, none of that matters now, especially after what you *did* tonight."

Andrew entered the drawing room at the mention of his name, lingering by the doors. Charlotte met his eyes, and behind her faux-confused smile, her eyes were filled with pure venom.

"This woman is *insane*, I can assure you," she said to the other guests, who were all staring intently at Julia.

"I've put out your little fire," Julia said as she begun to pace the room, glancing at the peephole. "At first I couldn't figure out why you would want Andrew back here, especially when you already had a perfectly good groundskeeper, but then it struck me. You didn't care about Andrew, but you knew what he cared about. You knew he loved this castle, and that was all he had. After your father cold-heartedly sacked him, Andrew would have done anything to get his job back, even if he pretended he didn't want it anymore. Of course, you offered him more than his job to do what he did. You had to. Even the most desperate man wouldn't do what he did for the sake of a job. What did you offer him? *Money*? A slice of the castle? Whatever is was, Andrew, I doubt she would have paid you."

"I honestly have no idea what you're talking about," Charlotte cried, laughing as blood rushed to her cheeks. "I've heard quite *enough* of this!"

"You told Andrew to get rid of Blair, no matter what the cost," Julia said, turning to look at the chef as she watched, just as confused as the guests. "But I guess you also told him to do the same to Mary. She was the only thing standing between you and owning this castle after your father's death."

"I *didn't* kill her," Andrew protested.

"I know you didn't," Julia said, dropping her eyes as sorrow swept over her. "But you're an accessory to all of this. I couldn't quite figure it out, but when I saw Charlotte tossing petrol around her father's bedroom tonight, it clicked. She sent you to burn the remains of Mary's car straight after she crashed so evidence of tampering couldn't be seen. There was something quite peculiar about the timing of Mary's death. Why let her come back to work and think everything was fine? Why send her away on *that* morning? Why *that* early? It's because you wanted a reason, and witnesses, wasn't it Rory?"

Rory suddenly sat up in his seat, after having been watching the whole thing unfold with mild interest. "What did you just say?"

"The fog provided you with a perfect cover-up for cutting the woman's brakes. We all saw her speed off that morning, but that's what you wanted. You made a public scene so that we all saw her drive off. You waited until four new guests checked in, and I wouldn't be surprised if they were all in the corner bedrooms just so they could see. Even the police believed it was an accident, but why wouldn't they? By the time she was found, her car was nothing more than a burnt-out shell. Petrol is quite a clever move, I must admit. It's not like the car wasn't full of it in the first place."

"It *wasn't* my idea!" Andrew blurted out. "*She* made me. She said if I didn't, I'd never work again! She was offering me half of this castle!"

"Oh, Andrew," Julia said, turning back to the groundskeeper once more. "You should never have believed her. Henry signed over the deeds to this castle well over a month ago, and I doubt Charlotte was just going to hand half of that over to you. While my sister and I were looking for evidence to pin Henry's death on Charlotte, we witnessed her putting the whisky decanter and tumbler on Henry's desk, which was stained with your DNA from your various secret meetings in the drawing room. She also had your mobile phone, and the wire cutters that I suspect Rory used on Mary's brakes."

Andrew suddenly patted down his pockets and looked desperately to Charlotte. She picked up her glass of wine and took a sip, unable to look anyone in the eye but her brother.

"I only told Rory to get rid of her," Charlotte said bitterly. "I didn't expect him to go so far. I had to clean his mess up somehow. For a lawyer, you sure are stupid, big brother. I didn't kill my father, though. That's where you are wrong."

"I believe that," Julia said. "Why would you want to? He was dying anyway, wasn't he? The man had *cancer*. It was only a matter of time. He decided to get rid of Mary so he could leave the castle to you, the only heir who wanted it. My guess is he was a proud man, and you were the only one to carry on his legacy, even if he could barely look at you. Of course, when you secretly took over, you realised that clueless Mary had run the business into the ground, and the castle would be worth more to you through the insurance pay-outs, which I suspect is what you and Rory have been up to these last couple of days. Making sure everything was watertight just in case you needed to resort to that. I can't imagine selling a failing castle would be very easy, so the next logical step is to burn it to the ground and make it look like Andrew did it in a deranged act of revenge against your family. That's why you wanted him back here so badly, to be your scapegoat. Who were the police going to believe? A grieving businesswoman, or a disgraced drunk? You weren't happy enough just using the man as your puppet, you wanted to frame him for this and run off into the sunset with the money before any of this could catch up with you."

Charlotte furiously sipped her wine, her nostrils flared. Julia expected her to try and defend herself, but she didn't say a word. All eyes looked expectantly to Julia to fill in the other pieces of the puzzle.

"Of course, you're not the *only* heir to your father's castle," Julia said. "You had competition."

"I never wanted this place!" Rory exclaimed. "It's crumbling beneath us!"

"I wasn't talking about *you*," Julia said with a heavy exhale. "Blair, who is the father of your baby?"

Blair shook her head and looked down at her fingers, which were frantically knotting around her apron. Julia turned back to Charlotte, who subtly arched a brow as she waited to hear what else Julia had to say.

"I don't think you knew Blair was pregnant with your father's child until recently, but when you found out, you knew she was carrying your baby brother or sister," Julia said, turning back to Blair and resting a hand on her shaking shoulder. "You wanted to get rid of the girl so she wouldn't cause any problems to your plan, but when you realised that wouldn't work, you decided to step things up a notch. I suppose your meeting with Andrew this afternoon influenced your decision to resort to plan B."

"I told her I wasn't gonna kill a lassie," Andrew said, pointing harshly at Charlotte. "'Specially one with a bairn in her tummy!"

"I believe you," Julia said. "I don't think you're a bad man, Andrew, I just think Charlotte is a very persuasive woman. She was raised without a real mother, instead having to settle for a revolving cast of stepmothers, and a father who couldn't look at her because she looked too much like the only woman he loved. You said it yourself how much they looked alike. I'm not surprised you turned out as cold and heartless as you did, Charlotte. With Henry McLaughlin as a father, it was almost to be expected."

Charlotte sucked her cheeks into her mouth before rolling her eyes and leaning back in her chair.

"You're not the first, y'know," Charlotte said to Blair, sounding more authentic than Julia had heard her. "He's been knocking girls up since as long as I can remember. He paid them off or convinced them to get rid of the baby, but you were stubborn, or he was getting soft in his dying days."

Blair rested her hand on her stomach, and out of the corner of her eye, Julia noticed Sue doing the same. She swallowed the lump in her throat and inhaled deeply.

"I *thought* you shot your father, Charlotte," Julia said. "But when I found out *when* Seirbigh Castle became yours, I realised there was no need for you to be that reckless.

Maybe you would have if it hadn't been for the cancer, but you didn't."

"So who did?" Charlotte asked, sitting up and checking her manicure. "I've been *dying* to know since it happened. Let us in on your secrets, Julia, since you seem to know *everything*."

Julia walked over to Charlotte and rested her hand on her right shoulder. She squeezed hard, and Charlotte let out a small yelp before slapping Julia's hand away.

"A hunting injury," Julia exclaimed as she walked around the table, glancing to Blair as she did. "People don't realise the power a gun can have. They can cause quite the painful injury if you don't know what you're doing."

Julia walked back to where she had been sitting. She picked up her wine glass and took a sip, making sure to dampen the sides as she did.

"Can you hold this, Benjamin?" Julia asked.

Benjamin reached out with his left hand. He awkwardly gripped the wine glass, but it slipped from his fingers and smashed against the wooden floor. He looked down to it, his face burning bright red.

"Some people are quite ambidextrous," Julia said quietly. "You are *not* one of those people, Benjamin."

"Ben?" Blair whispered, looking up at her brother.

"He said it himself. Charlotte was a terrible hunter, hence her injury from a simple rifle. You had never fired a gun before coming here, had you Ben? You had to learn your technique on the internet, and I don't doubt you picked it up quite well, which is why you decided to shoot Henry, rather than smother him in his sleep, or slip some poison into his food. You didn't quite realise how much more powerful a shotgun was over a rifle, which is why you have been using your left hand this entire time. The awkward handshake, dropping the magazine, chopping wood one-handed, throwing the screwdriver badly, dropping this wine glass. You're *right*-handed, not left-handed, but you've been trying not to use your right hand because of the pain in your shoulder. If a simple rifle can create a bruise as large as Charlotte's was, what did Henry's shotgun, which he made sure to let everyone know was loaded, do to your shoulder? Did it dislocate it?"

Benjamin lifted his left hand awkwardly up to his right shoulder as he stared down at his sister. He mouthed something, before looking up at Julia.

"You would have done the same," Benjamin said to Julia before directing it to the rest of the room. "She is only *nineteen*! *Any* of you would have done the same."

"How did you find out?" Blair asked, both of her hands clutching her tiny stomach.

"I suspect he overheard one of your conversations with Henry. It wasn't like you weren't in his room three times a day serving him his food. Benjamin had a knack for discovering this castle's secret passages, so I don't doubt he found the one leading up to Henry's bedroom from the courtyard. Those types of secret passageways were built to be easily accessed in case of emergencies, which was why Henry's was in his closet. You snuck up there to see where it led, and you overheard a conversation between Blair and Henry about their baby. You decided then you were going to kill the man, you were just waiting for your moment. You snuck into his bedroom when he wasn't there, took the gun from his wall, and you waited for him to return. You shot him, and then you ran back down the passage, disposed of the gun, no doubt in the loch, and you carried on with your day. Nobody knew you knew about the network of secret passages here. Why would anybody ever suspect the new groundskeeper?"

"He was *threatening* her!" Benjamin cried. "He told her if she didn't get rid of the baby, he would make her regret ever being born!"

"Blair got you this job here, so she wasn't going to go through this alone," Julia said, smiling down at Blair. "She was going to keep her baby regardless. She wanted to have the same relationship with her child as your mother did with you. It wasn't like Henry was going to be around for much longer. You hoped if you concealed your pregnancy for long enough, nobody would ever figure out who the father was, and you could save as much money as possible. Even if you had known the castle was up for grabs, I don't think you would have taken it. Out of all the people who lived in this castle, you were the only one who wanted to do the right thing."

Benjamin dropped to his knees and grabbed both of Blair's hands in his. He tried to look at her, but she couldn't bring herself to return his gaze. Julia's heart broke for them both. She understood why Benjamin did what he did, and if it was her and Sue in their situation, she wasn't sure if she could say she wouldn't have done the same.

"I didn't know he was dying," Benjamin said as he started to cry. "I'm so sorry, Blair."

"Why are you sorry?" Charlotte cried. "You did us all a favour. Is this over yet? I'm exhausted."

"It's over, Charlotte," Julia said before turning to the bookcase. "*DI Fletcher*, you have to give the door a *good push*!"

The bookcase creaked open and DI Fletcher, followed

by five uniformed officers walked into the room, all of them sharing the same dumbfounded look as they blinked into the light.

When Charlotte saw the uniformed officers, she suddenly jumped up from the chair and made for the door, but to everyone's surprise, Andrew stepped in her way and grabbed hold of her.

"If I'm going down, *yer* coming wi' me, lassie," he snarled through gritted teeth. "I've hated yer guts since the day you were born."

DI Fletcher handcuffed Benjamin, while the other officers advanced on Andrew, Charlotte, and Rory. Rory instantly started spouting about being a lawyer and how he was going make them all lose their jobs. Charlotte thrashed and screamed against Andrew, but despite everything, he did the right thing and held her securely until she was handcuffed. He immediately offered his hands for cuffing.

When they were all taken away, Julia let out a relieved sigh and turned her attention back to the table. Dot gulped down her wine, and then Charlotte's leftovers, before picking up her spoon to dig into her Cranachan.

"No point wasting good dessert," Dot announced, giving the rest of the guests an encouraging nod to join her. "I must say, the spa really *is* rather excellent, because I didn't notice any of this going on. Top notch work again, Julia, my love."

Julia collapsed into Rory's chair and reached across the table to grab Sue's hand. They both looked at their gran as she wolfed down her dessert, and all they could do was laugh.

* * *

AS THE OFFICERS WORKED THEIR WAY around the drawing room to take official statements of what everybody had heard, Julia hung back near the window, sitting in Charlotte's armchair. She stared out at the loch, wondering what would become of the castle that had seen so much death and destruction in the last week.

"I owe you an apology," a soft voice came from behind her.

DI Fletcher sat in the armchair next to her and joined her in looking out at the dark loch. In the reflection of the glass, she caught him glancing at her.

"It's not needed," Julia said, shaking her hands dismissively.

"You have a brilliant mind," he said, his tone heartfelt. "I couldn't piece any of that together. The police force needs more people like you."

"I just keep an ear to the ground and an eye on the shadows," Julia said with a small shrug. "I'm happy being a baker."

"Well, you must be an amazing baker," he said as he stood up. "Your man back home is pretty lucky. Now I can see why he couldn't resist letting you run his investigation. You're *quite* the force to be reckoned with, Miss South."

"He's not too bad himself," Julia said with a wink. "Do you mind helping me up, Detective Inspector? I can barely move in this dress."

She held out a hand, and he yanked her up. She pulled down the ruffles in her dress, surprised to see him holding out a hand for her to shake.

"I promise I'm actually left-handed," he said playfully as he glanced down at his open palm. "Drive safely back home."

They parted ways, and Julia was happy she had sensed the mutual respect between them. She felt bad for assuming he couldn't do his job because of his age, but she knew it had taken some guts to drop everything on her request and follow her down a secret passageway to wait for a confession that might or might not happen at the end of a long meal.

"So, let me get this straight," Sue said as she appeared behind Julia and rested her chin on her shoulder. "Charlotte told Rory to get rid of Mary, which he took to mean '*kill Mary*', which he did willingly. She also told Andrew to destroy the evidence of her brother's crime, and he did that willingly too. Then, Benjamin killed Henry, completely unrelated to the rest of the family, because Henry had gotten Blair pregnant, but he was dying of cancer anyway so he should have just waited and none of this would have happened?"

"I think that's about right," Julia said with a nod. "Although, you missed out how great the spa was."

They both looked back to their gran again and chuckled as she grabbed the dessert across the table from her and started her third helping of Cranachan as she gave her statement, no doubt embellished with dramatic twists that never happened and recommendations for great wrap treatments and cucumber facials.

"What now?" Sue asked, linking her arm with Julia's.

"We go to bed," Julia said, letting out a small yawn. "We have a long drive home tomorrow. Are you going to tell her?"

Sue rested her hand on her stomach as they walked out of the drawing room and towards the entrance hall.

"*Soon*," she said. "I think I'm enjoying this being our

secret for now. It's just like being kids again."

"But with tighter dresses and more murder."

They made their way up to their bedroom, and after Sue peeled the dress off Julia, she wiped off the remnants of her red lipstick and collapsed onto her bed, ready to dream of nothing else other than what was waiting for her back in Peridale.

CHAPTER 15

J ulia didn't set an alarm for the next morning, but she still rose with the sunrise, as did Sue and Dot. It wasn't long before they were fully packed and loading their mountain of luggage back into her tiny car.

"Do we need to check out?" Dot asked, looking back at the grand castle entrance.

"There's nobody to check out with," Sue reminded her. "The entire family has gone. Just like that."

"Probably for the best," Dot said airily with a shrug. "They were *all* pretty awful."

Julia and Sue both gave each other the look they did whenever their gran said something outrageous. One of them usually attempted to correct her so she could see why what she had said was inappropriate, but it seemed neither of them actually disagreed with their gran, even if they wouldn't have said it out loud themselves.

After forcing the car boot shut, and squashing the hatbox Sue still hadn't had a chance to open, Julia turned back to the castle and inhaled the cool, crystal clear heather-scented air once more. As though the loch knew what had happened, the skies were vibrant and cloudless, and the water was calm. In the distance, she thought she saw a deer sprinting across the horizon, but it could have been her mind playing tricks on her. Despite everything, it was still a beautiful place.

"Get the car started," Julia said, tossing her keys to Sue. "I have something I need to do."

Sue nodded her understanding and climbed into the car, leaving Julia to head back into the castle. She wasn't entirely sure where she would find Blair, but she decided the kitchen was the best place to start. When she pushed on the door, she saw the young girl sitting at the counter, her mousy hair down for the first time, and in much more casual clothes.

Blair looked up at her with a smile, letting Julia know there were no hard feelings. Julia climbed into the seat next to her, and they sat in silence for a moment.

"I'm sorry about your brother," Julia started.

"I'm sorry I ever asked him to come here," Blair said with a small laugh. "I was just so lonely and scared. Henry was a persuasive man. I never should have been so stupid."

"None of this is your fault," Julia whispered, nudging Blair with her shoulder. "*You're* the victim in all of this, but you have something to look forward to. *A new beginning*. I think there are some good lawyers out there who could make a worthy case for you inheriting this castle considering the only other heirs are soon to be serving long prison sentences."

Blair looked around the kitchen, and Julia actually thought she was considering it for a moment. She shook her head and looked down at her stomach, resting her hand on the tiny bump.

"A new beginning," Blair agreed with a nod. "I never belonged here. I'm going home to my mam in Blackpool. She's always wanted grandkids."

"That's a good idea. You're wise for somebody so young."

"Not wise enough to turn and run the first time Henry tried it on," Blair said softly. "Do you know what Seirbigh means in ancient Gaelic? It literally translates to doom. This is *Doom Castle*. I was doomed from the second I arrived here. It sucks you in with the beautiful views, but nothing good happens between these walls. You've set it free, Julia."

Blair took Julia by surprise and hugged her. When she let go, Julia could feel the tears welling up, but she forced them down.

"If you're ever near Peridale, pop into the cafe and say hello," Julia said, before looking at her stomach. "Both of you."

"I promise we will," Blair said with a nod. "I think I should go and pack. I don't suppose you're driving past Blackpool, are you?"

Julia nodded and held her arm out for Blair. They set off up the castle stairs together, both of them more than ready to go home.

* * *

AFTER DROPPING BLAIR OFF WITH HER mother, who was more than overjoyed at her daughter's surprise return, they set off towards Peridale leaving them to have a much needed conversation.

They arrived in Peridale just after six in the evening as the sun started to wane in the sky. As Julia drove through the village, she made sure to slow down and really soak up every tiny detail. Just seeing her café, even if it was closed, gave her butterflies.

She dropped Sue off with her gran. Just like with Blair and her mother, they also needed to have a serious conversation. Dot invited her in for a cup of tea, but she declined in favour of heading straight home.

When she pulled up behind Barker's car, she could barely contain her smile as she killed the engine. She inhaled, relieved to smell manure from the surrounding fields, and not heather. She grabbed her single bag from the boot and walked around Barker's car, which was now sporting a giant dent where the registration plate should have been.

Using her key, she unlocked the front door, dropped her bag on the doorstep, closed her eyes, and smiled. She was home.

She followed the sound of music and laughter into the kitchen. She walked in, surprised to see Barker and Jessie completely covered in flour.

"*Julia!*" Barker exclaimed. "You're home!"

"I am," she chuckled. "*Dare* I ask?"

"We're having a food fight," Jessie said with a shrug.

"We were trying to bake you a cake."

"But *you* said I always burn cakes."

"So she dumped a bag of flour on my head," Barker

said, dusting the flour off his hair. "And then I tossed the batter at her, and I guess – *welcome home!*"

Julia didn't care about the mess. She walked between them, taking them into an arm each. Jessie eventually wriggled free, leaving Julia to wrap her arms fully around Barker's waist. He kissed the top of her head, before lifting up her chin with his forefinger to kiss her softly on the lips. Time suddenly stopped, and everything that had happened over the past week no longer mattered.

"So, how was it?" Barker asked. "Did anything exciting happen?"

"Nope," Julia said, as she dusted the flour off her front. "It was actually quite boring. *Uneventful,* you might say."

Barker stared at her suspiciously, but he didn't question her. He wrapped his hand around her shoulder, and they both watched as Jessie sat down at the counter, her eyes glued to her tablet. Mowgli crawled in through the open kitchen window and nudged Julia's arm to let her know he was happy she had returned, before looking at the flour and sauntering straight back out into the garden.

"We should go away sometime soon," Barker suggested as he rested his head on hers. "Just you and me."

"I'm *exactly* where I want to be right now," she said, smiling at Jessie who looked peculiarly up from her tablet. "Here, with you two."

"Did you bump your head in Scotland?" Jessie mumbled as she tapped on her screen. "I heard too much fresh air can actually be bad for you."

Julia laughed as she picked up the kettle. Staring out into the garden, she flipped open the lid and began to fill it with water. She caught Barker's eye in the reflection of the glass, and they smiled at each other. As Barker began to sweep up the mess, and Jessie ignored them both in favour of her new gadget, Julia's mind wandered to her sister's pregnancy. Without realising she was doing it, her hand rested carefully on her stomach as the kettle overflowed, and for the first time in a long time, she began to wonder if that would be her one day.

ESPRESSO AND EVIL

BOOK 6

CHAPTER 1

"Cheap, sugar-filled *nonsense!*" Dot exclaimed, turning to face the room as she crushed a Happy Bean coffee cup in her fist. "This is *not* what Peridale is about."

There was a murmur of agreement among the dozen people in the village hall. Barker squeezed Julia's hand reassuringly as they listened from the front seats.

"We *cannot* let these corporate bullies push us around!" Dot cried, tossing the cup vehemently to the floor. "We *must* protect our way of life!"

Julia looked around the village hall, glad to see some of the familiar faces she hadn't seen since the new chain coffee shop had sprung up in the village, seemingly overnight.

"You may nod your head *now*, Amy Clark, but you're no better than the rest of them!" Dot pulled a small notepad from the breast pocket of her white blouse, licked her finger, and flicked through the pages until she landed on what she was looking for. "I saw you on Thursday, walking to the library with one of *their* cups in your hand!"

Amy Clark dropped her head and glanced apologetically at Julia. She smiled back to try and let her know it was okay, even if she did feel a little betrayed.

"And *you*, Shilpa Patil!" Dot cried, turning on her heels and extending a finger into the sea of faces as she flicked to the next page. "Don't think I didn't see you sneaking back into the post office with one of *their* sandwiches!"

Shilpa opened her mouth to defend herself before catching Julia's eyes and joining Amy in looking down at the floor.

"Processed *rubbish!*" Dot exclaimed as she tucked the notepad back into her blouse. She began to pace the small village hall as she adjusted the brooch holding her stiff collar in place, her pleated skirt fluttering side to side and her sensible shoes clicking on the polished wooden floor. "Doesn't this village mean *anything* to any of you?"

There was another murmur as all eyes landed on the floor. Julia wasn't sure if it was from remorse or out of fear of what Dot would do if they continued to stare at her.

"It's open a lot later than Julia's café," Father David offered, still in his black robes and dog collar. "I'm usually at the church late in the evenings."

"And it's cheaper," Imogen Carter dared to mumble. "Julia doesn't make chai lattes, and I really like them."

"You only had to ask," Julia said, the hurt evident in her voice. "I would make anything for any of you. You should know that."

They squirmed in their seats, glancing guiltily at each other. Harriet Barnes from the florist mouthed an apology to Julia, which she was grateful for. Julia clenched Barker's hand tightly, turning back to her gran as Dot stared out at the room with crossed arms and pursed lips.

"When that place opened up two weeks ago, you all *swore* you wouldn't desert my granddaughter!" Dot started again, her tone suddenly softer. "But one by one, like sheep being led to slaughter, you've betrayed the only woman in this village who has been there for every single one of you since her café opened! Two years of service, and for what?"

"*Gran*," Julia said with a shake of her head. "That's enough."

"No, she's *right*, Julia!" Jessie, Julia's young apprentice and lodger cried, jumping up from her seat next to her. "You said it yourself! The café's sales have never been so low!"

Julia squirmed uncomfortably in her seat, her cheeks blushing from embarrassment. She had been ignoring that the sales had barely been covering the bills since the coffee shop had opened across the village green, but hearing Jessie say the words aloud only cemented how much trouble her business was in.

"It's not *just* us!" Emily Burns, Julia's closest neighbour called out. "The tourists have been going there too."

"But it's not the tourists who keep the café afloat when it's cold, or raining," Dot said, pinching between her eyes. "It's *you* people. The villagers. Julia's café is the beating heart of Peridale, and *you're* happy to watch it die."

"We came to this meeting, didn't we?" Amy Clark, the elderly organist from the church said, suddenly sitting up, her brows furrowed. "Why else would we be here if we didn't care?"

"Because *she* threatened to cut the heads off my beloved roses!" Emily said, pointing at Dot.

"And she told me she'd start catching the bus to a post office out of the village if I didn't come!" Shilpa said. "I'm a local business too!"

"Do you serve coffee, Shilpa?" Dot asked.

"Well, no, but –"

"Then this meeting isn't about you!" Dot snapped as she began to pace back and forth again. "Do you people want to help, or not?"

"What can we do?" Emily asked.

A devious grin spread across Dot's face. She scurried across the hall to the table at the side of the room, which usually contained refreshments for the different village meetings. Instead of refreshments, there were two large brown cardboard boxes that Julia hadn't noticed until now.

"We *protest*!" Dot announced as she pulled a Stanley knife from her small handbag. "This Saturday!"

Julia's heart sank to the pit of her stomach. She exhaled and looked up at the ceiling, wondering if the last two weeks had been nothing more than a cruel nightmare. When she looked back at Dot as she sliced the knife down the tape holding the box together, she knew it was all too real. She had dreamed of owning a café since she was a little girl, and she could feel that dream decaying crumb by crumb.

"Isn't that illegal?" Amy asked, shifting in her seat. "I'm not going to prison for the sake of a café, no offence, Julia."

Julia shook her head to let her know no offence was taken.

"It's not illegal if we don't block the road, harass people, or stop entry to the building," Barker announced, letting go of Julia's hand to stand up and face the group. "I've already asked a couple of boys at the station to supervise, and they're more than happy to help."

Julia stared curiously at Barker, and then at Jessie. It was clear Dot had already let them in on her plans. Dot pulled a white t-shirt out of the box and let it hang proudly down her front.

"'*Choose Local Coffee*'," Dot announced, reading upside down from the black slogan on the t-shirt. "I got the idea from that campaign George Michael did in the eighties. We wear these on Saturday, and we let people know that there is an *alternative* to that soulless machine! Are you getting all of this, Johnny?"

Johnny Watson, who had been scribbling down everything Dot had just said for an article for *The Peridale Post* looked up and nodded. He adjusted his glasses and returned to his note taking.

"I *foresaw* this would happen!" Evelyn from the B&B announced as she clutched at the glittery brooch holding her purple turban in place, apparently channelling her psychic powers once more. "The cards mentioned a disruption in the village! I should have taken them more *seriously!*"

People looked awkwardly at each other as Evelyn began to hum and rock back and forth with her fingers pressed at her temples. As though to provide a distraction, Barker dragged off his tie and unbuttoned his shirt to reveal that he was already wearing one of the t-shirts. Jessie pulled off her black hoody and stood defiantly next to Barker in her own t-shirt.

"This is *important*," Jessie called out, planting her hands on her hips. "Whether you like it or not, you're all responsible for keeping local businesses open. Who is with us?"

A couple of people mumbled, but nobody immediately stood up. Julia looked out into the sea of faces, wondering if any of them would have come if Dot hadn't threatened them. Emily Burns eventually stood up, dragging Amy Clark up with her. Julia's heart warmed a little.

"Of course, we are with you, Julia," Emily called out, looking encouragingly at the others. "We just didn't realise the harm we were doing."

"I only really drink Moroccan tea, but I'm sure you'll put that on the menu if I give you some more," Evelyn said as she darted up, her purple caftan fluttering dramatically around her. "I'm with you! The cards predicted I would join a cause this week. How *exciting!*"

One by one the people in the room stood up and stepped forwards to collect a t-shirt from Dot. As they passed Julia, they all mumbled their apologies with their t-shirts clenched in their hands.

"Is this a private meeting or can anybody join?" a voice called from the back of the room, turning everyone's heads.

When Julia saw Anthony Kennedy's face, she suddenly felt sick. Jessie stepped forward, her fists clenched by her side, but Barker put out a hand to hold her back.

"You are *not* welcome here," Dot called, pushing through the crowd so that she was face to face with the man who had brought Happy Bean to the village. "*Get out!*"

"'*Choose Local Coffee*'?" Anthony read aloud, a smirk tickling his lips as he ran his fingers through his blow-dried blonde hair. "You realise I am local, don't you? I was born in this village, and I've lived here for sixty-two years!"

Barker wrapped his hand around Julia's again, squeezing harder than ever before. She was unable to look at the man who was single-handily destroying her business.

"You're a *traitor*!" Dot cried, wagging a finger in his face. "This village isn't about franchises and corporations. It's about *real* people. You know how much Julia loves that café!"

"It's not personal," he said, stepping around Dot to look at Julia. "It's *just* business."

Julia avoided Anthony's eyes. She knew the betrayal hurt so bitterly because her gran was right; Anthony did know how much Julia had always wanted to run her own café.

"You were the best man at Julia's father's wedding!" Dot announced, turning back to the crowd to make sure they were listening. "You've known her since the day she was born. This *is* personal."

Julia's stomach squirmed uncomfortably. She wanted nothing more than to retreat to the safety of her cottage and bury her head in some baking to take her away from the stress.

"Julia, love," Anthony called out, stepping around Dot. "It *is* just business!"

Daring to look up, Julia met Anthony's eyes, but she didn't see an ounce of compassion or remorse in his eyes, she just saw the cold and ruthless gaze she had come to know from the man. She looked away, scared she was going to say something she would regret in front of the people who were here to help her.

Anthony laughed coldly and dropped his gaze. He turned on the spot, his Cuban heels squeaking on the polished floor. Before he reached the door, he stopped in his tracks and looked into the crowd. He opened his mouth to speak, before shaking his head and marching out of the village hall as he pulled a packet of cigarettes from his jacket's inside pocket. Julia looked in the direction of what had caught Anthony's attention. She was surprised to see Anthony's teenage son, Gareth Kennedy, among the faces there to support her.

"How do you even know that guy?" Jessie asked. "He's a slime ball."

"He was my father's business partner," Julia said as her heart rate slowed down. "They ran the antique barn together."

Julia swallowed a lump in her throat, knowing he had been much more than that. She had called him Uncle Anthony, even after she had figured out that he wasn't really her uncle. He was as much a part of her childhood memories as her mother and father, or Dot and her sister, Sue.

"Come to *spy*?" Dot asked Gareth, marching towards him in a similar fashion she had his father. "You can get out too!"

"I agree with you," Gareth said, catching Julia's eye. "It's not right what he's done."

Julia didn't know Gareth that well, but she appreciated the support all the same. He was seventeen, the same age as Jessie, and had come to Anthony and his wife, Rosemary, later in life, which had surprised everyone, including Julia. Anthony had never made it a secret that he never had any desire to have children.

Dot pursed her lips at the young boy before throwing him a t-shirt and scurrying back to the front of the group.

Gareth looked down at the shirt in his hands as he chewed the inside of his cheek. There was no denying he was his father's son. Gareth's hair might have been styled a little more modern than his father's blow-dried mullet, but it was still the same golden hue. They also shared the same blue eyes, strong nose and jaw, and broad frame.

"We'll meet at midday on Saturday!" Dot announced, waving her hands to hush the chattering group. "*Spread the word!* We need all of the people we can get."

There was a final murmur of agreement before people filtered out of the room. When they were alone in the village hall, Julia let out a sigh of relief as she sat back in her seat.

"Are you sure this is a good idea?" she asked, looking down at the t-shirt in her hands. "It seems a little extreme."

"You've worked *too* hard for this," Dot said, sitting next to Julia and taking her hand. "This was all you talked about as a little girl. Even when you were in London for all those years, you'd still tell me on the phone how you were desperate to run your own café one day, even if Jerrad didn't care about what you wanted."

Dot suddenly bit her tongue, her eyes widening when she realised what she had said. They both turned to Barker, who looked confused at the pair of them.

"Who's Jerrad?" he asked quickly.

Julia opened her mouth, unsure of what to say. It had been five months since she had met Barker, but the time had never felt right to tell him about her twelve-year marriage. Her cheeks burned brightly as her mind turned to soup.

"*Did I miss it?*" Sue called out as she hurried into the village hall, her hands in the small of her back with her small bump poking out of her blue nurse's uniform. "The traffic was *murde*r!"

An audible sigh of relief left the mouths of Jessie, Dot, and Julia. Glad of the distraction, Julia hurried over and kissed Sue on the cheek before passing her a t-shirt.

"We're protesting," Julia said, glancing at Barker out of the corner of her eyes as he continued to stare suspiciously at her. "On Saturday. How's the shrimp?"

"According to Neil, it's now the size of a lime," Sue said as she rubbed the small, yet definite bump. "He's been reading books in the library, bless him, although it feels more like a melon at the moment. I have my twelve-week scan next week."

The conversation stayed firmly on Sue's pregnancy while they stacked the chairs. As they left the bright lights of the village hall and walked out into the warm summer's evening, it hadn't gone unnoticed by Julia that Barker was unusually silent.

"Don't worry, Julia," Dot said, squeezing Julia's shoulders as she looked across the village green at her dark café. "We'll fix this."

She smiled and nodded, turning her attention to the coffee shop, which was still illuminating the village green. Half a dozen people were lining up at the counter to get their drinks, some of them clutching white t-shirts in their hands.

Sue climbed into her car, and Dot hurried across the village green towards her cottage, leaving the three of them standing outside the village hall. Julia glanced at her aqua blue Ford Anglia, which was still parked next to her café. She pulled her keys from her pocket and turned to Barker, expecting him to repeat his question from earlier.

"Let's get a takeaway," Barker said, setting off towards Julia's car. "I'm starving."

"I want Indian," Jessie said, nudging Barker in the ribs with her elbow. "You picked last time. Can I drive home, Julia?"

"You failed your test!" Barker said with a chuckle as he climbed into the passenger seat of the car. "You almost killed that woman!"

"She was faking it," Jessie mumbled with a roll of her eyes as she sat in the back seat. "I *barely* hit her."

Julia pushed her key into the ignition. Her heart fluttered as she breathed freely, glad he had chosen not to push the subject at that moment. She knew she had to tell Barker the truth about her divorce eventually, but the longer she left it, the harder she knew it would be to reveal the only thing she had been keeping from him.

As she drove past Happy Bean, she dared to throw a glance in its direction. Her heart skipped a beat when she spotted Anthony staring out at them in the dark, his eyes trained on her car. A cold shudder ran down her spine. Even though she was hopeful, it felt like it was going to take more than a protest to turn her fortunes around.

CHAPTER 2

J ulia rose with the sun on Saturday morning. She had nervously baked four different cakes and over fifty cupcakes before Jessie's alarm rang, which she subsequently ignored for almost ten minutes before finally dragging herself out of bed. She grunted at Julia as she stumbled into the bathroom, the hood of her black dressing gown pulled low over her scruffy hair and half-closed eyes.

While Jessie showered, Julia made two cups of peppermint and liquorice tea. It had become a ritual for them to drink Julia's favourite tea with breakfast as they discussed the day ahead, even if Jessie never finished a full cup. Julia's hands were shaking with nerves, but she wanted to keep things as normal as possible for the both of them, even if the sky was falling in.

She sipped the tea, and its familiar sweetness soothed her. Mowgli, her grey Maine Coon, squeezed through the open kitchen window and padded across the counter towards her, leaving behind a trail of muddy paw prints and bringing in the scent of lavender from the garden. He nudged her, before jumping down to his bowl and loudly meowing. She grabbed a pouch of food from Mowgli's cupboard and squeezed half of the meat into his bowl. A knock at the door startled them both.

Julia looked up at the cat clock above her fridge with its swinging tail and darting eyes. It was only a little after seven. She scratched the top of Mowgli's head before walking down the hallway and to the front door.

Through the frosted glass, she saw a tall, broad man. The lack of a red jacket let her know it was probably a little early for the postman. She pulled her soft dressing gown across her pink silk pyjamas, tucked her curly hair behind her ears, and unlocked the door.

"*Dad*?" she said, the surprise loud in her voice. "What are doing here?"

Julia's father, Brian, smiled awkwardly down at her as he glanced back at his car, which he had parked behind her own. His expensive vehicle only served to highlight how dated her vintage wheels were.

"Your gran called," he said, reminding Julia that he rarely referred to her as '*mother*'. "She told me what was happening with Anthony."

"*Oh*," Julia mumbled, unsure of what to say. "Do you want to come in?"

He nodded, so she stepped to the side to let him into

her cottage. He wiped his feet on the doormat as he looked around the house he had never visited before, despite Julia having been living back in Peridale for well over two years now.

"You've got a nice place," he said with a nervous laugh as he closed the door behind him. "Your mother would have loved this."

Julia's stomach squirmed at the mention of her mother, but she smiled all the same. Her relationship with her father had improved in recent months, but it didn't erase their years of being practically estranged after her mother's death all those years ago.

"How's Katie?" Julia asked as she led her father through to the kitchen, avoiding referring to her father's wife as her 'step-mother'. "Tea?"

"Yes, please," he said as he took a seat in one of the stools at the counter, his head almost touching the low-beamed ceiling. "She's doing really well. Recovered from all of that business with her brother."

Julia refilled the kettle. It felt like a lifetime ago that Katie's brother, Charles, had been murdered during a garden party at their home. He had been protesting Katie's plans to turn their family manor into a spa, and it had been Julia who had uncovered the culprit after falsely accusing Katie of her brother's murder. Months had passed, and spring had turned to summer, but Julia hadn't seen her father, or Katie since, which made his appearance at her cottage feel stranger.

"I was surprised to hear from your gran," he said as she handed him a cup of tea. "Did you put sugar in this?"

"You've always taken two sugars."

"Katie's got me on no-sugar," he said with an

apologetic shrug. "Thinks I'm at risk of diabetes because of my age."

Julia took back the cup and tossed it down the drain, not needing another reminder that her father was sixty-four, and his wife was thirty-seven, just like Julia. She quickly remade the tea before leaning against the sink with her own tea.

"You know I don't get into the village much, so I was surprised to hear what Anthony had done," he said after taking a sip of the hot tea. "The rumour mill doesn't seem to make its way up to Peridale Manor. I wanted to show my support and let you know that I'm here for you."

Jessie appeared in the bathroom doorway, a towel tucked under her armpits with her wet hair hanging over her face. Brian turned in his seat, causing Jessie to scurry off to her bedroom.

"Still got the lodger?" he asked as he turned back.

"She's more than that," Julia said, her tone sharper than she intended. "Jessie is like family to me."

Brian nodded and took another sip of his tea. Julia could have cut the tension between them with a knife. Despite the man in front of her being her father, they were practically strangers to each other. After her mother's death, he had buried himself in his work, travelling the country hunting for antiques while Anthony ran the shop. Julia had learned very young not to rely on the man.

"Why are you surprised Anthony would do something like this?" Julia asked, looking down at Mowgli as he chewed his food contently, unbothered by the presence of the stranger in his house. "We both know he's always been a ruthless businessman."

"And not a very good one," he said, leaning forward

343

and clasping his fingers together. "The man conned me out of my share of the business we built together, but last I heard he was almost broke."

"He must have come into some money," Julia said, not wanting to admit she had researched the staggering amount it would cost to start a Happy Bean franchise. "You know it only takes a couple of decent antiques to turn things around."

"That's just the thing. The man was completely useless," he admitted, cupping his hands around the mug as he stared down into the golden surface of the tea. "Wouldn't know a Shigaraki Kiln Soy Vase from a Zsolnay. It was always my knowledge that propped the business up. I told him how much things were worth, and he sold them with his charm and charisma. He was good at that. Always had the gift of the gab, that's for sure."

"Well, he's certainly doing his best to make sure he's eliminating the competition," Julia whispered after sipping her tea.

Brian pulled his wallet out of his pocket and looked down at it for a second, weighing it up in his hands. He pulled it open to reveal that it was bursting with more red fifty-pound notes than Julia had ever seen in one place. He pulled them all out and pushed them across the counter.

"Your gran said you were struggling," he said, tapping a finger on the cash. "It's not a lot, but it'll tide you over."

Julia couldn't decide if she was offended or flattered. She stared down at the money, her mouth ajar. It would help, but she couldn't help but think the money had come from Katie's family fortune and not his pocket. After all, he had admitted that Anthony had conned him out of his business and Julia knew he hadn't worked since marrying

Katie over five years ago. It wasn't like he needed to. Katie was sitting on the Wellington fortune, and with her brother dead and her father wheelchair bound, it wasn't going to be long before she inherited the family pot of gold.

Before she could respond, Jessie came out of her bedroom dressed for work, already wearing her protest t-shirt. She hovered back before Julia gave her a supportive nod. She walked cautiously forward and sat at the counter, leaving a seat between them. She reached out for her tea, her eyes widening when she spotted the money.

"I should get going," he said, standing up and pushing his unfinished tea away as he checked his gold watch, no doubt designer. "Katie will be wondering where I've gone. She told me to invite you and your sister to lunch next Sunday."

"I'll let Sue know," she said, not giving him a definite answer as she wondered if it was really Katie who had asked that. "I'll show you out."

She walked her father to the door, leaving Jessie with her tea in the kitchen. When they reached the door, he turned and opened his mouth, but closed it again.

"I appreciate you coming to see me," Julia whispered, resting a hand on his shoulder. "You're always welcome here, you know that."

"I know," he said, his fingers closing around the door handle as though he couldn't wait to get back to his manor. "Just be careful today. Anthony won't think twice about playing dirty."

Her father left her cottage and walked back to his car. Before he drove away, he waved, and she waved back. When he drove down the winding lane, she exhaled, hating how awkward things were with the man she had adored as a child. She looked out to Emily Burns' cottage across the road. She waved with her rose pruning shears in her hands. Just like Jessie, she too was already in her '*Choose Local Coffee*' t-shirt. Julia waved back a little less enthusiastically as Emily craned her neck to see if she recognised the car speeding away from them.

"There's five hundred quid here," Jessie said, wafting the red notes in her hand. "He must be minted."

Julia sighed and took the money from Jessie. She hadn't wanted to keep it, but she hadn't been able to bring herself to flat out refuse either.

"I forgot to give it back," Julia said, unsure if that was true. She flicked through the notes before rolling them up and stuffing the bundle in the biscuit tin with the custard creams. "Hopefully, we won't need it."

***

"*Save Peridale!*" Dot's voice crackled out of the megaphone and floated through the open café door. "This faceless coffee shop is *destroying* local businesses!"

If Julia wasn't completely rushed off her feet trying to keep up with her full café's orders, she might have asked her gran to calm down a little. Even though things had started off quietly and it had just been Dot and a couple of her friends outside the coffee shop, there were now over twenty people there, all wearing the t-shirts, and holding signs written out in Dot's handwriting.

"If you want *real* coffee, go to my granddaughter's café," Dot cried out. "*Real* coffee, made by *real* people. Support local business!"

"We've not been this busy in weeks!" Jessie whispered excitedly as she hurried past Julia with a tray of tea and scones for a group of women who were curiously staring around Julia's café. "Dot's nutty plan *actually* worked!"

Julia took down another large food order and hurried through to the kitchen, where Sue was spreading butter on bread rolls as fast as she could.

"Not how I thought I'd be spending my first Saturday off in months," Sue said as she dabbed at her red face with a tea towel. "I bet they can hear her in Timbuktu!"

Julia hurried back through to the café, pleased to see Barker pushing through the crowd and making his way towards her.

"It's nice to see this place full again," he said as he approached the counter, his eyes darting up to the chalkboard menu behind her. "I'll take a large Americano to go. I'm on the clock."

"It's just one day, but it's a good sign."

"Your gran is certainly determined," Barker said with a chuckle as he pulled change from his pocket. "She needs to watch what she's saying though. She's crossing the line between protest and slander, and if Anthony officially complains, she could be arrested."

Julia pitied the poor officer who would try to put cuffs on Dot. Her gran might have been eighty-three, but she was the feistiest and most exuberant woman in the village. Her tongue may have been razor sharp, but the fact she had organised this protest to try and help Julia only proved how big her heart was.

She quickly made Barker's Americano and bagged up a chocolate cupcake for him to take away. When he reached into his pocket to grab more change, she rested her hand on his to stop him.

"You more than deserve it," Julia said, pushing the bag

into his hand. "It's the least I can do."

"I didn't do anything," Barker said as he peeled off the plastic lid from his coffee to add a sachet of brown sugar. "When Dot told me her plan, there was no way I wasn't going to help. I know how much you love this place, and I love you, so it was a no-brainer."

He leaned across the counter to give her a quick kiss before pulling away with a playful smirk, his teeth biting his lips. He turned on his heels and headed for the door with his coffee and cupcake, making way for more customers to walk into Julia's café.

"Take these outside," Julia said, handing Jessie a tray with an assortment of cupcakes on them. "Free samples. People might be in here today, but we want them to come back."

Jessie finished making a latte before taking the tray, hurrying through the café and out onto the village green. As Julia watched her approach the people to offer them free cupcakes with a smile, pride swelled through her. It hadn't been that long ago that Jessie had been homeless and breaking into Julia's café for her cakes. Julia didn't want to take any credit for Jessie's transformation, but she was glad she had given her a chance that she might not have gotten otherwise.

"Who's that boy talking to Jessie?" Sue asked as she appeared behind her with a plate of sandwiches for one of the tables. "He's a little close."

Julia squinted into the sun at the boy. Even though she couldn't see his face, the red tracksuit and baseball cap gave him away.

"Billy Matthews," Julia answered. "He's quite smitten with Jessie. I don't think she wants to admit that she likes him too. He's persistent."

"Is that the serial killer's kid?" Sue asked on her way back, pausing to grab one of the cupcakes from the cake stand. "The one that Barker sent to prison all those years ago before he moved to Peridale and left that funeral wreath on Barker's doorstep as a threat before a man was actually murdered? I'm surprised you're letting her associate herself with people like that."

"Jeffrey Taylor was found innocent," Julia reminded her. "He's an okay guy. Barker and he have gone for a few pints in The Plough since. I think it's more to prove that there's no bad blood between them. Jeffrey is trying to set a good example for Billy."

"Didn't Billy put a brick through your café's window?" Sue mumbled through a mouthful of cake as she arched a brow. "And didn't he try to steal your handbag too?"

Julia watched as Jessie walked away from Billy, but he followed her like a lovesick puppy. Jessie tossed her hair over her shoulder and shouted something at him, which only made him laugh and follow her even closer.

"He's not been in trouble with the police for months," Julia said tactfully. "You shouldn't judge a book by its cover. Everybody deserves a second chance."

"Speaking of books, Neil got this book from the library that said my lime is going to turn into a small pumpkin," Sue said uneasily as she rested a hand on her small stomach. "A *pumpkin*, Julia! I don't think I thought this through."

"You're going to be fine," Julia reassured her. "If it were that bad, Mum would have stopped with me."

Sue looked like she was about to argue, but she appeared to think about it for a second before mentally agreeing with Julia. She hurried back into the kitchen to start on the next order, leaving Julia to continue to watch Jessie and Billy. Her heart stopped when she spotted Anthony marching out of his coffee shop and across the village green towards Jessie, his open shirt flapping against his bronzed chest in the summer breeze. He tiptoed awkwardly on top of the grass as though he didn't want to get his expensive shoes dirty. Without a second thought, Julia abandoned her post and joined him in running towards Jessie.

"You need a permit to hand out street food," Anthony exclaimed smugly as he shielded his eyes from the sun with one hand while the other clicked at Jessie like she was a dog about to perform a trick. "I *assume* you have the right paperwork from the council?"

"Kiss my –"

"*Jessie!*" Julia cried, interrupting her before she said something Anthony could use against her. "Go back to the café. I'll deal with this."

"I could take him," Billy offered as he cracked his knuckles. "I've knocked out bigger."

"*Billy!*" Julia cried. "You get to the café too. What would your dad say?"

Billy scowled at Julia before rolling his eyes at the same time as Jessie. Despite Jessie's protests that she couldn't stand Billy, they were more alike than Jessie would like to admit.

"Aren't you going to offer me one?" Anthony asked, reaching out for the tray.

Jessie swiftly pulled it out of his way, but not before he managed to grab one of the red velvet cupcakes. He took a step back and began to slowly unpeel the casing, making sure to take his time to peel the paper away from each ridge in the tiny cake. Dot and the rest of the protestors had suddenly gone silent and were making their way across the village green towards them.

"Looks *delicious*," he mocked, winking at Julia. "Did you bake this yourself, Julia?"

"Julia bakes *everything* herself," Dot announced through the megaphone. "*Everything* at Julia's café is home baked! Unlike Happy Bean's cakes, which are *filled* with chemicals and have shelf-lives that will outlive the cockroaches and Cher herself!"

The people who had been making their way across to Julia's café stopped to observe the commotion. Julia watched as Anthony slowly lifted the cake up to his lip, his eye contact unwavering. It unsettled her that this was a man she had known since the day she was born, and yet she saw none of that recognition in his icy blue eyes.

"Get on with it, man!" Billy cried, stepping forward and cracking his knuckles again. "You're not getting any younger."

Anthony bit into the cake, and Julia was surprised to see the same look of pleasure she would expect to see from one of her paying customers. For a moment, she thought her baking had worked at healing the rift between her café and the new coffee shop, and she almost felt foolish for not trying to work with the new business, rather than against it.

But suddenly, Anthony's face contorted, as though he had just bit into a sour wedge of lemon. He crushed the cake between his teeth painfully slowly as a hand reached up to his mouth. A gasp rattled through the crowd when he pulled something red and shiny from between his lips. He wiped the wet cake mixture off it and held it up to the sun.

"*A red fingernail!*" Anthony explained, barely able to

hide the smugness in his voice as he twisted the piece of acrylic in the light. "As you heard yourself, ladies and gentlemen, Julia *does* bake everything herself. We might buy our cakes from the wholesaler at Happy Bean, but I can *assure* you, we follow the most *basic* food safety standards."

Julia looked at Jessie, who looked as confused as she felt. Julia lifted up her fingers, but they were natural and free of any nail polish, as were Jessie's.

"I don't even wear fake nails!" Julia cried. "He *planted* that!"

"You *all* saw me!" Anthony said, directing his attention to the gathering crowd. "I couldn't have possibly planted anything in that cake."

"You're gonna pay for –" Billy cried, launching himself forward, only to be dragged back by Jessie.

"I'll leave you to make up your minds," Anthony said with a sneer, tossing his hands out as he turned back to his coffee shop. "I gather you're all *intelligent* people."

Anthony pocketed the nail and screwed up the cupcake wrapper before dropping it to the grass. Julia watched in disbelief as he sauntered slowly back to his coffee shop, followed by most of the people who had been standing and watching. They were all looking at Julia in disgust, but she couldn't summon the words to defend herself. Her father had been right about Anthony being a good salesman and a dirty player.

"Emily! Amy! *Plan B!*" Dot cried through the megaphone before she tossed it to the ground and set off running towards the coffee shop, overtaking Anthony and the customers in a flash.

Before anybody could figure out what was going on, Emily and Amy stepped forward, pulling long metal chains from their tiny handbags. Dot stood in front of the coffee shop and in an instant, as though it had been rehearsed, Emily and Amy chained Dot's arms and legs to the front of the coffee shop before padlocking them in place.

"*Wicked*," Jessie whispered with a grin.

"That woman has *style*," Billy said, as he draped an arm around Jessie's shoulders. "I can still punch him for you, if you want, babe?"

"Shut up," Jessie said as she rolled her eyes and tossed his arm away. "Here comes trouble."

Jessie nodded in the direction of two uniformed officers who had been watching the protest unfold. They walked over to Emily and Amy, presumably asking for the keys to the padlocks, but they both shrugged, before linking arms and hurrying up the lane towards Emily's cottage.

"I will *not* be moved!" Dot cried. "This is a *peaceful* protest!"

"What about when she needs to pee?" Jessie whispered into Julia's ears as they walked across the village green. "Won't her arms get tired?"

Julia didn't know what to say. She turned back to her café, which was emptying as though the building was on fire. Sue darted between the tables trying to make them stay, but it was no use. She exhaled heavily, wondering how things could have gone so dramatically wrong.

It only took a couple of minutes for one of the officers to arrive with a pair of bolt cutters to cut Dot down. The trapped customers inside of the coffee shop scurried out, only to be replaced with the ones trying to flee Julia's café after seeing her contaminated cakes.

"*Call my lawyer!*" Dot cried as they pulled her arms behind her back and handcuffed them in place. "*Call the press*!"

Julia pinched uncomfortably between her brows as the officers forced Dot into the back of a police car. Barker mouthed his apology to her, with a look of '*I told you so*', but she shook her head to let him know it wasn't his fault.

The second Dot was driven towards the police station, the protest party dispersed, smiling their awkward apologies to Julia. She wasn't angry with them for leaving; she would have done the same. They had tried, and that mattered to her.

"Are they going to charge her?" Jessie asked.

"I doubt it," Julia said. "I'm sure Barker will do his best, although he might want to make her sweat a little first."

Julia turned her attention to Anthony, who was sitting at one of the sterile metallic tables outside his coffee shop, smoking a cigarette as he watched the scene come to an end. He looked mildly amused more than anything. It hurt Julia that somebody could be so callous and care so little.

Julia spotted Anthony's wife, Rosemary Kennedy, storm out of the coffee shop towards her husband, wearing one of Happy Bean's barista uniforms with her greying hair pinned at the back of her head in a tight roll. Julia was sure the woman was past retirement age. He grabbed her wrist and pulled her in, attempting to kiss her on the cheek, but she tugged her arm away and stormed off. She yanked her apron over her head and tossed it to the ground before tossing her hands in the air. Julia noticed her red nails, particularly the lack of one on her left index finger. Anthony chuckled and shook his head as though that too amused him.

"What now?" Jessie whispered as the crowd

354

disappeared, leaving them alone on the village green.

Julia looked back at her café, her heart heavy. She thought about the five hundred pounds in her biscuit tin at her cottage, the likelihood that she would need to use her father's money increasing. Julia linked arms with Jessie, and they set off back towards her café.

Before she reached the door, she turned back and looked at Happy Bean. A man had joined Anthony at the table with two coffees in their signature white and green cups. Anthony offered the man a cigarette, but he declined with a wave of his hand and a toothy smile. Julia's heart stopped for a moment. Did she recognise that smile? She shielded her eyes and squinted across the village, but her heart eased when she realised it was her imagination playing tricks on her.

"Too much hair," she whispered to herself as she shook away the suggestion.

"*Huh?*" Jessie asked.

"Nothing," Julia said, wrapping her arm around Jessie's shoulder as they walked back into the café. "Let's clean up. You never know, there might be a second wind."

Jessie nodded enthusiastically, even if both of them knew it was more than a little unlikely. As she gathered the half-finished sandwiches and cakes from the tables, she looked around her café, wondering if her dream was coming to an end. If her gran's protest couldn't save her café against the corporate machine, she didn't know what would. She wasn't going to hold her breath for a miracle.

CHAPTER 3

Later that night Julia was on her sitting room floor with Jessie, and her two new college friends, Dolly and Dom.

"I promise it won't hurt," Dom said as he smeared the jet-black charcoal face mask on Jessie's face. "Just sit *still*!"

Julia attempted to chuckle as Jessie squirmed under Dom's forceful touch, but he had already attacked Julia with the black mask ten minutes ago, and it had completely frozen her face.

"Is it meant to burn?" Jessie asked when Dom had finished.

"Drama queen," Dolly said as she rolled onto her back

on the hearthrug, the spoon from the ice cream tub still in her mouth. "We saw Billy earlier."

Jessie's eyes darted to Julia, and then to her fingers, which were suddenly fiddling with the drawstrings on her black pyjama bottoms.

"*So?*" she replied, attempting and failing to frown through the face mask. "I don't care."

"You *so* love him," Dom said, ribbing her with his elbow. "I bet you're blushing under there."

He went to peel the mask, but Jessie batted his hand away and snatched the ice cream spoon from Dolly to fill her mouth with the chocolatey goodness. The sleepover had been Jessie's idea, but the ice cream had been Julia's. After the day she had endured, she needed the distraction and the dairy.

"It's almost midnight," Dom announced as he climbed onto the sofa and tossed his head upside down to squint at the clock on the mantelpiece. "Remember how Cinderella turned back into a witch at midnight? You're going to be the opposite when we're finished with you, Jessie!"

"She wasn't a witch," Dolly mumbled as she tapped her fingers against her black, frozen cheeks. "She was a slave."

"She was a servant," Jessie corrected them, much to everyone's surprise. "*What?* I grew up in foster care, not on the moon!"

Jessie's expression remained stern for a moment before she broke out laughing. They all attempted to chuckle, wincing through the pain of the masks that Dom had insisted would make them all look and feel ten years younger. Considering Julia had twenty years on the three of them, she wasn't sure how much younger they could look without having to crawl back into nappies.

"How's college?" Julia asked, fondly remembering her days in the patisserie and baking course. "Is Mr Jackson still there?"

"*Jacko*?" Dom asked. "He's properly ancient! He creaks when he walks."

"Leaves a trail of dust," Dolly cackled, amused by herself. "He's practically mummified."

Jessie joined in the laughing, which in turn made Julia laugh. When Jessie had first told her she had made friends at college, Julia had been a little surprised, not because she didn't think Jessie was capable of making friends, but because she didn't think Jessie would want to, especially with kids her own age. When Jessie brought Dolly and Dom to the cottage a couple of weeks ago, Julia had been even more surprised to see that her new friends were impossibly tall, platinum blonde twins who wore every colour in the rainbow at all times. Julia loved them. They always had something funny to say, and their spirits were so pure. She wasn't sure they could manage to say a bad word about anyone if they tried.

"If you're not going to chase after Billy, I might try," Dom said as he twirled a blonde curl around his index finger. "In for a penny."

"I'm not chasing anybody," Jessie mumbled with a roll of her eyes.

"*He's* chasing you though," Dolly exclaimed as she took the spoon from Jessie to dig out a huge brownie chunk. "What do you think of him, Julia?"

"Erm, he's – *nice*," Julia said, everything she knew about Billy racing through her mind. "He's growing up."

Jessie snorted her disagreement before snatching the spoon back from Dolly and finishing the last of the ice cream. Dom let out a long yawn, which was echoed by Dolly, and then Julia. Jessie seemed to be the only one who wasn't tired.

"Do you have any Saturday jobs at your café?" Dom asked, looking at Julia upside down as he dangled off the edge of the sofa. "Our tutor at college said we should try and find Saturday jobs because the bakery we work at doesn't open on the weekends."

"No, there isn't," Jessie jumped in, her eyes darting uneasily at Julia. "I *told* you not to ask."

"In for a penny," Dom said again with a shrug and a smile, not fazed by the rejection. "I wonder what Billy is doing right now."

Jessie sighed and tossed the spoon into the ice cream tub. Julia thought Jessie was about to launch into an argument with Dom, but they were interrupted when Julia's mobile phone vibrated on the side table. They all jumped and looked at the phone, Dom and Dolly immediately bursting out laughing.

"It's *midnight!*" Dolly exclaimed. "Maybe that's Billy looking for his princess?"

Jessie picked up a cushion and launched it at Dolly, who didn't even try to dodge it. It hit her square in the face, which only caused more hysterical laughter, which was only interrupted by another yawn.

Julia rolled across the floor and grabbed her phone from the table. She looked down at the unknown contact and frowned, the mask pinching her forehead. It didn't resemble a phone number she had ever seen. She was about to reject the call and toss it back onto the table because of the late hour, but she suddenly remembered what the number was.

"It's the security alarm at the café," Julia mumbled under her breath. "It calls me when the alarm is triggered. Gran convinced me to get it after Billy put a brick through my window."

"Was it a *love* brick?" Dom asked, twiddling Jessie's hair.

"No, it was a *brick* brick," Jessie said, batting his hand away. "Is it serious, Julia?"

Julia answered the call, and as expected it gave her an automated message that her alarm had been triggered a minute before midnight. She glanced at the clock and sighed as she forced herself up off the rug, her knees creaking a little.

"Just stay here," Julia said as she headed for the door. "I won't be long. It's probably nothing."

Julia slipped her feet into her sheepskin slippers, tied her dressing gown around her waist, and grabbed her car keys.

"You've still got your mask on," Jessie mumbled through her tight face. "I'm coming with you."

"You're not," Julia said as she turned to the hallway mirror to tug at the mask's edge. "*Ouch!* What is this made of?"

Jessie joined her in the mirror and tugged at her mask. She yelped, and immediately let go, tears lining her eyes.

"Satan's flesh," Jessie mumbled darkly. "Let's just rip it off. Like a plaster."

Julia nodded and met Jessie's eyes in the mirror. They both yanked up from the bottom of their cheeks, but they stopped before they had even passed their mouths. Julia wiped away the tears as they streamed down her glossy black cheeks.

"I'll wash it off when I get back," Julia said, blinking through the pain as her fingers closed around her car key. "You're not coming with me."

"They'll already be asleep," Jessie whispered. "*Please.*"

"It's been less than a minute," Julia said, walking past Jessie and back into the sitting room, where Dolly was fast asleep on the rug, and Dom was draped across the sofa with his hand on his stomach and his head still hanging over the edge, his mouth gaping open. "*Unbelievable.*"

"It's some freaky talent they have," Jessie said as she pulled her usual black hoody over her pyjamas. "It's probably a lack of things going on in their head."

Julia and Jessie shared a little grin for a second before she reluctantly opened the front door, letting Jessie walk through first. She locked Dolly and Dom in and walked towards her car, hoping they were heading towards nothing more than a false alarm.

"In for a penny," Julia whispered.

***

When Julia drove into the village, she immediately heard the blaring siren and saw the red flashing lights coming from her café. As she pulled up outside, the lights in the bedrooms across the village green flicked on, including her gran's, who had been released from the police station with a caution after only an hour of questioning.

"The door is open," Jessie mumbled as she scrambled for her seatbelt. "I'm going to *murder* whoever it is!"

Julia killed the engine and struggled to undo her seatbelt. She caught a glimpse of her shiny face in the rear-view mirror, realising how ridiculous she looked.

She slammed her car door and hurried over to her café. The small pane of glass in the door had been smashed, the fragments on the doormat. Pulling Jessie back, Julia edged into the dark café, immediately making her way to the alarm system. She punched in the code, which was the date she had rescued Mowgli, and the alarm finally stopped.

"*Hello?*" she called out into her empty café.

"Come out, you *rats!*" Jessie cried, bursting past Julia and running into the kitchen. "They've gone."

Julia hurried after her. To her relief, the kitchen was empty. She flicked on the light to see what had been taken but was surprised to see everything where she had left it, including all of her expensive professional baking equipment that had cost her a pretty penny when first opening. She turned and looked through the beads into the café, but the till was still there too.

"*Odd,*" Julia whispered. "Maybe it was an accident?"

"There's no such thing," Jessie said, storming out of the café and turning on her mobile phone's flashlight.

She scanned it across the village green, and down the alleyway between the café and the post office. Julia followed her, but she couldn't see anybody.

"Maybe a bird flew into the window?" Julia suggested.

"There's no blood," Jessie said bluntly. "Somebody is trying to scare you."

Before Julia could ask who, she looked over to Happy Bean, her stomach turning when she saw that all the lights were still on. She knew they opened late, but not this late.

"Get in the car," Julia ordered.

"*Fat chance!*"

"Jessie!"

"*What?*"

"Do as you're told."

"Have we met?" Jessie replied with a clenched jaw. "I'm not leaving your side, cake lady."

In their pyjamas and charcoal face masks, they edged towards their rival, sticking to each other's side like Velcro. Jessie illuminated the path in front of them, her Doc Martens clunking on the cobbled road underfoot. When they were feet from the coffee shop, Julia noticed that the door was slightly ajar.

"We should call the police," Julia whispered, holding her arm in front of Jessie. "This doesn't feel right."

Jessie pouted before stepping around Julia's arm. She set off straight for the door. To Julia's surprise, she pulled her sleeve over her hand before pushing on the door. Julia suddenly remembered the time she had caught Jessie breaking into her café before they had known each other, and she realised she had more expertise than Julia had given her credit for.

All the lights in the coffee shop were switched on, but it appeared empty. Julia followed Jessie inside for the first time, making sure not to touch anything. She looked around at what her competition had to offer, initially impressed until she took a couple of steps inside. Everything looked like it was trying impossibly hard to appear comfortable and relatable, but it all felt a little sterile. On closer inspection, the exposed brick walls were just wallpaper, the leather sofas were pleather, and the framed pictures on the walls were nothing more than generic stock photography and bland prints of utilitarian paintings. Even the menu above the counter was eerily barren, with calorie contents and prices in tiny black text, making her chalkboard menu look like a piece of art.

"Julia," Jessie said with a gulp as she peered over the counter. "You might want to see this."

Julia's heart suddenly stopped in her chest. She recognised the fear and shock in Jessie's eyes. She had felt it herself more times than she cared to remember recently.

Taking her steps carefully and slowly, Julia walked towards the counter where Jessie was pointing the light. She looked over, and jumped back with a gasp, having not expected to see the eyes of Anthony Kennedy staring back up at her, glassy and vacant.

"Is he dead?" Jessie asked.

"I think so," Julia gulped, nodding her head as she dared to take another look. "We should get out of –"

Her voice trailed off when something on the counter caught her eye. She leaned in and peered at what had caught her attention, realising that it had been her own name. Perfectly aligned under the spotlight above the counter sat two sugar sachets, one brown and one white, both inscribed with glossy red writing.

"'*Murder*'," Julia read aloud, her throat drying up. "'*Julia did it*'. We really should get out of here."

To Julia's surprise, Jessie pressed a couple of buttons on her phone before taking a picture of the sugars. When Julia shook her head to ask her what she was doing, Jessie shrugged and pocketed her phone.

"It's *evidence*!" Jessie cried defensively. "It looks like it's been written in blood."

Julia took a step back, but something sharp pierced through her sheepskin slippers and stabbed into the sole of her foot. She yelped and jumped back. She looked down at a long metal screw, which was sticking up on the ground and covered in white dust. She felt her foot, but it didn't appear to be bleeding. Jessie bent down to pick up the screw, but Julia quickly held her back.

"Call the —"

Before Julia could finish her sentence, a hot light flooded the coffee shop. It took Julia a moment to realise that the burning brightness was coming from outside. They both turned around, their hands shielding their eyes from the white light. Julia opened her mouth to say something, but she couldn't see a thing beyond the brightness.

"*Come out with your hands up!*" a stern and angry voice cried over a megaphone. "*Don't try anything stupid!*"

As Julia walked towards the coffee shop door, she caught the reflection of their covered faces in the window. She knew things couldn't look any worse if they tried.

"There's a dead man in here," Julia called out, her hands above her head. "Somebody broke into my café across the village green, and I saw this door open and came to see what was happening. We haven't done anything wrong."

An officer stepped away from a police car, his baton in one hand and a pair of handcuffs in the other. Jessie shifted in closer to Julia, her hands also high above her head. Despite her bravado, Julia could feel fear radiating from every fibre of Jessie's being.

"We haven't done anything wrong," Julia repeated, daring to take a step forward as another officer circled the car, the headlights still blinding her.

"*Stay where you are!*" one of them called.

Before Julia knew what to do or say, both of them were in handcuffs and being driven past her café and through the village to the local police station, still in their increasingly tight charcoal face masks and pyjamas.

"We're done for, aren't we?" Jessie whispered.

"I think so," Julia replied, not knowing how she could sugar-coat their situation. "*I think so.*"

CHAPTER 4

The sun burned Julia's eyes as she stumbled out of the station with Jessie by her side. The moment she saw Barker sat on the bench outside the closed pub across the road, Julia ran straight into his arms, the tears lining her lashes.

"*Oh, Julia*," he said as he clenched her face to his chest. "I came as soon as I heard."

"It was horrible," Julia whispered, her fingers clinging to the back of Barker's shirt. "They've been questioning us for most of the night."

"They wouldn't let me anywhere near the interview rooms. It's procedure when we're so close to a –"

"*Suspect?*" Jessie asked as she joined them outside The

367

Plough. "You can say it."

Barker smiled sympathetically at Jessie before pulling away from Julia and holding her by the shoulders. He stared deep into her eyes, as though to calm her, but she could see the deep-set panic in his pupils.

"Why didn't you call me when the alarm went off?" Barker asked with a sigh. "I could have sorted this sooner."

"Sorted it?" Jessie asked.

"The only reason they've let you go without charging you is because I've been running around the village trying to prove your story. One of the girls at the station called me first thing this morning and told me everything that had happened, and how they were treating you like murder suspects. She said you were wearing balaclavas?"

"They were charcoal face masks," Julia said, her fingers drifting up to her still stinging cheeks after having the masks forcibly removed by the arresting officers. "*Dolly and Dom!*"

She clasped her fingers around her mouth as guilt surged through her. In all of the commotion, she had completely forgotten about the houseguests she had locked in her cottage.

"If you're talking about those two blonde kids asleep on your floor, they're still there," Barker said, a little confused. "They're curled up in a giant ball with Mowgli in the middle of them."

Julia pulled the plastic bag out of her pocket that contained her phone, car keys, and watch, the possessions that had been confiscated during her arrest. She squinted at the small watch face, surprised that it was already two in the afternoon. She looked around the village, suddenly realising that it was buzzing around her, and she was still in her pyjamas.

"I suppose they're just like two cats," Jessie said absently, her eyes glazing over as she stared into space. "Cats in clothes."

"How did you prove our story?" Julia asked as she reattached her watch. "They were acting like we had conspired to kill Anthony. They knew all about what happened with the fingernail earlier in the day, but that's Peridale for you."

"After that nasty business with the wreath on my doorstep, I had security cameras installed all around my cottage," Barker said nervously. "They caught you driving by at four minutes past midnight. I was banging on Shilpa's door at six this morning to get her post office footage. I don't think she likes me much right now, but it proves the rest of the story. You arrived in the village, went into your café, walked out and then went to Happy Bean. That's when the officers turned up. One of the residents called them when they heard your alarm. I have a good mind to have those jokers fired! They were one step away from tasering you, I'm sure of it!"

A cold shudder spread across Julia's shoulders. She pulled her dressing gown across her body and tucked her scruffy hair behind her ears, never one to be self-conscious, but also not one to wander around the village in her nightclothes.

"We're out now," Julia said, trying to force a smile. "That's all that matters."

"I'm not finished," Barker said, appearing a little excited and nervous at the same time. "The footage spotted somebody leaving Happy Bean, run to your café, and then head off into the night."

"Who?" Julia asked.

"I don't know," he said through a gritted jaw. "They were hooded. It's not the best quality. They went through the back door of the coffee shop, killed Anthony, and fled through the front. I've already checked, and there are no cameras covering the back entrance. If this were London, we'd have every corner covered, but it seems Peridale is quite resistant to surveillance."

Julia's mind flashed back to an uproar that had happened soon after she had moved back to the village. The council had been trying to erect cameras around the village green to target petty crime, but the backlash from the villagers had been so great, they had eventually backed down. It turned out the residents didn't like the thought of being spied on, which Dot had said was because everybody had something to hide.

"I just want to go home, shower, and sleep," Julia said after a long yawn, glad that it was Sunday, meaning she didn't have to think about her café. "I think we've earned it."

"There's more," Barker said, the concern growing in his voice. "They found something in the cake display case in your café."

"Found what?" Jessie asked loudly. "Because if it's a library book on American desserts, I swear I didn't know it was overdue!"

"They found a bottle of something," Barker said, his eyes meeting Julia's. "They've blocked me from this case, but I know the detective they've brought in from Cheltenham to lead the investigation, and he told me that their early tests suggest it's a poison of some kind."

"The murder weapon?" Jessie asked. "In Julia's café?"

"That explains the break-in," Julia theorised. "Why *my* café?"

Barker arched a brow and tucked his hands into his jacket. He cocked his head back and smirked dryly at her.

"You're taking this rather calmly," Barker said. "If I didn't know you, I'd think it was because you were involved, but I do know you, so what are you thinking?"

"Somebody is trying to frame me," Julia said, forcing down the lump in her throat. "I've had all night to come to that conclusion. The sugar at the scene proved that."

"Sugar?" Barked asked, proving how little he knew about the case.

Julia was about to explain, but Jessie pulled her own plastic bag containing her phone out of her pocket. She pressed a couple of buttons before a highly exposed and slightly blurry picture filled the frame. She pinched the screen and zoomed in on the shiny red writing on the sugar packets. Barker gulped and looked up at Julia.

"It's blood," Jessie whispered. "*Human* blood."

"'*Julia did it,*'" Barker whispered, tugging at his shirt collar. "That might explain a few things. Julia, you need to promise me that you're going to stay out of this investigation. You're still a suspect until they say otherwise. They're going to do everything they can to work around the evidence to make it fit their story. I should know, I work for them."

"I promise," Julia said as she stuffed her hands into her dressing gown. "I honestly just want to go home."

Barker kissed Julia gently on the forehead as he ruffled Jessie's hair. She batted his hand and ducked out of the way with a scowl. Julia chuckled, glad to see things going back to normal.

"I need to get to work," Barker said. "Somebody stole Imogen Carter's favourite garden gnome. They've put me on the case."

"Ever the *exciting* life, *eh*, Detective?" Jessie mocked.

"Watch your tongue, young lady," Barker said with a wink. "I could always go in there and fix it up so they charge you. I *know* people."

"Bite me."

Julia laughed, kissed Barker one more time and turned to watch him walk into the station. When they were alone, Julia let out a sigh of relief.

"Your fingers were crossed in your pocket when you made that promise, weren't they?" Jessie asked flatly.

"No," Julia said as she quickly uncrossed her fingers. "But somebody has gone to great trouble to try and frame me for murder, and I'll be damned if I sit back and let them get away with it. Security footage or not, I need to clear my name before the mud sticks."

"Mine too," Jessie said with a firm nod.

Julia was about to tell Jessie to stay out of things, but she closed her mouth. She would be a hypocrite if she broke her false promise to Barker while also forcing Jessie to make the same promise. As she linked her arms through her young lodger's, she realised they were far more alike than either of them probably recognised.

***

Julia and Jessie walked into the heart of the village arm in arm. Her chest tightened when she spotted her café. Blue and white crime scene tape circled the small building, a forensics team swarming in and out like flies. She thought about them touching all of her baking things, and her heart hurt a little.

"I don't mind going to prison," Jessie said as she pulled away from Julia and clenched both of her fists. "I reckon I could take out *at least* three of them before they call for back-up."

Julia rested her hand on Jessie's to let her know she appreciated the gesture but she would rather they both stay as far away from the police station as they could until they were handing over the real murderer.

Turning away from her café, she looked in the direction of Happy Bean, which had similar men in white costumes combing over the scene. Her mind flashed back to Anthony Kennedy lying on the floor in his coffee shop. Despite everything that had happened, it upset Julia to think a man had needlessly died, especially one she had known for so long. She thought back to the way he had looked at her on the village green the day before, with his glowing orange tan and porcelain white teeth, devoid of any real emotion. It wasn't so different from the look she had seen on his dead face.

Julia linked arms with Jessie and they set off. The thought of climbing into bed, even if she knew she wouldn't be able to sleep, was all that motivated her. She knew Anthony's untimely death wasn't going to be her café's saviour. Like most corporate beasts, another head always grew back when you cut off the first, and the second was usually much, much worse.

"Is that Dot?" Jessie asked, stopping in her tracks and looking at the village hall next to St. Peter's Church.

Julia shielded her eyes from the sun and squinted in the direction Jessie was looking. Her heart sank when she saw her gran, with a group of the other elderly villagers, marching towards her café with new t-shirts and protest signs.

"*Free Julia!*" Dot bellowed down the megaphone in the direction of the bewildered forensics team. "You can *try* and lock me up, and you can *throw* away the key, but we will not settle until she is *released!*"

"Maybe we should just leave her," Jessie whispered, holding Julia back. "It's too funny to spoil."

Julia considered it for a moment but shook her head. She looked down at her pyjamas and slippers, realising how silly she must look walking around the village.

"*What do we want?*" Dot cried.

"To free Julia!" the gang replied.

"*When do we want it?*"

The girls looked at each other, unsure of what the correct response was.

"*Now!*" Dot replied for them, pursing her lips and frowning heavily at her group. "*We want it now! Unleash* my granddaughter from your *evil* clutches or else I will – *Julia?*"

Julia smiled awkwardly as she walked forward. Dot, as well as the rest of the protesters, stared at her with bewilderment, as though she was walking on water, or had just risen from the dead. Dot immediately dropped her megaphone and pulled Julia into a suffocating hug.

"I'm fine, Gran," Julia gasped through the grip. "We're fine."

"Oh, *Julia!*" Dot cried into her ear. "We've been fearing the worst! Shilpa called and told us what Barker said about you being arrested for *murder!* I was on the phone first thing to the printers to get new t-shirts."

Dot tugged proudly at her t-shirt, which spelled out

'*FREE JULIA*' in giant letters.

"I couldn't bear the thought of you locked up in there," Amy Clark exclaimed as she pulled open her pale pink cardigan to reveal her t-shirt. "*I* should know what it's like."

"You robbed banks, Amy, you didn't bump off coffee shop owners," Emily Burns whispered, making Amy Clark nod meekly and pull her fluffy cardigan back across her chest. "It's good to see you back, Julia. Are those pyjamas?"

"It's a long story," Julia said, glancing through the window of her café as a man in a white suit swabbed her cake stand. "I'm sorry you wasted money on new t-shirts."

"No money wasted!" Dot announced with a grin. "I got them for free at the print shop on Mulberry Lane! Mr Shufflebottom was more than happy to accommodate our needs."

"You *did* blackmail him," Amy whispered, lifting a finger as she stepped forward.

"I *simply* said if he didn't do them, I would reveal his secret," Dot said with a shake of her perm as she glanced over her shoulder at Amy. "Do you have to be such a little snitch, Amy? I thought shacking up with the other criminals in cellblock H for a twenty stretch would have taught you better!"

"What secret?" Jessie asked.

"Oh, I didn't know one," Dot said with a smirk as she leaned into Jessie's ear. "But between you and me, *most* people have one, so it's a good tactic to use, kid." Dot winked and pinched Jessie's cheek. "He started blabbering about his gambling addiction before I had even finished my sentence. Worked a *treat!*"

Julia didn't know whether she should be flattered or

horrified at the lengths her gran had gone to for the sake of protesting her arrest. She knew Dot cared, but part of her knew she was enjoying stirring the troops and protesting something. Dot's arrest had no doubt lit a rebellious fire under her feet. Julia made a mental note to make a tiramisu for Mr Shufflebottom, which she remembered was his favourite after sitting next to him in The Comfy Corner restaurant for Dot's birthday dinner last year.

"Well, I've had enough murder, blackmail, and extortion for one day," Julia said, another yawn escaping her lips before she could stop it. "I appreciate the effort, Gran, but you can put your feet up until the next worthy cause passes you by."

"*Nonsense!*" Dot cried as she unclipped her handbag and pulled out a black marker pen. "I'll just *change* them! There's more work to be done."

Dot ripped open Amy's cardigan, crossed out '*FREE*' and scribbled '*IS INNOCENT*' under '*JULIA*'. Julia stepped forward to object, but Amy shook her head to let her know it was probably best to let Dot do what she wanted. Leaving her to finish correcting the group's t-shirts, Julia walked past her Ford Anglia, which was still parked where she had left it the night before. She realised it probably wasn't wise to try driving home on the little sleep she had had. For the second time that day, they set off back towards their cottage.

When they reached Happy Bean, she was surprised to see a woman with messy caramel hair laying a bouquet of pink lilies outside the coffee shop. Julia stopped in her tracks, her stomach knotting tightly. The woman wiped away a tear from her raw eyes with a sodden tissue before standing up. She too stopped in her tracks when she saw

Julia, and to Julia's surprise, her top lip snarled and her nostrils flared. She looked as though she was going to say something, but she pushed through them and marched across the village, her head low and her hands tucked into her jacket pockets.

"I think she works at the hospital with Sue," Julia whispered to herself as she looked down at the flowers. "Word really does get around. She thinks I'm guilty."

"Forget her," Jessie mumbled, dragging Julia away from the flowers. "What other people think of you is none of your business."

"That's very wise, Jessie."

"Read it on a sticker on a bus once," she said casually. "C'mon, Dolly and Dom might slip into a coma if we don't go home soon."

As they walked up the village lane, Julia couldn't shake the way the woman had looked at her. It didn't matter that she had been released from questioning for the time being, she knew the news of her arrest at the murder scene would be spreading around the village like wildfire. It didn't matter that she was innocent, the blame would be attached to her until the real culprit was discovered. Julia owed it to herself and Jessie to be the one to clear their names, no matter what it took.

She unlocked the door of her cottage and walked inside, glad to be home. Mowgli trotted out from the kitchen and circled her feet to let her know she was late putting his breakfast down. She peeped her head into the sitting room, where Dolly and Dom were still fast asleep exactly as they had been when they had left them the night before.

Jessie clapped her hands together, causing the twins to

dart up, dribble on their cheeks, their blonde hair sticking up in every direction, and their eyes half-closed as though they hadn't had any sleep at all.

"What's for breakfast?" they asked in unison as they squinted at Jessie and Julia, none the wiser to what had happened.

Julia chuckled to herself and walked through to the kitchen. She fed Mowgli, made four peppermint and liquorice teas, and got to work making four full English breakfasts. She had been kidding herself that she was going to be able to sleep; she had far too much to think about.

CHAPTER 5

Mondays in Julia's café were always the quietest. Julia almost decided not to open, especially considering what had happened over the weekend. It had been Jessie who had convinced her that she should open, and as it turned out, they ended up taking record sales for a Monday. She knew it was because people wanted to get a look at the woman who killed Anthony Kennedy, but she was surprised by how little she cared about that. The till rang out all day, and that's all that mattered at the moment. Every extra penny prolonged her café's lifespan.

When she finally closed the café, she pulled the cottage pie she had prepared that morning out of the fridge, along with a strawberry pavlova she had managed to bake in one of the few quiet spells during the day.

After sending Jessie home, Julia drove across the village to Anthony Kennedy's cottage. She pulled up outside and yanked up the handbrake as she stared at his beautiful house. He had lived there for as long as Julia had known him, but it had undergone many transformations in that time. It was one of the bigger cottages in the village, with a beautifully presented garden in the front, and a large glass conservatory in the back. Grabbing the food from the back seat, she checked her reflection in the mirror, which looked considerably better after a good night of sleep and a nice hot shower. She could almost convince the world that everything was fine.

Julia wasn't sure how her visit was going to be received by Anthony's wife and son. Despite not having done anything wrong, she knew gossiping was intertwined with Peridale's DNA. Taking a deep breath, she unclipped the white gate and walked slowly down the garden path, hoping the rumour mill hadn't reached this far out yet. Balancing the cottage pie and strawberry pavlova in one hand, she pressed the doorbell. It rang out through the house, and she was surprised when the door opened almost instantly, giving Julia no time to second-guess her visit.

"*Julia?*" Rosemary Kennedy exclaimed, dressed as though she had just been about to go out. "What a surprise!"

Julia was glad Rosemary didn't immediately attack her, but she was a little unsettled with how put together the woman looked, considering her husband had died only the day before. Gone was the Happy Bean barista uniform, to be replaced with a well-fitting pair of black jeans, which hugged her figure beautifully. She had paired it with an orange blouse, which was tucked into the waist of her jeans, hanging over a little. Her lips were stained with red lipstick, and her shoulder-length grey hair was neatly curled and tucked behind her diamond-studded ears. She might have been a woman in her mid-sixties, but she looked effortlessly stylish.

"I brought you a cottage pie," Julia said, offering forward the dish. "And a pavlova. I didn't think you'd want to be worrying about cooking today."

"Come in," Rosemary said, stepping to the side to let Julia into the cottage. "That's incredibly sweet of you. Come through to the kitchen."

Julia followed Rosemary down the impeccably decorated hallway to the glossy kitchen, which faced directly into the conservatory, which in turn looked over their beautiful garden, complete with a swimming pool. Julia had never seen so much natural light flooding into a house before, and yet it lacked an ounce of charm that the exterior would suggest it possessed.

"I hope you don't mind me showing up here," Julia said as she pushed the food onto the counter. "I know I'm probably the last person you want to see right now."

"Oh, not at all!" Rosemary said with a small laugh. "I know *you* didn't kill Anthony, my love."

The joviality of Rosemary's laughter disturbed Julia, but she was glad she wasn't placing the blame on her for suddenly becoming a widow.

Rosemary made them two cups of tea, which she took through to the conservatory. The sun was high in the clear July sky and beating down on the glass, not that Julia could feel it. A small air conditioning unit hummed quietly in the corner, keeping the glass room nice and cool. They sat in two wicker bucket chairs and stared out at the garden as they silently hugged their tea.

"How are you feeling?" Julia asked, breaking the awkward silence. "Stupid question, I know."

"Honestly?" Rosemary asked, inhaling deeply as she continued to look out at the garden. "I feel free."

Julia opened her mouth to speak, but she had no idea what to say. She stared at Rosemary, and free seemed like the perfect word to describe the content expression on her lightly make-up covered face. When Julia had seen Rosemary on Saturday ripping her apron off after denying her husband a kiss, she had looked like she had had the weight of the world on her shoulders. Julia's eyes wandered down to her fingers. Just as she had suspected, she was missing her left index finger acrylic nail. What was left behind looked painful and coarse, as though it had been ripped clean off. The only time Julia had ever endured acrylic nails was when she had been Sue's maid of honour. She had guilt-tripped Julia into believing she needed them to complete the wedding, so she reluctantly went along with it. The extensions had been so cumbersome and alien, she had felt completely incapacitated for the entire day. Not being used to them, she had banged them more than a couple of times and the pain was incomparable to anything she had ever experienced. She couldn't imagine how it would feel to have one ripped off.

"I suppose you know I was the one to find Anthony's body," Julia started, pausing to check Rosemary was even listening beneath her calm exterior. "Somebody planted a bottle of poison in my café, and they left a message there, pinning the murder on me."

"Arsenic poisoning," Rosemary mumbled, her brows twitching, her expression still vacant. "That's what the police are saying. They're still running tests."

"Do you have any idea who would want to frame me for Anthony's murder?" Julia asked, edging forward in her seat, her heart beating as she got straight to the point of her visit. "I know me and Anthony didn't seem like the best of friends. He was trying to destroy my business after all, but I would never resort to *that*. I know he didn't like me, but I knew him too long to truly hate him *that* much."

"You're right," Rosemary said, suddenly turning to face Julia. "He didn't like you. He didn't like anyone. All he liked was himself, and money. *Look* at that swimming pool. I can count on one hand how many times he used it, but he made sure to swindle as many people as he could to pay for it. I hope the next people who buy this place fill it with cement."

"You're selling the cottage?"

"Of course," Rosemary said with a soft chuckle. "Just look at this place. It's devoid of any personality. It's him all over. Any personality this place had when we moved in, he stripped it away and replaced it with glass and metal."

Julia looked down at the white marble tiles, not wanting Rosemary to see how uncomfortable she looked. She was talking as though she had just divorced him, instead of what had really happened. Julia wondered if she was in denial. If she was, she couldn't blame her. What unsettled Julia the most was how lucid and present she looked.

"Will you stay in Peridale?" Julia asked.

"Perhaps," she said with a shrug. "Maybe I'll move somewhere new. Somewhere where I can *be* somebody new."

Footsteps signalled the arrival of Gareth, their son. He walked into the conservatory as though he was about to say something but he bit his tongue when he saw Julia.

"*Oh*," he said, his cheeks burning red. "Hello."

"Hello, Gareth," Julia said. "How are you feeling?"

The teenager shrugged, and even though he looked a little less relieved than his mother, he didn't look particularly distraught either. Julia suddenly remembered his presence at the protest meeting at the village hall, and wondered what could have led him to being there.

"Dad's business partner is outside," Gareth said, looking past Julia to his mum. "He's talking to that guy from the station."

"He's early," Rosemary said, grabbing a photo frame from the window ledge to check her reflection. "Thanks for the cottage pie, Julia. I'm eating out tonight, but I'm sure Gareth will enjoy it."

Gareth shrugged and stuffed his hands into his pockets. Rosemary sprung up like a woman half her age. Julia couldn't be sure, but she was sure Rosemary looked like she was about to go on a date.

Julia followed Rosemary down the hallway and back to the front door, feeling none the wiser as to who could have wanted to frame her for murder. She had been racking her brain all day in the café trying to think of people she had wronged, but she couldn't think of any rivalry that would result in a murder charge. The only person she could think of who might have gone to those extremes was the man who was now lying on a slab in the morgue.

Rosemary grabbed her handbag from the bannister, unclipped it, and pulled out a small bottle of perfume. After dousing herself in the sweet, floral scent, she checked that she didn't have lipstick on her teeth in the hallway mirror, slid her feet into simple black heels, and opened the door.

When Julia saw Barker standing at the bottom of the garden talking to another man, the wind knocked out of her sails, and the rug pulled from under her feet. She was aware that Rosemary was saying something to her, but she couldn't hear a thing other than the intense beating of her heart. All she could do was stare, until Anthony's business partner turned to face her, as though in slow motion. She hadn't seen that smug smirk in so long, but she recognised it in an instant.

"Jerrad, you're early," Rosemary said as she walked down the path. "Julia, are you coming?"

"I thought I'd surprise you," the man said with a leer as he pushed his suit jacket away to stuff his hands into his trouser pockets. "Hello, *Julia*. It's been a while."

Julia swallowed and walked forward, her legs like jelly. She met Barker's eyes, and he looked at her with a confused smile. She tried to smile back, but she wasn't sure her lips moved beyond a shivery twitch.

Jerrad was thinner and his hair looked different, but there was no denying who she was looking at. She realised she hadn't imagined things when she thought she had seen him talking with Anthony outside the coffee shop on Saturday afternoon.

"You know each other?" Rosemary asked, stopping in front of Julia and looking curiously down at her from her heel-elevated height. "It's a small world, isn't it?"

"You could say that," he said, his smirk growing wider and wider. "She's my wife."

"*Ex*-wife," Julia blurted out, her blank mind reacting

on impulse rather than thought.

"I think you need to speak to your lawyer, darlin'," Jerrad said, barely able to contain his pleasure as he reached forward to unclip the gate for Rosemary. "I never signed the papers. We're still married. Are you ready, Rosemary?"

Julia watched as Rosemary followed Jerrad towards a flashy sports car she didn't recognise. He opened the door for her, but he wasn't able to take his dark stare off Julia. Looking as though she was just as flummoxed, Rosemary craned her neck to stare back at Julia as Jerrad practically forced her into the car. Before he climbed in himself, he sent her a final wink, which turned her entire body to stone. It wasn't until the car sped away and vanished into the countryside that she could even bring herself to look at Barker.

"I can explain," she mumbled feebly.

Barker looked as though he was going to speak, but no words left his lips. He pinched between his brows, exhaled heavily, and turned with a shake of his head, as though he couldn't look at Julia; he looked disgusted. He pulled his keys from his pocket, jumped into his car, and sped in the opposite direction without a second look at Julia.

She didn't know what to say, or what to feel. Her past and her present had just collided so heavily, she couldn't imagine how there could possibly be any future.

"How long do I cook this thing for?" Gareth called through the still open front door.

Julia didn't realise she was crying until she wiped the tears away. She turned and walked back inside to help Gareth cook the cottage pie.

CHAPTER 6

"You *silly* girl," Dot said as she looked over the paperwork in her hand. "You should have checked to make sure everything was final!"

"I know," Julia mumbled, unable to look at the letter her lawyer had sent to her.

"Just because you signed the papers, it doesn't mean you're divorced," Dot said as she tossed the paper onto her dining room table. "Didn't your lawyer explain that to you?"

"I know that now," Julia said, trying not to get frustrated with her gran. "It's not like I've been divorced before. Jerrad had been badgering me so much through my lawyer, I just thought he'd already signed his half. I dragged my heels for so long before signing them."

"When did you sign them?" Dot asked.

"March," Julia mumbled pathetically. "They were on my kitchen counter for months before I could even open them."

"It's only July!" Dot cried. "Oh, Julia. You silly, *silly* girl. It needs to go before a judge before it's official, and that's only if you've both signed the agreement." Dot was just echoing what the lawyer had told her on the phone the night before. "Eat your dinner. You can't go hungry."

Julia looked down at the lamb chops and mash, but she wasn't hungry. She had been pushing the food around the plate, as had Sue, who looked as upset as Julia at everything that had happened. Julia tried to smile at her sister, to reassure her that she was fine, but she knew her eyes betrayed her.

"I can hit him," Jessie remarked suddenly after pushing her plate away. "Or even better, I'll get Billy to do it."

"What good will that do?" Sue asked with a shake of her head as her hands rested on her bump. "Violence doesn't solve anything."

"It will make me feel better," Jessie mumbled. "And a black eye might make Julia feel better."

Julia wasn't sure what would make her feel better. She picked up her phone and called Barker for what felt like the hundredth time that day. It had been an hour since his phone had stopped ringing, now going straight through to his voicemail. Julia had tried to leave a message more than once, but she knew nothing she could say would fix the mess she had caused.

"There's still a murderer out there," Dot said softly, reaching out to touch Julia's hand. "That should keep your mind off things."

"Is that supposed to cheer her up?" Sue asked with a laugh. "Half of the village think Julia did it, and the other half think Jessie did it, and the rest think both of them did it together."

"You can't have more than two halves," Jessie corrected her with a roll of her eyes. "That baby has pickled your already tiny brain."

Sue sat up in her chair, clearly offended. Julia let out a small laugh. It was the first time she had felt an emotion all day that wasn't dread. Sue dropped her stern expression and joined in the laughing.

"Leave my little lime out of things," Sue said with a rub of her stomach.

"I don't like limes," Dot mumbled thoughtfully. "Lemons, on the other hand, they're a real fruit. They taste delicious and are great for polishing silverware."

"They taste the same," Jessie fired across the table. "Both sour."

A heated debate about the difference between lemons and limes started across the table, but Julia had already tuned out. She was glad they were talking about something other than her divorce, or lack of one. She picked up the letter and read over the legal jargon that her lawyer had sent special delivery overnight, just confirming what he had told her on the phone.

When the debate died down, neither side having won, Julia helped Dot clear away the dishes, while Sue and Jessie went through to the sitting room where the café's leftover cakes were waiting for them.

"I think Rosemary is dating Jerrad," Julia thought aloud as she scraped her dinner into the bin. "She's twenty years older than him."

"Men are fickle," Dot replied as she filled the sink with water and washing up liquid. "One minute they want someone younger because they feel old, and then they want someone older because they realise twenty-year-old girls have empty heads and nothing in common. What did Rosemary have to say for herself?"

"Nothing much," Julia said as she closed the bin and placed her plate on the pile of others. "She didn't seem to care that her husband was dead. If she had suspected me of actually killing him, I'm sure she would have thanked me."

"I don't blame her," Dot mumbled as she snapped on her pink rubber gloves. "Your father and Anthony were cut from the same cloth. Both selfish, money-obsessed fools. If they can't throw money at something, they're not interested."

Julia thought about the five hundred pounds still sitting in her biscuit tin. She knew her father's vision was clouded by money, but she knew he wasn't as bad as Anthony had been.

"Did you know Anthony's mum?" Julia asked.

"I still do," Dot said as she put the first plate on the draining board. "Not that I've seen Barb in a while. She doesn't get down from the nursing home that often. We used to be quite close. Brian and Anthony were the best of friends from being knee high, right up until that nasty business with Anthony taking your father's share of their company. I didn't speak to Barb again after that, just on principle. I might not be your father's biggest fan, but I have my integrity."

"I should speak to her," Julia said, almost to herself. "She might know something useful."

"I doubt it," Dot said as she added the second dish to the draining board. "Her and Anthony were never close. She once told me she looked for the mark of the devil on his forehead when he was sleeping. But, if you want to talk to her, we'll go now."

Dot snapped off her rubber gloves and tossed them on the side, leaving the rest of the dishes for later.

"Now?" Julia asked as Dot grabbed her coat from under the stairs. "I don't think it's a good time."

"No time like the present!" she announced as she pulled on her beige coat. "It will keep your mind busy. *Girls*, we're going out. We'll be back in a jiffy. Don't touch my good biscuits!"

Julia almost protested, but her gran was right. She needed something to take her mind off things, and talking to Anthony's mother provided that distraction, if only temporarily.

***

Oakwood Nursing Home sat on the outskirts of Peridale, surrounded by acres of sprawling countryside and no other signs of life for miles. They took a small winding lane up to the old manor house, which dated back to the early 19th century, according to Dot. It looked like a luxury hotel, rather than a place where the elderly would spend their twilight years.

"If I start dribbling and you need to put me in a home, I'd like it to be this one," Dot whispered as she looked up at the canopy of oak tree leaves above them. "Not that *you'd* ever be able to afford it."

Julia's tyres crunched against the gravel as she followed

the signs for guest parking, which took her around the back of the building. When they parked next to the half a dozen other cars, they walked back to the entrance, pausing to stare at the beautiful stone water feature directly in front of the grand doors.

Once inside, the scent of flowers hit them immediately. They walked along the marble floor of the grand entrance hall towards a reception desk, which was filled with fresh, white lilies.

"*This* is the life!" Dot exclaimed excitedly into Julia's ear. "Luxury at its finest! Ol' Barb has done alright for herself here."

Julia approached the reception desk while her gran marvelled at the grand chandelier glittering above. Applying her friendliest smile, Julia waited until the well-dressed young nurse behind the reception desk looked up from a copy of *Sense and Sensibility*. She waited until she finished the page she was reading, before turning and looking up with a smile so wide, it looked too bright to be anything but genuine.

"Hello," she cooed softly. "Welcome to Oakwood Nursing Home. How can I help you today?"

"We want to speak with Barb," Julia said, realising she didn't even know the woman's surname "Barb Kennedy?"

"Barbara?" the nurse asked with a nod. "We have a *Barbara* here."

"She went by Barb in my day," Dot mumbled out of the corner of her mouth. "Probably too common for lady muck now."

"Are you on her approved visiting list?" the nurse asked, her smile still beaming. "Is she expecting you?"

"What is this?" Dot asked, slapping her hands on the

desk. *"Prison?"*

The nurse's smile faltered for the first time as she recoiled her head. Her smile bounced back in a second before she rolled across the marble floor in her chair to the computer.

"They're going to ask us to take our shoes off and send us through scanners next," Dot whispered. *"Ridiculous!"*

"Rosemary?" the nurse asked, looking up at them.

"Yes, that's me," Dot said quickly, pushing Julia out of the way, plastering a smile on her face. *"I* am Rosemary."

"Barbara wasn't expecting you until tomorrow, but I'm sure she won't mind the early visit," the nurse said as she typed away at her keyboard. "And *you* are?"

"This is my daughter," Dot said before Julia could answer.

"Gareth?" the nurse asked, her brows arching as she stared suspiciously at Dot.

"It's short for *Garethina,*" Dot blurted out, stamping on Julia's foot to let her know not to say a word. "It's a very common name in Germany."

"You're German?"

"Fräulein uske-be clair!" Dot chanted enthusiastically. "May we enter your *fine* establishment now?"

"Barbara is in the television room enjoying a cup of tea," the nurse said as she pressed a button under the desk, which buzzed and unlocked the nearest door. "Through there, follow it down to the bottom, and take the first right."

"I'm sure we'll find it," Dot mumbled, slipping her hand through Julia's and dragging her to the door, before pausing and turning back to the nurse. "You're only a receptionist, you know. You're not holding the keys to heaven."

With that, Dot tugged Julia through the door before the young woman could reply. Julia didn't need to see her face to know she had probably lost her bright smile.

"I didn't know you spoke German," Julia whispered as she pulled her hand free.

"I don't," Dot said with a shrug. "That was complete nonsense, but it sounded good, didn't it? You've got to think on your toes, Julia! Honestly, I don't know *how* you've cracked so many murder cases! I'll chalk this one down to you having a lot on your mind. *Ah*, here we go! The television room."

From what Julia knew of nursing homes, the television room was usually a dark and depressing space where the silent elderly faced a tiny, ancient TV, while watching *Cash in the Attic*, *Songs of Praise*, and *Countdown* in between bouts of medication. What she hadn't been expecting was an airy, open room, lined with bookshelves, and filled with chatter and laughter. Comfy chairs cluttered the room, facing in every direction other than the TV, which appeared to be there purely for background noise. A group of men were gathered around a pool table in the middle of the room, taking it in turns to pot the ball, while the rest of the residents looked on, chatting in between pots and cheering when a ball made its way into a pocket.

"There she is," Dot whispered, marching forward to a group of women who were sat in a cluster of armchairs in the corner of the room as they played a game of chess.

"You're *cheating*, Barb!" one of the women exclaimed. "You're *far* too good at this!"

"Just because I'm about to win, it doesn't mean I'm cheating," Barb replied with a wicked grin. "*Checkmate!*"

The other woman sat back in her chair and sighed, while Barb sat back and crossed one tan-tight covered leg over the other, looking pleased with herself. Julia wasn't sure if she had been expecting a frail old woman, but that's not what Barb was. Just like her gran, she looked to be in her eighties, and also like her gran, didn't look like she was ready to slow down and accept old age just yet. She was wearing a white and pink floral blouse, and her white hair, which looked impossibly long, was swept up into a giant bun that sat neatly on the top of her head, not a single hair out of place.

"*Dorothy?*" Barb called out. "Is that *you?*"

"It is, Barb," Dot said. "You're looking well."

"As are you," Barb said through a strained smile. "Ladies, excuse me."

Barb got out of her low armchair with ease, nodding to the women in her group as she did. She hooked her arm through Dot's and led her through open French doors and into the never-ending garden.

"I didn't realise Oakwood was taking applications," Barb said as Julia lingered behind. "It's good to see you, old friend."

"I'm just here visiting," Dot said. "Well, we're here to see you, actually. This is my granddaughter, Julia."

Barb sat on a low wall overlooking the saturated vegetation ahead of them, its hue impossibly vivid. She smiled her recognition at Julia, before narrowing her eyes, and snapping her fingers together.

"Brian's daughter?" she asked, looking Julia up and down. "I haven't seen you since you were in nappies! How's your mum?"

"Dead," Julia answered.

"Of course," Barb mumbled, tapping her chin with her finger before it drifted up to her temple. "The memory fades with age. I'm sorry, dear. I didn't mean any offence. What's the reason for your visit today? I'd like to say it was to rebuild old bridges, but I know you don't do anything for nothing, Dorothy."

"It's *Dot*, now," she corrected her. "As you are now Barbara."

"We all change, Dorothy," she said, ignoring her gran's correction. "You don't look a day over eighty-nine!"

"I'm only eighty-*three*," Dot seethed through pursed lips. "You know I'm five years younger than you."

"Ah, yes," Barb said, tapping her temple once more. "The memory."

Dot glanced at Julia out of the corner of her eye, giving her the impression it was nothing to do with her memory, and more to do with this being how Barb was.

"I assume you've heard?" Dot asked.

"About my son's murder?" she replied coolly. "Of course. News travels fast in this village."

"You don't seem upset," Dot said bluntly. "He was your son."

"You know we weren't close," she said with a wave of her hand. "One reluctant flying visit every Friday for ten years doesn't constitute a close relationship. He looked at his watch the entire time. I was a chore to him. Nothing more, nothing less."

Julia was struck by the woman's coldness, despite delivering everything with a sweet smile. She couldn't imagine her gran being so callous if her own son died, no matter how strained their relationship was. Julia wasn't a mother, so maybe she didn't understand the complexities that came with it, but she had Jessie, and no matter how far apart they might drift, they were connected forever, and if anything ever happened to Jessie, Julia wouldn't be able to brush it off as something as trivial as a change in the weather.

"The thing is, Barb, somebody is trying to frame my granddaughter for your son's murder," Dot said, glancing uncomfortably at Julia. "Naturally, she didn't do it, but she found the body, and there is some rather - let's say - *incriminating*, evidence."

"Okay?" Barb replied, glancing back at the television room as though she wanted nothing more than to return to her game of chess. "How can I help?"

"We were just wondering if you knew if Anthony had any enemies," Julia asked, speaking up for the first time. "I just want to piece things together so I can clear my name."

Barb leaned forward and looked at Julia, her lips twisting as though she was containing a laugh. She held it back for a second before letting it burst free as she looked between the two of them.

"How long have you got?" Barb asked with a chuckle. "My son's favourite hobby was making enemies. From the time he first realised that money equalled power he was out for himself. He was a lovely baby, you know. He first stole from my purse when he was four. Took a shilling and six pence and used it to con one of his friends out of their Slinky. Sold it on to another for half a crown. Sometimes, I wonder if there was anything I could have done, but some children just come out wrong."

That sounded like the Anthony Julia knew. Even when she had been a child, he would dig through the toys her mother would buy her from car boot sales to see if any of them were rare or worth a penny or two.

"We were looking for some specific names," Julia asked.

"Ask your father," Barb snapped, her smile dropping. "How did you even get in here anyway? Neither of you is on my list."

Barb looked like she was going to continue with her rant, but a young nurse with long dark hair appeared behind them, holding a silver tray with a cup of pills and a glass of water.

"*Ah!* Yelena!" Barb exclaimed, clapping her hands together. "Just in time. Dot, it was nice catching up. Julia, good seeing you again. I must go and take my pills. You know what it's like at this age."

"I didn't want to interrupt," Yelena said, her accent clearly Eastern European. "But you said –"

"You're not interrupting anything," Dot mumbled as she scratched the side of her head, her brows high up her forehead. "See you around, Barb."

With that, she pushed off the wall and walked back into the television room, followed by Yelena who smiled meekly at Dot and Julia over her shoulder. Julia looked on in disbelief as Barb took her pills, shooed Yelena away, and started another game of chess. Just like Rosemary, she was totally unfazed. She wondered if this was a natural reaction she was going to receive from anybody close to Anthony.

"Imagine being that evil that your own mother doesn't mourn your death," Dot said. "Let's get out of here. I can feel them trying to absorb your youth like a nicotine patch."

They hurried back through the television room, back down the corridor, and into the entrance hall. The receptionist jumped up and ran forward, clutching something in her hands.

"Take a brochure?" she asked Dot with a bright smile. "We offer competitive rates."

"Thank you," Dot said, taking the thick, green volume before walking towards the exit and dumping it straight into the small bin next to the door. "I take it back, Julia. If I ever need putting in one of these places, take me to the fields and shoot me like a horse with a broken leg. Did you see how cheery they all were? It's practically sickening!"

Before Julia could reply, her heart stopped when she saw Barker's familiar car drive past, its tyres crunching on the gravel. Julia waited for him to park and make his way around to the front. When he saw her, he looked surprised that she was there. He stopped in his tracks and looked over his shoulder as though he was deciding if he should turn around. To her relief, he didn't, and he pressed forward.

"I'll wait in the car," Dot whispered as she slipped the keys from Julia's pocket. "*Barker.*"

"Dot," he replied with a curt nod. "*Julia.*"

"Barker," Julia said, hating how they suddenly felt like strangers again. "How are you?"

"I'm fine," he said, his eyes vacant and slightly red. "You?"

Julia almost responded with an automated answer, but her heart and mind were racing, trying to overtake the other.

"I'm sorry," she said. "I was going to tell you."

Barker gulped and looked down at the car keys in his hand. For a moment, she thought he might start crying, or even shout at her, but he looked up, his expression blank. She would have preferred anger over indifference.

"Why are you here?" he asked her.

"Visiting an old friend of Dot's," Julia said, hating that she was telling a lie to cover the fact she had lied about her promise not to investigate. "You?"

"Smashed window," he said. "Some kids from the Fern Moore Estate. Nothing too serious. I should get inside. They're expecting me."

Julia nodded and stepped to the side, staring at him and willed him to look back at her with the kind eyes she had come to know and love.

"I *really* am sorry," Julia called after him before he opened the door. "I honestly thought we were divorced."

Barker dropped his head again, before turning and looking at her. She knew that wasn't the point. She knew she should have told him either way. She caught a glimpse of the kindness she loved, and it sent her heart racing rapidly. No sooner had it returned did it vanish again.

"I just want you to be happy, Julia," he said heavily, dropping his eyes once more. "I need some space to think."

Julia nodded her understanding, even if she didn't want to. She wanted nothing more than to grab Barker and hold him until everything was fine again, but she wasn't entirely sure that he wouldn't push her away in an instant.

"Okay," was all she could think to say.

Barker half-smiled before pulling on the door and slipping into the nursing home. When he vanished, she grabbed fistfuls of her hair in frustration as she stared up hopelessly at the sky.

"Jessie sent you a text message," Dot said, Julia's phone in her hand as she climbed into her car. "She's back at your cottage. How are things?"

"Not good," Julia said before twisting the key in the ignition and reversing so quickly her wheels spun hopelessly against the gravel. "But can you blame him?"

Julia didn't realise she was driving fast until she pulled up outside her gran's cottage minutes after leaving the nursing home. Dot invited her in for some tea, but Julia declined, just wanting to be at home. She sped up to her cottage and walked through the unlocked door. She headed into the kitchen, surprised to see Jessie and Billy.

"*Oh*," Julia said. "Am I interrupting something?"

"Billy was just leaving," Jessie said through gritted teeth. "Weren't you, Billy?"

"Alright, alright," he said, backing away with his hands in the air. "Call me, yeah, babe?"

"I'm not your '*babe*'," Jessie said with a roll of her eyes. "Just clear off, will you?"

Billy winked at Jessie before doubling back and leaving the way Julia had just arrived. When they were alone, Julia went straight for the kettle and made herself and Jessie a cup of peppermint and liquorice tea.

"Are you okay?" Jessie asked softly, a hand resting on her shoulder. "He just turned up here. I didn't invite him."

"I'm fine," Julia lied, forcing back the tears and injecting a smile into her voice. "It's your home too, Jessie. You can invite anyone you want here. Grab the ice cream from the freezer. We can eat it with a film. You can pick."

Julia took the two teas into the living room where Jessie was waiting with two spoons, an open tub of vanilla ice cream, and the *Breakfast at Tiffany's* DVD menu on the screen. Julia was touched.

"I know it's old and boring, but it's your favourite film," Jessie said meekly.

Julia sat next to Jessie, rested her head on her shoulder, grabbed a spoon, tucked into the ice cream, and pressed play on the film. Even if Barker wasn't there with her, she was going to try and enjoy her evening with three of her favourite people: Audrey Hepburn, George Peppard, and Jessie.

CHAPTER 7

Wednesday evenings had become one of Julia's favourite days of the week. It was the day Jessie spent at college studying towards her apprenticeship, and when she came home, she brought Dolly and Dom with her for dinner. Cooking for the three of them had become a routine Julia looked forward to because having a house full of teenagers was something she never thought she would experience. This Wednesday, however, there was a space at the table where Barker should have been. Julia had even set a place for him before she remembered.

If Dolly and Dom noticed the lack of Barker's presence, they didn't mention it. Julia wondered if Jessie had told them not to bring him up, but she wasn't sure they would remember not to if she had. It always amused Julia how much they attempted to probe Barker about his cases, and how he always tried his best to dodge their questioning, answering them as a politician would; by not answering them at all. If he had told them he was investigating the murder of a rainbow coloured elephant, they probably would have lapped it up.

"This casserole is top quality," Dolly mumbled through a mouthful of food, barely pausing for air. "Thanks, Ju."

"It's *Julia*," Jessie corrected her without missing a beat. "Ju-li-*a*."

"I like Ju more," Dom added, also barely pausing. "Rolls off the tongue. *Juuuuuuu*."

"Ju-Ju," Dolly added. "Sounds like chew-chew."

Jessie rolled her eyes, but Julia chortled. Most of the time, the twins spoke their own language of childlike gibberish, but it distracted her, and she needed that. They made Jessie look completely adult in comparison, despite being the same age.

After dinner, Jessie helped Julia take the dishes through to the kitchen. It hadn't gone unnoticed to Julia that Jessie had glanced at Barker's empty space more than once.

"Did you invite him?" Jessie asked as she scraped the leftovers into the bin.

"He said he needed space," Julia said, trying to stay as calm as possible. "It's the least I can do."

"He'll come 'round," Jessie said, smiling at Julia hopefully in the dark reflection of the window. "He's not so bad."

Julia smiled back, but she wasn't as sure as Jessie. She had seen the hurt in his eyes, and she had caused that. She looked down as she filled the sink with water, hoping she could hold back the tears until she was alone. Why hadn't she just been honest with him from the start?

"Why is *he* even in Peridale?" Jessie asked. "I thought Jerrad lived in London?"

"I don't know," Julia said, not having given him much thought because of Barker consuming her thoughts. "I haven't seen him again."

"Happy Bean is back open," Jessie reminded her. "Do you think he's involved with that?"

The thought had crossed Julia's mind, but she couldn't figure out why Jerrad was interested in investing in a small chain coffee shop in a village that barely featured on the map. Jerrad dealt with high-stakes property investment, which had helped him get very rich over the years.

"He looked different," Julia said. "Like it was him, but it wasn't him. He seemed thinner and taller, and he looked like he had more hair."

A knock at the door interrupted their conversation. Julia pulled her hands out of the soapy water and wiped them on a tea towel, leaving Jessie to take over. She popped her head into the dining room, where Dolly and Dom were thumb wrestling; neither of them seemed to be winning.

"Hello, Julia," her father said when she opened the door. "Are you busy?"

"I've just finished dinner," she replied, glancing over her shoulder to the kitchen and spotting Jessie craning her neck around the side of the fridge. "Is everything okay?"

"Everything's fine," he said, tucking his face into the high collar of his overcoat. "Do you want to come for a walk?"

Julia didn't question him. She swapped her slippers for

her comfortable shoes, told Jessie she would be ten minutes, and followed her dad out of her garden and onto the winding lane. Instead of walking back towards the village, he walked up the lane towards Peridale Farm, which was the last stop before the village ended.

"It's a lovely night," he said quietly as he tucked his hands into his jacket pockets and looked up at the dark sky, the last streaks of the pink sunset lingering on the horizon. "I need to get out more. I miss a lot being cooped up in that old manor."

Julia bit her tongue. She almost reminded him that it had been his choice to marry a woman the same age as his eldest daughter and join her reclusive family, who lived in Peridale but had never been part of the community.

"How's Katie's father doing?" she asked, deciding it was better to continue with the small talk until he got to the point.

"He's as good as he can be," he said, sucking the cool night air through his teeth. "He's comfortable. Since that last stroke, he hasn't said a word, but Katie keeps trying. I think he knows she's there, but it's difficult for her."

Julia thought back to the time Katie's father, Vincent Wellington, had saved her life when she was being carried to her death by the murderer of Katie's brother. If it hadn't been for him pressing the emergency call button and waking everybody up, she would have followed Charles out of the window and down to her death.

"Your gran called," he said as a car passed them on the narrow lane, the headlights blinding her. "She told me about Anthony, but half the village had already called by that point. I think people put two and two together and guessed I might know something because we used to be in business together."

"You used to be more than that," Julia said, remembering what her gran had said about them being friends from childhood. "He was your best man."

"I was blind," he said, dropping his head. "I wasted my life working with that man, avoiding my problems."

A lump rose in Julia's throat. She thought about all the times she had sat by her gran's sitting room window waiting for her father to return from his many business trips. It hadn't taken her long, even as a child, to realise the gaps between the visits home were growing and the time spent at home was shrinking. Their relationship had never repaired beyond that point. Seeing him twice in one week felt unusual for Julia, but she appreciated the effort he was putting in. She knew it would have taken a lot for him to swallow his pride and knock on her door.

"Why did you come here, Dad?" Julia asked, stopping and leaning against the wall before they reached Peridale Farm. "It's not like you were passing by."

He laughed softly and joined her in leaning against the wall. He ran his fingers through his thick, blow-dried hair, which was styled similarly to how Anthony's had been, but brown and grey instead of yellow blonde.

"Your gran asked me about Anthony's enemies," he started, turning to look at her. "I apparently gave her the same answer as Barb. He wasn't on a lot of people's favourite's lists, mine included."

"Are you upset he was killed?"

He thought for a moment, looked up at the sky, and shrugged meekly with tight lips. Julia could tell that he was upset, which was more than she had seen from any of the man's family so far. She knew it meant something deep down that the best man at his wedding was now dead, even if they hadn't spoken in years.

"I wrote down a couple of names," he said, ignoring the question. He reached into his pocket and pulled out a small hand-written list, which was on thick Wellington monogrammed paper. "I know you're looking into it. I gave the same list to the police, just to be fair."

Julia looked over the names on the list, all of them belonging to men. She didn't recognise any of them.

"Do any of these men live in Peridale?" Julia asked, knowing how far an antique dealer's net could stretch.

"These two do," he said, pointing to the top two names on the list. "Timothy Edwards and Mike Andre. I called some of my old contacts and they were more than forthcoming with names. According to them, Anthony had stopped trying to be even a little honest in the last couple of months and had been conning every single person he came into contact with. There's definitely more, but this is a start."

"It's a good start," Julia said, pocketing the list. "Thank you. Who do you think killed him, Dad?"

He sucked the air through his teeth once more and looked dead ahead at the horizon as the sky completely faded to black. Julia could make out the lights lining the motorway in the distance as the cars whizzed up and down the lanes, but they were too far away to hear.

"He was a cold man," he said. "He'd been unfaithful to Rosemary for years, and I think she knew it."

Julia thought about how unbothered she had been, and the apparent date she had been on with Jerrad. Julia almost told her father that her estranged husband was in the village, but she realised they had only met a couple of times over the course of their twelve-year marriage.

"Do you know any of the women who were his mistresses?" Julia asked as they set off back to her cottage. "That might help."

"Not *just* women," he said, his brows darting high up his lined forehead. "Anthony was never fussy when it came to *that*. The last I heard, he was seeing a woman from the hospital, but that was when we were still on speaking terms."

Julia almost dismissed the information because it had been so long ago, but she suddenly remembered seeing the woman laying flowers at the coffee shop and how she had been sure she had seen her at the hospital Sue worked at. Julia had been so tired, she had thought the woman was just blaming her with her eyes because of the gossip she had heard, but as she thought back, she could see the grief burning behind the woman's glassy gaze.

"I should be getting back," he said, pausing at Julia's gate before going any further. "Don't forget Sunday lunch at the manor. Have you asked Sue yet?"

"We'll come," Julia said, not wanting to admit she had completely forgotten about the lunch, or to ask Sue. The look of hopefulness in her father's eyes surprised her, and it made it impossible to refuse the invitation. "I promise."

He nodded and backed away, before turning and walking down the winding lane towards the village. Across the road, Julia noticed Emily twitching at her net curtains. Julia waved, which caused Emily to quickly retreat back into the safety of her living room.

"What did he have to say?" Jessie asked as she wiped her hands, the washing up completely finished. "Didn't want his money back, did he?"

"He came to give me information," Julia said, clutching the note to her chest before passing it to Jessie. "Recognise any of those names?"

She knew it was a long shot, and she didn't actually expect Jessie to know any of the men on the list, so she was shocked when the girl's eyes opened wide and she nodded her head.

"Mike Andre," she said with certainty. "He was a tutor at my college. Emigrated to Australia a couple of months ago. Who are these people?"

"Potential enemies of Anthony Kennedy," Julia said as she pinned the note to the fridge under a cat magnet. "People my dad thinks might have been conned enough to resort to murder. If Mike Andre left Peridale months before the murder, that only leaves one other name on his list in the village."

Julia pulled a pen from her kitchen's clutter drawer, pulled the cap off with her teeth, and circled '*Timothy Edwards*' until it was the only name she could see.

"It's a good start," she said, echoing what she had said to her dad.

"I'll grab the phonebook," Jessie said, already walking into the hallway. "I'll start ringing those other names to see if any of them were near Peridale this weekend."

Julia almost stopped her, but she let her return with the blue public directory phonebook. She knew all Jessie wanted to do was make herself useful, so if this were what she wanted to do, she would let her; it would keep her out of any real trouble.

While Jessie started ringing through the numbers in the dining room with Dolly and Dom, Julia took her mobile phone into the bathroom and called her sister.

"Sue? It's me. Do you know a woman who works at your hospital who might have been having an affair with Anthony Kennedy?"

CHAPTER 8

Peridale ran through Julia's veins. It was the village she had been born in, along with generations of her family for as long as anybody could remember. Even though she had been living back in Peridale for two years, Julia still felt like a fool for running off with a charming man to the big, bright city. It had taken two years back in her natural habitat to realise the lure of something entirely different than what she had always known was what had tempted her so strongly. Now that she was back where she belonged, nothing could make her leave again.

During their marriage, Jerrad had made his feeling on Peridale clear. He thought it was a backwards, dead-end village, where things went to die and ideas were stifled.

What he had always failed to realise was that it was a buzzing community filled with life and laughter. Julia had never forgotten that.

Remembering this made it even stranger to look out of her café window and see Jerrad across the village green clearing a table outside Happy Bean. Since opening an hour ago, four different villagers had come in to tell Julia that Anthony's secret business partner was now running the coffee shop, which only confirmed her suspicions as to Jerrad's sudden appearance in the village. The question she couldn't stop asking herself was why? Why a coffee shop? Why in Peridale? Why now?

"We've run out of semi-skimmed milk," Jessie said as she poured the last of it into a latte for Roxy Carter, one of Julia's oldest friends from childhood, who was now a teacher at St. Peter's Primary School in the village.

"He looks different," Roxy said, tucking her flame red hair behind her ears as she joined Julia in staring out of the window at Jerrad as he slowly wiped a table, no doubt to taunt Julia. "I know I only met him a couple of times, but he looks different."

"I know," Julia mumbled. "I can't figure out why."

"You don't still –"

"Have feelings for him?" Julia scoffed, the suggestion turning her stomach. "That's the *last* thing on my mind right now."

"*Milk!*" Jessie cried with a roll of her eyes as she tossed the empty carton in the bin and poured the steamed milk in with the espresso shot.

Julia took Roxy's money and handed over the latte, before taking a five-pound note from the petty cash and joining Roxy in walking out of the café.

"He's looking over," Roxy said, squinting into the sun as she sipped her hot latte. "*Mmmm*, you've trained that girl well, Julia. She knows how to make coffee."

"Jerrad doesn't even like coffee," Julia remembered aloud. "Why a coffee shop?"

"Even the dying towns have busy coffee shops," she said before taking another sip of her latte. "Although you know I'll always be loyal to you."

Julia nodded her appreciation. After a fluke busy spell on Monday in the wake of the murder, Julia's café had returned to the ghost town it had become since Happy Bean had opened. Only a few of her most loyal customers were still popping in daily, Roxy being one of them.

"You don't think it's something I'm doing, do you?" Julia asked. "Maybe I'm just not good enough."

"You're the best baker this village has," Roxy said as she darted in to peck Julia on the cheek. "Things will return to normal soon. The novelty will wear off and people will realise they miss your fresh cakes. You'll see. I need to get back to the school, but I'll see you tomorrow."

Julia hoped she was right. For the sake of her business and keeping a roof over hers and Jessie's heads, she prayed Roxy was right.

After grabbing four large bottles of milk and having a little chat with Shilpa, who was trying to tell Julia she thought Anthony poisoned himself out of guilt for what he had done to the village, Julia returned to her café. The hairs on the back of her neck immediately stood on end when she saw Jerrad sitting at the table nearest the counter, staring around her café with a look of contempt.

"I tried to get him out," Jessie said desperately. "He won't budge."

"Threatened to '*bash my head in*'," Jerrad said with a little chuckle, his fingers performing the air quotes sign, something he used to do all the time to mock Julia. She had forgotten how much it irritated her. "Where did you find this one, darlin'?"

"Jessie lives with me," Julia said proudly as she marched back to the counter with the milk bottles in her hands. "And I'm not your '*darlin*'', okay?"

Julia performed the air quotes, which only roused a small smirk from Jerrad. His right brow, the only one he could arch, darted up his forehead, and Julia was sure it reached closer to his hairline than she remembered.

"You did always have a thing for the waifs and strays," he said as he picked dirt from under his nails. "Couldn't pass a homeless person without tossing a quid at them. I always told you, you'd be better off ignoring them, so they learn their lesson."

Julia clutched her hand around Jessie's, which was shaking violently with rage. She squeezed hard, letting her know he wasn't worth it. She was sure if Jerrad knew the truth about Jessie, and the months she had spent homeless and how many of her friends had been murdered on the streets, it wouldn't have made a difference. It probably would have launched him into one of his political rants, where he was the only person allowed a valid opinion. Julia kept her mouth firmly shut, which was something she had learned to do many years ago. This time, however, it was to spare Jessie.

"Why are you here, Jerrad?" Julia asked flatly while Jessie busied herself putting the milk in the fridge under the coffee machine.

"Oh, you know," he said, suddenly standing up and

pacing back and forth. "Just to check out the competition."

"I meant why are you in Peridale?"

"The same reason you are," he said, as though it was obvious. "For a fresh start."

Julia's stomach churned painfully, just as it had when she had first seen him. Not because she was learning that he was sticking around, but because that's what she had suspected all along. It seemed like the sort of cruel twist of fate that she was due, considering what she had kept from Barker.

"You *hate* this village," she reminded him. "It's *my* home."

"It's not *so* bad," he said with a shrug as he ran his finger along the shelf containing Julia's Peridale themed trinkets. He rubbed his fingers together, pretending to see dust, but Julia knew Jessie had cleaned that shelf only an hour ago because she was so bored. "Once you get used to it, it's almost – *quaint*. I can see why you were so obsessed."

"How did you ever marry this guy?" Jessie whispered as she listened from under the counter, stocking the fridge with the milk cartons as slowly as humanly possible. "He's a total *pig!*"

"I see you're still doing your baking," he said, walking over to the cake stand to peer inside. "Perhaps you and I could do some business? Since I'm running the coffee shop, it would be nice to appeal to the locals a little more."

"And put me entirely out of business?" Julia replied, suppressing her laughter. "You're out of your mind if you think I'd *ever* trade with you."

"I'd pay you reasonably," he said smugly. "What's the going rate these days? I can never keep up with the minimum wage. Always going up, while the effort goes down. That's what's wrong with our country. People are paid far too much for the most basic jobs. It's holding us back from growing."

Julia sighed, glad that Jerrad had cut his speech short. It was nothing she hadn't heard before. She used to tune it out, and nod and hum her agreement every so often, throwing in *'yes, dear'*, and *'you're right'* so he didn't question her. She couldn't believe she had ever been that woman.

"This *isn't* you," Julia said, looking around her café. "Peridale *isn't* you. You're a Londoner."

"I'm very adaptable," he said, meeting her eyes, his dark pupils looking right through her. "As are you. Taking in a young girl, hooking up with the local detective inspector. People do like to talk in this village. I hear you've become the woman to come to in a sticky situation too. Solving murders? That's not the Julia I knew."

"You don't know me," she reminded him, her voice stronger than it had ever been talking to him. "You only knew what you wanted to know."

Jerrad rested a hand on the counter, his eyes meeting hers, his lids flickering for a moment. She didn't recognise the look in his eyes. It made her anxious. She darted her eyes down to the counter, catching a flash of silver on his left hand. He was still wearing their wedding ring. Julia instinctively touched her own ring finger, which had been absent of a ring from the moment he had packed her things in bin bags and left a note on the doorstep. She had never regretted the decision to toss the ring in the River Thames. She thought about how much money she could have sold the diamond-studded band for, and how it would help keep her café afloat while she thought of new ways to tempt the customers back in. Just like the bundle of red notes in her biscuit tin, it was tainted money she would rather do without.

"We're going to have to learn to live alongside each other," he said as he stuffed his hands into his trouser pockets, making Julia wonder if he knew she had noticed the ring on his finger. "I'm staying at the B&B with some bonkers psychic woman offering me card readings every morning at breakfast. It's temporary until I find somewhere more permanent."

"You really are staying here," she whispered, her voice dark and suddenly angry. "You twisted little piece of –"

"I've invested every penny I've got into this business," he jumped in, his voice suddenly lowering as he leaned across the counter. "Anthony fleeced me, and now this is my way to get that money back. I'm not missing that chance, darlin'. Not for you, or anyone else in this village. See you around."

Jerrad's leather shoes squeaked on the tiled floor, and he sauntered slowly out of her café, making sure to eye up every small detail with a curl in his lip.

"Not missing his chance, eh?" Jessie said, bouncing up from the floor and folding her arms against her apron as they watched him walk across the village green. "Sounds like a motive for murder if ever I've heard one."

"It really does," Julia said. "For the man I remembered, the kind of money it takes to invest in a business like that is pocket change. If he's sunk all of his money into that coffee shop, he must not have had a lot to throw away in the first place. Did he seem a little desperate to you?"

"Reeked of the stuff," Jessie said, wriggling her nostrils. "And an aftershave that stinks of old men. Gross."

Julia sniffed up, his scent still lingering. Even after twelve years, the spicy fragrance that reminded her of the kind of detergent they used in hospital bathrooms still had the ability to churn her stomach.

"He's up to something," Julia whispered to herself as he walked back into his coffee shop. "And I'm going to find out what."

***

After closing the café, Julia drove to the hospital where Sue worked. She sat in her car, as instructed during their call the day before, until her sister came out of the front doors. Sue wafted the clouds of smoke from the smokers as she hurried through, jumping straight into Julia's distinctive aqua blue Ford Anglia.

"She's here," Sue said as she pulled her phone out of her pocket. "It was hard to snap a picture of her, but I managed to get one when she was getting a coffee at the vending machine. My flash went off, but I blamed it on baby brain. She didn't ask questions."

Sue swiped through several blurry pictures of her feet and the hospital floor before landing on a perplexed looking woman who was staring straight at the camera while she slotted a coin into the coffee machine.

"That's her," Julia said. "She's the woman I saw laying flowers at the coffee shop after I was released from the station. What do you know about her?"

"Her name is Maggie Croft. She's forty-seven, and she's worked here for the past twenty-five years from what I can gather. She's nice enough, but a little quiet. She likes to keep to herself, but the walls talk. She left her husband six months ago, and they're already divorced. People have been saying she's been having an affair for years. I stayed out of it, but she's the first person I could think of when you called. I'm sure I even saw Anthony here a couple of times now that I think about it."

"Dad said Anthony was having an affair with a woman at the hospital back when they were still friends, and I saw her at the scene of his death, so there's no denying it."

"Do you think she *killed* him?" Sue asked. "She collects ceramic figures of pugs. I was her secret Santa three years ago. That's all I could get out of people. Bit weird, don't you think?"

"I don't think a person's tastes in ceramics makes them capable of murder," Julia said with a laugh. "But if she was having an affair with him, and she left her husband, my guess is she expected Anthony to leave his wife too."

"And when he didn't, she poisoned him?" Sue asked, her eyes widening. "That's the last time I accept a coffee from her on a night shift. How are things with you and Barker?"

Julia squirmed in her seat, wanting to talk about anything else but Barker.

"Not good," Julia said, her chest aching. "He can barely bring himself to look at me."

"I can get my Neil to talk to him," Sue offered, resting a hand on Julia's knee. "A man to man chat at The Plough over a pint? That usually does the trick."

"Thanks, but this is something I need to sort out myself," Julia said, smiling appreciatively at her sister. "Jerrad came into my café to gloat today. He's acting like he's sticking around to run the coffee shop."

"He's moving to the village?" Sue asked, twisting in her

seat. "But he *can't*!"

"He can, and he will. He said he sunk all of his money into the business and he's not going to see it wasted."

"Oh, Julia," Sue whispered, grabbing her hand and squeezing hard. "I'm so sorry."

Julia squeezed back. She was sorry too; sorry she hadn't dealt with Jerrad sooner. She had realised that if she hadn't prolonged signing the papers for so long, Jerrad might have signed his half and they would have been divorced. If she had told Barker that earlier in their relationship, it might have been easier to face Jerrad being in the village with the man she loved standing by her side to support her.

"Barker will come around," Sue said. "I promise. He loves you, and that's all that matters."

"And what about honesty?"

"You didn't *lie* to him," Sue said, chewing the inside of her lip. "You just didn't tell him the *truth*. There's a difference."

"I don't think he sees it like that."

"Men usually don't," Sue said as she pocketed her phone and pulled on the door handle. "They see the world in shades of black and white and nothing in between. It's us girls who are cursed with that grey area. It makes us overthink, but it's also what makes us compassionate, caring creatures capable of brilliance. Barker sees that. He knows you, and he'll forgive you, given time. Men are like plants. You water and feed them, and the rest takes care of itself. The leaves may wilt, but a little tender love and care and they bounce right back. I need to get back. Debbie is covering for me. I said I was only nipping to the loo. I checked the schedule. Maggie finishes in ten minutes. She usually lingers outside for a cigarette before walking to the bus stop. You never heard any of this from me."

"Gotcha," Julia said, tapping the side of her nose. "Thank you."

"Don't ever forget that you're brilliant," Sue said into the car before closing the door. "My beautiful, brilliant, big sister. I'm going to go before I burst into tears. The lime is messing with my emotions today."

After a little pat on her bump and a final wave to Julia, she retreated back into the hospital, dramatically wafting her hands once again as she slipped through the cloud of smoke billowing from the patients.

Julia waited a couple of minutes before locking her car and walking towards the entrance. She checked her reflection in a car window, and dusted flour from her chocolatey curls.

She lingered back by the pay and display machine, smiling awkwardly at visitors as they glanced suspiciously at her while they tried to pay for their parking. After ten minutes, she began obsessively checking her watch, as more patients tossed their cigarettes to the ground and withdrew back to their wards, only to be replaced with more seconds later. She considered calling Sue to ask if she was sure she had the right time, until she saw Maggie slip out of the hospital.

Julia held back for a moment and observed the woman. Her eyes were stained red, her caramel blonde hair looked ratty and unwashed, and the duffel coat she was wearing over her blue uniform looked like it needed a trip to the dry cleaners. Compared to Rosemary, it was the difference between night and day. Julia watched as she fished her cigarettes out of her pocket, lighting one with shakier hands than some of the patients struggling to balance their crutches and their lighters. When her cigarette was lit, Julia took her moment.

Holding her breath through the smoke cloud, she looked ahead at Maggie, realising why she had recognised her as working at the hospital. She lifted her fingers up to the faint scar near her hairline where she had been struck by Charles Wellington's murderer in March. Maggie had been the nurse to remove the stitches. If it had been for the stitches alone, Julia might have forgotten her face entirely, but it was also the day she had signed and posted her divorce papers, so every detail of that day was engrained forever in her memory.

"*Maggie?*" Julia asked softly as she walked forward, her hands in her pockets. "Can I join you?"

Maggie scowled at Julia for a moment before a flash of recognition burned through her strained eyes. She pulled her cigarette out of her mouth and blew the stale smoke into Julia's face.

"*You!*" she sneered, venom in her voice. "What do *you* want?"

"I know what you've heard about me, but I can assure you, it's not true," Julia said, standing next to Maggie uninvited and leaning against the sign that told patients not to smoke at the entrance. "I didn't kill Anthony. I know you loved him."

"What do *you* know?" Maggie scoffed before sucking hard on her cigarette, tiny lines framing her lips. "How did you find me here?"

"I know you were in a relationship with Anthony Kennedy for many years before he died," Julia said, ignoring Maggie's second question. "I know you left your husband, probably in the hope that Anthony would do the same with his wife so you could be together."

The cigarette dropped from her lips and tumbled down her uniform. She stared at Julia for a moment before quickly dusting the grey ash off the blue fabric. She stamped on the cigarette and instantly pulled a fresh one from the packet. To Julia's surprise, she offered her one, which she politely declined. Roxy Carter's older sister, Rachel, had once persuaded Julia to try a cigarette when they were teenagers, but after one baby inhale she knew it hadn't been for her and one had never passed her lips since. Rachel was now in prison serving a life sentence for stabbing one of Julia's customers, but Julia didn't like to think the cigarettes were linked to the murderous streak, even as she was watching the woman at the top of her suspects' list light another cigarette.

"Anthony *loved* me," Maggie whispered through the side of her mouth as she struggled to light the tip with trembling fingers. "*Dammit!*"

She tossed the lighter to the ground, her hands disappearing up into her unkempt hair. She rested her head against the wall and clenched her eyes, the unlit cigarette falling from her lips as she began to cry.

"I don't think you were the only one," Julia said. "I don't know that for certain, but I've known Anthony for a long time."

"His wife *manipulated* him," Maggie said desperately, letting go of her hair and opening her eyes. "She *blackmailed* him to stay. He *couldn't* leave."

Julia thought back to the stylishly dressed woman who looked like she had had the weight of the world lifted off her shoulders in the wake of her husband's murder. It broke Julia's heart to think Maggie was another woman, just like her, who had allowed herself to be hoodwinked by a ruthless man.

"I think we both know Anthony wasn't going to leave his wife, and even if he did, he wouldn't have run into your arms."

"You don't know *anything*!" Maggie laughed coldly. "He used to laugh at you. The stupid little café girl with ideas above her station. He put you right in your place with his new business. He was going to bring me into it when it was doing better. He was going to open another location and let me run it. He loved me."

Julia knew it was no use trying to convince Maggie otherwise. Anthony might have been dead, but his ideas were well and truly alive in the poor woman's mind. Julia just prayed she would wake up and realise she was better than that before it broke her.

"I may just be a stupid little café girl, but I'm not going to sit back and take the blame for a murder I didn't commit," Julia whispered, leaning into Maggie so that nobody could hear her. "Where were you on the night Anthony was poisoned?"

Maggie stared at Julia for a moment as though she couldn't decide if she should take her seriously or not. A small laugh escaped her lips, but her nostrils flared, her expression flattening in an instant.

"I can't remember," she whispered, her bottom lip trembling. "Anthony had been ignoring my calls all week. He said he was busy, but I tried to go and see him that Saturday in the coffee shop. He told me to get out. I was upset, but I knew he'd come around. He always did, he just had a temper. I remember buying the bottle of vodka, but the next thing I remember is waking up in my flat the next morning. I didn't know he had died until I turned on the TV."

Julia hadn't been expecting such a frank confession, and from the horrified look that consumed Maggie's face, she hadn't expected to give it. Like all of the best secrets, it was almost impossible to keep them bottled up forever. Dirty laundry had a habit of floating to the top; Julia had learned that the hard way.

"Have you told the police any of this?" Julia asked.

"The police haven't spoken to me," Maggie said, stepping away from Julia. "If you tell anybody what I just told you, I'll say you're lying. Leave me alone."

Maggie pulled her cigarettes out of her pocket and headed towards the bus stop, asking every person she passed on the way for a lighter. Before she found one, a double decker bus eased into the stop, and she jumped on board. She sat by the window and glanced in Julia's direction before disappearing.

Julia hurried back to her car, the stench of cigarettes clinging to her pale pink peacoat, but her mind was whirring too quickly to care. She climbed into her Ford Anglia and set off back to Peridale, feeling like she had made a real breakthrough for the first time since Anthony had died.

CHAPTER 9

Sue reacted just as Julia expected she would when she sprung it on her that they were going to their father's for Sunday lunch, which is why Julia decided it was best to wait until late on Saturday night to tell her so she couldn't wriggle out of it, even if she tried her best to make every excuse in the world.

As they walked up the peaceful country lane to Peridale Manor, Julia could sense the tension between them, which was manifesting in as many passive aggressive comments as Sue could muster.

"I suppose Katie hired caterers," Sue said, reaching to the low hanging tree above and tearing off a leaf. "I can't imagine that woman knows how to cook."

"You mean our *step-mother*?" Julia asked playfully, knowing how they both hated the term as much as each other. "After the last Sunday lunch, I'm surprised we're even being invited again."

"The one where Gran dumped the bowl of mashed potatoes over Katie's head when she dared to call Gran an '*old woman*'?" Sue replied as she twiddled the leaf between her fingers. "Ah, good memories."

"That explains why she wasn't invited today."

"It doesn't explain why *we've* been invited though," Sue said, tossing the leaf. "I hope Dad is okay. You don't think he's sick, do you?"

Julia felt like she had been hit with a brick. Her father had been acting nicer than usual, but she hadn't connected it to anything serious. Her mind flashed back to the day their mother had tried to explain her cancer diagnosis to them and how she wasn't going to be around forever. Anxiety knotted inside her.

"I'm sure he's fine," Julia said, gulping down the lump in her throat. "He looked fine when he came to my cottage."

"Did you check his temperature?" Sue asked jokingly. "If he had shown up unannounced at my house I would have demanded it. I'm sure the only time he's stepped foot in my cottage was on my wedding day. He said I looked '*nice*'. *Nice*! I was wearing a two thousand pound dress that I couldn't get out of to pee, and if I had fallen into a body of water, I would have drowned from the weight. I looked like a *movie star*!"

"At least you're modest."

"*Nice*," Sue echoed. "*Huh*. I bet nobody called Princess Di's dress just '*nice*'."

The conversation died down when Peridale Manor came into view. Like Oakwood Nursing Home, it was a grand and looming building that stood like a Goliath in the middle of the countryside. Julia had always thought the building had far too many windows to feel comfortable with.

"Ready?" Sue inhaled, her hand resting on her bump through her baggy shirt.

"I don't know."

"Well, it's too late for that," Sue strode up to the doorbell and pressed it three times before stepping back. "It's now or never."

As expected, it wasn't their father or Katie who answered the door, but their elderly housekeeper, Hilary Boyle. She poked her head out of the door, her black liner-circled eyes bulging out at them as she polished a silver candlestick with a yellow rag.

"*You're late*," she barked, before swinging the door open and shuffling into the depths of the house.

"I wonder if they just keep her around because she's ingrained into the place?" Sue whispered as they closed the door behind them and shuffled into the giant manor.

A sweeping marble staircase spread up to the landing, providing all of the drama it was probably intended to. Julia couldn't imagine living in such a huge house, especially when there were only three of them. She wondered if they could go days without ever needing to see or speak to each other.

"*Girls!*" their father said, appearing from his study, dressed in a full tuxedo. "You made it."

Julia and Sue both looked down at their simple clothes. Julia had opted for a modest pastel green summer dress. Sue wore fitted jeans and an oversized t-shirt, which almost hid her bump. Julia suddenly realised Sue probably hadn't told their father the news of her pregnancy.

"I didn't realise there was a dress code," Sue mumbled through a smile. "Julia *forgot* to mention it."

"You're fine as you are," he said awkwardly as he adjusted his cufflinks. "Why don't you come through to the sitting room while Katie finishes getting ready?"

They followed their father through the large house, glancing awkwardly at each other as they did. Julia could feel the nerves radiating off his body, and it was making her nervous in turn. She couldn't shake what Sue had said about him being sick. She wasn't sure a tuxedo was the appropriate attire to break bad news to someone, but their father had never been one for convention.

"Wine?" he asked, already uncorking a bottle.

"I'm driving," Julia said, hoping the little white lie passed and that her father hadn't noticed that her car wasn't outside. "And Sue is doing this thing for work, aren't you Sue? What's it called? *Dry July?*"

"*Yeah,*" Sue mumbled, frowning at Julia as she nodded, the cogs in her brain clearly working overtime. "We're not drinking alcohol for charity."

"I thought you did that in January?" he asked, pouring himself a glass.

"It was so successful, we're doing it again!" Sue exclaimed, clapped her hands together. "Cheers to that!"

Brian lifted his glass and tipped it to them before taking a sip as he stared curiously at his daughters.

"*Dry July?*" Sue whispered when their dad walked over to the drinks cabinet to put the red wine back.

"It was the best thing I could think of!" Julia replied

quietly. "I was *trying* to help. Maybe today is a good time to tell him that's he's going to be a grandfather."

Sue pursed her lips, her cheeks burning even brighter. When their father returned, they both plastered artificial smiles on their faces as he handed them glasses of orange juice. Moments later, Hilary shuffled into the room and loudly cleared her throat. Their father nodded, and followed Hilary out of the room, motioning for them to follow him.

"He's acting stranger than usual," Sue whispered into her ear as they followed him into the dining room. "Are you sure you don't know what's going on?"

"You know as much as I do."

"It feels like a trap."

Katie was already waiting for them in the dining room. She was sitting at the head of the long table, wearing a strapless white dress, which was cut low over her ample cleavage. Her face was plastered in makeup, and her plump lips were smothered in so much nude gloss, they were reflecting every light in the room. Her peroxide blonde hair, which looked like it had been encased in rollers all day, bounced out of her scalp at an angle that didn't look like it had grown out of her head.

"*Girls*!" she squeaked, clapping her hands together. "*Welcome*! Please, sit."

There were only four places set on the impossibly stretched out table. One at either end for Katie and their father, and two in the middle for Julia and Sue. Julia walked around the table, taking the one in front of the fireplace so she could keep her eye on the door in case they were planning any surprises.

Once they were all seated, they sat in stifling silence.

Katie beamed out like a Cheshire cat, glancing from Julia to Sue as though it was their place to make conversation. Their father cleared his throat as he spread a napkin on his knee.

"No Vincent today?" Sue asked as she circled her finger around the lip of her orange juice.

"He wasn't feeling up to it," Katie replied quickly. "He's not himself at the moment."

Silence fell again until Hilary pushed in a trolley containing four bowls of tomato soup. Julia was glad of the distraction, even if it would only last until the bread rolls had run out.

"Delicious," Julia said. "Did you make it, Katie?"

Sue looked up from her bowl, pausing with the spoon next to her lips to send Julia a little grin. They both looked up at Katie, who appeared to be blushing under her caked-on makeup.

"Cooking isn't my strong point," she said with a shrug, her high-pitched voice reminding Julia of a little girl. "My talents lie in other areas, don't they, Brian?"

Sue choked on her soup, spluttering the red liquid all down her black t-shirt and onto the tablecloth.

"Katie is a great business woman," Brian said, smiling across the table at his wife, either ignoring or not noticing his daughter's reactions. "Tell them about your new venture."

"*Fake tan!*" Katie exclaimed, holding out her arms for them to see her luminous glow. "After the spa idea failed to get off the ground, I decided to go into product development. We're currently working on our first batch of '*Glow Like Katie*', but it should be hitting shelves soon!"

"Fake tan?" Sue asked, arching a brow. "Is that why we're here? For a sales pitch?"

"Well, no," Katie mumbled, looking a little hurt. "But it's something that is important to me. You could sell it in your café, Julia, and get the whole village glowing like Katie!"

Julia smiled politely, but she knew she wasn't going to let a bottle of the stuff pass her threshold. Just from the way Katie said it made it sound like Julia should be grateful for the proposal.

Instead of being a conversation starter, silence fell as they finished their soup. Sue appeared to have mentally checked out. She had started tearing her napkin into tiny pieces, something she did when she was anxious. Julia kicked her under the table and nodded, letting her know it was her time to speak. Sue mouthed '*ouch!*' and shook her head, so Julia kicked her again, but in the other shin this time. Sue jumped, her knees hitting the table, causing the cutlery to jump. Brian and Katie both turned to look at her.

"I *guess* I have something to share," Sue mumbled, looking under her brows angrily at Julia. "I'm –"

"*Roast dinner!*" Katie exclaimed as Hilary pushed into the room with another trolley full of food.

She displayed the giant chicken in the middle of the table, and surrounded it with roast potatoes, honey-roasted parsnips, mash, boiled cabbage, stuffing balls, sweetcorn, and a giant vat of gravy. By the time they had finished passing the various items around the table and were tucking in, the food had almost turned cold.

"What did you want to say?" Katie asked as she slowly lifted a piece of chicken to her glossy lips.

"*Oh,*" Sue mumbled, blushing and stuffing her mouth full of cabbage. "*I'humpfergant.*"

"*Huh?*" Brian asked, tensing his brows and pointing his

ear to Sue. "I didn't catch that."

Sue held her finger up, bobbing her head as she finished chewing. She looked at Julia, and rolled her eyes as she swallowed.

"I said I'm –"

"*Pregnant*," Katie blurted out.

"*What?*" Julia mumbled, choking on a piece of chicken as she turned lightning fast in her seat.

"That's *my* line," Sue cried, looking from their father to Katie, bewilderment deep in her face. "*I'm* pregnant."

"*We know*," Katie and Brian said in unison.

"How?" Sue asked, dropping her knife and fork and sitting back in her chair.

"We saw you at the maternity ward last month," Katie said, her hand reaching down to touch her white dress under the table, a distinct bump suddenly appearing before Julia's eyes. "I'm pregnant too."

Sue's nostrils flared, as anger clearly washed over her. Julia was too stunned to know what to say to calm her sister. The last time they had been invited to the manor house was with the rest of the village for a mystery announcement. Julia had expected Katie to announce she was pregnant then, not that she was attempting to turn the manor into a spa. That plan had been put to bed after her brother objected to the plans and was murdered. The thought of them having a baby hadn't crossed her mind since.

"I'm five months," Katie said, an excited squeak escaping her mouth as she stood up. "We're so happy, aren't we, Brian?"

Brian peered over his wine glass at his daughters, looking anything but happy. He seemed more concerned by their reactions than anything. His sudden reappearance in Julia's life, along with his unexpected compassion suddenly made sense.

"It's a little boy," he said, a smile breaking through his concern. "You're going to have a little brother!"

Sue's lips trembled as she attempted to speak, but the shock had silenced her.

"Congratulations," Julia said flatly, unsure of how she felt.

"*Yeah*," Sue mumbled, her eyes vacant as she stared at the butchered chicken carcass. "My brother is going to be two months older than my son."

"He'll *technically* be his uncle," Katie announced proudly as she cradled the bump, which was double the size of Sue's lime, with both hands. "Aren't you excited?"

Julia trained her gaze on Sue, willing her to make eye contact. Instead of saying anything, Sue screwed up her napkin, pushed out her chair and stormed out of the dining room. Brian jumped up, but Julia shook her head.

"Leave her," Julia said. "She's just in shock. We both are."

"A baby is an *amazing* thing," Katie said, apparently confused by Sue's reaction. "It will bring everyone together."

Julia stared at the bump, trying to imagine the fact she was suddenly about to have a baby brother who would be almost forty years younger than her. It only reminded her that she hadn't fulfilled her own dream of having kids. She tossed back the rest of the orange juice, wishing she had asked for wine after all.

When Julia didn't attempt to reassure Katie, she too stormed out of the room, leaving Julia and her father alone in silence. Hilary popped her head in, but quickly backed out when she caught Brian's firm gaze.

"Why does Sue *always* have to act like that?" Brian asked, the anger clear in his voice.

"Do you *really* need to ask that?" Julia asked, taking her turn to stand up and screw up her napkin. "You weren't there for us growing up, and now you're having another baby at the same time as you're about to become a grandfather. Are you honestly *that* blind?"

He gritted his jaw and flared his nostrils. He looked like he was going to try and defend himself, but he opted to drink the rest of his wine. Julia sighed and shook her head as she headed for the door.

"*Julia!*" he called after her. "Wait."

She almost didn't stop, but that little girl waiting at the window for her father was still buried deep inside. She stopped in the doorway and turned back to face him as he slowly stood up.

"I'm sorry," he said, holding out his hands. "I own up to everything. I know I haven't been the best dad, but I'm not about to let that happen again."

"Good," Julia said with a firm nod. "Because he deserves better. But it doesn't change the past."

"We can change the future," he said. "It's not too late for any of us."

Julia nodded and half-smiled, wanting so desperately to believe that. She tried to imagine Sue seeing it the same way, but she would be surprised if Sue ever spoke to either of them ever again.

"I'm happy for you, Dad," Julia said, bowing her head. "I do mean that."

Julia walked out of the dining room and towards the

open front door, where she could see Sue sobbing on the doorstep. She hurried along the marble tiles, her tiny heels echoing around the cavernous hall.

"Julia," her father called again. "I should have told you this before, but I've had a tip-off from a friend about Timothy Edwards. I think you'll want to speak to him. He lives in a small flat above Pretty Petals on Mulberry Lane."

Julia didn't turn around. She almost couldn't believe her father was taking the moment to give her information on the case, even if she did make a mental note to remember exactly what he had said.

After closing the door, she slowly approached Sue, not wanting to startle her. She crouched down, wrapping her arm around her shoulders.

"That was supposed to be *my* news," Sue cried as she smudged her mascara streaks across her cheek. "She couldn't *wait* to jump in and ruin it. She ruins *everything*."

"It's just your hormones," Julia said, hugging her close to her chest. "It doesn't take anything away from your little lime."

Sue nodded through the last of her staggered tears. Julia unclipped her handbag and wiped away the mascara with her white handkerchief. When her face was clean, Julia hooked her thumb under Sue's chin and lifted her face up. They both smiled, and Julia knew they were both thinking the exact same thing: no matter what happened, they would always have each other.

"Let's get out of here," Julia whispered. "The Comfy Corner puts on a good carvery on Sundays."

Sue smiled through her sadness, the thought of food cheering her up. As they walked into the village, Julia stayed two steps behind, pulled her little recipe notebook out of her bag along with her small silver pen, and scribbled down *'Timothy Edwards – Pretty Petals'*. Out of all of the information she had learned at Sunday dinner, she knew that could prove to be the most useful.

CHAPTER 10

S till full from the carvery, Julia walked through the village to Mulberry Lane after walking Sue home. It was a lovely summer day with a clear blue sky above and a nice cool breeze bringing in the scent of freshly cut grass.

Mulberry Lane was the oldest known street in Peridale, with its mushed together cottages and shops, made from golden Cotswold stone, dating back to the 1700s. Its boutique shops were usually buzzing with life, but as Julia turned the corner onto the winding street, it was eerily quiet. At the end of the lane stood the antique barn, where she had spent a lot of her childhood with her father before her mother's death. If she had visited it since, she had no memory of it. She wondered what would happen to it now that Anthony was dead.

Keeping Anthony fresh in the forefront of her mind, she walked to Pretty Petals, the only florist in the village. After peering through the window at the beautiful display of coloured carnations in the window, she spotted a small, bright yellow door next to the shop. She pressed the buzzer on the intercom system and waited.

"*Hu-hello?*" a voice mumbled through the speaker system, barely audible. "*Who's there?*"

"I'm Brian South's daughter," Julia said, hoping that was enough. "My name is Julia. I wanted to ask you a few questions about Anthony Kennedy."

The intercom crackled again as though the man was pushing down on the button, but he didn't say a word. Julia wondered if she had just approached the whole thing entirely wrong, until the yellow door clicked and unlocked.

The stairway up to the small flat above the shop was dank and musty. It smelled like it was in a good need of an open window and a can of air freshener. Julia pushed on the door, hoping she would be able to breathe freely, but the theme continued throughout the flat.

Julia squinted into the dark. Despite it being the middle of the day, the curtains were tightly drawn, and there were no lights turned on. It took a moment for her eyes to adjust. When she saw the figure sitting in an armchair, she jumped back a little, her fingers clenching around her bag strap.

"Timothy Edwards?" Julia whispered, taking a deep step forward. "My name is Julia. Julia South."

The man reached out and clicked on a small lamp. Julia almost gasped but stopped herself. The man didn't look well at all. He was pale, and sweaty, with purple circles suffocating his eyes, which were straining from the light. He went to speak, but he erupted into a coughing fit. Julia hurried forward, placing her hand on the man's back, but he batted her away.

"I'm *fine*," he insisted through his suddenly mauve face as he fought back another attack of coughing. "I'm *f–f–*"

Julia hurried across the tiny flat to the kitchenette lining the back wall. The counters were covered in Chinese takeaway containers and unwashed plates. The low hum of buzzing flies filled her ears, making her shudder. She opened the cupboard above the kettle, relieved to see a clean cup. She filled it with water from the tap and returned.

Timothy sipped the water and it appeared to ease him a little. He sat back in his chair and rested his thinning hair on the headrest. He looked completely exhausted from the fit of coughing. Julia perched on the edge of the cluttered sofa next to him. On closer inspection, he didn't appear as old as she had first thought. He was in his late forties at the most.

"I'm Julia South," she repeated.

"I *know* who *you* are," he snapped as he slowly opened his eyes. "What do you want? I'm not well."

"I can see that," Julia said, edging forward and resting her hands on her knees. "I wouldn't have bothered you if I would have known, but I need to ask you some questions about Anthony Kennedy."

"What about him?" Timothy said with a small cough. "He's dead."

"I know. Somebody is trying to frame me, rather unsuccessfully, I might add, but I'd like to clear my name before the gossips keep running with the story."

"*Poisoned*," he said, which he followed with another bout of coughing. "Doesn't surprise me."

He attempted to laugh, but it was replaced with more coughing. He suddenly sat up, and the smell that wafted Julia's way made her wonder when he had last showered. It reminded her strangely of garlic.

"My father told me you and Anthony weren't on good terms."

"I wasn't always living here, you know," he said, staring down at the floor. "I'm *embarrassed.* I had a nice cottage and a family until Anthony came along."

"What did he do to you?"

Timothy met her eyes with a venomous gaze. She gulped, trying not to let the fear register on her face. She looked back to the door to the staircase leading back to the bright safety of Mulberry Lane, glad she had left it slightly open for an easy escape if needed.

"He *conned* me," Timothy said. "What else? That's what he did. I thought I was different, but I should have known."

"Conned you how?"

"Nothing that man said was true," he continued, his eyes glazing over as he stared at the large stack of copies of *The Peridale Post* on the table, the latest sporting the headline '*COFFEE SHOP OWNER POISONED*'. "He had this way about him. He sucked you in and made you believe whatever he wanted. He could sell ice to the Eskimos. Rinsed me for all I was worth. I inherited valuable antiques from my mother. He told me they weren't worth the scrap money, but he offered me what he called a *good* deal. *Ha!* The man didn't know the meaning of the word. I trusted him, and then I lost everything. I lost my job, my wife, my kids, and for what? He's not even here now. To top it off, he came back for the painting because he knew I was a desperate man. He knew I would accept pennies for it."

"What painting?" Julia asked.

Timothy started coughing again, but this time it didn't subside. He stood up, instantly clutching his head. He swayed on the spot for a second before opening his eyes and stumbling across his flat and into the bathroom. Julia flicked on a second lamp, relieved at a little more light. It only showed how truly filthy the place was. She stood up and looked down at the couch, which was covered in a variety of different stains and smelled like it had spent a year or two in a swamp. She picked up the top newspaper, ignoring the article written by Johnny Watson, which also included details of her arrest and the ill-fated protest meeting. She put it down on the couch and sat, tucking her dress underneath her. She glanced at the bathroom as the sound of a flushing toilet echoed through the flat. Turning back, Julia's eyes landed on something that was sitting on top of the stack of newspapers that had been hiding under the most recent edition. It was a photo frame. She reached out and picked it up, glancing back at the bathroom as she did. The picture that looked up at her shocked her so much that her hand drifted up to her mouth.

Anthony Kennedy stared back at her with his glowing tan, yellow hair, open shirt, and pearly white teeth, with his arm around who appeared to be a much healthier, more youthful looking Timothy. Their heads were touching as Timothy reached out to take the photograph. She recognised Blackpool's south pier in the background.

The bathroom door opened and Julia quickly

attempted to place the photograph back where she had found it, but it was too late. Timothy hobbled over and snatched the frame from her hands, his eyes wide with rage.

"What do you think you're doing?" he growled, clutching the frame close to his chest. "How *dare* you come into my flat and touch my things."

"I didn't mean to," Julia mumbled. "I'm sorry. I should go."

She stood up, but the sick man loomed over her, his face nothing more than a shadow with eyes. Her heart thumped in her chest as she tried to remember where the door was.

"You were more than just friends, weren't you?" Julia asked, remembering what her father had told her. "You and Anthony were close in *another* way."

The flicker of his lids confirmed all Julia needed to know. She knew the look all too well and had felt it her fair share of times over the last week; it was heartbreak.

"He *used* me," Timothy croaked as he looked down at the picture. "He sensed my weakness. He used it against me, all to get to my antiques."

"That's awful," Julia whispered, reaching out and resting her hand on his, the fear subsiding. "I'm so sorry he treated you like that."

Timothy looked as though he was going to smile, but he coughed again. Julia decided she wasn't going to ask where he had been on the night Anthony was murdered. She didn't want to add insult to injury.

"You mentioned something about a painting?" Julia urged, nodding her head in hopes of encouraging him.

"It doesn't matter now," Timothy said, tossing the frame to the ground before collapsing into the chair. "It's too late."

Julia looked down at the frame. The glass had cracked right down the middle, separating the two. Just looking at Anthony's face made Julia's blood boil. She knew he was cold, but she didn't think even he would prey on somebody's emotions for his own financial gain.

"I should go," Julia said, realising she wasn't going to get anywhere with more questioning. "Are you sure you're going to be okay?"

"It's just a cold," he said before coughing again. "I can't get the taste of metal out of my mouth. Don't mind if I don't show you out."

Julia stepped over the broken frame and towards the door. She turned back at the same moment Timothy flicked off the lamps, sending himself into darkness once more. She didn't know the man, but it broke her heart to leave another human being in such a state. This was something not even one of her cakes could fix.

Julia pulled her notepad and pen out of her handbag as she made her way down the stairs. When she opened the door, she was glad to inhale the fresh country air again. It took her eyes a second to adjust, but the moment they did, she was scribbling down every detail Timothy had told her.

"*Julia?*" a familiar voice called out.

When she saw Barker walking down the street towards her, her heart skipped a beat. She smiled, never gladder than she was right then to hear Barker say her name. All she wanted to do was run into his arms, but she restrained herself.

"What are you doing here?" she asked, pocketing the notepad.

"I could ask you the same question," he said as he

looked sternly down at her bag as she clipped it shut. "Somebody called about a hanging flower basket that's been stolen, so I thought I'd check it out."

"A hanging basket?"

"Sentimental value," Barker said quickly with a shrug. "Or so they say. I'm glad I've bumped into you. There was something I wanted to tell you."

"*Oh?*" Julia replied quickly, barely able to contain her smile.

"It's about the case."

"Oh," she said, the smile vanishing. "Here to arrest me?"

"The opposite, actually," Barker said as he stuffed his hands into his trouser pockets and rocked back on his heels. "You've officially been dropped as a suspect. You'll probably get a call tomorrow to confirm, so just act surprised."

"Why?" Julia asked, crossing her arms. "Has somebody been arrested?"

"I'm not at liberty to say."

"It's not your case."

"It's still an active case, though," he said, holding back the usual grin he gave her whenever she questioned his authority. "Since an arrest would be public record, I can tell you that you won't find anything if you go looking."

"Why have they dropped me?" she asked again, curious to know what vital piece of information had ruled her out of the running.

"I shouldn't be telling you this," he said, glancing over his shoulder to make sure they were alone. "The toxicology report came back. It showed that the arsenic that killed Anthony had built up in his system over a long period of time. The theory is that he was given small doses, little and often. Not enough to kill him in one go, but enough to be eventually fatal. It just so happened that his body gave in on that night, and whoever had been doing the poisoning had been keeping a watchful eye on him."

"And they tried to pin it on me because of the rivalry," Julia said. "Quite clever."

"My guess is whoever killed Anthony started doing it long before he found a fingernail in one of your cakes," he said reassuringly. "You were just in the wrong place at the wrong time."

"What are the symptoms of arsenic poisoning?" Julia asked.

"You don't think you've been poisoned, do you?"

"I feel fine."

"Good," Barker said, a genuine smile warming his lips. "I worried you might have been targeted as collateral damage. The symptoms are wide and varied, depending on how long the poisoning has been going on. It can remain undetected at first, but when somebody is succumbing to the toxin, they'll start sweating out of control, get stomach cramps, headaches, dizziness, vomiting, excess saliva, and a weird metallic taste in their mouth. The most peculiar one is that they might smell of garlic, which I almost couldn't believe when I heard."

Barker chuckled, but Julia wasn't laughing. She mouthed the word '*garlic*' to herself as she turned back to Timothy's door. Her heart stopped in her chest as she thought about the man she had just left alone in his dark flat. Julia hurried over to the door and pressed the buzzer over and over. When he didn't answer, she banged hard with her fists.

"We need to get in," Julia said. "I was visiting Timothy

447

to ask about Anthony. They were having a love affair, which resulted in Anthony conning the man out of his valuables."

"So?" Barker asked, his brows creased low over his eyes.

"He had *those* symptoms!" she cried, her fists beating on the wood. "He said he had the taste of metal in his mouth! He thinks he has a cold, but he looked like he was on death's door."

Barker's eyes suddenly widened and he pushed Julia to the side. Before she knew what was happening, Barker's body collided with the door and it burst open with one swift bang. Julia scrambled after Barker as he ran up the stairs. He opened the door to the dark flat and felt on the wall for the light switch. By the time he had flicked on the light, Julia was right behind him.

"Don't look," Barker said, holding out his arm.

She stepped to the side, her mouth drying in an instant. Timothy was slumped in his chair, the photograph from the frame resting on his chest. There was no doubt that the man was dead.

Without bothering about anything that had happened, she buried her face into Barker's chest.

CHAPTER 11

J ulia barely slept a wink. She couldn't shake Timothy's
pain from her thoughts, no matter how many times she
tossed and turned. Just like Maggie, he had been
deceived by Anthony's lies, but the bubble had burst
for Timothy, which seemed to have taken a much worse
effect on him than Maggie.

When she crawled out of bed on Monday morning
ready to start another week at her café, her mind was filled
with questions. Who had poisoned Timothy, and why?
What did he know that could have led the police to the
murderer if they had asked the right questions?

Julia skipped breakfast and sent Jessie to open up the
café alone, deciding it was time she stopped avoiding her

problems and talked to the one person who might actually be able to give her some answers to what was going on.

She burst through the doors of Happy Bean. There was already a line of people to the door, but that no longer surprised her. She made sure to look into the eyes of the people who used to be her customers as she passed them.

"*Hey*, there's a line – *Oh*, hello, Julia," Johnny Watson from *The Peridale Post* said, blushing as he adjusted his glasses. "I was just grabbing a coffee for research. It's for an article."

"Sure," Julia said, trying her best to smile, but not really caring any more about the reasoning behind the mass abandonment of her café. Ignoring the disgruntled people she had just pushed in front of, Julia turned to the frazzled barista, who didn't look like she had a clue how to cope with such a huge line.

"Where's Jerrad?" Julia demanded, glancing down at the floor where Anthony had died. "I need to speak to him."

The girl didn't say a word. She squeaked and pointed a shaky finger to a door at the far side of the coffee shop. Julia ignored the '*STAFF ONLY*' sign and burst in.

"*Julia*," Jerrad said, looking around the young boy he was speaking to. "What a *pleasant* surprise."

The boy turned around. It was Gareth Kennedy. He smiled meekly at Julia, barely looking her in the eyes.

"You can pick up your uniform on Friday," Jerrad said as he scribbled something down in a book on his desk. "Tell your mum I'll call her tonight."

Gareth nodded and shuffled out of the office without saying a word. Julia waited until he had gone before slamming the door and standing in its way so neither of them could leave.

"He seems like a good kid," Julia said. "You better not be corrupting him."

"I'm merely giving the lad a job here," Jerrad said, barely looking up from whatever he was writing. "He's at college with that street urchin you've got in your café. He was doing some stupid catering course, but I set him straight. After Rosemary quit, and rightly so, it was time to get some fresh blood in the place. A coffee shop this busy doesn't run itself. You should know that. Actually, never mind."

"His father died last week," Julia said, ignoring his bait.

"They were practically strangers," Jerrad scoffed, snapping the book shut. "The boy barely knew the man. Why are you bursting into my office on a Monday morning? Come to reconsider my offer of a job? I'm sure it won't take *too long* to train you up to Happy Bean's standards. Old dogs *can* be taught new tricks, despite what they say."

Julia's nostrils flared, her fists clenching by her side before she even realised it. She wondered if Jessie's theory about giving Jerrad a black eye would make her feel better. She relaxed her fists, deciding it was the wrong time to find out.

"I need to hear everything you know," Julia demanded. "Another man has been poisoned, and I know you're hiding something."

"I don't remember you ever being so '*bossy*', darlin'," he said, performing his finger air quotes once more. "Take a seat and relax."

"I won't relax!" Julia cried, slamming her hand on the desk and startling Jerrad back into his chair. "Two innocent men are dead, you idiot. I need to stop this before anybody else is killed!"

"Me-*ow*," Jerrad purred, his brows darting up and down. "Where was this woman when the spark left our marriage?"

Julia recoiled, disgusted with the man in front of her. She wondered if it was possible for a person to be that ignorant to somebody's flaws for twelve whole years, or if Jerrad had just gotten worse in the two they hadn't seen each other.

"I'm not playing games," Julia said firmly. "Tell me everything."

Jerrad stood up and grabbed his car keys from a rack above the computer. He walked to the back of the office, where a back door opened onto the alley behind the coffee shop. Julia realised this was the entrance Barker had theorised that the murderer had used to gain entry to the coffee shop.

"Not here," he said, holding the door open and nodding out into the alley. "Let me take you out for breakfast. I've found this place that looks like a dump, but the food is fairly decent. I think it's called The Comfy Corner. Dreadful name."

"You must be out of your mind."

"Do you want me to share information, or not?" he asked with a leer. "Come on."

Jerrad walked through the door and turned into the alley. Julia looked back at the coffee shop, wondering how desperately she wanted to crack the case. If it hadn't been for seeing Timothy clinging onto the photograph of a man he had loved and been cheated by, Julia might have retreated to the safety of her dying café.

She didn't want to believe she would follow him, but that's just what she did.

The Comfy Corner was the only place in Peridale that could call itself a real restaurant. It was tucked away on a small backstreet directly across from the tiny library where Sue's husband, Neil, worked. From the outside, the restaurant wasn't much to look at, but everybody in the village knew it had the best food in Peridale, if not the whole of the Cotswolds.

Julia climbed out of Jerrad's sports car, glad to be in the fresh air again. The new car smell had practically knocked her sick when coupled with his erratic driving and overly spiced aftershave.

He held open the door of the restaurant, and she couldn't help but feel he was trying to take her out on a date, which was the last impression she wanted to give him.

The Comfy Corner was run by Mary and Todd Porter, two kind villagers in their sixties. When people talked about true love in the village, Mary and Todd were usually the standard that people looked up to. They had met when they were children at St. Peter's Primary School, and had been married since they were eighteen. Unlike Julia and Jerrad, Mary and Todd seemed just as in love as the day they had married.

"*Julia!*" Mary exclaimed. "Couldn't get enough of the carvery yesterday? Good to see you."

Mary's eyes landed on Jerrad and they bulged so hard out of her face, they practically popped out and rolled across the carpet. Julia wondered if Mary would wait until she had left to call everybody she knew to tell them Julia had been in there with a man that wasn't Barker. If gossiping were a sport, Mary would take the gold medal. She seemed to know everything before everyone, and it was known that you only said things in her presence that you were happy for the whole village to find out. Dot had suggested on more than one occasion that Mary had planted bugs around the quaint eatery, but Julia didn't quite believe that.

While Jerrad helped himself to three of everything from the breakfast buffet, Julia settled on a single slice of toast. She didn't want to give Jerrad the idea that she wanted to be there, even if her stomach did grumble as she walked past the bacon, sausages, beans, and scrambled eggs.

"Watching your figure?" he commented as they took a seat in the corner. "Probably for the best. You're creeping up to your forties."

Julia reminded herself why she was there and inhaled a deep, calming breath. She wished peppermint and liquorice tea were on the menu because she needed a cup to soothe her.

While Jerrad wolfed down his breakfast, Julia slowly buttered every millimetre of her toast, if only to figure out what she wanted to know first, and if he could be trusted.

"Where did you meet Anthony?" Julia asked, starting easy. "Sometime in the last two years I'm guessing?"

"Six months ago at a franchise convention in London," Jerrad mumbled through a mouthful of beans. "We bumped into each other by accident. He dropped all of his paperwork, and when I saw that he wanted to open a Happy Bean in Peridale, I knew I couldn't pass it up."

"You said you sunk all of your money into the project,"

Julia said, trying to remember everything Jerrad had already told her. "How much?"

"Everything I had," he said, pausing for air before tucking into the next sausage. "It wasn't cheap keeping up with the younger women. Hair transplant, new teeth, abdominal sculpting. It all cost money."

"I *knew* you looked different!" Julia exclaimed, snapping her fingers together as she peered at his lower and thicker hairline.

"If I would have known the upkeep, I might not have switched."

Julia knew by '*switched*' he meant from her, a normal thirty-something with a normal body, to a young, blonde, skinny twenty-something. It had been a long time since Julia had realised that Jerrad had done her the biggest favour of her life. Deciding not to mention this, she thought about the next question.

"What did Anthony promise you in return for your investment?"

"That we would take over the world," Jerrad said sternly. "I should have known it was too good to be true. He told me we would have a location open in every town in England before Christmas, if only I –"

"Put up the money?"

"*Bingo*," Jerrad said. "He was good at the sale, I'll give him that."

"You're not the only person he conned," Julia said. "It was all he knew. Does the name Timothy Edwards mean anything to you?"

Jerrad paused, a slice of bacon hovering near his open mouth. He looked up at Julia for a second before cramming the meat into his mouth and chewing slowly. She took his silence as a yes.

"That's who died," she continued. "Did you know about his *real* relationship with Anthony?"

"I guessed something *funny* was going on," Jerrad said, as though he found the situation comical. "I heard a man's voice sometimes in the background of phone calls, and then when I came to the village, I realised it was him."

"You've met Timothy?"

"I went to his flat with Anthony about a month ago after one of our meetings," Jerrad said with a shrug. "Total cesspit. I don't know how a man could live like that."

Julia thought back to their apartment in London. It had been barren and devoid of any real personality, except for the calculated pieces Jerrad had approved. She wasn't surprised he had gotten on with Anthony so well.

"Did it have something to do with a painting?" Julia asked.

"So, you know about *the painting*," Jerrad said with a roll of his eyes. "Everybody wants to know about *the painting*."

"What do they want to know?"

"How they can get their grubby hands on it."

"Is it worth something?"

"Oh, like you wouldn't believe," Jerrad said, his eyes sparkling. "Anthony reckoned it could go for around a million."

"Certainly enough to murder somebody for," Julia said before taking a bite into her toast, which was now stone cold. She chewed it slowly and let her words stew in the silence. "Where is the painting?"

Jerrad crammed an almost full sausage into his mouth, his nostrils flaring angrily. From the way he looked glassy-eyed down at the plate, she knew his exact answer.

"You don't know," Julia said, sitting back in her chair with a small laugh. "*That's* why you're *here*. You want to get your hands on it."

"He wouldn't let me see it!" Jerrad snapped, leaning in across the table. "He made me wait outside the flat until he covered it up. I helped him carry it down, but he had chained sheets all around it. He only gave Timothy five hundred quid for it. He didn't know what it was worth. It's his own fault really."

"He *loved* Anthony," Julia snapped back, tilting across the table and meeting him halfway. "Anthony tricked him into falling in love with him for the sake of robbing him. It wasn't *his* fault. We all do stupid things in the name of love."

Jerrad narrowed his eyes before leaning back in his chair. He pushed his empty plate away, his right forefinger and thumb twirling the ring around on his left hand. Julia wondered if he even knew he was doing it.

"The slimy git could have hidden the painting anywhere," Jerrad said. "I wouldn't even know if I passed it in the street! I just know it's worth something, and he *owes* me that money! He turned me upside down and shook every last coin out of my pockets. I lost it all. That car outside is a rental. A *rental!* I'm disgusted with myself. He didn't put it in the business account like he promised. There's barely enough in there to keep that place afloat. We're running day to day."

"Not a nice feeling, is it?" Julia replied, thinking about the money in her biscuit tin once more. "Where does Rosemary come into this? I assume you're together?"

"*Casually* so," Jerrad said, his eyes tapering. "For now."

It took Julia a minute to realise what that meant, but a light bulb quickly sparked above her head, a crucial part of the puzzle slotting neatly into place.

"You're hoping she knows where the painting is!" Julia exclaimed, shaking her head as she held back the laughter. "Oh, Jerrad, you're no better than Anthony. You're using a widow for the sake of money."

"It's almost a million quid, darlin'," Jerrad remarked, his eyes widening with excitement. "It's only what I'm *owed*. She knows about the painting."

"But she doesn't know where it is either?" Julia asked. "Who else knows about the painting?"

Jerrad shifted uncomfortably in his seat. He glanced at the gold watch on his wrist, motioning for Mary to send the bill over.

"Gareth knows, doesn't he?" Julia responded for him. "That's why you've given him the job. You're hoping one of them is going to lead you to the pot of gold like a truffle pig."

"Kids soak up things," Jerrad mumbled as he pulled a twenty-pound note from his wallet and tucked it under his plate. "He *must* know something. They're bound to slip up eventually."

Julia couldn't believe what she was hearing. Dumping her things on the doorstep of the home they shared for twelve years was one thing, but using a boy and his mother to get to a dead man's treasure was a new low she wouldn't have thought even he was capable of.

"Why Peridale?" Julia asked. "And don't tell me you wanted a fresh start. If you invested with Anthony, you thought he was going to run the business and make you rich. You're not the type to get your hands dirty."

Jerrad stood up and fastened his suit jacket. He picked up a knife and held it up to his face. First, he checked his teeth in the reflection, which looked to have been replaced with a full set of veneers, and then his thick hair, which had been balding and receding the last time Julia had seen him.

"Why do you think?" he replied, a sudden softness taking over his voice before he turned and walked to the door.

Julia didn't move until she heard the roar of his sports car tearing down the road. She wondered what he had meant by that, but she didn't want to go there. The way he had touched his wedding ring had made her wonder if there was still a shred of the human being she had married in there somewhere.

"You've barely touched your toast, love," Mary said softly as she approached. "Would you like another go at the buffet? I won't charge extra."

"Thank you, but no thank you," Julia said as she stood up. "I have somebody I need to warn."

Julia headed straight for the exit and set off across Peridale, taking every shortcut she knew. She hurried down a small path and came out in front of Rosemary's cottage, her legs covered in nettle stings. She didn't care. She had already spent twelve years of her life making a mistake, she wasn't about to let Rosemary repeat that mistake. Jerrad might have shown an ounce of humanity beneath his ruthless exterior, but it wasn't enough. It only reminded Julia of how much she loved Barker, and how Rosemary deserved somebody like that, even if Barker could never bring himself to forgive her.

Julia unclipped the gate and hurried down the neat garden path towards the front door. Her finger lifted to the doorbell, but she stopped when she heard raised voices drifting through the slightly open sitting room window. She almost pressed the bell to make herself known, but she paused and decided to listen first.

"He's *gone*!" she heard Rosemary exclaim. "We can do what we want now. Be who we *want* to be. We don't even have to stay here."

"What if I *want* to?" she heard Gareth reply.

"Is it for that painting?"

"*No!*"

"Because if it is, we're never going to find it," Rosemary snapped, the freeness and contented calm gone from her voice. "Your father hid that thing good and proper, which means he died for nothing, but I *don't* care! We can start *fresh*! You and me, somewhere new. We can go to the coast! You always said you wanted to live by the sea."

"You're just as bad as him!" Gareth cried, his voice cracking at the top of his register. "All you care about is yourself!"

A door slammed, making Julia jump back. She thought about pressing the doorbell, but she had only come to warn Rosemary away from Jerrad. From the way she was talking, she wasn't the damsel in distress she had assumed she was.

Julia tiptoed down the garden path and back the way she had come, stinging her shins with the nettles once more. Wherever the painting was, Julia hoped it was beautiful enough to explain why it had driven everybody in Anthony's life to insanity.

CHAPTER 12

"All of this for a painting," Sue said as she sipped her raspberry lemonade at the table closest to Julia's counter later that afternoon. "I wonder what it looks like."

"It's probably some boring landscape," Jessie mumbled as she wiped down the tables for the fourth time since Julia had returned, despite there having been no customers. "Expensive art is always stupid. Galleries are pointless."

"It's a shame Rachel Carter is in prison for murder," Sue said with a heavy exhale as she remembered the owner of Peridale's only art gallery, which had remained closed since she had been locked up. "She would have been able to help."

"Are you forgetting the part where you destroyed her irreplaceable Georgia O'Keefe painting?" Julia reminded her with a playful smile.

"You asked me for a distraction!"

"And what about that priceless vase at Seirbigh Castle in Scotland?" Julia added, tapping her chin. "That was a family heirloom you sacrificed in another *distraction*."

"I'm clumsy," Sue said with a shrug as she rubbed her stomach. "What happened in Scotland stays in Scotland."

"What happened in Scotland?" Jessie asked, a confused expression on her face.

"*Nothing*," Julia and Sue replied in unison, having sworn not to mention the murder they had solved several weeks ago during a spa trip to Scotland, which their gran had won as part of a radio contest.

"Who are your suspects?" Sue asked, draining the last of her raspberry lemonade and shaking the cup for a refill. "You must have quite a few by now."

"I wish I did," Julia said with a sigh as she walked around the counter with the freshly pressed lemonade. "It seemed Anthony wasn't in short supply of people who wanted to kill him."

"It had to be somebody who knows about the painting," Jessie said. "So that could be practically anybody in the village the way people 'round here talk."

"We know Rosemary and Gareth know about it after what I heard this morning," Julia said, pulling out her notepad to read the things she had scribbled down. "And Jerrad, obviously. I don't know if Maggie knew about the painting."

"She could have still killed him though," Jessie suggested as she tossed the cloth down and took the seat across from Sue. "I saw people do the craziest things on the streets when they were drunk, especially on vodka. It always made them so angry."

"I totally forgot about that," Sue said, pulling her phone out of her pocket. "After you told me about Maggie's story, I remembered a text Debbie sent me. I never put two and two together until last night when I was in bed going through my messages. My storage was full, so I was deciding which ones to delete. *Ah*, here it is! '*You'll never guess who just turned up at my door drunk as a skunk*' with the crying laughing face emoji. That was at half ten on the Saturday night. I was asleep, but I woke up at four to throw up. Lime trouble." Sue paused to rub her stomach before continuing. "I sent her a message saying '*Omg! Who?*' with the confused face emoji at four minutes past four, and she replied '*Ceramic Pug Maggie! Came in and crashed out on my couch and then just jumped up and left ten minutes ago!*' with the shrugging girl emoji and the cocktail emoji, so I replied '*Omg! No way!*' with the shocked face emoji, and then *she* replied —"

"*Alright!*" Jessie cried. "*We get it!* I can't take anymore."

Sue pouted, locked her phone and tucked it away before crossing her arms and sulking.

"It rules her out," Sue said. "Anthony died before midnight, and she was at Debbie's between half ten at night and four in the morning."

"That's when he died, but that's not when he was murdered," Julia whispered, drumming her fingers on the counter as she hovered over Maggie's name with the pen. "Whoever poisoned him did it over a long period of time. She had access. It just means it wasn't her at the scene of the crime."

"What if Timothy poisoned Anthony and then poisoned himself?" Jessie suggested, her finger tapping thoughtfully on her chin. "Romeo and Juliet style, except everybody is dead when they say they are."

"You know Romeo and Juliet?" Sue asked suspiciously.

"Julia made me watch the film," Jessie replied, staring down her nose at Sue in a way only Jessie could. "The one with the dude from *Titanic*."

"That doesn't count!"

"It *totally* counts."

"It doesn't matter," Julia butted in before a full-scale fight broke out. "It's a good theory, brilliant in fact. It just doesn't feel right. I looked into his eyes, and I don't think he would try to frame me in the process."

"Who else knows about the painting?" Sue asked, staring off into the corner of the café.

"What painting?" a voice asked through the open door.

They all turned and watched as Brian ducked inside, a sheepish smile on his face. Sue looked like she was about to bolt and make for the door, so Julia hurried around and stood between them, smiling kindly at both of them.

"Thanks for coming, Dad," Julia said, apologising with her eyes to her sister. "That is actually a question I was hoping you would be able to answer. Tea?"

"Yes, please."

Julia quickly made him a pot of tea. She put it on a tray with a cup, saucer, milk, and sugar, before remembering what he had told her about the sugar. She quickly removed it and carried it to the table, which he had taken directly next to Sue's. She was trying her best to look in every direction apart from his.

"So, you want my antique expertise?" he asked as he

pulled off the teapot lid to check if the tea had steeped. "I can't say I've been asked for that in a while. What's this painting? Something you've found in your attic?"

"Not *exactly*," Julia said, pulling up the chair across from him and catching Sue's eye to let her know it was okay to speak. "We don't actually know what the painting is, or where it is."

"Is this connected to Anthony?" he asked as he poured himself a cup of tea.

"You know the painting?" Jessie asked.

"No, but everything seems to be connected to him at the moment, which is why I guessed you called me here."

Julia smiled her apologies. She wondered if a small part of him had thought she had called him to talk about what had happened at Sunday dinner. That was currently the bottom of Julia's priorities list, even if she had noticed it was a good opportunity to get her sister and father in the same room again.

"What does it look like?" he asked. "Who painted it?"

Julia looked at Jessie, who looked at Sue, who stared down at her nails.

"I need a manicure," she whispered absently.

"We don't know," Julia said, pursing her lips at her baby sister. "We don't know anything other than that it could sell for nearly a million pounds, and it's worth slowly poisoning a man for."

"A *million*?" Brian replied, sucking the air through his teeth. "Not many paintings fetch that. It has to be something special by one of the greats. That narrows it down slightly."

"Do you think you would be able to make some calls?" Julia asked hopefully, nodding her head, feeling like she was clasping her fingers around one of the final puzzle pieces.

"It won't be *that* easy," he said after sipping his tea, ripping that puzzle piece away from her. "Anthony didn't exactly work by the book. If he were buying a painting to sell it, he wouldn't have been going through the proper channels. Do you know who the previous owner was?"

"Remember how you gave me Timothy Edwards' name?" Julia asked, the name sticking in her throat. "He was poisoned yesterday. I'm certain it's connected to this painting."

"Edwards, you say?" he said, furrowing his brow and looking down at the teapot. "*Edwards. Edwards.* How do I know an Edwards? I got Timothy's name from an old friend, but now that I think about it, I know an Edwards of my own. I'm sure the name rings a bell."

Julia stared hopefully at him and waited for a grand revelation. After less than a minute of thinking, he shrugged and resumed his tea.

"Have you asked Rosemary if she knows anything?" he asked, setting his cup back onto the saucer. "From what I can remember she wasn't all that bad at antiques. She had style and taste, and that accounts for a lot. You can buy something worthless and give it worth by the way you position it or frame it. She used to help out in the shop with your mother when I lacked inspiration."

Sue suddenly sat up straight in her chair at the mention of their mother. She whipped her head to face him to let him know he shouldn't have dared to speak about their mother. Julia pleaded with Sue with her eyes to calm down, but it didn't seem to make any difference.

"I overheard Rosemary saying they would never find the painting," Julia said, hoping the detour would give Sue a moment to calm down.

"That doesn't mean she doesn't know *what* it looks like," he suggested as he filled his teacup again and added more milk. "Or at least *who* painted it."

Julia sat back in her chair, realising he was right. She stood up and hurried behind the counter to grab her car keys and coat.

"I won't be long," she said to Jessie. "Sue will stay and keep you company, won't you, Sue?"

Sue grumbled and nodded, not looking up or speaking as she obsessed over her nail beds once more.

"Dad?" Julia called as she opened the café door. "Are you coming?"

"Oh," he mumbled, draining the last of his tea before standing up. "Right. Am I coming with you?"

"You're the expert," Julia said.

"I suppose I am," he replied with a nod as he hurried after her. "See you later, girls."

They both grunted back, neither of them seeming able to communicate like proper human beings when the time called. Ignoring that, Julia unlocked her tiny car and she set off towards Rosemary's cottage for the second time that day.

When they were outside the cottage, Julia was surprised to see a removal van parked outside, and she was even more surprised to see that they were taking things into the cottage, instead of out.

They jumped out of the car and followed the movers through the open front door. The men carried an ornate chair up the stairs, but Julia and her father slipped through to the bright, open-planned kitchen.

"Julia?" Rosemary exclaimed from the stove where she was stirring something in a pot. "I was just making lunch. Brian, is that you?"

Rosemary turned off the gas and squinted at Julia's father.

"It's me," he said. "Long time no see."

"What has it been?" she asked with a chuckle. "Twenty-five years? Or even longer? I haven't seen you since – *well* – you know."

Rosemary's eyes flickered sympathetically to Julia. She knew exactly what Rosemary was talking about, but she let it glide over her head because she had more pressing things to discuss.

"I'll make some tea," Rosemary mumbled as she shuffled over to the kettle to distract herself. "Still take two sugars, Brian?"

"Katie's got me on the no-sugar thing," he said, patting his small stomach. "Diabetes scare."

"Ah, yes," Rosemary said, grinning over her shoulder. "The *younger* model."

Unlike most people, Rosemary didn't look offended that Brian had married a woman almost twenty years younger than him. Instead, she almost looked proud. It took Julia a moment to realise there was probably a similar age gap between Rosemary and Jerrad. It sent a shudder down her spine. Not because of the difference in age, but because Rosemary seemed pleased with the man she had managed to catch. Julia wanted to tell her there and then that no matter how much younger Jerrad was, she deserved far better, especially being such a stylish and vivacious woman.

They took the tea through to the conservatory, and Julia stopped in her tracks when she saw Barb sat in one of the wicker bucket chairs, staring out at the garden while the young nurse from Oakwood painted her nails red. Unlike when she had seen her at the nursing home, her thin grey hair was out of its bun and flowing down her shoulders. It was so long it rested in her lap.

"Barb, you remember Brian and his daughter?" Rosemary asked jovially as she set a cup on the table next to her mother-in-law.

Barb looked Brian up and down, a strained smile twisting her lips. When she spotted Julia, she smiled a little easier, but there was still a flicker of confusion at their visit.

"Barb's moving in for a while," Rosemary said, the smile growing from ear to ear, her cheeks blushing a little. "Thinks I need the help."

"It's the least I can do," Barb said as she looked down at her freshly painted nails. "Yelena, will you be a dear and fetch my blood pressure pills from upstairs? I think I'm due a top up."

"Of course," Yelena said with a soft smile, her Eastern European accent sticking out. "One moment."

The tall and pretty young nurse excused herself from the room, smiling at Julia as she passed.

"Yelena was kind enough to leave Oakwood to be my private nurse," Barb explained when she met Julia's eyes after she had watched Yelena hurry down the hallway and up the stairs. "She's a lovely girl. You find the Ukrainians are very grateful for the jobs."

Julia was a little shocked when nobody picked up on her casual racism. If it had been her gran, she would have corrected her immediately, but she held her tongue because it wasn't her place.

Rosemary pulled two more chairs from the side of the room, and she took the one next to Barb where Yelena had been sitting. Julia and her father sat across from them, awkwardly sipping their tea as they sat in silence. She was almost glad when she heard Yelena padding down the carpeted stairs, if only for something to break the silence.

She returned with a packet of pills in her hand, from which she popped out two. She passed them to Barb, who slotted them between her lips with shaky hands. She sipped a little of her hot tea before tossing her head back. Without the safety of her chess-playing friends to surround her, she looked frailer and much older than Julia first remembered.

"I'm surprised you've left Oakwood," Julia said after sipping her tea. "You seemed to enjoy it there."

"They'll keep my room open," Barb replied with a smile as she reached out and grabbed Rosemary's hand. "I might not have been close with my son, but Rosemary and Gareth are the only family I have left now."

Rosemary smiled sweetly while glancing down at Barb's bony fingers. Julia wasn't sure if she was imagining it, but Rosemary seemed to want to do nothing more than pull her hand away.

"There is a purpose to our visit," Julia said as she rested her cup on the window ledge. "We hope you could help us with some information regarding Anthony."

"*Information?*" Rosemary asked, a shaky smile covering her lips. "About what?"

"A painting," Brian jumped in. "A valuable painting that your husband bought and intended to sell for an incredible profit. Do you know anything about that?"

Barb didn't react, instead looking at Rosemary, whose

lips were shaking out of control as she attempted to smile. She sipped her tea and swallowed hard before tilting her head and smiling a little firmer.

"I'm sorry, I don't know anything about a painting," Rosemary said, avoiding Julia's gaze and staring right at Brian. "I didn't get involved with Anthony's work."

Julia almost called her a liar right then, but she gritted her teeth and forced herself to keep quiet. If she revealed what she knew, it would out her eavesdropping earlier in the day.

Rosemary opened her mouth to say something, but the sound of smashing glass startled them all.

"What are they doing with my things?" Barb cried, jumping up and scurrying down the hallway with Yelena hot on her heels. "Not my glass vase! What am I paying you for?"

Rosemary continued to sip her tea, smiling as though nothing was wrong. Compared to the free smile Julia had seen the day after Anthony's death, this one was as fake as they came.

"Do you know Timothy Edwards?" Julia asked, her eyes trained on Rosemary's.

Her lips twitched, her smile freezing as she considered her response. She sipped her tea again, swallowing as though she was drinking a cup of sand.

"No," Rosemary said, her hand patting her chest as she forced it down. "Will you excuse me for a moment?"

Rosemary put her tea on the table next to Barb's and hurried out of the conservatory.

"She's lying," Julia whispered. "Why is she lying?"

"Maybe she's found the painting?" her father theorised.

"In a couple of hours?" Julia replied with a shake of her

head. "No. She was talking about fleeing Peridale this morning, and now she's letting her mother-in-law move in. I don't understand."

"That's just the kind of woman Barb is. It's almost impossible to say no to her. I know she says she didn't like Anthony, but he didn't like her much either. He visited her out of guilt, even if he didn't really understand the concept of guilt."

Leaving her tea almost untouched, Julia stood up, deciding nothing Rosemary said could be trusted anymore. They slipped out of the cottage as two men heaved a chest of drawers up the stairs while Barb dictated from the top.

"If you hear anything about the painting, make sure to call me," Julia said as she dropped her father off outside Peridale Manor. "Tell Katie I said hello."

He assured her that he would, seeming touched by the gesture. Julia knew it was going to take more than a baby to build long since burned bridges, but it was a better place to try than any.

As she drove back to the café, she racked her brain to try and figure out the truth about what had happened on the night her café had been broken into. She felt like the answer was staring her straight in the face, but she was missing a vital piece of information that was wriggling right under her nose.

CHAPTER 13

When Julia returned to the café, Sue was standing behind the counter flicking through a gossip magazine. She let out a yawn before looking up and spotting Julia.

"Jessie's gone for a driving lesson with Barker," Sue said as she flicked through the magazine. "Do you think I'll suit this dress after I've pushed out the pumpkin?"

Julia shrugged. She hung her jacket on the hook in the kitchen and tossed her car keys on the counter. She smiled to herself, glad that Barker wasn't taking his anger out on Jessie. She was an innocent party stuck in the middle of two people who didn't know what to say to each other to make everything right.

"He asked where you were," Sue said, slapping the magazine shut as she stretched out, letting out another yawn. "Told him you'd gone off somewhere with Dad. Wasn't sure if you wanted him to know you were snooping."

"I wasn't snooping," Julia said with a roll of her eyes. "I was just asking some questions."

"Same difference," Sue said with a chuckle. "He seemed pretty upset that you weren't here. I think he wanted to talk to you."

Julia thought back to the brief moment they had shared after finding Timothy's body. She had buried her head in his chest, and he had put his arm around her, holding her silently until the police arrived at the scene. As soon as the scene was secured, they parted ways, and she wasn't sure how they had left things. She hoped it would have brought them closer together again, but she also knew it was possible it was a momentary blip, and Barker might never want to touch her again.

"Are you just assuming he was upset or did he actually look upset?" Julia asked as she dropped a peppermint and liquorice teabag into a cup.

"He pulled this face." Sue scrunched up her face and pushed out her bottom lip. She looked like a Cabbage Patch Kid. "And then he started sobbing and fainted to the floor screaming '*Julia*'!"

Julia tossed a dry teabag at Sue. It hit her on the side of the face.

"I'm glad my life is so amusing to you."

"Oh, cheer up, big sis," Sue said, tossing the teabag back. "Okay, so I might have stretched the truth *a little*, but he did look disappointed. And he's spending his lunch break giving Jessie a driving lesson. That must mean something."

"Jessie hasn't done anything wrong."

"Neither have you," Sue said with a shrug. "Still being married to a pig isn't a crime. So what that you didn't tell him? I bet he hasn't told you every detail of his past."

Julia dropped her head guiltily as she poured hot water into the small cup. She thought back to the time Barker had shared his past with her, about how his fiancé had died. She had almost shared her own past with him after that revelation, but it felt cheap in comparison. He had told Julia she was the first woman he had loved since, which dug the guilty knife even deeper into her chest.

She pulled on the string of the teabag and bobbed it up and down in the water as she gazed out of her café window at the quiet village green. People seemed to be heading to Happy Bean's, avoiding looking in her café's direction. She wondered if it was time to accept her fate and start thinking about another route she could take, but it ached to think she wouldn't have her café to come to every day.

"Maybe I could do corporate events," Julia thought aloud before blowing on the hot surface of the water. "Or wedding cakes."

"*Boring!*" Sue exclaimed. "I went for my scan this morning. I was going to tell you before, but Dad came, and I didn't want to show –"

Screeching tyres interrupted Sue before she could finish her sentence. They both turned to the window in time to see Jessie drifting around the corner of the village green in Barker's car. Dot, who was tearing out the weeds that were poking through her garden wall, jumped back, tumbling over the low wall and into her garden. Julia caught a flash of

Jessie's hand waving her apology before she sped off again, turning and speeding past St. Peter's Church like she was drag racing.

"For the sake of Peridale, I hope that girl *never* passes her test," Sue said with a nervous laugh. "She's *lethal!*"

"She's learning," Julia said, as hopefully as she could muster. "You failed your test three times, remember?"

"But I didn't kill anybody in the process!" Sue exclaimed as she grabbed her handbag from under the counter before pulling out a bottle of red nail polish. "I hit that cat, but it sprung right up and ran away with eight lives still intact. Barker is braver than me to get in a car with her. What do you think of this colour? Does it clash with the bump?"

Julia chuckled as she sipped her tea. She looked out of the window at the village green again, and something outside Happy Bean caught her attention. She craned her neck in time to see Jerrad bolting out of the coffee shop as the stressed young barista from earlier burst through a crowd of people, tossing her apron to the ground as tears streamed down her face. She ran across the road, narrowly missing the bonnet of Barker's car as Jessie made another erratic lap of the village green.

"Drama at Happy Bean," Julia whispered over the top of her tea. "Looks like she's just quit."

"You could sound *a little* less happy about that," Sue replied with a wink. "Serves the man right."

Julia sipped her tea, letting the peppermint and liquorice warm her throat, the familiar sweetness perking her mood after the disjointed morning. She watched the girl sprint across the village green, mascara streaking her cheeks. Julia put down her tea, and walked around the counter.

"Stay here," Julia said. "I won't be long."

"*Again?*" Sue cried as the red-tipped brush touched her thumb nail. "Where are you going?"

"To gloat," Julia said with a shrug and a twinkle in her eye. "If you can't beat them, join them."

Leaving Sue in the café to paint her nails and attend the non-existent customers, Julia hurried across the village, waiting until Jessie had passed to cross the road. A little smile tickled her lips when she looked through Happy Bean's window and saw Jerrad behind the counter, attempting to work the complicated computer screen till while a line of frustrated people tapped their feet

"Having some staffing trouble?" Julia asked, trying her best to sound concerned.

"The little brat quit!" Jerrad cried, hovering over the screen, his eyes scanning the dozens of different options. "What did you say you wanted?"

"A caramel latte with an extra shot," Jeffrey Taylor, Billy's father, said. "Oh, hello, Julia. Is that your Jessie bombing around the village in that car? She's almost as bad a driver as my Billy. I've tried teaching him, but he's a lost cause."

"Let's hope they never get in a car together then," Julia said, trying to smile through her disappointment that Jeffrey hadn't come to her café for his usual order.

Jerrad peered under his brows, his eyes almost pleading with Julia to help. He somehow managed to put the order through the machine before taking Jeffrey's money with shaky hands. When he turned to the coffee machine, he wiped the visible beads of sweat from his forehead with one hand while the other rubbed the faint stubble on his jaw.

"*Erm,*" he mumbled. "Coffee. *Right.*"

Julia exhaled heavily, not wanting to believe what she was about to do. She walked around the back of the machine and slipped behind the counter, pushing Jerrad out of the way.

"You like it quite strong, don't you Jeffrey?" Julia asked over her shoulder with a smile. "No custard slice today?"

"Watching the figure," he said with a pat on his completely flat stomach, which she knew was smothered in inky tattoos under the fabric.

Julia quickly made the order with ease. It was a little more complicated than the machine in her café, but it did the same thing. She had always wondered why steaming milk and filtering ground coffee needed so many buttons and knobs.

While Jerrad figured out the drinks orders on the till, Julia quickly produced them, switching with ease between coffee, cold drinks, and tea. She wasn't sure if she was working to Happy Bean's standards, but she knew she was working to her own, which had been good enough for the village until recently. When the last of the customers took their drinks, Jerrad turned to Julia with a relieved smile covering his sweaty face.

"We make quite the team," he said with a smirk. "You just saved my bacon."

"Don't get any funny ideas," Julia said, extending a finger in his face. "Even I couldn't watch you try to figure this out. I did it for the customers, *not* for you. They might have stopped caring about me, but that doesn't mean I've stopped caring about them."

Jerrad held his hands up, before clasping them together and bowing his head in thanks.

"I rather like this new, feistier Julia," he said, taking a

step forward. "You've changed."

"I've grown."

"We both have."

Julia held back the laugh. She looked at his fake hairline, fake teeth, and impossibly flat stomach, which used to poke out of his shirts.

"There's a difference between growth and change for the sake of change," Julia said with an arch of her brow. "I need to get back. I have an empty café to run."

Julia slipped around the side of the coffee machine and walked across the sterile coffee shop towards the door.

"*Wait!*" Jerrad called after her. "Let's talk."

"About what?"

"Us."

Julia didn't suppress the laughter this time as Jerrad walked around the counter after her.

"Unless you want to talk about us actually getting divorced, there is no '*us*'," Julia said, folding her arms across her chest.

Jerrad reached out and grabbed her hand, his cold wedding ring burning against her skin. She was so stunned, she didn't immediately pull away.

"Don't you feel it?" he asked, pulling her in slightly. "The spark?"

"I think it's just indigestion, *darlin'*," Julia said, ripping her hand away as she stared into Jerrad's eyes, sure that he was just about to kiss her. "I think you need to read the instruction manual before your next wave of customers floods through the door."

Julia turned on her heels, pleased with her confidence. She had never had the guts to stand up to Jerrad, but looking into his eyes and saying exactly what she wanted felt refreshing. Barker had never tried to censor her, and she knew it had made her a better, stronger woman.

She pulled on the door and set off down the street, feeling Jerrad hot on her heels.

"*Julia*!" he cried after her. "You're *still* my wife."

"We're separated," she called over her shoulder. "It's just a piece of paper. It doesn't mean anything."

Knowing that Jerrad was going to chase her right back to her café, where she would be stuck in a room with him, she made a detour and cut across the village green, glancing in Sue's direction to make sure she wasn't being bombarded with customers; she wasn't, and she was still paying close attention to painting her nails.

"You *need* to listen to me," he cried, jogging to keep up as she hurried across the grass.

"I don't *need* to do anything."

To her surprise, Jerrad's fingers wrapped around her wrist, yanking her back. She stopped in her tracks, feeling a little pop in her shoulder. She tried to pull away, but his grip was firm.

"I said, you need to listen to me," he said, his voice darkening as he stared deep into her eyes. "You're my wife, and I made a mistake."

Julia stared down at the fingers tightening around her wrist, turning the skin there white, and her fingers bright red. She pulled again, but he was holding on tightly.

"Let *go* of me," she said, her free hand clenching. "Now."

"You're my wife!" he repeated, as though it meant something. "Twelve years, darlin'. It means something. You and me, the dream team."

"It was a nightmare," Julia said through gritted teeth as

she continued to yank. "I said, let go –"

Screeching tyres interrupted her, making them both turn to face St. Peter's Church. Barker's car burst over the concrete lip of the village green, landing with a crash on the grass. Instead of stopping, the car sped up, racing towards them at lightning speed. Frozen to the spot with Jerrad still gripping her, Julia closed her eyes and waited.

There was another screeching, as tyres and grass collided. Julia peeked through her lids, and let out a huge sigh of relief when she saw the car had ground to a halt only steps away from them. Through the pounding of her heart, she let out a small nervous laugh.

The driver's door opened. What Julia saw was even more shocking than the car racing towards them. Jessie wasn't the one who had been driving, it had been Barker.

"Get off her," Barker snapped as he slammed the door before marching towards her.

To Julia's surprise, Jerrad did let go of her in an instant, but instead of stepping back and apologising, he walked towards Barker, meeting him halfway. Julia clutched her sore wrist, turning as Jessie jumped out of the passenger seat.

"Or *what*?" Jerrad sneered, laughing in Barker's face as their chests bumped together. "You gonna arrest me, PC Plod?"

Barker smiled down at Jerrad, who was several inches shorter than him. He blinked slowly, the smile growing, before turning into a sneer. Julia noticed Jerrad's fingers tucking into his palm. She stepped forward, unsure of what to do.

Before Barker could do anything, Jerrad reacted first, his fist striking Barker hard in the stomach. He doubled over and stumbled back before falling to the ground. Julia screamed out and ran to his side.

"You *idiot*!" she cried up at Jerrad, her hands clutching Barker's shoulders.

"She's *my* wife," Jerrad said, before spitting at Barker's feet on the grass. "Nobody is going to –"

Jerrad didn't get to finish his sentence. Jessie's fist struck his nose, and with a crack and a spurt of blood, he fell to the ground completely unconscious. Jessie doubled back, clutching her fist to her stomach as she winced in pain.

"*Ouch*!" Jessie mumbled through her red face. "I knew he was a bonehead."

Barker stumbled to his feet with Julia's help as he caught his breath. Julia looked around the village as people ran from every direction, including two police officers.

"If anybody asks, I punched him," Barker said, tapping Jessie on the shoulders. "Get out of here."

A car pulled up in front of Julia's café just as Sue ran to the door, her eyes wide. Their father climbed out of the car and looked down at Sue. Instead of explaining anything, she grabbed his hand and dragged him to the scene, with her other hand clutching her tiny bump.

"What did I miss?" Sue cried, her arm wrapping around Jessie's shoulders as she looked confused between them. "Jessie, are you okay?"

"I think I've broken my thumb," she muttered, looking down at her hand, which she was still clenching. "But it was worth it."

"You need to ice it," Julia's father said.

"There's ice at Happy Bean," Julia replied, glancing down at Jerrad as he started to come around with a groan.

"He's not dead."

"Shame," Jessie mumbled as they walked towards the coffee shop. "I was hoping to hit him so hard he flew out of Peridale and landed on the moon."

Barker held back, pretending to clutch his hand as he began to explain what had happened to the two police officers, who Julia recognised as the ones who arrested her and Jessie. Barker caught her gaze, and they shared a smile. He winked at her, before reapplying his fake hurt expression. She had a feeling things were going to be okay after all.

Once they were in the empty coffee shop, Jessie and Sue sat in two of the pleather armchairs, while Julia hurried behind the counter and scooped a handful of ice into a tea towel, which she secured in place with an elastic band from a bag of chocolate flakes. Julia's father hovered back, following her as she walked towards Jessie and Sue. He looked like an excited child who was dying to tell her something.

"Let me see," Julia whispered, prying Jessie's fingers off her sore hand. "You didn't have to do that."

"I did," Jessie said. "Are you angry with me?"

Julia smiled. She didn't want to let Jessie know that she had been right about it being highly satisfying to watch Jerrad be punched in the face. If it were anyone else, she wouldn't have condoned the violence, but she hoped Jessie might have knocked some sense into the deranged man.

"I'm not angry with you," Julia said softly as she rested the ice against Jessie's bright red hand. "I think we need to take you up to the hospital."

"Julia?" her father mumbled.

"Just a second," Julia said as she wiped the tears from

Jessie's cheeks. "I feel like the appropriate thing to say right now would be not to do it again."

"Or just not to tuck your thumb in when you punch somebody," Sue suggested as she blew on her still wet nails. "But also, what Julia said. *Naughty!*"

"You're going to make an ace mum," Jessie said, before glancing at Julia. "Must run in the family."

Julia rested her hand against her chest, her heart swelling at the sentiment. Looking into the young girl's eyes, it put everything into perspective. She didn't need her café to feel complete, it was just a nice extra to have. She glanced at Barker on the village green as the police officers handcuffed Jerrad and not Barker. She might not have done things the same way as her sister, but she had created a life for herself, despite having thought she had wasted her years with the man being dragged towards the police car.

"Julia?" Brian muttered again, his hand dragging over his chin as he glanced from her to the wall behind her.

"What?" she snapped, not wanting to leave the special moment.

"The painting," he said, glancing behind her again. "I think I've found it."

"*How?*" Sue cried, jumping up, careful not to touch her nails.

Instead of saying anything, their father nodded at the wall he was staring at. They turned around together, their mouths opening when their eyes landed on the giant landscape painting in the gold frame on the wall among the stock photography.

"Are you sure?" Julia asked. "I thought it was a print."

"It's a Murphy Jones," Brian said with so much certainty, Julia felt like he had just muttered a name she should have heard of, but hadn't. "And that's one of his pre-war landscapes from when he lived in Peridale briefly in the early 1900s. They're rare to come by, and the last time one was discovered, it sold at auction for well over a million."

Sue gasped, her hand clasping over her mouth, the money making her completely forget about her nail polish. Julia stared at the dull, dreary painting. She took a step forward, the thick brush strokes jumping out at her.

"Anthony is a clever swine," Brian mumbled, sounding a little impressed. "He hid it in plain sight. Most people wouldn't know a Murphy Jones if it hit them in the face, especially his early work."

Julia crept forward, her eyes honing in on the missing screw on the left side of the painting.

"*The screw!*" she cried, lifting her foot up and clasping her sole.

"I beg your pardon?" Sue exclaimed.

"I stepped on a screw the night we found Anthony," Julia said, glancing back to the counter where she had stepped on the sharp object. "They were trying to steal the painting, but something interrupted them."

"Your café alarm," Jessie mumbled, still clutching the ice to her hand. "It spooked them."

"They've been waiting until the scent died down so they could come back for it," Julia said with a nod as she stared at Sue's red nail polish. "Jessie, do you still have that picture of the sugar on your phone."

Jessie nodded and pulled her phone out of her jeans, wincing as she did. Julia unlocked it and opened the gallery. She was surprised to see that the most recent picture was a selfie of Jessie and Billy smiling up at the camera. Julia suppressed a little grin as her heart fluttered. She glanced at Jessie who didn't seem to remember the picture was there. Julia flicked through to the picture of the sugar sachets. She zoomed in on the blurry red writing, and then at Sue's nails.

"I know who killed Anthony Kennedy," she whispered as she pocketed Jessie's phone. "Sue, take Jessie to the hospital. Dad, you're coming with me."

Thankfully for Julia, nobody argued. She hurried back over to her own café, quickly flipped the sign from '*OPEN*' to '*CLOSED*', before jumping into her father's car.

"How did you know the painting was in the café?" Julia asked as they sped across the village.

"I didn't," he said with a knowing smile. "That part was by accident. But I remembered why I knew the name Edwards. Oh, Julia, you're not going to believe this one."

CHAPTER 14

For the third time that day, Julia found herself at Rosemary Kennedy's cottage. When they pulled up outside, the van was gone and the front door was closed. She peered through the window into the sitting room. Gareth was sitting on the couch, a laptop on his knee.

"How do we get inside?" Julia asked. "We can't just knock on the door after turning up earlier and then leaving."

"Why not?" her dad asked, already getting out of the car. "It's not like we don't know them."

Julia scratched at her legs, remembering the nettle stings from earlier in the day. The sun was starting to wane in the sky, but the long summer night was far from over. She hoped to have put an end to the whole sorry affair by the time the sun drifted past the horizon.

Giving up on trying to think of an excuse, and half wishing she had had the foresight to bake a cake to bring if only to have something to hold, she got out of the car and followed her father down the garden path.

He pressed the doorbell and her heart pounded in her chest. She wondered if she had pieced things together correctly, knowing that if she hadn't, she was about to embarrass herself. She thought back to the painting in Happy Bean, still not able to believe it had been sitting under everyone's noses the whole time.

Gareth answered the door, his laptop in his hands. He barely looked up from it as he grunted. Julia guessed he was asking what they wanted and why they were there. Living with Jessie had given her plenty of practise translating 'teenager' to 'adult English'.

"Is your mother home?" Brian asked, his voiced commanding authority.

"No," he said, snapping his laptop shut and looking up at them. "She's gone out with Barb."

Julia and her father glanced awkwardly at each other, but to their surprise, Gareth doubled back into the cottage leaving the door open. Not wanting to question the invitation, they stepped inside, closing the door behind them.

They followed Gareth through to the kitchen, where Yelena was slicing a loaf of tiger bread into small slices. She looked up and smiled before continuing with her work. Gareth put his laptop on the counter and yanked open the fridge. He grabbed a carton of orange juice and drank directly from the spout. Julia inhaled deeply, stopping herself from correcting him like she would Jessie.

"I don't know when they're coming back," Gareth said as he wiped his mouth. "Could be ages."

"They've gone to get food," Yelena said with a sweet smile. "Barb is cooking as a thank you to Rosemary."

Gareth looked at the nurse out of the corner of his eyes before tossing the carton into the fridge. He scooped up his laptop and walked through to the conservatory, sitting in one of the wicker chairs so that he was just in view.

"He looks just like his father," Brian whispered as they stared around the blindingly white and clean kitchen. "Got his attitude too."

"He's not so bad," Yelena said, glancing at the conservatory. "Hormones. I remember my son at that age."

"You have a son?" Julia asked, not knowing why the information surprised her.

"Two back in Ukraine," Yelena said with a nod. "They are with my mother."

She pulled her phone from her pocket and flicked to a picture of a teenager with his arm around a toddler, both with dark hair like their mother. They were beaming up at the camera with pure and innocent smiles.

"They're beautiful," Julia said, ignoring the usual pang she got whenever she saw a young baby. "You must miss them."

"I send money home. I do this for them."

Julia nodded her understanding as Yelena resumed slicing the bread. When she was done, she looked through the cupboards until she found the one with the plates. She scooped up the slices and displayed them neatly in the middle of the kitchen island.

Much to Julia's relief, the front door opened and Rosemary and Barb returned with shopping bags. They walked into the kitchen, both of them staring curiously at Julia and Brian, although they appeared to be trying their best to hide it behind smiles.

"I think I left my phone here," Brian said quickly before tapping his empty pocket. "Have you seen it?"

"I don't think so," Rosemary said as she put the bags on the counter. "I can have a look around if you like?"

Brian patted down his jacket, rolling his eyes and laughing as he pulled his phone from his inside pocket.

"What am I like?" he asked, blushing a little as he glanced at Julia. "I must be getting old."

Barb climbed up onto one of the stools at the island, her long hair back in the signature bun it had been in when Julia had first met her. She exhaled heavily and rested her head against her hand. It looked like she had endured a long and stressful day.

"Did you get everything moved okay?" Julia asked.

"I wouldn't recommend that company, let's just say that," Barb said through pursed lips. "Wouldn't know how to be gentle if they tried. You'd think I wasn't paying them."

"Can I invite you to stay for dinner?" Rosemary asked airily, making it more than obvious she wanted them to refuse and was just trying to be polite.

"Yes," Brian said quickly before Julia could answer. "That would be lovely. Thanks, Rosemary. It'll give us a real chance to catch up."

Julia tried her best to smile, but she looked at her father and widened her eyes. He gave her a look that read '*just go along with it*', so she didn't question him, she just hoped he knew what he was doing.

***

Julia ate her dinner of beef casserole uneasily, wondering if it was possible to taste arsenic in food. She used more bread than she usually would, hoping it would soak up the poison if it had been slipped in while cooking.

"What made you want to work at Happy Bean?" Julia asked Gareth when they had finished eating at the kitchen island and were now sipping their drinks in awkward silence. "I thought you were at college?"

Gareth shrugged, glancing awkwardly at his mother. She smiled across the table as she tucked her neat grey curls behind her ears before sipping her wine, not taking her eyes away from her son.

"Money," Gareth mumbled with a shrug.

"Anthony didn't leave us a lot," Rosemary explained. "He wasn't the best businessman when it came down to it."

There was a murmur of agreement, which explained to Julia why Anthony's murderer was so desperate to get their hands on the painting.

"Does Jack still own the antiques barn?" Brian asked Rosemary after sipping his wine.

"He died last year. His son has taken it over now," Rosemary said, almost glad for the change of subject. "I have no idea what he'll do with it. I was almost relieved when Anthony told me he was opening a coffee shop, if only to get out of the antique business."

"It's not so bad," Brian said.

"Well, it turns out what he got into was a lot worse," Rosemary said, glancing at Gareth again. "He made sure to tear as many lives apart as he could before he died."

"Like Timothy Edwards," Julia said casually. "It's a shame he had to die too."

There was an uncomfortable shuffle around the table. As though Julia had just dropped a conversational bomb, Rosemary and Yelena stood up at the same time picking up their plates.

"I'll do it," Barb said, standing up and grabbing the plate from Yelena. "It's only fair I pull my weight if you're going to be putting me up here."

Rosemary passed her plate around to Barb and sat down again. She stared blankly at Julia as she tossed back the rest of her wine.

"Gareth, why don't you go and clean up the living room so we can go through?" Rosemary asked, glancing at Barb as she washed up the plates as Yelena passed them to her.

Gareth huffed and slid off his stool. He pulled his phone out of his pocket and walked through to the living room. Julia looked through the conservatory as the sun started to slowly edge closer to the horizon, making the dim spotlights under the counter and above the island struggle to keep up.

"I heard your boyfriend hit Jerrad," Rosemary said. "His nose is broken."

"Does that upset you?" Julia asked.

"I'm sorry?" Rosemary replied, recoiling her head a little. "What do you mean?"

"Well, Jerrad is now your boyfriend, isn't he?" Julia asked. "Or is it not that serious?"

Rosemary lifted her glass up to her lips, but it was empty. She looked at the equally empty bottle of white wine in the middle of the table before sliding off the stool, appearing to be avoiding Julia's stare at all costs.

"I'll grab another one from the cellar," she said as she walked over to a door, which she quickly slipped through.

"Can you grab my pills, Yelena?" Barb ordered. "They're upstairs on my bed."

Yelena nodded and slinked out of the kitchen, disappearing down the dark hallway. The sound of the TV drifted in from the living room, but the prickly silence in the kitchen was impossible to ignore. Brian sipped his wine as he quickly looked at Julia with a small nod.

Julia slid off her stool and gathered up the rest of the plates. She took them over to the sink and placed them with the others as Barb washed them, her painted fingernails bobbing in and out of the bubbles.

"That's a pretty colour," Julia remarked as she leaned against the counter. "What's that shade called?"

"Blood Rose," Barb replied with a polite smile as she grabbed the next plate. "She has a dishwasher, but I prefer to keep my hands busy."

"I find dishwashers don't get things quite clean," Julia said. "Blood Rose. That's an interesting name. It almost looks like blood, doesn't it?"

Barb looked up at Julia, a slight arch appearing in her brow, lining her wrinkled skin.

"It's one of Yelena's," Barb said with a shrug. "It's one of those long-lasting ones."

"Still keeps its shine though."

"I suppose it does."

"Almost like real blood," Julia said as she pulled Jessie's phone from her pocket. "That's what I thought this was."

She pinched the screen and zoomed in on the red

writing on the sugar before showing it to Barb. She glanced at the picture, but a reaction didn't register on her face.

"What's that?" she asked as she looked down at the water.

"Just a little something somebody knocked up to frame me for Anthony's murder," Julia said as she slotted the phone away. "Arsenic poisoning is quite a nasty way to kill somebody, don't you think?"

"I haven't given it much thought."

"Are you sure?" Julia asked, folding her arms across her chest as she leaned into Barb's ear. "I think the problem is, you gave it far too much thought, at least every Friday when Anthony visited you at Oakwood Nursing Home."

"Excuse me?" Barb cried with an awkward laugh as the plate slipped from her hands and into the water. "What are you talking about, you silly woman?"

"A lot of people don't know that you can slowly poison somebody with arsenic," Julia said. "I didn't know that. Did you know that, Dad?"

"I didn't," he called across from his seat at the island.

"The funny thing about arsenic is that it can stay in your system and wreak havoc. A little bit can get in your bones, and stay there. It can kill a person quite slowly if left undetected, but if you're being given a drop in your coffee, let's say, every Friday, it can be quite dangerous. Of course, you knew that, didn't you Barb? That's why you poisoned your son."

Barb pulled her hands out of the sink, her eyes trained on Julia. She grabbed the tea towel and wiped the suds off her fingers, before tossing it onto the island.

"I've heard quite *enough* of this!" Barb snapped. "Your mother was a fantasist too."

Julia gulped hard at the mention of her mother. She glanced at her father, his gaze giving her the strength she needed.

"Oakwood Nursing Home is rather expensive, isn't it?" Julia asked. "That's why you plotted to kill your son when you found out about the painting. Was the pension fund running out a little quicker than you expected, or did you not think you'd live this long?"

Shaking her head, Barb walked across the kitchen, but she stopped in her tracks and turned to face Julia.

"You have no idea what you're talking about," Barb said. "You're just a silly little baker with ideas above her station."

"That's funny because you're not the first person to say that," Julia said, walking forward so that she was face to face with Barb in the dim light. "Would I be right in guessing you heard that from your son? The son who visited you every Friday out of guilt. He might have been a conman, but you were still his mother, even if it was a flying visit. What was it? Ten minutes a week? He sipped his coffee, told you what he was up to, and left?"

"He checked his watch the whole time," Barb said bitterly, echoing what she had said at the nursing home. "Babbled on about antiques even though he knew I didn't care. His father was in antiques too, and just as useless at it as he was."

"Except the day he slipped into the conversation that he had acquired a rare Murphy Jones painting, I bet your ears pricked up for the first time in years. I suppose he didn't think you'd know who he was. I'd never heard of him. Why would I have? But he was quite famous, or so my father says."

"For people of a *certain* generation," Brian said with a firm nod. "They used to teach about him at school."

"You knew all about Murphy Jones, and his days before the war, painting the Peridale landscape," Julia said, tapping her finger against her chin. "You knew *at least* enough to know those paintings were valuable."

Barb's jaw clenched as she stared ahead at Julia, her face becoming nothing more than a shadow as the sun drifted past the horizon.

"The fool was stupid enough to tell me exactly where he'd hidden the painting," Barb scoffed darkly. "Thought he was clever."

"This painting has caused quite a storm in a teacup," Julia said with a sigh. "Everybody wanted to get their hands on it. Rosemary, my ex-husband, even Gareth perhaps, you all thought you were entitled to a slice of the money, but only *you* knew where it was, so you slipped arsenic into your son's coffee once a week, and you waited. You watched and waited until he died, so you could slip in and steal the painting. You even managed to get one of the screws out, but you were startled. Somebody broke into my café, and the alarm scared you off. You fled, and you've been waiting ever since to go back and take it, knowing that nobody had a clue it was there. They might not have noticed it was even missing."

Barb laughed coldly and shook her head. Her bony hands drifted up to her hair, which she checked to make sure was all still in the bun.

"My son underestimated you," Barb said with a sigh. "It's almost a shame nobody will believe you against a little, frail, old woman."

"They might believe me though," Rosemary said, her

voice echoing around the stairway down to the cellar as she slipped out of the shadow. "Did you really kill my husband for the sake of keeping your room at the nursing home?"

Barb turned around and faced her widowed daughter-in-law. Julia almost expected Barb to put on her forgetful old lady routine and try to wriggle out of things, but her steely expression didn't falter.

"They've been threatening to evict me for weeks," Barb snapped. "They want *thousands* a month! I gave birth to the boy!"

"It doesn't give you the right to kill him," Rosemary said, her voice cracking with sadness for the first time since her husband's death. "I might not have liked the man, but that's low, even for you, Barb."

"I would have shared the money!" Barb cried desperately. "We *deserved* it. It's not too late, Rosemary. The painting is still there. We can *deal* with this!"

"Like you dealt with Timothy Edwards?" Julia called out, forcing Barb to spin around again. "I suppose he was somewhat surprised to see you turn up at his flat. You didn't have time to poison him slowly, so you did it in one go. I watched the man die."

"I'd known about their seedy affair for years," Barb whispered. "He was just *one* of them. When he mentioned that he'd bought the painting from Timothy, I realised it was only a matter of time before he realised the true value."

"You killed him to keep him quiet."

"He was *nobody!*" Barb cried. "He was just one of Anthony's playthings!"

"He *loved* your son," Julia said, the anger bubbling in her voice. "He loved Anthony more than any of you did, and you punished him for that. Were you going to go after

Maggie next? I'm sure you wondered if there was a chance he had told her too."

A flash of amusement flashed across Barb's thin lips before she turned on her heels and ran for the door. Another figure appeared from the shadows, stopping her dead in her tracks.

"How could a mother murder her own son?" Yelena mumbled as she held Barb in place after dropping the bottle of pills to the ground with a clatter. "You're a monster."

"I've been *good* to you!" Barb cried. "I brought you with me! Let go of me, you *stupid* girl!"

Tears lined Yelena's eyes, but she didn't let go of Barb's shoulders. In the distance, the piercing screech of police sirens shot through the air.

"Just in time!" Julia announced, clapping her hands together. "Thanks, Dad."

Brian waved the phone, winking warmly at her. Barb looked around the room before she began thrashing against her nurse, but it was in vain. Yelena was a mother, and she understood what it actually felt like to love her son.

Seconds later, the police burst through into the house, shouting and waving their flashlights as they did. Barb was in handcuffs in an instant despite her struggling. Yelena collapsed into the wall and began to sob.

"Julia?" Barker's voice called down the hallway. "I got your dad's text. Are you okay?"

"We're fine," Julia said as he burst into the kitchen, pushing past the officers as they dragged Barb down the hallway. "Thanks for coming."

"Why wouldn't I come?" Barker asked, pulling Julia in and squeezing her tight to his body. "Oh, Julia. I was so worried. Why do you put yourself in these situations?"

"Because it's the right thing to do," she whispered. "And I should have done right by you and told you the truth when I had the chance."

"I don't care about that," he whispered, hooking her chin up to kiss her. "I don't care about any of that. I love you."

***

Julia returned to her empty home after giving her statement, but only momentarily. She grabbed what she wanted, fed Mowgli, and it wasn't long before she was back at Rosemary's cottage.

Once she had given her statement, Rosemary shuffled into the kitchen and collapsed into a seat. She grabbed the bottle of wine she had brought up from the cellar, and instead of pouring it into a glass, she drank from the bottle.

"I always hated her," Rosemary said, wincing through the alcohol. "I think she always hated me too. All of that nicey-nicey stuff earlier was just because she had nowhere to go. I never even suspected she knew about the painting."

"But *you* did," Julia said, letting Rosemary know she knew about the lie earlier in the day. "You're not perfect in all of this, Rosemary. The second you found out about your husband's painting, it consumed you too. Did Jerrad bring it up?"

"It was all he talked about," Rosemary said with a sigh. "I don't know how you were ever married to the fool, Julia. He's incessant."

"You were using each other for information, but the ironic thing was neither of you actually knew anything," Julia said with a soft smile through the dark. "Is that why you forced Gareth to take a job at the coffee shop?"

"I thought Jerrad had to slip up eventually if he found out where the painting was."

"And he thought the same of you," Julia said with a sigh. "Two wrongs don't make a right."

"I'm done with him," Rosemary said after taking another swig of the wine. "It was nice dating a younger man, but they have nothing to talk about. I'm going to focus on my son and me from now on, and if I find another man, he will be somebody who loves me for me. I thought Anthony did once, but I was young and blind. There have been people like Maggie and Timothy since the start of our marriage. I even thought your father was in on the action too, but he loved your mother too much for that. You and your sister are too hard on him, you know that?"

Julia suddenly felt guilty. She thought about the boys on Yelena's phone, and then about the little boy in Katie's stomach. She owed it to that baby to unite her family so he didn't grow up in the same situation she had.

"I know," she said. "Am I okay to use the bathroom?"

Rosemary nodded and wafted a finger towards the staircase in the hallway. Julia crept up the stairs, but instead of going to the bathroom, she opened and closed all of the doors until she found the one containing Yelena.

"I never even got to sleep here," she said. "It's nicer than the room at Oakwood."

"You know you can't stay here," Julia said.

"I know," Yelena said, looking up at Julia with a soft smile. "Why didn't you tell them?"

Julia laughed softly as she sat next to Yelena. She picked the woman's hand up and nodded to the photo frame on the nightstand, the only thing she had unpacked.

"When I figured out the writing on the sugar packets was your nail polish and not blood, I knew Barb hadn't acted alone. My sister painted her nails red, and it reminded me that I'd seen you painting Barb's nails the same colour. She might have been cunning, but there was no way she could have darted across the village like the person I saw on the security footage. You broke into my café, and you tried to frame me, but I suspect it was only on Barb's request."

"She said she didn't know how her son died," Yelena said, glancing at the sweet boys in the picture. "She said we were framing you to cover our tracks, just to be safe. I was going to send my part of the money to Ukraine. She said if I didn't help her, she'd have me fired from the nursing home. I didn't have any choice coming here with her. She was broke. She wasn't even paying me to be her personal nurse, I was just scared of what she would do if I didn't come."

"I know," Julia said, reaching into her handbag to pull out the rolled up stack of red notes. "This will be enough for a flight home, and hopefully some for you to start a new life. It's only five hundred pounds, but it's all I have."

"I cannot take this," Yelena said, holding up her hands and shaking her head.

"Somebody gave it to me to help, and I was ungrateful, so now I'm passing it on to somebody who it can *really* help," Julia said, forcing the money into the nurse's hands and closing her fingers around it. "I'll be fine. I always am."

Yelena looked down at the money and smiled as a tear tumbled down her cheek. She didn't say anything, instead pulling Julia into a tight hug. When the women finally parted, Julia wished her luck and slipped back downstairs, where Rosemary was with Gareth in the sitting room.

"I'm so sorry," Rosemary said as she hugged her son. "I let money blind me, just like your father. You can stay at catering college and live your life for you. I love you."

Gareth mumbled something before pulling away and shuffling out of the room and up to his bedroom. Rosemary and Julia smiled at each other, both of them understanding the complexities of teenagers.

"Does that mean you're staying in Peridale?" Julia asked, leaning in the doorframe.

"I owe it to my son," she said, looking up at the ceiling. "I always wanted children, but I thought I had left it too late. I went along with Anthony because he didn't want anything weighing him down. I was forty-eight when I fell pregnant. It was a miracle. Doctors called me a 'geriatric' mother! *Ha*! They said I was a '*rare*' case, and the chances of me carrying him full term weren't great. Having Gareth made me believe in something bigger and better. I should have plucked up the courage when he was a baby to leave Anthony, but it was all I ever knew."

"Some men have a habit of making us think there's nothing better out there," Julia said, knowing that feeling all too well. "But trust me, there is, and you deserve it."

Rosemary smiled her thanks as Julia backed out of the sitting room. She walked towards the front door feeling lighter and freer than she had in weeks. When she walked out into the dark, her heart fluttered when she spotted Barker's car.

"Can I offer the lady a lift?" he called through the open window with a soft smile from ear to ear.

Without a second thought, Julia climbed into the car and kissed Barker. Her past might have been in the village having his nose plastered up, but her future was right in front of her. She deserved to be happy, but so did Barker, and she was never going to jeopardise that ever again.

CHAPTER 15

The next morning in the café, things seemed to go back to normal. Happy Bean was closed and her café was full again with all of the regular faces. It turned out more than a couple of people had their own stories to share about Barb, and even though Julia didn't care for the gossip, she was glad they were doing it in her café once again.

"This is *impossible!*" Jessie cried as she attempted to hold a wooden spoon with her arm encased in a cast from elbow to fingers. "I feel like the tin man."

"But you look like the scarecrow," Dom exclaimed. "Please will you let me put highlights in your hair?"

"No," Jessie snapped.

"They'll bring out your eyes," Dolly added.

"My eyes are fine where they are," Jessie said with a roll of her eyes.

Julia shuffled past them and grabbed the fresh chocolate cake she had baked that morning from the fridge. She knew it might only be temporary that her café was busy, but she wasn't going to miss what could be one of her last chances to feed the villagers her baked creations.

She headed back into the café, pleased to see Barker walking in on his lunch break.

"Is that chocolate cake?" Barker asked with wide eyes. "My favourite!"

"Baked it especially," Julia said, glancing at the clock, glad that Barker had come in just on time. "One slice or two?"

"Two, please," he said after leaning across the counter to peck her on the cheek. "I've missed your baking."

Julia sliced two generous chunks out of the cake before placing it in the display case between a plate of éclairs and red velvet cupcakes. She quickly made Barker an Americano and placed them in front of him on the table nearest to the counter.

"Barb is singing like a canary," Barker mumbled through a mouthful of cake, chocolate cream on his chin. "Full confession. Turns out she got the arsenic from a resident at Oakwood who bragged about having some left over from the Second World War! It was totally expired, which explains why it took so long to kill Anthony, but still lethal."

"Has she mentioned Yelena?"

"Who?" Barker asked.

"Nobody," Julia said, containing her smile. "I suppose

the old woman had some compassion left in her after all."

While Barker finished the first slice, Sue and Dot walked into the café, followed quickly by her father and Katie. She was glad they were all on time.

"What's *she* doing here?" Sue mumbled out of the corner of her mouth as she glanced at Katie's large bump. "Is this a stitch-up?"

"No, it's a truce," Julia said, waving a small white handkerchief in the air. "A fresh start for the sake of the limes in your stomachs."

"Actually, mine is the size of a banana!" Katie squeaked proudly.

Sue shook her head and scowled in her direction, which Katie seemed to take offence to as she looked the other way, her arms folding under her enhanced bosom.

"What Julia is trying to say is, you need to get along for the sake of our family," Brian said, stepping between the two women as he rested a hand on each of their shoulders. "Because like it or not, we *are* a family."

"Does that include me?" Dot mumbled through a mouthful of the second slice of chocolate cake she had swiped from Barker's plate.

"Yes, it does, Gran," Julia said. "And Barker, and Jessie. We all need to be there for these babies, so they grow up in the most loving environment possible."

Sue and Katie both sighed before glancing at each other. Julia nodded to Sue, who reluctantly held a hand out in front of her father. Katie meekly accepted the hand, sending half a smile to Sue.

"Is that it?" Julia asked. "I didn't believe that."

"I'm not *hugging* her!" Sue exclaimed. "I don't know if what she has is catching."

"This is why I didn't want to come, Brian!" Katie cried, stamping her high-heels into the floor. "*She* is jealous!"

"Oh, for the love of chocolate cake," Dot cried, spitting crumbs everywhere. "I hate to say it, but Julia is right. It's not about you, it's about the babies."

Sue and Katie looked guiltily at the floor, and then at each other, their eyes lingering a little longer this time.

"Sorry," Sue mumbled.

"Yeah, me too," Katie replied.

"Wasn't too hard, was it?" Brian said, pulling them both into his side for a reluctant hug.

"This is good cake," Dot said as she licked the chocolate from her fingers. "I thought your baking had dipped over the last couple of weeks, but who could blame you considering the situation. It's back on top form though!"

"I'm surprised you're not upset you have nothing to protest," Julia said as she took the empty plate and put it on the counter. "Mr Shufflebottom is going to miss having you blackmailing him for t-shirts."

"Well," Dot said, standing up and unbuttoning her blue cardigan. "I went for *one* last trip."

She ripped open the cardigan, and a gasp came from everybody, except for Sue. Julia read the words over and over again until they sank in.

"'*I'm going to be a great-great-grandmother to twins!*'" Barker read aloud from the t-shirt.

"I tried to tell you yesterday before Jessie decided to play *Grand Theft Auto* in the village," Sue said as reached into her pocket to pull out a tiny black and white scan picture. "It turns out there are two limes."

Katie let out a horrified squeak before turning on her

heels and stomping out of the café. Brian shrugged his apology.

"I should go after her," he said as he pulled Sue into a hug. "Congratulations. I'm so happy for you, my little girl."

"Thanks," Sue mumbled, her cheeks burning.

"Oh, I almost forget to mention," he said as he headed to the door. "I spoke to Jack's son and he's agreed to let me take over the antique barn. I'm going back to what I know best. I realised I couldn't bring a child into this world and not teach him the value of work."

"That's great news," Julia said, happy to know her father would be in the village more often. "See you later."

"Bye, girls."

Julia and Sue turned to each other with a smile. It felt like a small victory, but it was like they both knew they had their father back.

"*Twins?*" Julia said, a smile beaming from ear to ear. "You're having twins!"

"*Surprise!*" Sue mumbled, her cheeks blushing.

Julia pulled her into a hug. She could feel her sister's nerves at the thought of having to give birth to two babies, but Julia couldn't contain her excitement.

"Babies are like buses," Dot exclaimed as she looked down at her t-shirt. "One doesn't come for ages, and then you have two at once."

After having a cup of tea, Sue and Dot left the café, leaving Julia and Barker alone. She sat across from him, but she instantly jumped up when Jerrad walked into the café, with two black eyes and a plastic support over his nose.

"I come in peace," he mumbled, his voice nasally and muffled. "*She's* not around, is she?"

"Jessie is in the kitchen," Julia said, resting a hand on

Barker's shoulder. "What do you want?"

Jerrad walked carefully into the café, looking around as though he was about to step on a land mine. He stopped in his tracks a couple of metres away from their table, and stuffed his hands into his pockets.

"I came to apologise," Jerrad said meekly. "I'm sorry."

"You're what?"

"Sorry."

"I heard that. It's just I've never heard you apologise before."

"Neither have I, and I think it might be the painkillers they've got me on, but for now I mean it." Jerrad paused and gently patted the structure holding his nose together. "She's got a mean right hook, I'll give her that."

Julia didn't say anything. Even though Barker had taken the blame for the punch and escaped charge free, Jerrad could have told the police the truth about what had happened, but he hadn't. Julia had spent the entire night expecting police to come knocking on her door to take Jessie away for assault.

"Well, I appreciate that," Julia said, still not wanting to be nice to him. "Anything else?"

"There is actually," he said, reaching into his inside pocket to pull out a folded manila envelope. "I got my lawyer to make another copy. Same terms as before, but I thought we could both sign them together so we know there's no backing out."

"Divorce papers?" Julia asked, her mouth drying as he pulled the thick wad of white paper out of the envelope.

"Unless you've had second thoughts?" he asked with a playful smirk as he handed the pen to Julia.

Julia snatched the pen out of his hand and scribbled

her signature faster than she had ever signed for something before. She watched carefully as Jerrad signed next to her name, making sure that he was using the right hand and it was his real signature. She was surprised when he didn't pull any tricks.

"I'll get these to my lawyer," he said as he tucked them into his pocket. "It'll take a while for it to be official, but you'll know when it happens."

"Thank you," Julia said, nodding at him. "I really mean it."

Jerrad smiled and glanced down at the floor. She noticed a pale white line on his finger where the wedding ring had been.

"Now we can both move on," Jerrad said. "For real, this time."

"What will you do next?"

"Go back to the city," he said, glancing over his shoulder at the coffee shop. "Why did I think I could run a coffee shop? I've spoken to Rosemary, and she said she's going to keep it and turn it into something else, so you don't have to worry."

It took all of Julia's power not to breathe a huge sigh of relief. The floor beneath her suddenly felt a lot firmer, and it had never felt so good.

"Well, good luck," Julia said.

"You too. Who knows, maybe I'll run into that painting on my way out? Wouldn't that be a nice stroke of luck?"

"Maybe," Julia said through a strained smile.

"Look after her, Barker," Jerrad said, turning on his heels and heading for the door. "She's a good woman, I just realised it far too late."

Jerrad left the café, leaving them both in a stunned silence. Barker reached up and squeezed Julia's hand, letting her know everything really was fine.

"Maybe I should have told him the painting was a fake," Julia said.

"*What?*"

"That's why my father turned up yesterday," Julia said with a knowing grin. "Timothy Edwards' grandfather was Martin Edwards, an infamous art forger. The painting was nothing more than an elaborate copy, and anybody with a million pounds to spend on a Murphy Jones painting would have known that. It turns out that Anthony Kennedy really was a terrible antiques dealer."

"So, all of this was for nothing?" Barker exclaimed with a stunted laugh. "He died for nothing? Have you told any of them?"

"No," Julia said. "I think it's better they all live with the shame of what that painting did to them. Might stop them from doing something stupid again."

Barker's eyes twinkled up at her for a moment before he started laughing.

"You're brilliant," Barker said as he stood up. "I hope you know that."

"You're not so bad yourself, are you?" Julia asked. "There was no stolen gnome, smashed window, or hanging basket, was there? You were investigating Anthony's murder, even if you weren't on the case. That's why you turned up at Rosemary's cottage, the nursing home, and Timothy's flat."

"Nothing gets past you," Barker said as he fastened up his jacket. "I couldn't sit back and do nothing while your name was being dragged through the mud. As usual, you were always two steps ahead of me."

Julia knew that Barker truly was a good man. Even though he had barely been able to speak to her or look at her, he had still gone out of his way to help her. She knew that's what true love was.

He left the café, so Julia walked into the kitchen, where Dolly and Dom were drawing pictures in flour on the work surface, their tongues poking out of their mouths.

"Where's Jessie?" Julia asked.

They both nodded to the back door, neither of them looking up from the masterpieces they were creating. Julia walked across the kitchen and pulled on the heavy door that opened onto the tiny yard behind her café.

Standing between the bins and the gate were Jessie and Billy, sharing their first kiss. Biting her lip, Julia retreated back into the kitchen without making a sound. It was a moment she wasn't going to interrupt.

"What's she doing?" Dom asked.

"She's been out there for ages," Dolly added.

"Nothing," Julia said, trying her best to conceal her beam. "Wash your hands. Let's bake something!"

If you enjoyed this book, why not sign up to Agatha Frost's **free** newsletter at **AgathaFrost.com** to hear about brand new releases!

OUT NOW! Julia and friends are back for another Peridale Café Mystery case in *Macarons and Mayhem!* Order on **AMAZON**.

92784088R00306

Made in the USA
Lexington, KY
08 July 2018